The Guilty Plea

Robert Rotenberg

W F HOWES LTD

This large print edition published in 2012 by
W F Howes Ltd
Unit 4, Rearsby Business Park, Gaddesby Lane,
Rearsby, Leicester LE7 4YH

1 3 5 7 9 10 8 6 4 2

First published in the United Kingdom in 2011
by John Murray

A CIP catalogue record for this book is available
from the British Library

ISBN 978 1 47120 074 8

Typeset by Palimpsest Book Production Limited,
Falkirk, Stirlingshire
Printed and bound in Great Britain
by MPG Books Ltd, Bodmin, Cornwall

For my parents
Gertrude Rotenberg, December 21,
1921–October 19, 1999
Dr Cyril Rotenberg, March 9,
1920–April 10, 2009
who always believed in me

Despite all the rules and objections and soft illusion of decorum, a trial was after all a savage and primitive battle for survival itself.

Robert Traver, *Anatomy of a Murder*

PART I
AUGUST

CHAPTER 1

Even for Arceli Ocaya, it was too hot to sleep. The heat wave had gripped the city for days and by six in the morning her tiny apartment was already steaming. Back home in Manila, her husband and their five children would never believe it could be so warm in Canada. By next summer when she brought them over, Ocaya planned to have a bigger place, and she knew they would never understand what it had been like – all these years alone with the summer heat, the winter cold, and the eternal loneliness.

It was good that she was up early. Her employer, Mr Terrance Wyler, would need all the help she could give him this morning. Poor man. Even though he was rich.

The bus she took every day to the subway arrived on time, but there was a delay on Eglinton Avenue where a film crew was making a movie. This happened so many times in Toronto. The trailers parked on the side of the road funneled the traffic. Ocaya saw a stone building with a new sign that said CIRCUIT COURT – BALTIMORE and police cars with the words BALTIMORE CITY POLICE on the side.

Unfortunately, most people on the subway were reading the transit newspaper, which had a picture of Mr Wyler right on the front page with his arm around his famous American girlfriend, the actress April Goodling. The headline read DIVORCE FROM HELL TRIAL STARTS TODAY. Why do they write such terrible things? Ocaya wondered. Her employer was the nicest person she'd worked for since leaving the Philippines.

At her last subway stop, Bayview Avenue, she rushed up the escalator. Oh, no, she thought when she got to street level and saw the back of the bus pull away, its tailpipe spitting out sooty black smoke. She decided to walk the six blocks to his house.

Marching up Hillside Drive, Ocaya couldn't stop thinking about that foolish headline. 'Divorce from Hell.' Try being separated from your family for six years and only getting to go home to see them once. That was hell. This divorce was silliness. Mr Wyler was an excellent father and those accusations his wife, Samantha, made against him last year were nonsense.

After three blocks she felt the sweat collect on the back of her neck. The lawns of all the expensive houses were turning brown at the edges from the long dry spell and most of the driveways were empty. For the next three blocks the street climbed at a steeper grade, but she refused to slacken her pace.

Ocaya had learned that in Toronto during the

month of August many people were on holiday, especially the wealthy ones. They called it 'going up north.' When Mr Wyler's son, Simon, was just a baby – and Mr Wyler and Samantha were still married – the family went up north to a cottage and Ocaya went with them. Why they would leave their air-conditioned home to spend a week in a wood-shed with an old refrigerator, a place with bugs and snakes outside, was a mystery to her. Strangest of all, one afternoon they caught seven fish and insisted on throwing them all back in the lake.

She arrived every day by seven-thirty. Mr Wyler was always up, his stereo on loud, prancing around the kitchen, chopping up fresh fruit. Sometimes he played his piano. On the weeks he had Simon, he would make breakfast while listening to a man named Billy Joel. Apparently Mr Joel played piano too. Her employer even named his dog Billy.

Simon had just turned four years old and was already learning to read. Short words, but Mr Wyler was so proud. A few weeks earlier he bought some colorful magnetic letters and put them on the front of his refrigerator. Each night he spelled a short word and when Simon came down for breakfast the boy would read it. First D-O-G, then C-A-T, then H-O-U-S-E, then T-R-A-I-N.

As she climbed the stone steps to the front door, Ocaya was surprised to see that the newspaper was still there. Usually Mr Wyler had read it by the time she arrived, and he often showed her an article he thought would interest her. This morning,

5

with so much on his mind, he probably didn't have time. She scooped the paper up and put her key in the door. It was unlocked. Mr Wyler had probably been outside earlier, before the paper came, and forgotten.

I'll bet the poor man couldn't sleep, she thought. His parents and two older brothers had been at the house last night for Sunday-night dinner, and Ocaya had been there to help out. The family had fought about their business. That, on top of the trial starting today, must have upset him.

It was quiet inside the house. There was no music playing. No clatter of dishes in the kitchen. No patter of Simon's little feet. And where was Billy? Every morning when the dog heard Ocaya come in, he would bark with happiness, stand up on his back legs to greet her.

The house was hot. Mr Wyler often forgot to put on the air-conditioning before he went to sleep, especially lately when he was so upset. She took off her backpack and slid it under the front hall desk. At last she heard the click of dog tags on Billy's collar. He poked his head around the corner of the living room.

'Billy, my favorite little doggie.' She clapped her hands together. 'Where's Simon?'

Saying 'Simon' always brought an instant response from the dog, but Billy seemed uninterested. He lowered his head. Must be the heat, Ocaya thought.

'I better get you some water.' She swung open

the kitchen door but the dog was reluctant to follow.

The first thing that hit her was the smell. Something strong. Horrible.

She saw the blood. A dark red splotch on the clean white tile floor. She would use one of the rags under the sink to wipe it up, she thought.

Then she saw Mr Wyler.

He was lying on the floor near the refrigerator. His eyes were open. Vacant. She ran to him. 'Did you fall, sir?'

There were cuts across his white shirt, the one she'd ironed for him on Friday. So many cuts. On his neck too. And the blood. All the blood.

Her heart was pounding. She was having trouble breathing. Thinking.

Wait, she thought, hearing the silence of the house.

'Simon,' she shrieked, louder than she thought she knew how to yell. And raced to the stairs.

CHAPTER 2

For some reason known only to him, every summer Homicide Detective Ari Greene's father insisted on repainting the railing on the front steps of his house. One of these years I'm going to scrape the damn things down, Greene thought as he grabbed two thin vertical bars and yanked them back and forth to make sure they were secure. The railing wobbled a bit. He'd need to fill in the cement too.

Even this early in the morning it was hot and the heat accumulated on the concrete steps. His dad had made Greene a fresh pot of tea and was drinking his usual instant coffee from an old Toronto Maple Leafs mug.

Greene laid out the morning's newspaper under the railing and opened a can of black paint with a screwdriver. The can had lasted two summers already. 'I think there's enough for one more year,' he said.

His father reached in with a long stir stick. 'Let's hope.'

Greene had just picked up a brush when the emergency beeper on his hip went off. He hadn't expected a call today, because he was number four on the handwritten list posted in the bureau of who was in line for the next murder. He picked up his cell phone and called in.

'Toronto's turning into Murder City,' the dispatcher said. Her name was Denise, a tough old battle-ax Greene had known for years. 'This is the fourth of the night.'

'Must be the heat,' Greene said.

'It's not the heat, it's the humidity.' Denise couldn't wait to fill him in on the details of the three other homicides. In the Jane-Finch corridor, shots were fired and a seven-year-old girl at a backyard birthday party was hit by a stray bullet. Downtown in the entertainment district, a med student up from Buffalo got stabbed when he jumped in to break up a fight. And a home invader out in Etobicoke beat a babysitter to death when she wouldn't open the family safe.

'What've I got?' Greene asked Denise.

His father took the paint can lid and tapped it back into place with the back of his brush. Greene had been on the homicide squad for five years and they both knew the drill. When a murder call came in, he dropped everything else in his life.

'You heard of Terrance Wyler, from the Wyler Foods grocery store?' Denise asked. 'The guy who's going out with April Goodling, the Hollywood star. She goes through men like water. Wyler's divorce trial was supposed to start today.'

9

Greene read the front page of the newspaper on the porch. 'Divorce from Hell trial,' he said.

His father picked up the paintbrushes and the stir stick.

'Lover Boy's dead. This morning the Filipino nanny found him stabbed in his kitchen.' Denise sounded excited to deliver the bad news. 'His four-year-old boy was asleep upstairs. Doesn't know what happened yet.'

'On my way,' Greene said after she gave him the address.

'I'll clean up,' his father said.

'Call you tonight.' Greene bent down and kissed his dad on his forehead, then jumped into his car and slapped the emergency light on the roof.

Ten minutes later he pulled his '88 Oldsmobile behind a police cruiser in front of 221 Hillside Drive and stepped out into the morning sunlight. Taking his time, he looked up at the house, which was elevated well above the street.

'Hello, Detective,' a young policewoman at the front door said when he got to the top of the stairs. She was a thin East Indian woman with a slender nose. 'P. C. Mudhar. I'm the first officer on scene.'

'Detective Greene.' He shook her hand. It was sweaty. 'Your first homicide call?'

'Yes, sir.'

'Where's the little boy?'

'Upstairs with the nanny.' Her voice was thin. 'I told her to keep him in the room.'

'You see him?'

'For a second. He was waking up. The nanny says she found Mr Wyler in the kitchen when she came to work this morning.' Mudhar had a palm-size police notebook, and she flipped it open. 'She said that was about seven-thirty. I checked the body. There are no vital signs.'

'You call for backup to cordon off the street?'

Mudhar shook her head. 'Not yet, sir.'

'Don't worry,' Greene said. 'I called it when I was driving over. Cars will be here any minute. Send someone to Tim Hortons to get a chocolate milk and a doughnut with sprinkles.'

'Yes, sir.'

'I told dispatch to hold off the ambulance until we get the boy out of here. Anyone else in the house?'

'No, sir. I checked. It's clear.'

'Good work.'

Mudhar smiled and closed her notebook.

'What's the nanny's name?' he asked.

She opened her notebook again. 'Arceli Ocaya. Says the boy's mother has been acting strange the last few weeks.'

As he'd driven to the house, Denise the dispatcher had briefed Greene on the recent police occurrences involving the wife. Samantha Wyler had been harassing her soon-to-be ex-husband with nasty voice messages and angry e-mails that were close to the line, but not actual threats. A pair of rookie police constables had warned her to stop. The usual stuff.

With four murders on the go, there'd be a scramble among the homicide detectives to grab good officers to work their cases. Greene called Daniel Kennicott, a smart young cop who'd worked with him on his last murder. Kennicott had his cell phone set so if Greene called it had a special ring tone.

'Detective Greene?' Kennicott said.

'Where are you?' Greene asked.

'On patrol. Started my shift about half an hour ago.' Kennicott sounded sleepy. 'First day back. What's up?'

The two men had a complicated relationship. Kennicott's older brother, Michael, was murdered five years earlier. At the time Kennicott was a lawyer at one of the top downtown firms. Twelve months later when the investigation stalled, Kennicott quit his law job and joined the force, determined to make the homicide squad in record time. It was Greene's only unsolved case.

'A new murder.' Greene gave him the address. He was going to start Kennicott off with the toughest assignment of the day: informing the family of the murder.

'Be there in ten minutes,' Kennicott said.

Greene turned to Mudhar. 'What's the name of the boy upstairs?' Beads of perspiration pooled on the side of the young policewoman's face. The reality of homicide work was that usually it was the greenest of the green cops who were the first to arrive.

This time Mudhar didn't need her notebook. 'Simon.' Her bottom lip began to quiver. 'It's gruesome.'

Greene put his hand on her shoulder. 'Stay here and cover the door.' He looked at the cloudless sky. There was a smell of mint in the air. He must have crushed some coming up the steps.

'Yes, sir.' The wash of relief across Mudhar's face was palpable.

Greene walked through the front hall and opened the kitchen door with his elbow. Already knowing what he'd see inside didn't make it any less disturbing. Wyler's fit, trim body was splayed out on the tile floor, arms flung to the sides, apparently helpless in the face of a knife attack that had lacerated his chest, the top of his shoulders, and his neck.

Greene bent close to the body without touching it. There were no obvious cuts to Wyler's fingers or forearms. Forensics would look for skin or DNA under his fingernails, but at first blush there were no defensive wounds. The smell in the hot room was overpowering.

Scanning the kitchen, Greene saw a half canta-loupe on the counter, fruit flies swarming all around it. The rest of the room was as spotless as the hallway had been. All the cupboard doors were closed. Greene put his hand inches from the dish-washer. It was cool. Same with the stove, where he noticed three dish towels draped over the handle. The first was red and white, and the second was

13

green and white. There was a gap the width of a towel and then another green one. A wooden block near the sink held a number of black-handled knives. The widest groove was empty. No sign of a knife on the floor or the counter.

There was nothing else Greene could do here until the forensic officer arrived. He had a sudden urge to be out of this room of death. He had to go upstairs to talk to a boy who no longer had a father.

CHAPTER 3

Ted DiPaulo opened the door to his law office and stared at his desk. What a fucking mess. Damn, he hated paperwork. Even more, he hated a boring week like the one coming up. Today nothing was doing, and he'd be stuck pushing that pile of paper around. Tomorrow he had a guilty plea for a drunk driver, Wednesday a sentencing on a fraud case, Thursday a meeting with a new client charged with stealing from his employer. Friday zip. He could do all this in his sleep.

If there was one thing DiPaulo couldn't stand, even more than dishonest prosecutors or incompetent judges, it was not having enough to do. Not having a big case on the go. Not getting into court to cross-examine a witness. Not having the press lapping up his every word.

Bloody summer. His law practice was too damn slow, as if everyone were on holiday. Even his best criminals.

DiPaulo needed to be in court the way an actor needed to be onstage. That's why he'd started his career as a Crown Attorney, where prosecutors

15

were on their feet all day long. With his love of doing trials and his great capacity for work, he had risen through the ranks fast. Became the youngest-ever head Crown of the Toronto office at the age of forty-one.

He'd thrived in the job. Couldn't get enough of the pressure. The profile. Then, five years ago, his wife, Olive, was diagnosed with liver cancer. She died in three months, and in the blink of an eye he had to take care of his two teenage kids. All those years before that, he'd been a part-time parent, practically living at the office. That was no longer an option. He quit and went into private practice so he'd have more time.

At first Kyle, then fourteen, and Lauren, twelve, clung to him. Wanted him home every night for dinner. Funny thing. Just as he got used to it and started to crave their company, they turned into full-fledged teenagers. On the go all the time. And perhaps they knew their dad was much easier to live with when he got his daily dose of the courtroom. Soon he was back to doing big cases, sleepless nights and crazy hours, with the added bonus of a new closeness to his children. But that was time-dated, like a container of yogurt in the fridge. Kyle was away on a six-week canoe trip and would be off to university in September. Lauren was home, taking a summer school course. Another year and she'd be gone too.

He stopped for a moment at the credenza near

his office door and picked up a framed photo. Olive died four months after their twentieth anniversary. On the first Mother's Day after her death, the kids gave him this picture of the two of them on top of Ayers Rock. They had taken the hiking trip to Australia to celebrate their forty-fifth birthdays, which were one week apart. Ted was very tall, over six feet six. And big. Olive was quite short, fine and delicate.

It was his private ritual to look at the photo every time he entered and exited the office. In a job where the demands on his time and emotions were so extreme, he was determined to keep this piece of his own life intact. Half a decade. He'd never forgotten.

He settled behind his desk and the phone rang. DiPaulo smiled. On Saturday night he'd been invited over to some friends' house for dinner and they'd introduced him to a woman named Chiara. She was an orthopedic surgeon, a few years older, smart and independent, Italian even, though a dark beauty from Sicily in contrast with his blond northern Italian blood. They'd joked about who started work earlier on Monday mornings, and as he was leaving, he gave her his card and said, 'Call if you want. Earlier the better.'

After Olive died, DiPaulo had waited a few years before he started dating. At first he made the predictable mistakes – talked incessantly about his late wife, his children, or his career as a criminal lawyer. Lessons learned. He wasn't going to blow this one.

He leaned far back in his chair. 'Hi there.' His voice was warm. Even sexy.

'Ted, so glad you are in early,' a male voice said. He recognized it immediately. It was Winston Feindel, a family lawyer who sent DiPaulo a lot of work.

'Winston, oh, hi.' He snapped straight up in his seat. 'You must be on your way to court.'

Feindel was an elderly British barrister who'd moved to Canada ten years earlier. Trading on his English accent, his well-tailored suits, and his courtly manner, he had quickly established himself as a leading light in the local family law bar. His specialty was representing women splitting up from rich husbands. When a client had to testify in a divorce trial, he sent them to DiPaulo to prepare them for court. DiPaulo had been working with Samantha Wyler, a particularly difficult woman, since the beginning of July, and her divorce trial was starting this morning.

'Unfortunately,' Feindel said. 'The trial has been canceled.'

This was Feindel's style. Very British. Understated. 'Canceled?' DiPaulo asked. 'Why?'

'My part in this matter has ended. Ms Wyler will now be your full-time client.'

'*My* client? Divorce isn't a crime.'

'Ah. But murder is,' Feindel said.

'What?' DiPaulo said. 'Who?'

DiPaulo had watched as Samantha, or Sam as she insisted on being called, had become increasingly unglued in recent weeks. What had she done?

18

'Ms Wyler's now *late* husband was found at his home this morning. Victim, it seems, of a great many stab wounds. Puts a crimp in the divorce action.'

'Oh, no.'

'I just received a phone call from a homicide detective, Ari Greene. You know the gentleman?'

'Good cop,' DiPaulo said.

'The detective was inquiring as to the whereabouts of our formerly mutual client.'

After all his years in the court, DiPaulo prided himself in his ability to take startling news in stride. But he needed a minute to absorb this. The air-conditioned office felt hot. 'Where's Sam?' The tumblers in his mind were locking into gear.

'She was sitting on the steps of my office a few minutes ago when I arrived,' Feindel said, as calmly as he'd tell a colleague where he'd gone for lunch. 'She's in my office now and most upset.'

And a dangerous client for you, DiPaulo thought. Feindel wanted to pass her off fast, like a real-life hot potato. His law chambers, as he insisted on calling his luxurious office, were in a brownstone in Yorkville, a trendy midtown location. Near all the best restaurants for his ladies-who-lunch clientele. It would be a short drive.

'I'll get right over there.'

DiPaulo reached for his old leather briefcase, grabbed a few pens and a clean pad of paper, and rushed out. Samantha Wyler could be questioned by the police, or even arrested, at any moment.

19

His office was on the eleventh floor. At the elevator, the numbers above the door were at six, then five, then four. To hell with it. He headed to the stairwell. Keeping one hand on the steel railing, he skipped down the concrete steps.

It wasn't until he got to the third floor that DiPaulo realized he hadn't paused at the anniversary photo on his way out. He gripped the railing. Then kept going down.

CHAPTER 4

It was a perfect room for a boy to grow up in, Ari Greene thought, closing the door behind him and grinning at the dark-eyed child nestled in the bed on the far wall. Tucked in next to him, a short woman was reading him a book called *Really Big Trains*. A large poster of Thomas the Tank Engine smiled down on them from above. On the wood floor a throw rug featured a print of Curious George forever being chased by the man with the yellow hat. In a bay window that overlooked the street the built-in sitting area was covered with a half-finished Lego construction of a tall building.

'Hello.' The boy smiled at Greene, remarkably at ease with a total stranger coming into his room. He patted a small black dog at his side.

'I bet you're Simon,' Greene said.

'Yep,' he said. 'Arceli told me someone would be coming to see me. She said my daddy had to leave early. This is my dog Billy.'

Greene kept a smile on his face. 'Arceli's a special friend.'

'When she reads about the train named Victor she says Bictor.' Simon laughed.

The nanny nodded at Greene and forced herself to laugh along.

The boy had deep, dark eyes. 'Have you ever been in a fire truck?' Greene asked.

'At day care they taught us "stop, drop, and roll."' Simon popped out of bed, stood erect on the carpet, dropped to the ground, and rolled over to Greene's feet.

Greene got down on one knee. 'Ever been in a police car?'

'I've got one.' Simon jumped up and pulled a basket out from under his bed. It was packed with cars and trucks and trains. He expertly extracted a black-and-white car.

'This one's my bestest.' He made driving noises – *vroom, vroom, vroom* – as he rolled it along the edge of the bed. 'Police emergency, police emergency,' he called out in as deep a voice as he could.

'Guess what?' Greene said. 'A police car's going to take you to Arceli's place.'

Simon turned back to Greene. A confused look on his face. 'This is zoo day at day-care camp.'

'It's so hot. The animals need to stay inside,' Greene said.

Simon thought about this for a moment. 'Arceli's apartment is hot too. She told me.'

'What do you want to take with you?'

Simon dove under his bed again and brought

out a plastic bucket. A moment of rummaging and he found a police badge. 'This,' he said, showing it to Greene. He grabbed a well-worn Sesame Street doll. 'And Bert.' He looked at the dog, who was still on the bed. 'And Billy. Are dogs allowed in police cars?'

'Sure. A policewoman bought you chocolate milk and doughnuts for breakfast. Arceli's going to go get them and you can eat here in your room.'

Simon furrowed his brow. 'My mom lets me eat in front of the TV, but Daddy says I have to eat in the kitchen or the dining room.'

'That's a good rule. But today we can do something special.'

The nanny left and Greene glanced out the bay window. The squad cars he'd ordered had cut off the street on both sides of the house. Greene pulled out a basket of Brio trains and wooden track. 'Do you want to work on this with me?'

'Sure.' Simon stretched out on the floor.

Within a few minutes they'd built a figure eight, with an extension looping off to an outer ring. A second spur line circled under a bridge and curled back to a painted wood station.

'You're fun to play with,' Simon said.

Greene reached back for more rails and felt something soft touch his arm. It was the boy's hand.

One Saturday afternoon when he was six years old, Greene's father came home early from work and they took two buses to get to a store called

George's Trains on Mount Pleasant Avenue. When Greene walked in he could hardly breathe, so overwhelming was the place. The walls were lined with hand-painted locomotives, and the salesmen, none of them young, wore gray-and-white-striped conductors' hats. Best of all, a large train ran all the way around the store, high up on the walls, toot-tooting every minute or so.

Greene's father could afford only one circular track, with a locomotive and a coal car. Greene spent countless hours in the basement, running the train around and around. There was a special liquid that came in a glass bottle, and three drops of it would produce steam once the engine warmed up.

The nanny opened Simon's bedroom door, quickly shutting it behind her. 'Here's your doughnut,' she said. 'And chocolate milk.'

Simon reached for the doughnut. 'Sprinkles.' He smiled.

'Drink your milk first.' She put a straw in the milk carton and held it out to him. 'Careful, no spilling.'

'This man likes trains, like my mom,' Simon said after he took a sip.

'Most people like trains,' Ocaya said.

'Arceli had to take a long airplane ride to get to Canada,' Simon explained. 'Her family is far away but she doesn't cry. My dad doesn't cry, but my mom always cries when I have to say goodbye.'

Greene got up from the floor. 'That's because she loves you,' he said.

'She kisses me at night when she thinks I'm asleep, and I know she's crying. Like she did—'

'Simon, take another sip,' Ocaya said. 'Enough talking.'

'I'm saying that Mommy cries.' Simon put the straw back into his mouth.

'Yes. Here's the doughnut.' She had it wrapped in a white napkin. 'Be careful. No crumbs on the floor.'

'She cried last night,' Simon said.

Greene and Ocaya exchanged glances. 'Silly Simon,' Ocaya said. 'Last night you were not at your mother's house, you slept here.'

'My mom came into my room here at my dad's house. She kissed me and she was crying.' Simon took a bite out of the doughnut and swallowed it. 'She said she wouldn't see me for a long time. How come?'

Instead of looking at his nanny, Simon looked squarely at Greene – the man who'd appeared in his life, built trains with him on the floor, and told him he wasn't going to day-care camp today.

He picked a red sprinkle off the doughnut. 'How come?' Simon asked again.

CHAPTER 5

'I'm looking for Wyler Foods.' Officer Daniel Kennicott jumped out of his patrol car and grabbed the arm of a muscle-bound man carrying a basket of fresh corn with both hands. Kennicott had just parked at the Ontario Food Terminal, a gigantic tract of land in the southwest part of the city.

'Main building.' The man indicated the direction with his chin. 'Turn right and right again. Can't miss it.'

'Thanks.' Kennicott took off at a run. The food terminal was one of the biggest fresh food depots in North America, and the lot was filled to capacity with farmers' pickup trucks and vehicles belonging to buyers from every corner of the province. One caught his eye: a paneled van painted in gaudy orange and green colors, the words IT'S WYLER FRESH standing out in old-fashioned block letters.

He was fighting the clock. 'You're going to notify the oldest brother, Nathan Wyler, the one you see on all those billboard ads,' Detective Greene had told Kennicott half an hour before when he had gotten to Terrance Wyler's house. 'The parents

26

and the middle brother, Jason, who's disabled by some rare disease, live northwest of the city. Too far a drive. Better to let Nathan tell the family. Throw on your siren and get there fast. I don't want him to hear about this from the press.'

Kennicott had looked at the other patrol cars that cut off the street. Greene could have grabbed any of those cops and given them this assignment. 'No problem,' he'd said.

The food terminal was a large warehouse with a huge open courtyard in the middle. Storefronts rimmed the perimeter on all four sides, with colorful names like Rosie's Bananas, So Green Organics, Romano Pasta Company, Upper Canadian Cheese.

A network of concrete paths ran around the complex, and a constant stream of electric trolleys, laden with all manner of produce, zipped in and out of stores. Their drivers beeped their high-pitched horns as they whirled around, like hepped-up go-cart drivers on a familiar track.

It was easy to find Wyler Foods. The garish façade featured the store's orange and green colors, with the words IT'S WYLER FRESH on a banner high across the entrance. Inside was a beehive of activity. A lineup of farmers brought in cartons of food to show Wyler employees, all dressed in orange-and-green aprons. Nathan Wyler was right in the middle of it all, pacing back and forth behind a long, rectangular table, his striped bow tie slightly askew. He barked out orders as he pawed through the trays of fresh food his minions brought up for inspection.

Kennicott recognized the man immediately. Wyler Foods was a well-known high-end food store in midtown Toronto. It had recently launched a billboard ad campaign across the city that featured a photo of Nathan with his sleeves rolled up, arms filled with fresh produce, wearing the distinctive bow tie. Behind him were old photos of two other men wearing the same tie and handling produce. Obviously these were his father and grandfather. The tagline read 'I'm Nathan Wyler. For three generations it's always been Wyler Fresh.'

'Fucking heat wave,' Wyler said. He was a big man, with broad, hunched-over shoulders. He grabbed a tray of blueberries from one of his employees. 'This stuff's all shriveled to shit.'

Kennicott strode up to the table. Despite the fact that he was in full uniform, no one seemed to notice him.

'Look at this scrawny stuff they're trying to hide.' Wyler dug through a carton of romaine and yanked a thin head of lettuce from the bottom row. It was brown around the edges.

'Excuse me, Mr Wyler,' Kennicott said.

Wyler fixed him with a pair of eyes that were a remarkable translucent green. He wasn't an attractive man. Up close, his brownish hair had the plastic look of cheap color. He had a deep double chin. But the eyes made the rest of his face irrelevant.

'Yeah?' Wyler didn't seem at all surprised to see a police officer in his store. Squeezing the ends of a cantaloupe, he heaved it back into its box and turned to another employee. 'These are good. Ask if he's got any honeydew.'

'Could I speak to you for a moment, sir?' Kennicott asked.

Wyler held an oversize avocado out to him. 'Organic, from Florida. Amazing stuff. What is it, Officer?'

'I'd rather speak to you in private.' Kennicott took the avocado. It had a thick, scaly skin.

Someone shoved a cluster of fresh basil at Wyler. He tore off a bottom leaf and popped it into his mouth. 'This is the best. Americans have this quick cooling method. Stuff stays fresh for ten days.' He took back the avocado from Kennicott and offered him a leaf. 'Try it.'

'No thanks, I really must—'

'Look.' Wyler spread his arms out at the train of food being brought up to him. 'Monday morning. Peak buying hour. With this heat, no one has enough supply.'

'Sir, this is urgent.'

Wyler's fingers danced over a basket of green zucchini. 'They're not great, but we better grab them. See if they have any yellows,' he said to yet another employee before he turned back to Kennicott. 'Officer, you must be new at the division. Go help yourself to whatever you want. Not a problem.'

'It's about your brother,' Kennicott said.

Wyler's eyes widened and his shoulders slumped. His hands tightened around a celery stalk. 'Jason? He in the hospital again?'

'Please, sir,' Kennicott said. 'Where can we talk alone?'

'Back in my office.' Wyler tossed the celery at another employee. 'They're fine,' he said. 'Try to get some carrots.' He turned to the front of the store. 'Paulette, I'll be in back for five,' he yelled.

A young redhead who was working the cash register looked up. She had a beautiful smile.

The office was a small cubbyhole tucked away in the corner. An old steel desk stacked high with order books sat against the back wall. A pinboard behind it had heaps of paper stuck on every inch. Two round black ashtrays were filled with butts, many of them half smoked.

'We're not fancy.' Wyler closed the door behind them. The room had a rancid smell of moldy fruit. 'My father and my grandfather worked out of here too. Where's Jason?'

Kennicott realized that Wyler had naturally assumed this was about his disabled brother. 'It's not Jason. I'm afraid it's Terrance.'

Relief washed over Wyler's face, his concern immediately replaced by frustration and anger. 'What bullshit charge did Samantha cook up this time?'

'She didn't charge him with anything.'

'What'd she do?' He looked genuinely confused.

'I have terrible news.' Kennicott spoke quickly. He'd done this once before, informed a family about a murder. It was best to be direct. 'Your brother Terrance was found dead in his house this morning.'

'Dead?' Wyler's jaw gaped open.

'He was killed.'

Wyler flinched. His green eyes bulged, then receded. The first shock wave of understanding hit and he stumbled back, as if he'd been smacked in the solar plexus with a two-by-four. 'Killed?' He struggled to get the word out.

'I can't tell you much more right now, but clearly it was murder.'

'Murdered?' Wyler's breathing was forced. 'Terry?'

'The nanny found him.'

'Arceli?' His hands went to his face. 'She was at Terry's house last night. We were all there for dinner. Jason drove her home.'

'This morning when she came to work.'

'Where's Simon? It's Terry's week with the boy.'

'He's okay. We've taken him to the nanny's apartment.'

'Who did this?'

'We don't know yet.'

Wyler was nodding. Dazed. 'That explains it,' he said. Almost a whisper.

'Explains what, sir?'

Wyler reached down to his belt. Kennicott heard a hard plastic click sound, and a second later Wyler tossed a battered BlackBerry at him.

31

'Terry and I talk and e-mail about twenty times a day, and I haven't been able to get him all morning. I figured he was distracted because of the trial starting today.'

Wyler's eyes were right on Kennicott. Piercing. Looking for answers. 'What about Samantha?' he said, anger shoving the shock aside. 'Where the hell is the bitch?'

CHAPTER 6

Ted DiPaulo swung his Lexus sedan into the gravel driveway behind Winston Feindel's Mercedes. The family lawyer's license plate read ALIM$. The front door was open, and Feindel's ground-floor office was at the front of the house. Samantha Wyler sat on a quilted couch. She wore a short black skirt, a loose-fitting cotton blouse, and a pair of sporty-looking sandals. Her arms were crossed, and she was rocking back and forth. Feindel was at his desk, the sunlight streaming in through the windows behind him.

Wyler gazed up at DiPaulo. Her dark hair hung down limp and dirty. She flicked her head to get it out of her face, a nervous tic that he'd noticed the first time they'd met. Her eyes looked tired, her face haggard and exhausted.

Even in her bedraggled state, Samantha was attractive. She had a long neck, broad shoulders, and a full face centered by warm brown eyes. He had learned over the last few weeks that for her, her natural good looks were more of a burden than a blessing.

'Ms Wyler hasn't said a word since she came in.' Feindel's voice was unusually restrained.

'We need to speak alone,' DiPaulo said.

'I anticipated that.' Feindel vaulted from behind his desk. He was a gawky man, all arms and legs. 'I'm off to the local Starbucks.' He made the *a* in the coffee shop's name almost sound like an *o*.

DiPaulo listened to Feindel's footsteps recede down the hall. When he heard the front door close, he pulled the nearest chair closer to the sofa. Wyler was looking at the floor, rocking harder now. There was a teapot on a side table, and the room had a gentle smell of some exotic tea.

'Sam,' DiPaulo whispered. 'We need to talk right away. The police are going to find you in a few minutes.'

She seemed to roll into a tight ball, her head above her knees. There was something in her hands that she was protecting, like a child cradling her special blanket.

'They're going to have a lot of questions.'

She looked at him, a thin line of mascara streaking down her cheeks.

'You have the right to remain silent,' he said. 'You don't have to answer any questions.'

She nodded.

'But that won't stop them from questioning you. They're going to want to know where you were last night. This is no time to be ashamed if you did something foolish. If you have an alibi I need to know it now.'

She froze.

'I don't care where you were and the police won't . . .'

Her body lurched. For a moment DiPaulo thought she was going to vomit. She opened her arms and held out a red-and-white dish towel.

He was about to take it. Then his lawyer's instincts kicked in and he pulled back. 'Sam, listen to me. Put that on the carpet and open it. Slowly.'

Fixing him with her eyes, she placed the towel down and unfolded the corners one at a time, like a jeweler unwrapping a precious stone.

DiPaulo felt a tingle at the edge of his fingers. Before she lifted the last layer, he could already see the outline of the object inside.

'It's from our kitchen,' Wyler said, speaking at last. She exposed a black-handled knife, stained from top to bottom with blood.

Our kitchen, DiPaulo thought. Interesting choice of words.

She looked at him, those dark eyes now swimming in confusion. 'I took it,' she said.

'Well,' DiPaulo said, fighting to keep his voice steady, 'we're going to have to find a way to give it back.'

CHAPTER 7

Right now, Margaret Kwon had to be statue still. The door of her hotel room, number 403, was open a crack, and she stood at the threshold, her camera tucked into her palm. Even after twenty years as a celebrity journalist for *Faces* magazine, chasing Hollywood stars all across the continent, she lived for moments like this.

She had gotten this prime location the night before, when, for fifty bucks, a Somali limo driver tipped her off that April Goodling wasn't holed up at the Four Seasons, the hotel usually frequented by stars who came to Toronto, but was here at the Gladstone, a boutique hotel in the west end.

This was typical of Goodling. A control freak, in Kwon's opinion, she complained bitterly about being hounded by the celebrity press, at the same time courting their attention at every turn. This was especially true when one of her new films was about to be released, or when she was showing off her newest boyfriend.

Last September, when she'd been here at the Toronto International Film Festival to promote her latest film, Goodling had met Terrance Wyler at the Wyler Foods Festival Picnic. Remet, to be exact. The pair had dated twenty years before, when they were students at a small college in Vermont, and hadn't seen each other since. For once, the attraction on Goodling's part appeared to be genuine.

Kwon, who came to Toronto every year to cover the festival, received a tip from an actor who had been a part-time waiter at the picnic and had snagged a picture of Goodling and Wyler kissing behind the tent. The story went international – everyone loved the old-flames-rekindled angle. Wyler and his wife had broken up the next week.

This morning Kwon knew that Goodling had an 8:15 pickup. The actress planned to slip out the side door to her limo. Kwon had positioned one photographer, dressed like a street person, in the bus shelter across the road. A second, wearing a tracksuit, was in the lobby. With her door opened a crack, Kwon had a clear sight line of Goodling's door, room 408, diagonally across the hall.

It was the part of the job Kwon adored. Catching the moment. No matter how rich and famous they were, there was no magical way for celebrities to get out of a hotel. No Scotty to beam them up. Sooner or later they had to walk the walk, and Kwon was going to be there.

Hard work. That's how she'd broken the Brad torn condom story, the Britney implant piece, and the Jessica sixth-toe blockbuster. In her pursuit of celebrity trash, Kwon bought off hotel workers, charmed flight attendants, and cajoled hospital workers. She would wait endlessly in nightclub parking lots, hotel lobbies, and illegally parked cars. Most of all, she outthought the dumb-ass actors and their entourages of arrogant handlers.

Of course, at her age Kwon really shouldn't have been doing this anymore. By the time they were forty-five, most reporters had graduated to being editors, content to lounge behind a desk and let the young guns stay up on all-night stakeouts or go through a celebrity's garbage before the truck arrived.

Her parents thought she was flushing her brains down the toilet. Last weekend she'd trekked out to Long Island for dinner. There were her two younger sisters, parked in the living room with their lily-white husbands and their kids in OshKosh and Ralph Lauren. All of them had been right on time, of course. Kwon was an hour late.

What did they expect? She'd just landed the Marc and Jennifer satanic fertility story, for God's sake. But all her family saw was Margaret, still single, with no professional degree behind her name. The night ended as they always did, with Kwon and her parents screaming at each other in full Korean rage.

Goodling's door opened a crack. Gotcha, Kwon thought.

She tensed. A stocky guy in a baseball jacket came out and looked down the hall in the other direction, toward the elevator. Kwon shut her door before he turned back her way. She counted on her fingers. She estimated that ten seconds was enough time for the bodyguard to check that the coast was clear and get Goodling into the hallway. She'd paced it out late last night: it was ten steps from her room to 408, then fifteen steps to the elevator.

Eight, nine, ten. Kwon stepped into the hall. Right away she knew something was wrong. The bodyguard was staring back toward room 408, looking concerned. Goodling was still inside.

Kwon had no choice. If she turned back, it would alert the guard. She'd planned to film a secret video with the handheld camera while they were in the elevator together. She started down the hall.

A few steps in she heard a voice coming from the room. 'No. No!' It was Goodling. She was screaming.

Kwon's heart beat fast. She kept going. Five more steps and she'd be at the door. Then she made a rookie mistake – she sped up.

Her quickened pace caught the corner of the bodyguard's eye. His head jerked around. Moving with surprising dexterity for such a big man, he lunged inside the hotel room.

He was slamming the door shut. There was only one thing to do. Kwon pressed the Video Shoot button and dove straight ahead, like a goalie in a soccer match reaching for a top corner shot. She heard Goodling scream out something and felt a whoosh of air as the door banged shut.

Kwon's chin hit the wood floor and her teeth rattled at the back of her jaw. Then her whole body crashed.

I really am getting too old for this, she thought, lying spread out in the middle of the empty hallway. She turned the camera toward her and switched it to display mode. A short video of Goodling played on the screen. Kwon played it again, this time frame by frame, like the Zapruder film of President Kennedy getting shot in Dallas.

Kwon could feel the adrenaline still in her body. Her chest and rib cage were sore, her chin was ripped open, and her back teeth felt tight. But it didn't matter. She'd hit pay dirt. Without a doubt, right there at frame thirty-four, was the next cover of *Faces* magazine.

CHAPTER 8

Ari Greene stepped out of the elevator on the eleventh floor of the office building at 350 Bay Street, right across from the Old City Hall courthouse, and checked his watch. It was 9:50. As usual, he was early. A narrow metal sign that read DIPAULO & PARISH, SPECIALISTS IN CRIMINAL LAW, 1105, pointed to his right down a poorly lit hallway.

The door to suite 1105 was a dull gray, and his opening it triggered an unseen bell that chimed out a high-pitched ding-dong. The law firm's lobby was a mishmash of old sofas and a smattering of dated magazines. On top of the pile, an issue of *The Hockey News* from last spring celebrated the Toronto Maple Leafs' unlikely Stanley Cup win. This summer the team released the veteran goaltender who'd been the surprise hero of the series. Instead they signed a young Swedish goalie. Greene's father had been apoplectic.

The reception desk was empty. The window behind it was covered by a dusty-looking blind clamped shut. Greene peeked over the edge and saw stacks of cardboard evidence boxes. An old-fashioned grandfather clock stood on the far wall, ticking as its pendulum swung back and forth.

'Ari.'

Greene turned to see Ted DiPaulo striding down the narrow corridor, the top button of his shirt open, his tie askew. The lawyer's whole face broke into a grin as the two men shook hands. He had one of those winning smiles that lit up every room he was in, which he used like a weapon when he was in court to cajole witnesses, ingratiate himself to judges, and charm juries.

DiPaulo held out his hand. 'Thanks for coming down. You're here early.'

'Bad habit,' Greene said.

He followed the lawyer down the hallway, thinking, as he always did when confronted with DiPaulo, how well the man's stature matched his big voice and big ego. They passed the office of DiPaulo's partner, Nancy Parish, who Greene knew from a previous murder trial. Her door was closed.

Greene well remembered when DiPaulo had been the head of the Downtown Toronto Crown Attorney's office. He'd been tough, even on the up-and-coming lawyers, who tended to idolize him. And he had loved big trials. The higher the profile the better.

'How're the kids?' Greene asked when DiPaulo had ushered him into his office.

Unlike the barely furnished dinginess of the rest

of the office, DiPaulo's space was beautifully laid out.

'Growing up too fast.'

DiPaulo motioned Greene to the far chair near the window and settled himself into the other one. He left the door open behind him.

'Your oldest must be in university,' Greene said.

'Good memory, Detective,' DiPaulo said. 'Only my daughter's left at home, and just for one more year.'

Greene scanned the room. On the credenza near the entrance was a picture of DiPaulo hiking with his late wife, Olive, a lovely-looking Chinese woman. There were photos of their kids at various ages. Beautiful children.

He returned his gaze to DiPaulo. Both men knew the time for their cordial chitchat was over. The defense lawyer had called him an hour earlier and asked if he could come over right away. 'Something urgent' was all he would say.

'Samantha Wyler.' DiPaulo checked his watch. 'She's my client. I assume you want to talk to her in relation to the death of her husband?'

'Seven stab wounds,' Greene said. 'I think murder's the appropriate word.'

DiPaulo nodded, keeping his face neutral, careful not to give away whether this was news to him or not.

'Know where I can find her?' Greene asked.

'I do. I need time to talk to her.' DiPaulo fiddled with his gold wedding band.

'If she has an alibi for last night, I'd like to hear it. The sooner the better.'

The lawyer sneaked another look at his watch.

He's stalling, Greene thought. Waiting for someone.

The outer door opened and Greene heard the ding-dong of the bell. DiPaulo's whole face broke into a grin.

Sharp footsteps pounded down the hall, and a moment later a pencil-thin black woman in a long dress and high heels stood in the doorway. She was young. In her hand was a plastic shopping bag with a LONGO'S FINE FOODS logo on it.

'Excuse me,' the woman said, out of breath. 'I'm looking for Detective Ari Greene.'

Greene stood and extended his hand. 'You found him.'

'Barbara Delacroix.' She gave him a surprisingly firm handshake for someone with such a slender arm. 'I'm a lawyer at Levine and Sundralingham.'

Greene looked at the bag. 'What can I do for you?'

'Uh, can I talk to you alone, please, sir? If you don't mind?'

DiPaulo popped out of his seat, his smile broader than ever. 'Let me show you two the boardroom.'

Seconds later Greene was in a small, windowless room, sitting across from Delacroix at an oval-shaped table.

'Detective Greene.' She put the bag on the table and spoke in an over-rehearsed monotone: 'The

44

firm of Levine and Sundralingham has been retained by a client who wishes to keep his or her identity anonymous. That client has instructed our firm to deliver to you the contents of this package.'

Delacroix passed the bag across to him. She looked as if she'd just gotten rid of something highly infectious.

Greene pulled the top back. There was a clear plastic bag sealed inside. It contained a red-and-white dish towel.

'I don't imagine you know what's in here,' Greene said.

'I . . . I'm instructed to tell you only what I've just said.'

'Is it heavy?'

'Not too . . . I'm not supposed to say anything else.'

'Sharp?'

'Yes . . .' She stopped. Her breath became forced. 'I'm sorry, Officer – I mean Detective. I was only called to the bar ten months ago.'

'You did fine.' Greene closed the outer bag. 'Tell the lawyers at your firm: mission accomplished. You delivered the bloody knife.'

Delacroix scurried out, and the door ding-donged again. Greene strolled across the hall and found DiPaulo behind his desk, hanging up the phone.

They both knew what had just happened. Samantha Wyler must have given DiPaulo the bloody knife, and he'd set up a double blind, lawyer's style. Step one: he hired Levine and Sundralingham. That way he was their client, and his identity was protected. Step two: he instructed his new lawyers to pick up the knife. Step three: he got Greene down to his office to facilitate the handover. This way no trail led back to his client Samantha Wyler.

'Interesting meeting.' Greene lifted the bag.

'Really.' DiPaulo flashed his golden smile and pointed to the phone. 'That was Ms Wyler.'

'Where is she?'

DiPaulo shrugged. 'I'd rather not tell you right now. Trust me, she's not going anywhere. As I said, I need to talk to her first.'

Greene thought of Parish's closed office door. He was pretty sure Wyler was in there.

'We both know she has no legal obligation to speak to you,' DiPaulo said. The smile was gone.

DiPaulo always played hardball. The guy loved to win. But to his credit, he played by the rules, and what he'd said was true. Greene had no power to force Samantha Wyler to talk to the police. If she didn't, his only option would be to arrest her. And then she'd probably shut up entirely.

'There's a knife and a red-and-white towel missing from the murder scene.' Greene lifted up the bag. 'I want to know where she was last night.'

A fragile trust develops between a good lawyer and a detective on a tough case like this. DiPaulo had moved quickly to get the bloody knife returned. It showed good faith. Sometimes it was better to leave a suspect's lawyer alone with his client. He might talk the client into being realistic, entering a quick guilty plea for the best possible deal.

'How much time do you need?' Greene asked.

'We have quite a bit of ground to cover.'

This was defense-lawyer code for 'Let me work on her. She's still in denial.'

'If I'm going to arrest her, I'll call you first,' Greene said.

'That's fair.'

'The longer it takes, the weaker her alibi becomes. Like fish, it starts to stink in a few days.'

'Don't I know it,' DiPaulo said.

He looked at the plastic bag in Greene's hand. He fidgeted again with his wedding ring. DiPaulo looked like a gambler who'd drawn a bad hand but was in too deep to pull out of the game. With nothing left to smile about.

CHAPTER 9

'**F**orty-nine, please,' Daniel Kennicott said to the woman standing next to the number display in the crowded elevator. He'd squeezed into the last available space among all the people in business suits. Most carried dark briefcases or expensive bags, and at least half of them were tapping away on BlackBerrys. The others were watching the elevator news.

This was me four years ago, he thought, remembering his days as a junior lawyer working his way up the big-firm ladder. Back then he would have fit in. Stylish suit. Handmade shoes. But now, in full cop uniform, he felt totally out of place.

The elevator accelerated upward and in moments he was deposited into the reception area of Anita Starr and Associates, Barristers & Solicitors, Specialists in Family Law. Across a shining marble floor, behind a rosewood desk accented by a bouquet of yellow roses, a young female receptionist wore a thin headset.

Kennicott took out his police business card. The woman put her hand over the microphone and smiled. There was a tiny diamond stud under her bottom lip.

'Daniel Kennicott, Toronto Police. I'm here to see Ms Starr.'

'She's expecting you,' the woman said. 'Would you like a cappuccino, herbal tea, bottled water?'

'I'm fine,' Kennicott said.

'Ms Starr's office is at the end of the hall. You can go straight in.'

Kennicott walked past a raft of modern paintings and photo prints. Starr's office was a huge affair featuring an enormous glass desk held up by four pillars made of the same marble as the front hall floor. More yellow roses rested on a side table. There was only one client chair in the room. It was covered in lush black leather.

Starr was a thin woman, dressed in a fine linen jacket and skirt. A jade necklace matched her earrings. Her hair, heavily streaked, was perfectly in place.

'It's been an unbelievable morning,' Starr was saying into the phone. She waved Kennicott in, motioning to the chair. 'No one can believe that this has happened to me.'

Cradling the phone on her shoulder, Starr pointed to two legal file folders on her desk. She lifted one and passed it to Kennicott. 'Can you believe it?' she said into the phone. 'I canceled our trip to Barcelona for this trial.'

The file was labeled WYLER, TERRANCE. It was

well organized, with different-colored folders for each section.

'Normie's ready to kill me.' Starr giggled. 'Oh, I guess I shouldn't say that. A police officer just came in. Hope I'm not a suspect. Tell His Honor I'm bringing the motion into his court in about an hour. You're a doll.'

She hung up and came around the desk. Kennicott stood to greet her.

'Anita Starr.' She stood near him and took his hand in both of hers. 'Good of you to come, Officer Kennicott. Terrance was such a wonderful client. I still remember the first day he came into the office. All the girls swooned.'

'We're hoping you can help us with this investigation.'

'Twenty-four years of practice,' Starr said, still holding Kennicott's hand. 'I've never had anything like this happen to me.' Her attention was drawn to a thin computer screen at the side of her desk. Every few seconds there was a faint ping. 'My phone, e-mails – it hasn't stopped. Everyone's asking me how I am handling it.'

Kennicott lifted the folder in his free hand. 'This for us?'

'Of course. I'll do anything to help with this investigation.' She patted his hand. 'I assume you know about Samantha's false charges against Terrance last year. Her e-mails and phone messages, how the police warned her.'

'We've pulled all the files,' Kennicott said.

'Her lawyer, Feindel, is no fool. But he lost control of his client. I'm sure you've talked to him already.'

Kennicott shook his head. 'I can't discuss the investigation with you.'

'Sorry. My husband, Norman, calls me a back-seat driver, even when I'm in the front seat. I feel so helpless.' She sighed and finally let go of his hand. Reaching for the other folder, she flipped through it with practiced ease. 'I organize every file the same way. Financials are blue, child custody assessments green, family court pleadings and affidavits are red. Yellow is correspondence.' Starr bit her lower lip. 'I was going to rip Samantha apart on the witness stand.'

'When's the last time you heard from Terrance?'

'Last night. We e-mailed back and forth all weekend. Feindel knew his case was going down the tubes, so on Friday morning he hit us with a last-minute offer. Samantha had been fighting for joint custody, and she didn't have a prayer. Now she wanted partial access, proposed a whole schedule. I told Terrance they were running scared and he shouldn't respond. Sunday night he e-mailed me that his family had been over for dinner and everyone agreed. No deal. This morning I checked my messages.' She reached for the BlackBerry on her desk and scrolled through it – '"Ms Starr. I know you'll be upset with me. I've accepted Sam's offer. This will be best for Simon. Sam's coming over in half an hour to talk through

the details. Thanks for everything you've done.'"
Starr was still standing close to Kennicott. 'I was
in shock.'

'When was that written?'

'I canceled my summer holidays for this.'

'The time of the e-mail?'

She shook her head. 'Twelve thirty-seven a.m.'
She walked back to her chair. Her computer screen
was ping-pinging away more than ever. Kennicott
sat down. He realized that by having only one
chair facing her, she made clients feel they were
getting her undivided attention.

Her hands flew across the keyboard. 'This is an
emergency ex parte motion to prevent Samantha
Wyler from having access to her son.'

'On what grounds?' I sound like a lawyer,
Kennicott thought.

Starr turned to him. 'That she's a danger to the
boy.'

He expected her to turn back to her computer.
Instead she looked right at him. 'I know you're a
lawyer. And I know why you became a cop. I went
to university with your brother, the joint LLM-MBA
program. Michael was the most brilliant person
I've ever met.'

This happened quite often. His brother had
been such a big presence in so many people's
lives. Kennicott often ran into his former friends
or colleagues. He decided to ignore her comment.
'Why do you say Samantha's a threat to her
son?'

Starr chuckled. She had a surprisingly guttural laugh. 'Because she killed her husband.'

'You know I'm not going to comment on that.'

'Okay. You want background?'

'This only happened a few hours ago. We need to find out everything we can.'

'I'll start with Samantha. From some small town up north. Middle of nowhere. Family ran a gas station. Scholarship student, real ambitious, worked for the bank and got recruited to work at Wyler Foods. Nathan, the oldest brother, was running the business into the ground.'

'That how she met Terrance?'

'He was living in the States and came back for the company barbecue. They had a whirlwind romance, and he moved back home. Terrance's mother planned a big wedding, but Sam talked Terrance into eloping. Before you know it, she's pregnant. They were so mismatched.'

'How's that?'

'Terrance had it easy his whole life. He didn't want to work that hard. When Simon was born, he was head over heels about the baby. Samantha wasn't into motherhood. And she hated the stupid social scene. The balls, the opera openings, sitting around that boring yacht club all summer. Sam didn't care about any of that crap. I give her credit for one thing: she actually worked.'

'What happened to their marriage?'

'Samantha talked Terrance into leaving Wyler Foods and starting up their own food store. A total disaster. Last year he met April Goodling and that was it. He went back to work with his brothers and was loving it.'

'You know the brothers?'

'Those Wyler boys. What a mess.' Starr ran a hand through her hair. 'Nathan, the oldest, is fifty-three and on his third wife. We'll see how long that lasts. And Jason has that terrible disease. Another year and he'll be on a feeding tube. Poor guy. In the Wyler family what good are you if you can't haul around a bunch of vegetables at three in the morning?'

'I met Nathan this morning,' Kennicott said. 'He's not fond of Samantha.'

'Hah,' Starr said. 'The whole family hates her.'

Starr hit the keyboard again and the printer started spitting out pages.

'How did Terrance react to Samantha's angry e-mails and voice messages? Was he upset? Furious?'

She shook her head. 'Not the vengeful type. I almost had to break his arm to force him to call the police. My husband calls me Anita the Hun. Says I make Attila look like a marshmallow.'

A marshmallow, Kennicott thought, that's burned to a crisp. He stood up and tucked the file under his arm.

Starr walked him to the door. She took his hand again. Her grip was strong. 'Your brother told me a lot about you.'

'Michael? Why would he talk to you about me?'

'I had a younger sibling too. My sister Arlene.' Starr dropped Kennicott's hand. 'She killed herself the first year we were at graduate school. Michael was great to talk to.'

A part of Kennicott didn't want to have this conversation. Another part couldn't pull away.

'Michael thought because your father was such a famous judge, your mother the high-profile journalist, and then he was so successful so young, it would be a tough act to follow. Like I was for Arlene.'

'Thanks, but we should really talk about this some other time.'

Starr didn't budge. She'd zeroed in on him, and he could see that she had laserlike focus when she needed it. He thought of her clients, sitting in the only chair facing her. Mesmerized.

'Michael said everything came so easily to you. He told me girls had been following you around since about grade six. You hardly worked at school and were always top of your class. But he was frustrated too. Said you never pushed yourself. I still remember it used to drive him crazy, that you were always late for things.'

Kennicott had been famous in his family for always being tardy. 'Meet Daniel, my great, always-late brother,' was how Michael used to introduce him. The last time they spoke, Michael told him to be at the restaurant at seven-thirty. 'And this time, surprise me. Be on time.' They had both laughed. He got there at ten to eight. Too late.

'With no family, I'm sure it's lonely.' Starr let go of his hand at last. 'I know he'd be proud of you now.'

'Thank you.' Kennicott took a step toward the door.

Starr rustled the papers from the printer. They were in her other hand. 'I'm going to get this order. Samantha won't be able to see Simon for the next seventy-two hours.' She was all business now.

'Why seventy-two?' he asked

'Takes us through the funeral on Thursday.'

'This investigation could last a long time.'

'You'll arrest her in a few days,' she said. 'No judge will let her see Simon while she's on trial for murder. Sam will try to con the jury, but it won't work this time. Once she's convicted this order will become permanent. I'm going to make sure she never sees her son again.'

CHAPTER 10

'Detective Greene just left,' Ted DiPaulo told Winston Feindel, who had picked up the phone on the first ring. 'Terrance Wyler was stabbed seven times.'

'More bad news on this end,' Feindel said. 'Anita Starr, Terrance's family lawyer, got an emergency order from the court prohibiting Samantha access to her son for the next seventy-two hours. Your client will not be pleased.'

'That's for sure.' DiPaulo thanked Feindel and hung up. Samantha was next door in Nancy Parish's office, and he should have gone to get her. Instead he wandered over to the credenza and picked up the picture of himself and Olive.

Late one night soon after Olive had been diagnosed with liver cancer, DiPaulo found himself sleepless, staring at the bookshelf in their living room. He pulled down his old college copy of the Elisabeth Kübler-Ross book *On Death and Dying*, wrapped himself in a Hudson's Bay blanket, and read straight through until morning. Denial, anger, bargaining, depression, acceptance: the five stages of dying. He had watched his wife go through them all.

He realized that his clients went through the same process. And it could take weeks, sometimes months, to coax them out of denial, cushion their anger, reason through their bargaining, nurse them through depression, and push them to acceptance. That the rest of the suite was shabby did not bother him. It was the inner sanctum that needed to feel safe. How they were handled at the first meeting was crucial.

When they came to see him they were almost always in shock. That's why he'd set up his office so it oozed comfort. His wooden desk was always clean, the window counter was covered with jade plants and small watercolors, and old film noir posters and artwork from various stages of his children's lives lined the walls. Two upholstered clients' chairs rotated so they could face each other. He insisted that clients sit in the far chair while he took the one closest to the door – never behind his desk, to start out.

DiPaulo went down the hall to get Samantha. He didn't have the luxury of time. If she had an alibi, he needed to hear it now. But what alibi could she have? After all, she'd brought the bloody knife with her to Feindel's office.

Sam followed him back to his office and flopped down into the chair closest to the door. She was the only client he'd ever had who didn't take the seat by the window. 'I don't like to have my back to the wall,' she'd said at their first meeting. 'I was attacked when I was a kid, in high school. I always have a Plan B.'

He closed the door and gave her a glass of water. She placed it on the coaster on the edge of his desk.

'You okay, Sam?' He took the chair beside the window and swiveled it to face her.

'No.' She studied the glass of water. Her voice was hollow, her eyes unfocused. Classic signs of shock.

'We have to talk.' He sounded neutral, not overly sympathetic.

She glanced at him, jarred by his unusually cool tone. 'Terry is dead, God knows when I'll get to see Simon, and . . .' Her voice faltered. She shook her head.

'Terry isn't just dead. He was murdered.'

She let her brown eyes rest on him. Even when they were in distress, those eyes warmed everything in their path.

'I didn't kill him.' Her voice was so faint DiPaulo had to strain to hear her.

This didn't surprise him. Most clients told him they were innocent at the initial meeting. He never let himself believe or disbelieve them. But he knew that denial runs deep. On the other hand, if she had an alibi, nothing would make him happier than running a murder trial he thought he could win.

'Sam, listen. We have almost no time and little room to maneuver. If you weren't in that house last night, I need to know where you were.'

She looked again at the water.

'They could arrest you at any moment.' He had to break through to her. 'The first question will be: Where were you last night?'

She didn't say a word.

Clients usually grew quiet when he got them out of the denial stage. Silence was often a form of surrender to the inevitable.

He pushed on, looking straight at her. 'Every murder case comes down to two things. Motive and opportunity.'

'Ha.' She laughed, catching him off guard. 'I have motive in spades. The divorce trial about to start . . . his movie-star girlfriend.'

Good, DiPaulo thought. She's talking. 'Those angry voice mails and e-mails you sent Terry. They don't help.'

'So it all depends on whether I had the opportunity?' She turned to the closed door beside her. For a second he was afraid she was going to bolt.

'Listen carefully before you say another word,' he said. 'I can't knowingly present false evidence in court. If you tell me you were in his house last night, you can't turn around later and testify that you were somewhere else.'

In fact, this was an overstatement. There were many ways DiPaulo could finesse the problem, especially if, like most clients, she told him more than one story. Then his position would be simply that he had no way of knowing what the truth was. But right now, he wanted to maximize the pressure he was putting on Samantha.

60

Her head bobbed. Her back was to him, but he knew he had her full attention.

'I can do great things with the truth, however bad it is,' he said. 'Nothing would be worse than for you to lie to me right now. I'd rather you say nothing.'

Wyler swung her chair back to him. She was silent. That seemed to say it all.

'There's one thing we can do,' DiPaulo said. 'If you're not sure of what to say to me, you can ask me a "theoretical" question and I can give you a theoretical answer.'

She finally spoke. 'So, theoretically, if I was in the house, that would mean . . .'

They were entering the danger zone. The fine line between preparing a client to talk to the police and coaching them about what to say. 'So, theoretically, you don't have an alibi?'

'Let's say, theoretically, I was in the house.'

'Then we better make a deal.'

'What if . . .' Wyler reached for the glass of water. She was putting her thoughts together. Teetering on the verge of something. Not quite trusting him.

'Theoretically. If I said I was at the house last night . . .' She tossed her hair off her face and took a sip before she turned back to face DiPaulo. Those dark eyes bore into him. 'But that I didn't kill him. Theoretically. Would you believe me?'

'It's not my job to believe you.'

She slammed the glass down. 'I need a lawyer who believes me.'

'That's the last thing you need.' DiPaulo kept calm. 'You need a lawyer who can defend you.'

She glared at him. Challenging.

He stared back. There was a moment with clients when they were ready to confess. It was human nature, this urge to confide in someone. That's why he hadn't responded a few minutes ago when Wyler said she didn't kill her husband. Didn't want her to feel trapped by her own words. He needed to keep his professional distance.

'Why did you go to the house?' he asked. 'Theoretically.'

'After midnight, Terry e-mailed me. I can show you if you want.' She pulled out her BlackBerry, scrolled through the e-mails, and passed it over to him. 'See. He said he'd accept my offer after all. Asked me to come to talk about it.'

DiPaulo watched her, transfixed. She'd dropped saying theoretically. Greene must have seen these e-mails on Terrance's BlackBerry before he came to DiPaulo's office. That's why he'd said *if* she has an alibi. He knew she didn't. This kept getting worse. 'You went over?'

'He was dead on the kitchen floor.' She was breathing hard now. 'The knife was right there beside him. I ran upstairs to see if Simon was okay. Then I left.'

'You left?'

'With the knife.' She sat statue still. 'I wrapped it in a dish towel. A red-and-white one.'

'Why?'

'To protect my son.' She opened her hands in a helpless gesture of resignation.

This couldn't be worse. The risk of having this type of theoretical conversation at such an early stage was that your client would lock into her denial. Now Samantha had convinced herself of a story that no jury in the world would believe. Especially if she spoke to them in this cold, remote tone.

'You didn't call the police?'

'I was in shock.'

'And you left your son alone in the house?'

Her body jolted. 'I panicked. He was asleep.'

'He's four years old.' DiPaulo felt a surge of anger. He was slipping into his old Crown Attorney role, cross-examining his own client.

The last major case he did at the Crown's office, he'd prosecuted a man who'd grabbed a young girl jogging in the Humber River valley, raped and strangled her, then left her dead in the woods. The man's pathetic explanation as to how his sperm was found in a fourteen-year-old's vagina? That he had been out running, happened upon her dead body, and had sex with it. The jury convicted him in less than two hours. Samantha Wyler's story wouldn't keep them out much longer.

'It's awful,' she said.

'The jury will hate you for it.'

She started to hyperventilate. Her face flushed. 'Okay. You want to make a list of everything I've done wrong in my life?'

'No, Samantha, I . . .'

She balled her hand into a fist and pointed her index finger at him. 'After my father died, I blamed my mother.' She flicked out her middle finger. 'Those teachers and librarians back home – I never showed any appreciation.' Her ring finger came next, the wedding ring still on it. 'Terry. It's true what they say. I hated his family. Couldn't stand how they controlled him.' Her baby finger. 'And I wasn't a great mother. For Terry it was the best thing, having a child. He wanted more kids and I wouldn't do it.' She yanked out her thumb. 'I've always been a misfit.'

With her open palm she slammed her hand down on his desk, barely missing the glass of water. 'But I'm not a murderer. I didn't kill him.'

She rolled her hand back into a fist and started to gnaw on the end of her thumb, almost like a child. DiPaulo had never seen her cry, but in a flash she was heaving tears. 'I want to see my son.'

He shook his head. 'I have more bad news for you. The Wylers have got a court order prohibiting you from seeing Simon for the next seventy-two hours.'

'What?' She was screaming.

'Unless you have an alibi . . .'

Wyler sobbed. It was as if some embedded plug in her emotions had been torn asunder. She cried for a few minutes and he watched her. At last she straightened her back and the tears stopped. She drank the rest of the water. 'No one will believe me.'

DiPaulo felt ill. Sam had been in Terrance Wyler's home. Left the child alone. Had the murder weapon. 'Where did you go after you left the house?'

'To my lawyer's office. Feindel.'

'He's miles away. How did you get there?'

'I walked. It's downhill. That's all I remember.' She looked frightened. Lost. 'It's true. You don't believe me, do you?'

From the beginning of his career, he'd lived by the mantra: a lawyer who believes everything a witness or his client says is a fool. It wasn't so much that everybody lied. But everyone had secrets. No one ever told the whole story, so DiPaulo never took anything at face value. Always had his own Plan B.

He got up and sat behind his desk. Samantha had her arms crossed in front, her hands clutching her shoulders. Logic dictated that he shouldn't believe a word she'd said. But with this woman who was so remote, so difficult to like, what was true? What was denial? What was manipulation?

He would work like hell to get Samantha to admit her guilt while he bargained for the best possible deal. And if she stuck to her story, he would be prepared to defend her with everything he had.

'Don't,' he said, looking Samantha square in the eyes, 'ask me that question again.'

CHAPTER 11

How many years have I waited to have a Monday morning like this? Jennifer Raglan wondered. She plopped her still-hot latte on the side table by the living-room couch and opened a new mystery novel, one set in Sicily. Bliss. Her two older boys were off at her mother's place for another week, her daughter, Dana, wasn't coming home from camp until this afternoon, and her husband, Gordon, was at work. It felt like the first time in decades that she'd been alone in her own house. On holiday from work. On a weekday. With no one to take care of but herself.

This past June she'd stepped down as the head Crown Attorney for the Downtown Toronto office, and since then she'd been luxuriating in the world of diminished responsibility. Raglan wasn't going to prosecute any more murder cases that could take weeks or even months out of her life. Instead she was assigned to short daily trials. And now that she didn't have to worry about the lives of fifty other lawyers, she could do her own work and go home.

Being back home was new too. A year ago the

stress of the job, the kids, everything overwhelmed her. She moved out and within weeks started a secret affair with a homicide detective, Ari Greene. Breaking up with him to move back and give her marriage another shot had been tough. She was trying her hardest with Gordon. This morning she'd walked up to Queen Street with him and they even held hands while waiting for his streetcar.

But the best part of the morning, she had to admit, was wandering on the street after he was gone. Cruising the bookstore, buying the novel, picking up her fresh latte. Time for herself. What an amazing concept.

The phone rang.

No, no, no, she said to herself. I'm going to ignore it. She opened her book and let the phone keep ringing until it finally stopped.

She read the first paragraph. The phone rang again.

Damn. Maybe it was the camp. Something about her daughter. The bus was due in at twelve-thirty.

There was nothing around to use as a bookmark, so she folded back the first page along the spine of the book and peeled herself off the couch. Maybe if I go slow enough, whoever it is will hang up, she thought as she made her way into the kitchen. No such luck. It was still ringing when she got there. Raglan picked up the cordless phone. 'Hello,' she said.

'Jennifer, thank God you're home.' It was Ralph

Armitage. Armitage had taken over as the head Crown two months ago. He called almost every day for advice. Even when she and Gordon were away in New England. It was too much.

'Ralph, please. I don't want to be rude, but I'm on holiday and—'

'You haven't heard?'

'Heard what?' she said, not able to resist.

'Last night. Four murders. Terrance Wyler, the food guy who was dating that movie star, was stabbed to death in his kitchen.' Panic was rising in Armitage's voice.

'Dana's coming back from camp this afternoon. I have to pick her up.' Raglan went back to the living room. Sun was hitting the place on the cushions where her body had made an indent.

'I hate to bug you. But you know how short I am on experienced Crowns,' Armitage said.

It was true, and partly Raglan's fault. Last spring she'd fired two of the top Crowns, Phil Cutter and Barb Gild, when they'd gone rogue. 'How about Fernandez?' she said, naming one of the best young Crowns in the office.

'Back in Chile, visiting his in-laws.'

Raglan asked about a few others she thought would be up to the task. All were either on holiday or assigned to the other three homicides.

'I know you're not doing any more murder trials,' Armitage said. 'I just need you to get things rolling. You know how important the first few hours can be.'

Armitage was right. It was crucial to have a Crown who knew what she was doing on the case right from the get-go.

'I'm picking Dana up at twelve-thirty at Yorkdale,' she said, referring to a shopping mall in the north part of the city.

'Give me one hour.'

Raglan sighed. 'Who's the OIC?' If the officer in charge of the case was lousy, something like this could turn into a nightmare.

'Greene, Ari Greene,' Armitage said. 'You ever done anything with him?'

'A few things.' Raglan was glad he couldn't see her blushing. She looked at her cooling latte and her unread novel, which had folded back shut.

'Okay,' she said. 'You've got me. One hour.'

CHAPTER 12

'We're here to see Phil Cutter,' Daniel Kennicott said.

He and Detective Greene were standing at the ultramodern reception desk of the law firm of Cutter & Gild, Specialists in Criminal Law. The thin blond receptionist reached for a sleek phone.

'Gents, it's been too long,' a voice called from down the hallway before the receptionist could say a word.

Kennicott looked over to see Cutter barreling toward them, his voice booming out ahead of him. As he approached, Kennicott was taken aback by his appearance. For years Phil Cutter and his partner Barb Gild were Crown Attorneys at the Downtown Toronto office, and Cutter was renowned for his cheap suits and squeaky soft-soled shoes. Now he wore a crisp blue Armani suit, matching tie and pocket handkerchief, wingtip loafers.

Cutter grabbed his hand and did the same with Detective Greene. 'Recession's a great time to start a law practice. We tied this place up for five years,

70

option for another five. Landlords were begging for us to come in. And best of all, crime's way up.'

'Lucky for you,' Greene said. Kennicott saw Greene's mouth turn in a subtle smirk.

A female voice from down the hall caught Kennicott's attention. 'Ari, Daniel. How are you?'

It was Barb Gild. If Cutter had changed his look from high school vice principal to downtown lawyer, Gild had gone from mousy librarian to high-end fashionista. Gone were her flat shoes, bulky sweaters, greasy hair tied behind her head, and the what-me-wear-makeup look. Now she wore high heels, and a pearl necklace swished across her patterned silk dress. Her cheeks were dabbed with rouge, and her red hair was a new shade of auburn, expertly coifed.

Gild approached and shook hands.

There was a moment of awkward silence. Cutter had been a hard-nosed prosecutor famous for his take-no-prisoners attitude, his nonstop nervous energy, and his outrageously loud voice. Gild was the office research guru. Last May they were pushed out because of their overzealous efforts to gain a conviction in a murder trial. It had been Greene and Kennicott's case.

Cutter clapped his hands together and rocked back and forth. The man never could stay still. 'I have to show you guys around.'

Gild turned to him and put up both hands, like a hall monitor calming down an overexcited student. 'Let's do it after,' she said. 'April's ready.'

'Mustn't keep our celebrity client waiting.' Cutter made an effort to lower his voice but wasn't very successful. 'We have this fantastic new espresso machine. I'll get the receptionist to make you a latte.'

'What happened to your famous coffee thermos?' Greene asked.

Cutter put his head back and let out a guffaw. As a Crown, he loved to brag about raising four kids on his civil servant's salary, and how he did it with bagged lunches and coffee from home in his battered old thermos.

'I'm in the marketing business now. Follow me to our beautiful boardroom.' He led them down the hall.

Kennicott noticed Cutter's fancy Armani pants were belted up too high, exposing a pair of cheap beige socks. He caught Greene's eye. The detective always dressed impeccably, and he could tell Greene had seen them too. He winked at Kennicott.

Goodling sat at the far end of a black-lacquered rectangular table. A heavyset man with almost no neck was seated beside her. The actress stood the moment they came in, making direct eye contact first with Kennicott, then Greene. Her hair, a reddish brown shade that matched her tan complexion, swept back from her forehead and was gathered in a confident ponytail over her left shoulder. She wore a glistening white shirt, with the collar up, under a green cashmere sweater. In her hands was a sheaf of legal papers that she held in front of her body like a shield. Her face was perfectly proportioned, high cheekbones, stunning eyes, slender nose. It was hard not to stare at her.

For the last decade Kennicott had had an on-again, off-again relationship with a fashion model named Andrea. A year earlier, things had finally ended for good when she moved to Milan to live with a photographer. In all those years, he'd learned what it was like for people who were born with natural beauty. How they developed the instinct to retreat, build their own walls of protection, crave privacy.

'Hello, officers.' Goodling extended her right hand across the table, keeping her paper shield in place with her left. 'Barbara and Philip speak highly of both of you.'

'Thanks.' Kennicott let go of Goodling's hand. Barb and Phil were now Barbara and Philip. He exchanged bemused looks with Greene.

Greene took the seat at the end of the table next to Goodling, and Kennicott sat beside him. Cutter and Gild walked to the other side. Cutter jerked his head, and the bodyguard got up and stood behind Goodling.

Taking his time, Greene opened his notebook, took out a micro-recorder, and placed it on the table. 'You don't mind if I record this?' he asked Cutter.

'Not at all,' Cutter said.

Greene checked his watch. 'It's five minutes after

73

eleven, Monday, August seventeenth. This is Homicide Detective Ari Greene. I'm here with Officer Daniel Kennicott at the offices of defense counsels Ms Barbara Gild and Mr Philip Cutter. They are here with their client Ms April Goodling and . . .' He nodded toward the no-neck bodyguard. 'Sir, your name?'

'Bluin. Pete Bluin.'

'Thank you,' Greene said. 'We're investigating the murder of Terrance Wyler.'

Kennicott was watching Goodling. As Wyler's name was spoken, he saw her shoulders twitch.

'I want it clear from the top,' Cutter said, his usually loud voice restrained and sober, 'that earlier this morning, acting on our client's instructions, I contacted Detective Greene and arranged this meeting.'

'That's correct,' Greene said.

'Question number one,' Cutter asked. 'Is my client a suspect?'

'Not at this time. We're at the early stages,' Greene said. 'That's why we want to speak to her.'

'April won't make any statements at this meeting.' Cutter's usually nervous body was calm, focused on Greene. Kennicott had seen Cutter like this in court, where his intensity could intimidate even the most confident witness.

Greene didn't look fazed.

'Barbara, pass out copies of our prepared statements,' Cutter said. 'April already has hers.' He didn't take his eyes off Greene.

Gild had a small stack of bound papers in front of her. She gave copies to Greene and Kennicott and Cutter and kept one for herself. Goodling fingered the copy in front of her.

'These sworn affidavits demonstrate Ms Goodling's complete cooperation with this investigation.' Cutter leafed through the papers. 'They're from the night desk manager at the Gladstone Hotel, from the head of security operations there, and from Mr Peter Bluin.' He pointed at the muscle-bound man standing behind Goodling. 'Mr Bluin is Ms Goodling's personal security guard. Between the hours of ten p.m. on Sunday evening, August sixteenth, and eight a.m. on Monday morning, August seventeenth, Ms Goodling was at the hotel and never left. She has a complete alibi.'

Greene read through the legal papers slowly. 'Ms Goodling,' he said, putting the pages down, 'where were you earlier in the day yesterday? Before you got back to the hotel.'

Kennicott thought she was about to speak when Cutter sliced his arm down in front of her, as if he were lowering a barrier.

'My client insisted on being here today. Against our advice, I might add. She was supposed to leave early this morning, but stayed. She's going back to the States tonight. We both know she's not legally required to answer any questions. I repeat, she'll make no statements.'

'I've every right to question her.' Greene was

calm. 'Whether she wants to answer me or not, that's her decision.'

'This meeting's over,' Cutter said.

Ignoring Cutter, Greene turned to Goodling. 'We solve crimes because citizens help. Here's my card. Call me.' He clicked his pen and wrote down a number. 'That's my personal cell. It's always on.'

Greene held out the card and she took it. He took out another card and turned it over. 'Now write your cell number for me. I'll never show it to anyone, but I'll put it in my contacts. When you call me your name will pop up and I'll know it's you.'

When you call me, Kennicott thought. His murdered brother, Michael, had been a master salesman. 'I always use the word "when,"' he once told Kennicott. 'That way a customer is already past the "if" stage.'

No one spoke. Greene clicked his pen twice. Goodling took it and wrote out her number.

'Thanks.' Greene reached for his tape recorder.

Cutter covered his hand with a meaty paw. 'I assume you're satisfied with the affidavit material,' he said.

Greene jerked his arm back and clicked off the recorder. 'Assume nothing. I expected more from you, Phil.'

The conference-room door opened, and the blond receptionist walked in with a tray. Five frothy-looking cappuccinos jiggled on top. She put them gently on the table.

'We don't need them.' Greene turned to Goodling. 'I thought that after you'd been with Terrance for a year, perhaps you cared about him.'

'Of course I did,' she said.

Cutter jumped to his feet. 'No statements.' This was the real Phil Cutter now, Kennicott thought. Tough and hard. So much for putting on a smooth show for his big-name client.

'I'd never heard of Terrance Wyler until this morning,' Greene said to Goodling. 'I didn't know much about you either until Officer Kennicott put together some articles for me to read.'

'Tabloid trash,' she said.

'No more questions,' Cutter said, his voice half a growl.

Goodling was staring straight at Greene. 'Our anniversary was in two weeks.' She pulled on her perfect ponytail.

'April, don't answer him.' It was Barb Gild. She was on her feet now too. Her thin lips were tight.

'Why were you leaving the morning of his divorce trial?'

'I didn't want to be a distraction,' Goodling said.

'April, we discussed this,' Gild said in a stern voice.

Something must have connected, because Goodling turned to her lawyers. 'Okay,' she said.

'Now there's no divorce trial, there's nothing for you to distract,' Greene persisted. 'Weren't you friendly with his son, Simon?'

Goodling flushed. 'I love Simon.'

'April,' Gild said.

'A few hours from now I'm taking that little boy into a studio at police headquarters so he can tell me on tape what happened last night,' Greene said. 'Then his family gets to tell him that his daddy is dead. If you care about the boy, why aren't you staying to support him?'

Goodling's mouth gaped open. 'Who are you to question me like this?'

Greene grabbed his notebook from the table. 'I'm a homicide detective. A child has lost his father and it means nothing to you.' He pushed his chair back and started toward the door.

Kennicott got up to follow.

'How can you say that?' For the first time Goodling looked angry. 'You don't understand what—'

'April,' Gild shouted. 'No.'

Greene stormed back to the table. 'A poor kid gets shot in one of the tough parts of the city, Jane and Finch or Rexdale. When no one talks to the police, all we hear is how awful "these" people are who won't cooperate with the authorities. You tell me how you're any damn different?'

Goodling was shaking her head.

'What's your excuse? There's no gang member lying in wait for you because you ratted out his friend. Silence kills,' Greene said. 'Believe me, I know.'

'That's enough,' Cutter bellowed at Greene.

'No, it isn't. I'm just getting started.' Greene

grew calm. He glared at Cutter. 'There's a fine line between advising your client and obstructing police.'

'You threatening me?' Cutter said.

'I'm watching you two like a hawk.' He nodded at Gild before he turned to the actress. 'You're going to talk to me, Ms Goodling. You know it and I know it. Because it's the right thing to do. Your high-priced legal help can advise you all they want. You have my number now. I expect to hear from you.'

He spun back around, strode out, and slammed the door behind him so hard that the frothy cappuccinos shuddered. Bits of white foam flew across the table.

'Quick, get a cloth,' Cutter shouted at the receptionist.

Kennicott made for the door after Greene. He grabbed the handle and stole one last glance at Goodling. She was sliding Greene's business card into her purse, like a child hiding a candy from her parents.

CHAPTER 13

For Jennifer Raglan, this was an odd moment. Walking back into her old office for the first time in two months. Until June, she'd been the head Crown for five stress-filled years. She'd loved it and hated it. Mostly loved it.

'Jennie, thanks so much for coming,' Ralph Armitage said with a nervous laugh, sitting up in her old chair. Armitage had been a camp counselor and had the annoying habit of giving everyone nicknames that ended in the *ee* sound. 'Feels odd to be sitting behind *your* desk.'

'Feels good to me,' Raglan said.

Armitage was a tall man, and even seated he dominated the room. Her old desk was spotless, in stark contrast to the usual clutter of files that always topped it when she worked there. The framed photo of Raglan's three kids, which used to adorn the credenza on the back wall, had been replaced by an array of pictures of Armitage and his very blond and equally tall wife on various athletic vacations – skiing in Switzerland, horseback riding in New Mexico, scuba diving in Belize. All the things couples without children could afford.

It was hot in the room. The office faced east, and the morning sun slanted in. An old air-conditioning unit that rattled away in the corner window was better at making noise than delivering cool air. Despite the heat, Armitage wore a full suit, tie done right up.

Ari Greene, in a pair of chinos and a short-sleeved shirt, stood calmly a few steps off to the right. His usual spot, slightly removed, everything in clear view. He carried his ever-present thin leather briefcase in his hand. Their eyes met for a moment and she flashed him a quick smile. Raglan hadn't seen him since June, and Greene's skin had a deep, tempting tan. Despite herself, she thought about his shoulders. Their first kiss had been in this office, right about where he was standing now.

'Ari,' Armitage said. How convenient for him that Greene's first name ended in a *ee* sound. No way even Armitage would call Greene Greeney. 'Jennie tells me you two've done a few things together.'

'A few.' He glanced back at her.

'She's not doing murder trials anymore, but she kindly agreed to come in and get things started with you.'

Tell me about it, Raglan thought. Get things started with Ari.

Armitage clapped his large hands together. Another one of his camp counselor habits. 'Why don't you two grab an empty office and go at it?'

Go at it, Raglan thought. Hmm.

They found an office with no windows. Someone had left a fan on, and it was rotating back and forth, doing nothing more than swirling hot air around.

'How're the kids?' Greene shut the door and slipped into a wooden chair tucked in the far corner.

'Better,' she said. 'Thanks for asking. How's your dad?'

'Difficult as ever.'

'You make it sound like a good thing.'

He laughed. 'It is.'

She'd tried to forget how much she liked his laugh. There was an awkward silence. Say something, Raglan told herself, her mind drifting. Like 'Nice to see you, Ari.' Or 'Ari, I missed you.' Or 'Ari, you look so tanned.' She thought of their first kiss. It had been late at night, and they were working together. She'd shut the door and gone right over to him. He hadn't looked surprised.

Now Greene was talking to her. 'We have to keep it totally under wraps,' he was saying. She nodded. Her heart was beating as if she were a teenager on a first date. Silly.

'No matter what, it can't get out,' Greene said.

Odd he should bring up their affair now, she thought. He was usually so understated, and they'd taken such elaborate steps to be discreet. She was convinced no one knew.

'The knife coming to us in that way. You never

know how it's going to help us,' Greene said. 'Besides, the press would go wild with it.'

Raglan kept nodding. What an idiot you are, Jennifer, she thought. He's talking about the case. Not you. Fuck. Hope I'm not blushing. 'Right,' she said. Remember, you broke it off with him. You wanted to be home. See the kids every day. Concentrate.

He summed up the rest of the evidence. The marriage breaking up, Samantha's e-mails and voice mails, the police warning her. On Terrance's BlackBerry he'd found the e-mail telling Samantha he'd take the deal and inviting her to come to his house. E-mails back saying she'd be there in half an hour. No signs of forced entry. No apparent defense wounds on the body. The child saying his mother had been in his room last night.

'Then this morning there was a call from your old boss, Ted DiPaulo,' Greene said. 'He's representing Samantha.'

'Ted?' DiPaulo had been the head Crown before she got the job. He'd mentored her since the beginning of her career. Handpicked her as his successor.

'Dragged me down to his office and had another lawyer give me the bloody kitchen knife wrapped in a towel,' Greene said.

'That's Ted. Always ethical. Wife have an alibi?'

'Don't know. DiPaulo's stalling for time.'

'Where is she?'

'I thought DiPaulo had her in his partner's office,

so I put on a surveillance team. He just drove her home. We'll follow her round the clock. I've alerted all the airports and the borders. Daniel Kennicott's working with me on this case. He swore out a warrant, so we'll monitor her phone, e-mails, et cetera.'

This was smart. If Greene rushed into an arrest, it would leave things open for the defense to accuse him of tunnel vision. Failure to eliminate other suspects. Besides, once she was arrested, Samantha would effectively be silenced. This way they could watch and listen to her.

'Terrance have any known enemies?'

'No. No criminal record. No police contacts. Sounds like everyone loved him.'

'Except his wife. Other suspects?'

'April Goodling, the movie-star girlfriend, seems to have an alibi. In her hotel room all night. Cutter and Gild are her lawyers.'

'That figures,' Raglan said. There was no love lost between Phil Cutter and Jennifer Raglan.

'The oldest brother works early mornings at the food terminal. Kennicott did the notification.'

Raglan knew why Greene had done this. The Michael Kennicott case was Greene's only unsolved homicide. It would be tough for Daniel to tell someone his brother was dead. Greene was testing him.

'The rest of the family live up north, parents and a disabled brother. We're meeting them early tomorrow morning. Right now we're going

84

door-to-door on Wyler's street. Most of the people are away.'

'Up north at their cottages, no doubt,' Raglan said.

'I'm trying to trace Samantha Wyler's movements for the last twenty-four hours. We checked the video in the lobby of her apartment. She left at nine forty-one on Sunday night and never returned. Doesn't have a license. The nanny says she never learned to drive. We're checking the cab companies, the videos at the subway. We'll interview the late-night bus drivers when they come back on shift. Nothing so far.'

'Where do you think she went?'

'I have a hunch. We're going door-to-door in Yorkville, where her family lawyer, a guy named Feindel, has his office. DiPaulo got that knife from her somehow. Makes sense to me she gave it to Feindel.'

Many homicide detectives took pride in making speedy arrests, but Greene had a way of seeing another angle to even the most straightforward set of facts. This time, though, Raglan wondered if he weren't being too conservative. 'She has motive and opportunity. You've got her e-mailing him that she's coming over, the knife, her son saying she was in the house. Then she disappears. What else do you need?'

Greene stood up. His eyes were a mesmerizing gray-blue. Easy to stare at. 'The boy's already lost his father,' he said. 'Last thing I want to do is make a mistake. Then he'll lose his mother. Let's see if she comes up with an alibi.'

That was so like him, Raglan thought. Any other detective would arrest her right now. But Greene didn't see Samantha Wyler only as a suspect, but as the boy's mother.

'What are you doing next?'

Greene looked at his watch. 'Going back to Wyler's house. The forensic officer is ready to walk me through the scene. Kennicott's meeting me there in half an hour.'

'Has the child been told?'

'The family's going to speak to him tonight.' Greene clenched his jaw. 'Before he's been told, I'm going to try to get him to tell me on tape what he said this morning. That his mother came into his room last night. If I can do that, the case is almost over.'

'Oh, Ari,' she said.

He looked away. 'I'm picking him up at four. We have a special room for kids at police head-quarters.'

The Old City Hall clock, which was in a spiked stone tower almost above their heads, rang through the four parts of its hourly chime and started to dong twelve times. It was noon. She had to hurry or be late to pick up her daughter.

Ari Greene, Ari Greene. Every time she thought she could reach him, he slipped away. Like a shadow over a cliff.

That night in her office, she hadn't been sure if

he'd let her kiss him. Raglan had heard women's washroom scuttlebutt about Greene over the years. Others had tried without luck. Thinking back, every detail was still so clear. The roughness of his hands. His clean smell. He hadn't been shy about her body.

What did she really know about him? There were all these gaps. Greene's parents were Holocaust survivors, and he was an only child. His mother had died last winter, and his father still lived in the house Greene grew up in. He didn't join the force until he was thirty. About fifteen years ago, he took a twelve-month leave of absence. One of those cop mysteries that no one could figure out. When he returned, Chief of Police Hap Charlton became his 'rabbi,' promoting him up the ladder fast. Greene liked to joke that this had special relevance, since he was the only Jewish homicide detective on the force.

Raglan knew that Greene had been in Europe, because every once in a while he'd mention an old town square he'd seen, an ancient bridge he'd walked across, a painting in a gallery. From all the French books in his house, she could tell he'd spent time in France. Two French stations were programmed into his old car radio.

One night when they went to a country inn for the weekend, he'd awakened in a sweat. She'd touched his back, and he jumped. '*Quoi?*' he said, casting his arms out in the air.

'Ari,' she asked, 'you okay?'

He had rolled over and looked at her in the dim light. Lost for a moment before he pulled her to him.

. . . Dong, dong, dong. The bell tower finished ringing out twelve o'clock. 'I'm glad for that boy that you're on this case.' Raglan was watching him.

Greene had an unconscious habit of licking the top of his lip for a moment before they kissed. She was sure he had no idea he did it. The edge of his tongue slid across his upper lip for a split second. He still wants me, she thought.

He flashed her that grin of his again. 'But we all know you're not doing any more murder trials.' Greene grabbed his briefcase and slipped out of the hot room, leaving the door open behind him.

Raglan leaned back on the desk, alone, replaying their last seconds together over and over, her hair sticking to her forehead in the heat.

CHAPTER 14

'Is much blood,' the identification officer, Brygida Zeilinski, said to Ari Greene and Daniel Kennicott when she met them at the front door of Terrance Wyler's house. A heavyset woman with thinning hair and a permanent frown, she spoke with a thick Polish accent. The book on her was that in her twenty-five years on the force, no one had ever seen Zeilinski smile, crack a joke, or laugh.

Greene took his notebook and wrote down the time. It was twelve-thirty. He'd arranged for Kennicott to meet him here to do a walk-through of the murder scene. Zeilinski led them inside.

'Is messy.' Her face assumed its perpetual scowl as they entered the kitchen. Zeilinski wore latex gloves on her stubby fingers and plastic booties over her shoes. She handed Greene and Kennicott fresh pairs of both to put on.

The spot where Terrance Wyler's body had lain earlier in the day was vacated. No one outlined a corpse in white chalk anymore – except in TV shows. When the forensic officers arrived at a murder scene, they videotaped everything, photographed the body in situ, and had it removed. The room was then measured and photographed to produce a scale drawing.

With Kennicott behind him, Greene followed Zeilinski's footsteps around the kitchen, their plastic booties squeaking on the tiles. The floor, the fridge, and the counters were covered in little metal numbered signs, with arrows pointing to bits of dried blood and other pieces of evidence. The room was hot, and the smell of death still lingered. Greene looked around.

On the right wall was an expensive-looking gas stove with thick black grates on top. Farther along was a deep double sink and a large window above it. The house was on a wide lot built into a hill. The driveway to the left climbed up and curled around, with space for three or four cars, level with the back. To the right was a manicured lawn. Instead of a fence, there was a row of mature cedars planted quite far apart. A well-worn footpath led through the trees to the neighbor's back door.

'Is one knife missing.' Zeilinski nodded toward the woodblock knife holder on the counter.

'I noticed that this morning,' Greene said.

'Is maybe one towel missing also.' She pointed to the stove handle, where there were two green-and-white towels, but only a single red-and-white one.

'Is one missing,' he said.

'And here.' She led them back through the door

90

frame between the kitchen and the front hall. 'Is contact stain. One hundred forty-seven point thirty-two centimeters. Four feet, ten inches from ground.'

Greene looked at Kennicott. A contact stain was usually from someone's hand. Probably the perpetrator fleeing the scene.

'More blood.' Now they were on their way out of the kitchen and going up the wide staircase. 'Is here, here, here, and here.' Walking up the stairs, she pointed to small droplets on the rails. 'And is here.' She brought them into Simon's room. On the Curious George carpet a label pointed to a small red dot on the man's yellow hat.

Greene and Kennicott exchanged glances again. Both were thinking about Simon saying that his mother had come to his room. 'Good work,' Greene said as Zeilinski trooped them downstairs.

Even though she'd been in the warm house all day, the woman looked as if she could keep going for another twelve hours, which she often had to do. Greene had seen identification officers go more than twenty-four hours without a break.

Her biggest regret in life, she'd told Greene when they'd first met on a case more than a decade ago, was that her parents left Poland when she was twenty-one. 'Is five years before, and I not have this accent.'

'Bad luck,' Greene had agreed.

A few years later, when she discovered that Greene was Jewish, Zeilinski was eager to set the record straight.

'Is no Nazi, my family,' she'd told him.

'Many Polish Christians helped Polish Jews,' he said. 'Three different families hid my father.'

'Is in Auschwitz, my father, whole war. First transport. Was political prisoner. Number four hundred and fifty-one. Name in museum in Jerusalem.'

The last time Greene had been to Israel, some of his mother's distant relatives – no one was left on his father's side – took him to Yad Vashem, the Holocaust memorial. There was this woman's father's name in the special tribute to Righteous Gentiles – Jozef Zeilinski.

'Now the outside doors.' Zeilinski showed them the front of the house. 'This door, no marks, no paint chipped, is no sign forced entry.'

This was often evidence that the victim knew the killer, or at least voluntarily let the person into his house.

'Blood,' she said, pointing to the door frame. 'Is contact stain.' A labeled tape measure ran up beside it.

'One hundred twenty-seven centimeters. Four feet, two inches from ground.' It was about the height of the stain on the door frame in the kitchen. Consistent with its being the same person.

'Back door.' Zeilinski paraded them through the house. 'Is sticky.' She grasped the handle and demonstrated how the painted wood door needed a shove to open and a yank to close it. There were no forced entry signs here either.

At the bottom of the door was another labeled tape measure. Greene couldn't see any blood.

'Bend down,' Zeilinski told them.

They followed her instructions. There was a scuff mark, like something from the sole of a shoe. It was thick on the bottom and thinned as it expanded up, like the Nike swoosh. A wisp of red was just below it.

'Is blood,' Zeilinski said. 'Twenty-five point four centimeters. Ten inches from floor.'

Follow the blood, it will tell the story, Greene thought. The killer knew the layout of the house, went upstairs to Simon's room, and then left by the front door. Simon said his mother came in last night when he was in bed and told him she wouldn't see him for a long time. Everything fit, except this last small bloodstain.

Zeilinski read his thoughts. 'Blood can last long time.'

'I know,' Greene said.

'Is not usually last long time in doorway. Especially in such clean house.'

Greene looked at her and then at Kennicott. They were all thinking the same thing. Had there been a second person in the house, who'd left by the back door?

CHAPTER 15

Jennifer Raglan sprinted up to the crowd of parents waiting calmly in the northwest corner of the suburban parking lot. It was after 12:35, and the heat was radiating up from the black asphalt. A wave of sweat wrapped its way around her body.

She'd spent the last half hour in her old Saturn, running yellow traffic lights and the occasional near-red one to get here on time. Driving through the city like a maniac wasn't a great thing for a Crown Attorney to do, but being late for her daughter was a worse option.

'Don't worry, the buses are never on time,' a woman with flabby arms, wearing a wide-brimmed hat, said to Raglan. She was sitting in a folding chair with a cup holder, sipping on a frothy-looking iced drink.

Raglan surveyed the other parents awaiting the buses. The women, with their stylish sunglasses and Capri pants or workout outfits, bespoke summer days lounging on a dock by the still waters of a northern lake. The men, laconic in their button-down shirts, speaking into their cell phones or scrolling through their BlackBerrys, were in no hurry at all. Didn't any of these people work?

She'd dug deep into her personal savings to send Dana away – in part to fulfill her daughter's long-standing wish to go to sleepover camp, in part to buy some time alone with her husband. For ten kid-free days they drove down through Vermont and Massachusetts to Cape Cod and doubled back through upstate New York. They even visited the Baseball Hall of Fame in Cooperstown. Gordon's long-standing wish.

As Raglan looked over the huge SUVs and snazzy imported convertibles parked nearby, she heard snippets of conversation: 'So frustrating. We have to wait another week to get the indoor motor repaired' . . . 'The screens on the porch were ripped to shreds by that windstorm' . . . 'Do you know someone who's good with wells?'

The travails of the rich, Raglan thought as the heat bore down on her. Last week when they were in Provincetown she'd bought a straw hat and wondered if she'd left it in the car. She was about to go back to look when a cheer went up from the parents. Three bulky buses came into view at the far edge of the lot.

Everyone started waving madly. Even the men put away their cell phones. Raglan stole a look at her watch. It was 12:45. She turned her BlackBerry to vibrate and slid it into her back pocket.

The BlackBerry was the thing her children hated the most. When she'd returned home, Raglan had

95

sat down with all three of them. 'I'm not the head Crown anymore,' she said, putting her hand on a mock Bible, like a witness at one of her trials. 'I solemnly swear, I'll turn the BlackBerry off the moment I walk in the door.'

The buses pulled up, the doors swung open, and controlled chaos ensued as girl after girl after girl bounded down three sets of stairs. There was no indication which bus held which kids, but the other parents somehow knew where to position themselves. Raglan was left at the back of the crowd. From her vantage point the children all looked the same. For a strange and terrible moment she thought, What if I don't recognize my own daughter?

After what seemed a long time, she felt a tug at her sleeve. Leave me alone, was her first thought. There was another tug. She looked down and saw Dana. Impossibly, her daughter was so much taller after three weeks. She wore a scrunched-down white hat and a filthy T-shirt. Her arms were ringed with handmade bracelets.

'My baby,' Raglan heard herself scream. She scooped up her youngest child. 'I missed you so much.'

'Where's Daddy?' Dana narrowed her eyes at her mother.

'He's gone to work. We had a great vacation in Cape Cod. Went to see a Red Sox game.' Raglan felt the BlackBerry buzz in her back pocket. Must be Ralph Armitage yet again, she thought. 'Where's your bag?'

96

'I want you to meet my counselor.' Dana pulled her sideways into the crowd.

Raglan smiled when they found a tall young woman with a deep tan.

'Hi, I'm Marcia.' She put her hand easily on Dana's head. 'Your daughter's terrific. No one could beat her in an argument.'

'That's my girl.' The BlackBerry in her pocket buzzed again. Raglan ignored it.

'She's really proud of you, I'll tell you that,' the counselor said.

'I'm proud of her,' Raglan said. She was trying to remember the counselor's name. Was it Marsha or Marlene? The phone buzzed a third time. What the hell was going on? Armitage must really be panicking about something.

'Says you're the most important lawyer in the city.'

Didn't say anything about what kind of mother I am, Raglan thought. 'Her letters were all about you and the cabin. I know she'll want to go back.'

'For sure,' Dana said.

It was worth all that money, Raglan thought as she located her daughter's bag and hoisted it over her shoulder. Please don't buzz again, she prayed silently to the phone in her pocket.

'Time to get you in the bath,' she said as they tromped across the parking lot. A layer of sweat was covering her back.

'Mom, aren't you going to work?'

'No.' Raglan tried not to sound too proud of

herself. She opened the trunk and threw the bag in. It felt good to get the weight off her shoulders. 'I bought some fresh corn for lunch.'

'Hey, what's this?' Dana said, slipping into the backseat and spying a baseball cap on the middle armrest. 'The Red Sox.'

'I got it for you at Fenway.' Raglan started the car. The air-conditioning needed to be fixed, but it would cost two thousand dollars. Instead, she rolled down the windows. The phone buzzed again in her back pocket. 'I bought some wild blueberries and fresh peaches.' She put the car in gear.

'Thanks,' Dana said, taking her camp hat off and twirling it in one hand. 'And Mommy . . .'

'What, sweetie?'

'I don't mind.' Dana plopped the Red Sox hat on her head backward. 'You can answer your BlackBerry.'

CHAPTER 16

Dealing with the press was Ari Greene's least favorite part of the job, but on a case like this it came with the territory. This morning, after getting Simon out of the house, he'd been able to avoid the media. But this afternoon, when he'd come back to the Wyler house with Kennicott to do the walk-through with Zeilinski, they'd had to run the gauntlet of the reporters and television crews teeming up against the police tape.

Greene promised to make a statement when he came out. It was a good idea to say something to the press rather than remain silent and let them speculate.

'Stand beside me,' Greene muttered to Kennicott as they exited Wyler's front door. 'Looks better if there's more than one cop at the scene.' This summer, when gun violence in the city ramped up, the force had sent all the homicide detectives to media training. Most of it was common sense: look straight at the reporters when you answer their questions, be factual when you can, keep it short.

'Detective Greene! Detective Greene!' reporters were shouting. He approached the yellow tape, in no particular hurry.

'I'll take questions now.' He held his hands up like a ringmaster at a circus quieting down a bunch of overexcited schoolchildren.

After the media training session, Chief Charlton had taken Greene aside. 'Forget all that crap. Reporters love two things – call them by their first name, and call them professionals. Tell them how much you'd love to talk, but you have a case to solve. Blah, blah, blah.'

'Kirt?' Greene said. Kirt Bishop was a smart reporter from *The Globe and Mail*.

'Who's your prime suspect?' Bishop asked, pen and pad in hand.

Greene smiled. 'Kirt, at the risk of using the oldest cliché in the book: the investigation's ongoing.'

Everyone chuckled.

'Zac?' Greene pointed to Zachery Stone, a short, aggressive reporter from the *Toronto Sun*.

'Where's Wyler's wife?'

'Hey, you're all professionals.' Greene grinned even more widely. 'Zac, cliché number two: I can't discuss the details of the case at this time.'

Now everyone laughed.

'Awotwe?' Awotwe Amankwah, a tough reporter from the *Toronto Star*, was the only black face in the crowd.

'Four more people killed last night makes

sixty-four so far this year. Twenty in the last two months. People are calling this the Summer of the Gun. What's going on?'

'We need to keep things in perspective.' Statistics were the other part of Greene's media training. Every week he was peppered with memos on how to talk down the latest body count. 'According to Statistics Canada, Toronto's the tenth most dangerous city in the country. Our homicide rate is half that of Winnipeg, which is the worst in Canada.'

There were a few reporters in the crowd he didn't recognize. Greene turned to address them. 'To the American journalists who are here, Toronto's twenty-eighth of all major North American cities in homicides, and we're the fifth biggest urban area after New York, L.A., Chicago, and Mexico City.'

An Asian woman who'd elbowed her way to the front caught his eye. 'Yes?' he said.

'Margaret Kwon, *Faces* magazine.' She had a strong New York accent. 'April Goodling – have you seen her?'

'I have,' Greene said.

'Where?' Kwon asked. She held up a slim digital recorder.

'On the cover of almost every magazine on the newsstand,' Greene said. That received the loudest laugh yet.

'Do you know where she was last night?' Kwon asked. Something about the question made Greene think this reporter already knew the answer.

He made a show of looking at his watch. 'Folks, we've got a long day ahead of us. I'll update you when we have more news.'

People dispersed, anxious to meet their deadlines. The television crews were happy because they'd gotten the shot of Greene and Kennicott coming out of the house. It didn't really matter what he'd said. Radio and print people had a few quotes. Greene watched Kwon, the American reporter on the other side of the police tape. She was in no hurry to leave. He nodded at her. She picked up the signal and lingered, writing in her notepad.

'Detective Ari Greene,' he said a few minutes later, when everyone else had gone. He reached out to shake hands.

She gave him an uncomfortable handshake, as if she were performing some outlandish ritual. Her hair was a deep black, her face rounded and her skin smooth. She wore a pair of narrow glasses that accentuated her piercing black eyes. It was difficult to guess her age. Greene put her in her early forties, though she could pass for about ten years younger. 'I come here every year for the film festival and I always have to get used to you Canadians being so polite.'

'Tough adjustment,' Greene said. 'You on the April Goodling story?'

She let go of his hand slowly. 'Twenty-four seven.'

He took her recorder and turned it off. 'Why do I have the feeling you know where she was last night?'

'Why do I have the feeling that you're a smart cop?' Kwon asked back. She hadn't resisted when he'd turned off her recorder.

'What can you tell the lead detective on the "Divorce from the North" case?' 'Divorce from the North' was the title of one of the articles Greene had read about Goodling. He'd asked Kennicott to grab him some celebrity magazines, and he remembered Kwon's name on the byline.

Her dark eyes lit up. 'You read my story.' She put her hand out, and they shook again. 'If I did have some information, what's in it for me?'

'How about exclusive access to the officer in charge of this case?'

'Deal.' She gave him a hard shake. 'Let's do this over dinner. Where can we go to escape the heat?'

Greene let go of her hand and gave Kwon back her recorder. 'I know a few interesting places,' he said.

'Why doesn't that surprise me,' she said.

CHAPTER 17

There was the familiar smell of jasmine tea in the air when Jennifer Raglan walked into the Thai restaurant on the south side of Dundas Street. She spotted the owner, a slight man who always wore khaki pants and a starch-white shirt. He bowed and pointed to her usual table, the one farthest from the window.

This all began a few hours ago when Raglan answered her cell phone, sitting in her steaming hot car in the Yorkdale parking lot. Dana sat in the backseat twirling her new Red Sox hat on her fingers.

'It's me. I'm sorry to keep calling,' a woman said without identifying herself. She knew Raglan would recognize her voice. 'There's something I really need to talk to you about.'

'I just picked up Dana from camp,' Raglan said.

'I know you're on holiday, but it's urgent. Can we meet when I get out of court?'

The fact that Jo Summers, a young and talented assistant Crown Attorney, wasn't identifying herself on the phone – or sending her an e-mail or a text – told Raglan this was something very confidential.

'Can't it wait till tomorrow?'

'I wish it could,' Summers said.

'Okay. The usual place at five.'

Last May, when Raglan was still running the downtown Crown office, Summers had helped her ferret out two renegade prosecutors, Phil Cutter and Barb Gild. Raglan had taken extra precautions to ensure that no one knew Summers was involved. When they needed to talk, instead of meeting for coffee at the Starbucks or the Timothy's franchises down on Queen Street, they'd slip out to this cozy Thai restaurant.

Raglan had spent the afternoon with Dana. Taken her home, given her an enormous lunch, put her in the bath, and made her go to her room and read. Gordon had cut out of work early. He'd never done that before. Raglan threw in two loads of laundry before rushing downtown.

Jo Summers sat at their usual table, slumped down in a wicker chair. She was a tall, high-cheekboned woman. Her most striking feature was the wild tumble of blond hair she always wore tied up above her head, held in place by an exotic wooden hair clip. Today she looked thin and drawn, her hair still up, but askew.

Raglan sat down across from her. The small restaurant was steamy. There were deep bags under Summers's blue eyes.

'What's wrong?' Raglan asked.

Summers knotted her fingers together in front of her mouth. 'Terrance Wyler – I knew him.' A

105

solitary tear slid from her left eye. 'Since I was a kid.'

Raglan's mouth dropped open. 'Oh, Jo.' She sprang up from her chair and rushed over to hug Summers. 'I'm so sorry.' She remembered that Terrance Wyler was forty years old. Summers was in her mid-thirties.

'I think I'm still in shock,' Summers said when Raglan sat down across from her again.

'How did you work today?'

'Our families sail together at the club.' Summers took a paper napkin from under her fork and blew her nose. 'I hate people looking at me.'

Summers had always been guarded about herself. Her father, Johnathan Summers, the head judge at Old City Hall court, was a bully who took pleasure in terrifying defense and Crown counsel in equal measure. Jo kept a low profile. Raglan knew she lived alone in a converted cottage over on the Toronto Islands, a small community across the water from downtown. 'Were you close?' Raglan asked.

'He left Toronto. I did too, but we kept in touch.'

Summers hadn't really answered the question. Raglan felt herself slipping into what her husband referred to as her cross-examination mode. 'Did you see him after he moved back?'

'I'd see him at the club. We sailed sometimes. And . . .' Summers looked away. She shook her head so hard that strands of hair slipped out from the clip and dangled across her face, like tails from a kite.

'Jo? What?'

'It's going to sound so bad.' She bit down hard on her lower lip. 'We had lunch every Friday if I wasn't stuck in court.' Her voice sounded hollow. 'Once a year we'd go to a restaurant together for a Christmas dinner. Our friendship was . . .' Summers sighed. 'It was private.'

You're not the only one with secrets, Jennifer, Raglan said to herself, thinking of Ari Greene.

Summers squeezed her hands around a ceramic tea mug. She had long, lovely fingers. Raglan always wished hers were slender like that.

'I assume his wife didn't know about this,' Raglan said.

Summers jerked her head up. 'No. But not for that reason. We were only just friends.'

'Okay.'

'See, it sounds stupid.'

'Why didn't the wife know?' Further cross-examination, Raglan thought.

'Samantha was so possessive of Terry. That's what everyone called him. Before he met her, Terry was close with his brothers, had tons of friends. She cut him off from everyone.'

Raglan saw Summers's wide mouth twist in anger. 'When's the last time you saw him?'

'We had lunch on Friday. And he came over to my place on the island on Sunday.'

'Oh.' Raglan felt the hairs stand up on the

back of her neck. This was going to make her a suspect.

Summers blanched. 'In the afternoon. He brought Simon and April Goodling. I assume you've heard of her.'

'The whole world's heard of her.'

'She's not as superficial as people think.'

'How long did they stay?'

'The afternoon. They avoided the ferry. Walter, the water-taxi guy, picked them up.'

'You'll have to be interviewed by the police,' Raglan said.

'I know. They'll want to know if I have an alibi.'

On a Sunday night, Summers was probably home alone. Like most people her alibi would be 'I was asleep.' When a murder took place in the middle of the night not many people had an absolutely foolproof alibi. I'm going to stop cross-examining you, Raglan thought. 'Leave it to the police.'

'Don't worry.' She gave a bitter laugh. 'I was with someone, and he's a solid witness.'

Summers had worked as a corporate lawyer at one of the larger firms in town before becoming a Crown. Raglan could imagine all sorts of corporate types who'd want to be with her. 'Listen, Jo, I don't want to pry into your personal life—'

'He's a cop. So damn cliché, isn't it,' Summers said. 'Female Crowns and male cops.'

Raglan gulped. Cops and Crowns. It was a cliché – something she'd kidded Greene about.

Summers took a long sip of her tea. 'I like my privacy.' Her hands were shaking. 'He's someone I've known for a long time. Nothing had ever happened between us. But last week he'd gotten back from a tough trip and Sunday night he wanted to talk . . .' She shook her head.

'Scorched earth,' Raglan said. 'It's always like this with a murder investigation. Everyone close to it gets burned. Privacy's the first casualty.'

'You know him, Jennifer. It's Daniel Kennicott.'

Raglan froze. Her mind scrambling. 'He's on the case,' she said.

'What?'

'Kennicott. I haven't had time to tell you. Ralph Armitage begged me to come in this morning to help get things started. I met with the detective who's handling the case. A guy named Greene. He told me Kennicott's working with him on this case.'

'Oh my God.'

Raglan was thinking fast. This always happened at the start of a murder investigation. Facts and connections flying at you from all directions. 'You understand what this means? You've been seeing a married man who's been murdered. Kennicott's your alibi. That can't be compromised, no matter what.'

'I wasn't *seeing* Terry like that.'

'Doesn't matter,' Raglan said.

Summers dabbed her eyes with the napkin, which now was rolled into a flaky ball. 'So I can't talk to Daniel?'

'Not a word.'

The color drained from Summers's already white skin. 'Jennifer, there's something about me and Terry that I need to keep secret. A lot of people could be hurt if this comes out. It has nothing to do with the case.'

'I can't promise—'

'He was my brother.'

'Who?'

'Terry. My half brother.'

'What?' Raglan felt her throat start to constrict. For a moment she couldn't speak. 'You mean—'

'My father. His mother. They told us when I was fourteen years old. Terry was nineteen. We were close, sailing together all the time. They were afraid we might get involved. Terry was so angry, he moved away for years.' Summers had grown calm.

'Who knows about this?'

'His two older brothers. They're sworn to secrecy. My mother doesn't know. It would destroy her. Nor does Mr Wyler. He's incredibly possessive. If he found out, it would be bad news for Mrs Wyler. Samantha doesn't know anything.'

'I see why you want this kept secret,' Raglan said.

They sat in silence. There was a clatter of dishes back in the kitchen.

Summers glanced up at her. 'What's this cop Greene like?'

Was that a knowing look? Despite everything

she'd done to keep her relationship with Greene secret, Raglan always worried.

'He's smart and honest.' You're being stupid, to say nothing of self-absorbed and narcissistic, Raglan told herself. Jo Summers doesn't know anything about your affair with Greene. Nor would she care right now. Her brother was murdered yesterday. 'I won't tell him about this unless I feel I have to. That's the best I can do.'

'Thanks.' Summers let go of the mug, put her elbows on the table, and buried her face in her hands. 'Can I ask you one more thing?'

'Sure.'

'Which Crown's going to prosecute this case?' Summers spoke between clasped fingers, her voice muffled.

Raglan looked at her young colleague. 'I am.' She stared at Summers. Dumbfounded. The words had escaped from her mouth like air from a balloon. And now it was impossible to put them back.

CHAPTER 18

The heat had finally broken late in the day. Cool wind blew into the city from across the lake, sweeping away the sticky sweat of the past week and breathing new life into the night air.

In Toronto, languorous summer evenings like this were the reward for the long winter months of cold and darkness, and Danforth Avenue, affectionately known as the Danforth, or the Danny by the older locals, was the perfect place for an outdoor meal. The heart of so-called Greektown, it was a wide thoroughfare chockablock with open-windowed restaurants, the smell of roasting lamb wafting across packed patios. On the crowded sidewalks, gaggles of girls tilting over their high heels, groups of guys out of their muscle cars, and well-dressed older European-born couples all promenaded while a traffic jam tailed on late into the night.

As a young patrolman, Ari Greene had enjoyed working the Danny. The shopkeepers, perhaps sensing his working-class roots, felt comfortable with him. One night he was in Pappas Grill, one of his favorite restaurants. He told Nick, the owner, that his father was a survivor of Treblinka – one of a handful of people who escaped in the only revolt at the death camp.

To Greene's surprise, Nick rolled up his pants on his right leg. He pointed to an ancient, deep scar. 'Damn Nazis,' he said. 'I was nine years old, and I snuck a few pieces of bread out of the German garbage. This blond one, he caught me. Kicked me so hard I still limp today.'

Word soon spread among the Danforth merchants about the Jewish cop who was a good guy, and it opened doors for Greene. A year later there was a shooting at a backroom poker game down the street from Nick's place, leaving one man dead. There were seven witnesses and no one was talking. After a few weeks had gone by, Greene dropped in to have a chat with Nick.

'The tax people from Ottawa are going to hit the Danny. Do some audits,' Greene said over a glass of ouzo. 'They think there's lots of cash floating around the restaurants.'

'The Danny, we're always taking it in the neck,' Nick said. 'Cops for everything. Parking. Garbage. We can't even throw out a bag anymore.'

'It's ridiculous,' Greene agreed. 'I know you've got nothing to hide, Nick—'

'Of course not—'

'I told them you were clean to save you the hassle. They're not going to bug you.'

Nick poured them both another glass, and the next day Greene had a name to give Hap Charlton, who back then was the homicide detective on the case.

'Detective, such a long time. Who's the beautiful young lady?' Nick said, walking with his usual limp to greet Greene in the doorway, taking Margaret Kwon's hand in his own and bowing to kiss it. He wore a black-and-white uniform, his thinning hair slicked back over his narrow skull.

'Nick, meet Margaret Kwon, a reporter from New York.'

'My pleasure.' He let her hand go but didn't take his eyes off her.

'My pleasure,' Kwon said. 'Keep calling me a beautiful young lady, I'll come here every night.'

Nick grinned at her, his eyes twinkling. 'I have cousins who live in Queens.'

'Nick has a cousin in every state in the union that a customer comes from,' Greene said.

They all laughed.

Kwon went to the washroom and Nick seated Greene at a small table tucked away at the end of the patio. The sound and smell of garlic sizzling in olive oil followed them through the big French doors.

'Detective, I have a question for you,' Nick whispered, slipping into the seat across from Greene. 'Most cops your age, I see them. Divorced. Always with the young ones. But you like more than a pretty face. And not so young.'

It was almost eight-thirty, and the sky was still

bright in the west. The last rays of sun lit up the clouds. Greene lifted the long menu. 'Brains. I like brains. You serve them?'

Nick smacked the table. He spotted Kwon coming onto the patio and waved her over. 'Here comes your special dish.'

Kwon smiled when she arrived at the table.

Nick stood and bowed again. Unlike the tables inside, which were made of dark wood, those outside were covered in gaudy plastic tablecloths. He took it off in three efficient folds.

'Why are you doing that?' Kwon asked.

Nick looked at Greene and grinned. 'The detective never eats in a restaurant with table-cloths.' He kissed her hand again and slipped away.

'I love the street life out here,' Kwon said.

'See that restaurant?' Greene pointed to the south side of the street. 'That's where they filmed the movie *My Big Fat Greek Wedding*.'

They ordered the house Greek salad for two and shared a plate of hummus and another of tzatziki, with olives on the side. Kwon told Greene that her two younger sisters were both doctors. 'I'm a failure in the eyes of my father,' she said, 'no matter how many cover stories I get.'

Greene laughed. 'The fate of all children of immigrants,' he said.

She slid an olive into her mouth. 'I've got some-thing to show you.' She dove into the oversize bag she'd slung over the back of her chair and pulled out a small digital camera. 'April Goodling in her hotel room at the moment she heard Terrance Wyler was dead.'

Greene looked away. He watched the stream of people walking on the Danforth. Not a care in the world.

'Don't you want to see it?' Kwon asked. 'I'm thinking of the headline: "April Rains."'

'Not my style,' he said. 'Invading people's privacy like that.'

Kwon dropped the camera on the table. 'Get over it,' she said. 'I've heard this same line for twenty years, and guess what, sales of celebrity magazines keep going up and up. Don't feel bad for these Hollywood types. They're the most superficial people in the whole world and they love the attention.'

'I met her today at her lawyer's,' Greene said.

'Piece of work, isn't she?'

'Not terribly cooperative.'

Kwon stood and came to his side. She lowered the back screen of the camera to his eye level and moved her thumb into position. 'Tell you what. I'll play it. You don't have to look.'

Greene put his fingers over his eyes, then opened them up a crack to peek.

She gave him a playful slap on the shoulder. 'I'm American. I'm aggressive. Get used to it.'

The image came on the screen. Goodling was holding a cell phone to her ear. Suddenly her face

116

contorted in pain, as if she'd been punched in the gut. With a jolt, she threw the phone out of the camera range and clasped her hands to her stomach. She shouted something. It looked as if her lips mouthed two words, but there was no sound.

'What did she say?' Greene asked when the short video was over.

'I don't know,' Kwon said. 'It all happened so fast. The bodyguard whipped the door closed and I landed on the floor. Here, feel this.'

She took his hand and guided it to the bottom of her chin. He touched the spot where her skin was scraped.

'I was told Goodling was going to leave today,' Greene said.

'She did,' Kwon said. 'Private flight from the back of Pearson Airport, at one eighteen. See, I've got good information for you.'

'I appreciate it.'

'This is a huge story now. I'm covering the funeral. The trial, when it happens. Everything. Goodling's going to come back here at some point, I'm convinced.'

'Let me know when she does.'

'It's a deal. Want to go to one of those bars across the street and have a drink?'

'I'm heading to the morgue in half an hour for the autopsy,' he said.

'Sounds like an exciting night,' she said.

'Comes with the territory.' Greene looked past

Kwon to the throng of carefree people strolling along the sidewalk, where a misty darkness had descended amidst the streetlights and shimmering storefronts.

CHAPTER 19

Daniel Kennicott smiled when he saw the white plastic bag on the handle of the side entrance to his second-floor flat. Inside the bag were fresh tomatoes, carrots, and cucumbers, a bright red apple, and a note from his landlords: 'In case the store be closed, Mr and Mrs Federico.' The couple lived downstairs, and Mr Federico was an avid gardener who constantly pushed food on his upstairs tenant. Unlike most cops his age, who owned town houses out in the suburbs, Kennicott had rented this place downtown for years. It was on Clinton Street, just north of College and the heart of Little Italy.

He put the Terrance Wyler file and the plastic bag on his kitchen table and pulled out a carrot. Kennicott had more than enough experience with sleep deprivation, first as a law student, then as a young lawyer in a top downtown firm, and now as a cop. It was important to eat.

The apartment was stuffy. He opened the windows at the front of the flat, then the back ones too. He tilted his head out into the cool night air. There was a chirp-chirp and a rustle of feet. Two black squirrels chased each other up Mr Federico's grapevine, which blossomed into a shaded awning over his concrete back porch every summer. Kennicott took out a bottle of vinegar and a rag from under the sink and wiped his leather shoes clean before he went to his bedroom to change.

Back in the kitchen in a clean T-shirt and shorts, he sat down. Even though there was a desk in his second bedroom, he liked to work here. He opened the Wyler file and started reading through the legal pleadings to get an overall view of the divorce case. There were long, detailed affidavits from husband and wife that were mirror images of each other. Classic 'he said, she said' stuff.

Terrance's affidavit was ten pages of dense prose detailing every faux pas and misstep. Samantha was a workaholic, she had never bonded with Simon, and she was a careless mother – as illustrated by the time in late July when the boy sliced open his cheek and had to go the hospital. She didn't even notify Terrance. Samantha was untruthful, as demonstrated by the 'patently false' charge she'd brought against Terrance, alleging that he'd threatened her with a knife. She systematically alienated Terrance from his family and almost bankrupted him two years ago with her ill-conceived plan to start a gourmet food shop.

Samantha painted an equally unattractive picture. Terrance was controlled by his family. He had lots of ideas to modernize Wyler Foods but no one listened and he was too weak to stand up to them. She started the food shop so he could realize his potential. Nathan Wyler used his contacts to undermine them and Terrance wasn't prepared to work hard enough for it to succeed. Even though Terrance was acquitted of threatening her with the knife, he wasn't the easygoing person he pretended to be, but was angry and potentially violent. He destroyed the marriage by leaving Samantha for the actress April Goodling.

Kennicott had seen this type of angry dispute over and over again. Two people who'd lived together, been intimate, had children, yet at the same time were secretly keeping score, like accountants at tax time.

The next file was marked E-MAILS. For some reason e-mail brought out the worst in people, especially when they were angry. There were three in a subfile marked 'Samantha E-mails for Police':

July 30
You're unbelievable. Simon gets three stitches on his cheek and you'd think he'd lost a limb. No I didn't call you about it because he's fine. Now you're trying to use this against me and it's pathetic. I bet your family is behind this. All they want is to get their hands on Simon.

121

August 7
Where the hell does your lawyer get off saying I'm an incompetent mother!!! That I'd be lucky to get supervised access to Simon once a month if we go to trial!!! I'm so pissed off. Your family will stop at nothing to try to take my son away.

August 12
One week from the trial and now your lawyer amends her pleadings and asks for full custody. Says it's not safe for Simon to stay overnight with me???!!! Who the fuck do you think you are? Just like you to stab me in the back. You want to go to war. Watch out. You're not the only one with a knife.

Kennicott read the last message over again. 'You're not the only one with a knife.' The prosecutor will love that line, he thought.

He yawned. It was three-thirty in the morning. Kennicott had been going nonstop since the initial radio call early this morning, and there were hours of work ahead of him: read the correspondence between the lawyers, listen to the voice mails, go through the other e-mails, and comb through the financial information. Greene was spending the night at the morgue observing the autopsy. He was going to pick Kennicott up at eight in the morning to go see the Wyler family and would expect to be fully briefed.

Kennicott kept eating carrots as he read. The last forty-eight hours he'd hardly had time to breathe or eat – or do what he wanted to do most of all: call Jo Summers.

They'd met years ago in law school and had stumbled upon each other again last winter at the Crown's office at Old City Hall. Kennicott was working on his first murder trial with Greene and Jo was running bail court. It was an embarrassing moment, because at first he couldn't remember her name. Not a good thing with a woman who you had a one-night stand with so many years ago and never even called afterward.

Throughout the spring and early summer they'd become friends, edging closer to each other. In the last week of July he went to Italy for three weeks to track down some clues to his brother Michael's murder. His parents had died in a car accident two years earlier. But now there were questions. Was it really an accident?

It had been a rough and disappointing trip. He had returned last Thursday and called Summers. She said the first time she was free was Sunday night. He took the ferry over to visit her on the Toronto Islands, not really knowing what to expect.

She met him at the landing. It was eight o'clock but still stifling hot. They walked along the outer boardwalk to a deserted part of the beach and looked out across Lake Ontario. There was no breeze. Sitting in the sand at sunset, she reached over and straightened the collar of his shirt.

They talked, it seemed, about everything but themselves. Even when the sun went down, the heat didn't relent. 'When's the last ferry?' he asked after what seemed like hours.

'You missed it.' There was just enough moonlight that he could see her mischievous smile. 'But you can always take a water taxi.'

He laughed.

'Truth or dare?' she said, laughing back.

'Truth.' Good, he thought. At last they'd talk about what was so unspoken between them.

'Truth. I was pissed that you never phoned after that night in law school.' She had her sandals off and scooped sand over her feet. 'But I was even more pissed, I think, when you walked into my office last winter and couldn't even remember my name.'

'Truth. I was an asshole.'

She touched his elbow. 'Truth. You weren't an asshole. Actually, you were kind. I'm not a prude, Daniel. I can handle a one-night stand. But there was something careless about you. It scared me.'

'Truth, then,' he said. 'Why are you sitting here with me?'

She kicked her feet out of the sand. 'Truth. Last winter in my office, remember I told you I thought about calling you after I heard about your brother's murder?'

'I was touched.'

'I must have picked up the phone ten times. I

wrote you three or four letters, but never mailed them. I wanted to reach out to that kind side of you, but I was afraid.'

'Of my careless side.'

She looked at him. Jo had wide blue eyes. 'Dare.' She jumped up. 'Remember the opening scene in the movie *Jaws*? There aren't any sharks in this lake.' With a snap she yanked down her shorts, in one move pulled off her T-shirt, and reached back and unleashed her mane of hair. Kennicott watched her for a moment in the moonlight, slack-jawed, before he stripped down and followed her in. It was so hot, there was no difference in the temperature of the air and the water and Jo's luminous skin.

Tonight a cool breeze blew through his apartment, driving out the stifling heat. Kennicott felt around his landlord's bag of fruit and vegetables, yanked out the apple, and sank his teeth into it. No matter what happened on this case tomorrow, he was going to find time to call Jo.

CHAPTER 20

Visiting the family of the deceased was one of the toughest parts of the job, but Ari Greene knew it was a prime opportunity to learn more about the victim and to find possible suspects. Right now, those were the two top priorities.

Timing was key. Wait too long and the family would feel abandoned. Nothing was worse in a murder trial than when the family lost faith in the police and the prosecution. But if you descended upon them too fast, people would be in shock, and there was a real danger of overwhelming everyone.

The afternoon before, he had called Nathan Wyler and offered to come see them all. But they'd agreed it would be better if he came in the morning. They needed some time to talk to Simon. Be alone together. Greene said he'd be there by nine.

Daniel Kennicott sat next to him as they drove past Woodhill, a town northwest of Toronto. This was, according to snobbish downtowners, 'nosebleed country.' As they rode, Greene and Kennicott updated each other on all they had learned the previous night.

'The autopsy was straightforward,' Greene said. 'Seven stab wounds, no defensive wounds, cause of death loss of blood. They're consistent with the kitchen knife. The cut that killed him was a small puncture to the neck, hit the carotid artery. He would have bled out real fast. Pathologist says four minutes tops.'

'I went over the divorce file,' Kennicott said. 'She was angry. Sent him some e-mails that were close to being threats. Said he'd stabbed her in the back and had better watch out. He wasn't the only one with a knife.'

Greene had seen more than his share of ugly family breakups that ended in criminal charges. 'These divorces get nastier all the time. Any news from the door knockers?' Door knockers were the division cops Greene had tasked to canvass the streets near Wyler's home and in Yorkville, where Samantha Wyler's family lawyer had his office.

'No one saw anything on Wyler's street. There were only a few people at home.'

'Not surprising, a neighborhood like that in the middle of the summer.'

'We got lucky down in Yorkville with one of the store owners.' Kennicott pulled out his notebook and flipped through a few pages. 'Allan Rupert. In business since 1968. Store called Chemise If You Please. Sells high-end men's shirts. Was in early to set up for the fall rush and the film festival. Noticed a woman, Caucasian, dark hair, estimated age early thirties, curled up on the doorstep of Winston Feindel's law office. Rupert knows Feindel. Both are British, like to go to the local pub to watch soccer matches.'

'What time?'

'A few minutes before seven. Knows the time because he always catches the BBC news at the top of the hour.'

'She gave the knife to Feindel. That's how DiPaulo passed it over to me so fast. But how'd she get downtown?'

'She's not on the subway videos. No cabbies picked her up and we showed her picture to every bus driver anywhere near the house. Nothing.'

In nosebleed country the streets were wide, the blocks long, and the sidewalks narrow or nonexistent. Greene hadn't seen a tree in Woodhill, just concrete and big-box stores, and there wasn't a pedestrian in sight. Sprawling subdivisions sported garish stone gateways, their pretentious names ending in words like 'estates,' 'manor,' and even 'domain.' Billboards announcing 'record sales,' and 'time-limited, must-buy-now' offers were surrounded by balloon-festooned flagpoles. Greene wondered who first hit on the notion that flags and balloons would induce people to slam on their brakes and go buy a new home.

'What'd you find about the Wylers?' Greene asked.

'Ran them all through CPIC,' Kennicott said, referring to the police database. 'The father, William Wyler, showed up. Been charged twice. Once by a farmer who got into an argument with him down at the food terminal. And a female employee claimed he cornered her in the back office and forced her to have sex with him.'

'What happened?'

'N.G. both times.' N.G. was police shorthand for not guilty.

'Big surprise,' Greene said.

'A few years ago his wife called 911. He'd been drinking and was throwing things around the house. She told the cops he hadn't hit her. They didn't see any injuries. The oldest son, Nathan, came over and the father calmed down.'

'Every unhappy family is unhappy in its own way.' Greene swung into Fieldstone Forest, the development where Nathan Wyler lived. It was a warren of winding streets. Wyler's mini-mansion was on a circular cul-de-sac between two other equally huge homes. Greene pulled his Oldsmobile into the driveway, where four sparkling clean cars were parked. A large Cadillac had the license plate name WFRESH 1, a black Lexus was WFRESH 2, a sleek Mercedes with a disabled notice in the front window was WFRESH 3, and a panel van painted in the corporate colors was WFRESH 4. Only the van had a transponder, a gadget that slipped on the windshield for use by frequent commuters on the 407 toll highway that led from the city to suburbia.

The front lawn was manicured, the trimmed flower beds filled with annuals in dull primary colors. A note on a plastic stake read 'Early-Bird Lawn – Weekly Maintenance – Monday, August 17, 5:00 a.m.' It listed about twenty categories of work that had been done the day before.

Greene bent down for a closer look. Wonder what I miss with my hand-push lawn mower, he thought, reading through the list of chores. Beside an illustration of a robin pulling a worm out of the ground a note read, 'Next Early-Bird Visit, Monday, August 24, 5:00 a.m.'

He suspected that not one member of the Wyler family planted a seed, mowed a lawn, pulled a weed, or raked a leaf. The chatter of crickets in the early-morning air was the only hint of real nature.

'Detective Ari Greene, Toronto Homicide.' He extended a hand to the big man who opened the front door.

Greene recognized Nathan Wyler from a long time before. They'd spent a few months in the same class during Greene's final year of high school, after Wyler was kicked out of his fancy private school. He'd been a real jerk back then, used to getting his way and throwing his weight around.

'Nathan Wyler,' he said. 'Nice to meet you.'

Wyler turned to Kennicott and shook his hand. 'I'm sorry I exploded at you yesterday when you told me the news.'

'No need to apologize,' Kennicott said. 'Losing a brother is a terrible thing.'

'I appreciate both of you coming. It means everything to my parents.'

Interesting how the mind works, Greene thought as they followed Wyler into the house. He could still remember Nathan's distinctive, lumbering gait, those massive shoulders hunched over, the way his large head jutted out. And the fight they'd had in the high school cafeteria.

It had been a few weeks after Wyler showed up at the school. 'Who spells green with an *e* on the end?' Wyler asked one day to a crowd of hangers-on around him. His voice was loud. Greene, who was skinny back then, sat across the long table, a few seats down.

He looked up at Wyler and waited. More people looked on. 'Someone Hitler couldn't kill,' Greene said, keeping his voice level. 'What did your daddy do during the war? Get rich selling lettuce and tomatoes while everyone else was off fighting?'

Wyler glared back at Greene. 'I get it,' Wyler said. 'It's *e* for greeny.' 'Greeny' was slang for a new immigrant.

The words were barely out of Wyler's mouth when Greene grabbed a pitcher of fruit punch and threw it at him. Without waiting, Greene jumped

131

on the table. Despite the fact that Wyler was so much bigger, Greene came down on him hard, hitting with all his might. It was the only time he'd ever punched someone.

After all these years, Greene would have recognized Wyler by simply walking behind him. He was sure Wyler wouldn't remember him.

'Everyone's in the living room.' Wyler led them across a bleached white wood floor into a large rotunda with a spiral staircase heading up through the two-story space, twirling around a massive chandelier. The living room was off to the side. Three enormous couches were packed with people around a square coffee table.

'This is Detective Greene and Officer Kennicott,' Wyler said. The chatter in the room died down instantly. He pointed to the couch on his left. 'My cousins.' Then to the second couch. 'My wife, Harriet, and some of her friends.' Finally he looked to his right. 'My parents and my brother Jason.'

Greene walked directly over to the parents.

Mrs Wyler stood as he approached and Greene grasped her hand. She was a surprisingly tall woman, with dark hair accented by a white stripe to the left of center. Her palm and fingers were cold. 'We'll do everything we can,' he said.

'It's unthinkable.' Her eyes, the same enchanting green as her oldest son's, were hooded in sadness.

'I don't have anything to say to make it easier.

I wish I did.' Greene never used the trite phrases they recommended at the police seminars, things like 'I'm sorry for your loss.'

Mr Wyler got up stiffly beside his wife. 'Damn knees are a mess. Too many years hauling around vegetable crates.' Like his oldest son, he was a big, hulking man. He wore heavy rubber-soled shoes, presumably to cushion his weak legs. His eyes were dark and cold. 'Call me Bill.' He gave Greene an unenthusiastic handshake. 'This was always my wife's greatest fear. To bury one of her sons.'

'My father lost children too,' Greene said. At the seminars they said you should never personalize what you say to victims' families. Advice he steadfastly ignored. The best thing he could do in this situation was be himself.

The third person in this grim receiving line was the middle brother, Jason. Unlike the other members of the family, he was short. He pulled himself to his feet with difficulty, grasping two well-worn metal canes to steady himself. Kennicott had told Greene that Jason lived on the ground floor of Nathan's house. Suffered from a rare degenerative nerve disease called spinal muscular atrophy, or SMA.

'This is our son Jason.' Mrs Wyler was watching him.

'Hello, Detective.' His voice was deep, but it was an effort for him to talk. He slipped one cane under his arm and gave a surprisingly firm handshake. Although his legs were weak and withered, his shoulders and arms were strong. 'We were all at Terry's for Sunday-night dinner.'

'I understand you're a close family,' Greene said.

'Very.' It was Nathan Wyler talking. He was still standing beside Greene.

'We put together a great meal,' Jason said.

'My boys all like to cook,' Mrs Wyler said.

'I made a vichyssoise,' Jason said. 'Nathan brought these amazing organic peppers.'

'We do everything together, even argue,' Nathan said. He turned to his brother, who was teetering on his canes. 'Jason, sit down.' He looked at Greene. 'What can you tell us?'

They all sat down. The worst part of these initial meetings was how little you could say at a time when the families were desperate for information. Greene always spoke directly. No cop lingo. He knelt down so he was at eye level with Mrs Wyler. 'We've worked around the clock since your son's murder.' Greene didn't sugarcoat anything. People always respected that. 'Let me tell you everything I can.'

For the next ten minutes he laid out some of the details: that Terrance had been found by the nanny on the kitchen floor, stabbed many times – he didn't say how many – that an autopsy had been performed and the cause of death was loss of blood. He made no mention of the Sunday-night e-mails between Samantha and Terrance, or Samantha's being in Simon's room, or of the bloody knife.

'Simon was asleep when Arceli arrived,' Greene said. 'We got your grandson out of the house before the press showed up.'

'Thank you for that,' Mrs Wyler said. 'He's in the basement with the nanny. Nathan told him the news last night and all he wants to do is play with his trains.' She looked at her disabled son. 'Jason drove to Terrance's house, and one of your young officers brought out the train set for him.'

Nathan cast his arms in a wide circle. He was still standing beside Greene. 'What about Samantha? We all know she was threatening him.'

'When are you going to arrest her?' It was Mr Wyler. His lips were upturned into an angry snarl.

'I don't want that woman anywhere near my grandson,' Mrs Wyler said. 'Ever.'

Greene had expected an outburst like this. The key was to stay calm. He was determined to interview everyone he could before making an arrest.

'The hardest part right now is that you're going to have to be patient,' he said.

'We're not a patient family,' Mr Wyler said, those cold eyes of his challenging.

'That's why Officer Kennicott and I are here. To move things along as fast as we can. We need

135

to speak to everyone individually. It'll probably take all day.'

Greene met the man's angry eyes and stared at him until William Wyler looked away.

CHAPTER 21

'You awake?'

Daniel Kennicott's eyes were half closed. He always slept with the window and the blinds open, and it was still dark outside. When the cell phone woke him up, he'd hoped it was Jo Summers. He'd left her a message on her voice mail the day before, but she hadn't called back. The ring tone told him it was Detective Greene.

'Getting there,' he said. 'What do you need?'

'The timeline. You update it last night?' Greene asked.

Kennicott snapped on the night-light by his bed. It was a quarter to five. Didn't Greene ever sleep? The timeline was the chronology the police assembled as an investigation moved forward. After each witness was interviewed, the information was added to the list, which Kennicott kept in a separate notebook.

'Yeah.' Kennicott rubbed a hand over his face. In his days as a young lawyer, when he was on an important case, Lloyd Granwell, the senior partner who'd recruited him to the firm, was like Greene. Pushing him day and night. 'You have the spark,

Daniel,' Granwell once told him. 'You see things most people don't even think about.'

'Good.' Greene sounded wide awake. Granwell was like this too. Indefatigable. 'Meet me in half an hour at the Caldense Bakery in Little Portugal, on Dundas West. Opens at five.'

'I know the place.' Kennicott resisted the urge to ask, 'Why not meet at police headquarters?' Greene always met with him in some restaurant or café, never the same place twice. And he always knew the owner, even had a few words to say in whatever language they spoke.

At first Kennicott couldn't figure this out. But now, four years in as a cop, he saw how Greene had his own personal map of Toronto, to which he was always adding details, filling in gaps.

Half an hour later Kennicott walked into the Caldense, a place that was much more than just a bakery. There were a dozen square tables on a blue, yellow, and white floor, and a TV in the corner, the volume up too high, broadcasting a Portuguese station – right now a couple wearing black were doing the tango. A long glass counter displayed fresh baked goods, sweet pastries, desserts, meat and cheese for slicing into sandwiches, and aged sausages. A separate glassed-in cabinet featured birthday and wedding cakes.

Greene was seated by the window, laughing with a bald man whose jet-black mustache matched the black vest he wore over an equally black shirt. A lineup of men in sweatshirts with LABOURERS –

LOCAL 183 logos on the back were ordering coffee at the front counter. They wore work boots, the top laces undone. Everyone spoke Portuguese. A crooked clock on the wall said it was exactly 5:15.

'Officer Daniel Kennicott, meet Miguel Oliviera, proprietor extraordinaire,' Greene said.

'My pleasure,' Oliviera said to Kennicott. He had a firm handshake and a musical accent.

'Have some of my croissant.' Greene pointed to a round white plate where a flat croissant was cut in half. 'It's fresh.'

'Cappuccino?' Oliviera asked.

Kennicott sat down. 'Please,' he said.

'Tea for the detective, of course,' Oliviera said. 'I buy one box for him, lasts me a year.'

'*Obrigado,*' Greene said. He waited until the proprietor moved out of earshot before he said to Kennicott, 'Here's my question on the timeline. When does the family leave Terrance's house on the Sunday night?'

'Dinner lasted until about eleven o'clock—'

'After they'd used the knives to chop up all those fresh Wyler vegetables for the vichyssoise,' Greene said.

Kennicott looked at the TV. A musical group was playing the song 'I Gotta Feeling' in Portuguese. Despite himself, Kennicott started humming 'tonight's gonna be a good night, tonight's gonna be a good, good night' in his mind.

'What happens next?' Greene asked.

'When the family leaves, Terrance e-mails his

139

lawyer. Confirms he's not taking Samantha's deal. Then at twelve thirty-five he sends Samantha an e-mail saying he's going to accept her offer after all and invites her over. She e-mails back that she'll be there in half an hour. I walked from her apartment to Terrance's house. Took fifteen minutes.'

'Good.' Greene ate part of his croissant. 'Here, share some more of this with me. They're way too heavy and sweet.'

Kennicott took a bite. Greene was right. The croissant tasted like sugary dough.

Greene put up his hand to caution Kennicott as Oliviera approached the table with a tray in hand. 'Here you go, gentlemen,' he said. 'One herbal tea.' He squinted his nose up in mock horror as he put a thin metal teapot in front of Greene. 'One lovely cappuccino.' Kennicott's drink had a white, foamy top, liberally sprinkled with chocolate bits that spilled over onto the white saucer.

Kennicott took a sip. It was sweet and watery. When they were alone, he continued. 'At twelve thirty-seven Terrance e-mails Starr and tells her he's taking the deal and that Samantha's coming over to his house. That's the final e-mail. Starr didn't see it until the morning.'

'Didn't the nanny say the family had a fight on Sunday night?' Greene asked.

Kennicott flipped back a few pages. 'Nathan said their billboard ad campaign, which was Terrance's idea, was expensive. Terrance wanted them to sponsor a reception at the upcoming film festival. They did it last year and that's where he met April Goodling. Everyone else was against it.'

Greene poured some tea into a white cup. 'These damn things always leak,' he said at the moment when the teapot did just that. He mopped up the mess with a napkin and braved another bite of the croissant. Kennicott had a funny thought: Maybe Greene got me down here just to help him with the Portuguese pastry.

'I had my friend Hamdi at my old law firm do a title search on Nathan's house,' Kennicott said. 'Place's mortgaged to the hilt.'

'Guy's on his third marriage,' Greene said.

'Sounds like Wyler Foods is in trouble too.'

'From the mansion to the millhouse in three generations,' Greene said.

'That's a good way to put it.'

'Not my phrase,' Greene said. 'Happens all the time. The grandfather starts a business, the father builds it, and the son squanders it all away. Nathan's broke and his little brother's on a spending spree.'

'Nathan e-mailed Terrance at five ten on Monday morning saying good luck today in court. "Even though we fight, I still love you" was the last line.'

'Could be a self-serving e-mail. The guy has a temper.' Greene motioned to the croissant in front of Kennicott. 'Eat up.'

Kennicott forced down a hunk of the doughy bread and washed it down with the watery coffee.

Now on the TV there were highlights of various soccer matches, each goal accompanied by wild cheering by the fans and players.

Greene took out his notebook and wrote. 'We have about a four-and-a-half-hour gap.'

Kennicott swallowed more of the croissant. 'From twelve forty to five ten. Between Terrance's last e-mail to his lawyer and Nathan's e-mail to him, which is never answered. What does the coroner say about the time of death?'

'Don't believe what you see on TV,' Greene said. 'They can never pinpoint it. The body was cold. Food in the stomach. Could have been dead two, three, four hours. No way to know.'

'Where does it leave us?'

'With a big black hole.' Greene went back through the pages of his notebook. 'Nathan Wyler – what time did he say he got to work?'

Kennicott turned back in his notebook too. 'About three o'clock.'

'You remember that Wyler Foods truck we saw in their driveway?' Greene asked.

'WFRESH 4. I saw it at the food terminal two days ago, when I notified him that his brother had been murdered.' Was it only two days ago? Less than forty-eight hours. Kennicott felt as if he'd been living in this case and Terrance Wyler's life for weeks.

'Perfect.' Greene picked up his cell phone and pushed a preset number. 'It's Greene. Who's in charge of toll road records?' He kept the cell in his ear but turned the microphone away from his mouth. 'Nathan's vehicle was the only one with a transponder, so we know he takes the 407. I want to find out what time he hit the highway and when he got off.'

'You think he was angry at his brother because of all the money he was spending—'

Greene put up his hand to stop Kennicott and swung the phone back in place. 'I have a license number I need you to trace on the 407. Rush job. Thanks.'

It was amazing how wide-awake Greene was, Kennicott thought as he looked around the bakery. A cooking segment had come on the TV and the chef was making an egg-based tart. Among the continual lineup of men buying coffee at the counter, he saw the first female customer of the morning. An older woman who purchased three loaves of white bread.

Greene turned the phone away from his mouth again. 'They photograph every license plate on the 407, whether the car has a transponder or not,' he said to Kennicott. 'Means we can trace when and where any vehicle got on and off that highway.'

He put his finger back up in the air, turned the phone back to his mouth, and wrote some notes. 'Good, okay, thanks,' he said and hung up.

Kennicott tried to read upside down what he'd written. It was a collection of numbers and times.

Greene looked at Kennicott, his eyes sparkling: 'Wyler got on the 407 at one fifteen, going east.

Remember, the non-toll highways were all cut off because of all the other murders that night. But he didn't get off at Highway 427, which you'd expect him to do if he was going down to the food terminal. He went all the way east to Yonge Street. Exited there at one forty-two.'

'Yonge Street,' Kennicott said. 'Near Terrance's house.'

'Right,' Greene said. 'But even closer to Samantha's place.'

Kennicott felt a hit of adrenaline spike through his system. This is what it takes, he thought, to make homicide. On the TV now, politicians were standing in the Portuguese parliament making impassioned speeches with exaggerated hand gestures. Greene tossed a twenty-dollar bill on the table. 'Let's go,' he said.

Kennicott got up. But Greene pointed back to the table. 'Finish your croissant.' A chunk was on the plate. By the time Kennicott tossed it into his mouth, Greene was already out the door.

CHAPTER 22

In his early twenties Ari Greene spent a summer in Israel. He visited with some of his mother's distant relatives and worked for a few weeks on a kibbutz in the Negev desert. That's where he met Natalya, a waif of a young woman who'd left in the first wave of Jewish exodus from the Soviet Union. Beautiful and secretive, she was perhaps the most manipulative person he'd ever met in his whole life. They had a lot of fun together. Six months after Greene got home, she showed up one day on the concrete doorsteps of his parents' house. Natalya wanted Greene to marry her so she could get into the country. When he refused, they had an enormous fight. She disappeared, only to pop up again in his life when he'd least expect it.

He'd never forget the first time he took her to a Canadian grocery store. It was the only occasion when she was totally unable to control her emotions. All the food. Fresh. Bountiful. The endless aisles of it. She started running back and forth to assure herself that all this really existed. She'd grabbed Greene and cried. All those gray years of deprivation, and here was a world full of everything.

He thought of Natalya as he walked into the sprawling Ontario Food Terminal. The produce, the smells, the color. This was the daily challenge of human existence: to get food from the ground to people's mouths.

Inside Wyler Foods, Nathan Wyler stood behind a long table, sorting through crates of fresh fruits and vegetables his uniformed employees brought up to him in waves. Greene stood back to watch him work.

Wyler's fingers flew over every tray of fresh goods like a concert pianist. He shouted out a cacophony of criticism of almost everything he saw, laced with profanities.

A buxom redhead who'd been at the cash register at the front approached Greene. The Wyler Foods uniform was tight on her. 'Can I help you?'

'I'm here to see Mr Wyler.'

'Detective Greene, what are you doing back there?' Wyler shouted. 'Paulette, bring him up here.'

Greene held out his hand as he approached the table and Wyler shook it.

'Angelo, take over for a while,' Wyler said to one of his many assistants. 'Detective Greene's in charge of Terry's case. We need to go for a walk.'

'I wasn't sure if you'd be at work today,' Greene said.

'It's the food business,' Wyler said, leading

Greene out of the shop. 'Never stops. This is how we were raised.'

'A hard way to live.'

'Only thing I know,' Wyler said. 'I'm not looking forward to tomorrow.'

'No one likes funerals,' Greene said.

'Maybe it will hit me at the graveyard. But I can't believe my baby brother's dead.'

Greene walked with him, not saying anything. A cart zipped around the corner and honked at the last minute. They jumped to get out of its way.

Wyler pulled out a cigarette pack before they got to the exit door. 'You smoke?'

'I quit in grade ten,' Greene said.

Wyler snorted out a laugh. 'That was smart.' Outdoors, he took another look at Greene before he lit up. 'Where'd you go to school?'

Greene was wearing a light Windbreaker. He stuffed his hands into the side pockets before he answered. 'Marlee High.'

Wyler took a long drag. 'Greene with an *e* on the end. Right?'

'That's me.'

'I bet you recognized me right away,' Wyler said.

'Remembering faces is a good thing if you're a detective.'

Wyler took another puff. 'You had a good punch.'

'You're the only person I've ever hit in my life.'

Wyler laughed. 'Hope you enjoyed it.'

'You know something?' Greene laughed as well. 'I did.' He took his hands out of his pockets.

'Any news?' Wyler asked.

'Not yet. I wanted to ask about your business.'

'It's a dogfight,' Wyler said. 'Let's get something to eat.'

He led Greene back inside to a greasy spoon tucked away in a corner. The old couple who worked there looked like they'd run the place for a few centuries. Wyler ordered bacon and eggs, and Greene got a muffin.

'Food business is going down the crapper.' Wyler dug into his meal the moment his plate came. 'Everyone's stealing from everyone else. The big chains are selling gas and books and housewares. The department stores, the gas stations, the bookstores, even the drugstores, for fuck's sake, are all selling food. No one's making any money.'

'Your store appeals to a higher-end market, doesn't it?'

'There's no brand loyalty anymore. Everyone wants a deal.'

'What was it like when Samantha and Terrance opened their own store?'

Wyler piled the food into his mouth.

'Total fuckup. Last thing we needed was more competition from our own family. Samantha thinks she's so smart, but I know all the suppliers. You think they'd deliver their grade-A stuff to that bitch?'

'You must have been angry at your brother too.'

Wyler eyed Greene carefully. 'Of course I was pissed off. Terrance always had things easy. Mr Handsome. Mr Top Athlete. Guy with all the beautiful girls. I'm sweating it out up here, he gets to go to school in the States. Comes back with money in his pocket so he can buy his house in the city, marries Sam, who treats our whole family like dirt.'

People in the restaurant were looking at their table.

'Let's go outside.' Greene took out a twenty-dollar bill and insisted Wyler let him pay.

Out in the parking lot, Wyler lit up another cigarette. 'What she did to my brother was unbelievable. My mom would make Sunday dinner, and Sam would cancel at the last minute. Find some asinine excuse not to come with Simon, and Terry'd show up alone. Pathetic.'

'I heard you argued with him at the Sunday-night dinner.'

Wyler's big shoulders shook with amusement. 'When didn't we argue? Family business. Terry thought there was always money for everything. Advertising. Film festival parties. You name it.'

Greene spotted a bench at the far end of the lot. 'What did you do Monday morning?' he asked in a neutral voice when they sat down.

Wyler looked around. For the first time he seemed to realize that Greene had isolated him.

'I don't know. I came to work.'

Greene had anticipated this evasive answer. He'd checked with the gatehouse half an hour before, when he arrived at the food terminal. 'You got here at three oh seven a.m.,' Greene said. It was important to make a suspect aware that you knew a lot about him. Keep him guessing.

'Yeah,' Wyler said. He stomped out his cigarette on the asphalt.

'That time of night, you could drive here from your home in what, half an hour?' Greene said.

'Twenty-four minutes, if I come straight here.'

'Fastest way is using the 407.'

'Yeah, the fucking toll saves me about five minutes.'

'But Monday morning you took the 407 all the way to Yonge Street at one forty-two. That's one exit away from Terrance's house.'

'I know.'

'Even closer to Samantha's place.'

Wyler pulled out another cigarette, clicked on his lighter, and took a drag. 'Just my luck.'

'You didn't think I'd find this out?'

Wyler looked back over the parking lot. 'It didn't even occur to me until a few hours after that young cop told me Terry'd been murdered. I guess I was in shock.'

'It didn't occur to you that you'd been at your sister-in-law's place—'

'What?' Wyler tossed his cigarette on the ground and butted it out. 'You crazy? Me at Samantha's

150

place? No one in my family would talk to that bitch in a million years. It's the redhead.'

'The redhead?'

'Paulette. The one on cash. Don't tell me you didn't notice her.'

When a homicide happened, time stopped and everyone near it was captured in one gigantic freeze-frame photograph. Inevitably, there was collateral damage. It looked as if Nathan Wyler had been caught, literally, with his pants down.

'Look, I've only been married to Harriet for six years,' Wyler said. 'She wouldn't sign a prenup. Another divorce will wipe me out.' He looked at Greene, almost pleading.

Greene thought about what Kennicott had told him. All of Wyler's debt.

'I park in the basement of the condo I've sublet for her. It's a new building. Costs me a thousand a month to put her up there. They've got video cameras and all that shit.' He pulled out his wallet and fished out a plastic card hidden under a leather flap. 'Here's my passkey. Records when I come and go. I left about ten to three. I know because I listened to the sports at the top of the hour. That time of night I get here from her place in less than twenty minutes.'

Greene took the card. 'Anything else I should know?'

'Those two other houses on the court where

we live. We used to own them all. Parents on one side, Jason on the other. We had to sell both of them. Now the whole family's under one roof, and the fucking mortgage is halfway up my ass.'

'What about the fleet of fancy cars?'

'Ha.' He had a loud, cackling laugh. 'Financed to the roof. Used to have transponders for all four, now just the van. Can't even afford the stupid toll. The gardener and all that junk, it's all for show. Dad's too damn proud. It would kill him if people knew.'

Greene remembered the time his father found himself on the 407 toll road. It was last winter, after Greene's mother had died, and his father got lost trying to visit an old friend. He'd ended up in the ditch, narrowly missing a light pole. Greene threatened to take away his license, and after lengthy negotiations his dad agreed to only drive during the day, and to stay off the highway.

To add insult to injury, his father didn't realize that the 407 was equipped with scanners that automatically read his license plate. Two months later, when the bill arrived for seven dollars and fifty-seven cents, he was outraged.

Wyler's story would be easy to verify. Greene slipped the garage key card into his pocket. 'I'll check out your alibi.'

'This comes out, I'm screwed.' Wyler reached

back into his cigarette pack, but it was empty. 'House will be gone for sure. Doesn't matter to me. I could live in a crate. But my parents, my sick brother, and now my nephew, Simon. Where they going to go?'

CHAPTER 23

Daniel Kennicott was staring at Terrance Wyler's casket at the front of the church. Attending the funeral was Detective Greene's idea. 'Go as a mourner, and keep your eyes and ears open,' he'd said. Kennicott knew the detective was testing him. Making him think.

But Kennicott was having trouble not thinking about Jo Summers. He'd left her a message on Tuesday morning and she hadn't called back. Yesterday, when he was out working, she left him a cryptic voice mail.

'*Daniel, I'm sorry I didn't return your call. Something's come up and I won't be able to talk to you for a while. I can't explain it now, maybe in a few weeks.*' There was a long pause. Was she crying? '*It's an awful time. This has nothing to do with you. With you and me, I guess. I mean. Please, don't call me back.*' And then she hung up.

He'd listened to the message over and over, and now he kept playing it back in his mind. Stay focused, Kennicott told himself. He opened the thin brochure he'd picked up on his way into the chapel. It had the title TERRY WYLER: SON,

BROTHER, FATHER. No mention that he'd been a husband for five years. Inside were photos of Wyler – with his mother on a sailboat, in a kitchen cooking with one hand and holding baby Simon in the other, a group family shot that didn't include Samantha. There were no pictures of her anywhere. In two pages of clichéd prose – he loved sailing, cooking, his family and friends, and most of all his son, Simon – her name wasn't mentioned.

Kennicott studied Terrance Wyler's face, which he'd seen plastered all over the newspapers for the last few days. He felt as if they'd met before, but he couldn't place it.

The church filled up and the noise level rose. You'd never know all these people were here for a funeral. The women behind him were particularly loud.

'Could you ever understand what Terry saw in her?' one of the female voices said.

Kennicott turned halfway around, pretending to look back up the central aisle. The woman had a thick neck and bulky arms.

'She's still pretty,' her friend beside her said. She was short, with dark hair. 'But so limited.'

'Did you ever see her at the club?' the first woman asked.

'Not once,' the second woman said.

'They're coming,' a third woman said. 'Look.'

Kennicott followed their eyes back to the chapel entrance, where people were assembling. Within seconds a silence descended on the crowd, as if some unseen net had fallen on them from its spot on the high wooden ceiling. The volume of the church organ rose, creating a cozy bed of sound.

Mr and Mrs Wyler led the procession, looking stern and exhausted. Next came the brothers: Jason, using his two canes, slow but determined, and Nathan towering over him, his face angry. Behind were Nathan's wife, Harriet, and other cousins Kennicott recognized from his visit with Greene to the Wyler house.

Once they were seated in the front row, Samantha Wyler entered. She wore a high-necked black dress that accentuated her long neck. Her face was stark white, in contrast to her dark hair, which was pulled back tight. She looked straight down the center aisle at the coffin. Walking beside her was a man who was obviously her brother. He had the same general features but was nowhere near as good-looking. His cheap suit looked at least one size too small, and the shirt was tight around his collar. Must be the first time in years he'd dressed up, Kennicott thought. Brother and sister didn't touch.

Kennicott looked to the front row, where the Wyler family was seated. Jason, the middle son, was the only one who turned around. He shot an angry glance at his former sister-in-law, then snapped his head forward.

The priest waited until everyone was seated before he rose. The service took a long time, and the church, filled to capacity, was hot. When it was over, Kennicott drifted out with the crowd to his car, which was parked near the end of a long line of vehicles. All had FUNERAL signs wedged into their front hoods.

A police motorcycle escort moved them through the city. As the cars turned south onto Mount Pleasant Avenue, Kennicott saw another funeral procession coming up the hill from the other direction. It created a bottleneck at the entrance to the cemetery.

People ahead of him began parking their cars on the side of the road, getting out, and walking. Kennicott pulled his vehicle over and ran down the street until he got to the bridge that went over the graveyard. He stopped halfway across, at its highest point. There was a concrete barrier topped by two parallel rows of metal railing and he leaned over the top rail. A road was underneath, about fifty feet below, and to the left was the open grave. There was no wind and it was hot.

He'd got there just in time. The back door of the hearse was open and the casket was out, being carried by eight pallbearers. Mr and Mrs Wyler walked behind it with their disabled son, Jason. Samantha Wyler and her brother stayed well back.

Kennicott was trying to keep his mind on the present. Not think about those other funerals. His own family, which had vanished in such a short time. He scanned the crowd below.

'Hello, Officer Kennicott,' a female voice beside him said.

Margaret Kwon, the American reporter from the impromptu press conference outside the Wyler house the morning of the murder, was standing beside him. She was taking pictures with a tele-photo lens.

'Hello, Ms Kwon.' Kennicott looked away.

'I imagine you don't approve, but this is my job. Don't you think the press should cover funerals?' Kwon hefted the camera up to her eye. Kennicott heard it go click-click-click.

'I didn't appreciate it when my brother was buried,' he said.

Kwon put her camera down. 'I'm sorry. It sounds trite, but I mean it.' She grabbed her bag, rushed across the bridge, and disappeared down a flight of stairs on the south side.

Kennicott looked back at the crowd. He'd noticed something just before Kwon spoke to him. It was a woman's hair, piled high on her head. For a moment he wished Kwon was still there so he could get a better look through her camera lens. But then the woman turned in his direction and he knew. It was Jo Summers.

Now he remembered why Terrance Wyler's face looked familiar. Last year, a few days before Christmas, Kennicott had run into Jo Summers on College Street. She was with Terrance, and they were going out to dinner, and he'd wondered if they were involved with each other. He thought of the funeral brochure photos of Wyler sailing. At Jo's house on the Islands, he'd seen a picture of her and her dad on a sailboat, holding up a cup they'd obviously won in a regatta. Her father, Judge Summers, made a big deal about being a sailor.

Maybe Samantha Wyler never went to 'the club,' Kennicott thought, but it looked as if Jo Summers did. Must be how she knew Terrance. Now he understood. Jo was seeing a married man who'd been murdered. That's why she'd said in her voice mail that this was such a bad time for her.

Kennicott caught Summers's eye for a moment before she looked away. So this was why she had to avoid all contact with him. Kennicott was with her all Sunday night when her secret boyfriend, Terrance Wyler, was murdered. He was her alibi. And the only way to maintain the integrity of an alibi witness was to cease all communication.

So that's the story, Kennicott thought. Truth or dare.

CHAPTER 24

After he'd been widowed, Ted DiPaulo became numb to funerals. They were simply something he had to endure, like his need for reading glasses since he'd hit his mid-forties. His goal was always to leave the services as quickly as he decently could.

Today he had a good excuse. Lauren had to take her final English exam on Friday, and he'd promised to keep all day Thursday open to help her study *A Midsummer Night's Dream*. But going with Samantha Wyler to Terrance's funeral was unavoidable. So he'd compromised. Gone to the church service, but not the cemetery. And he swore to his daughter that, no matter what, he'd be home by noon.

The country's first prime minister, Sir John A. Macdonald, said that Canadians understood that a good compromise meant that everyone went away a little unhappy. That's what happened this morning. Lauren didn't speak to him when she got up, and Samantha Wyler clung to him when he left.

Good to his word, it was a few minutes before

160

twelve when DiPaulo pulled into his driveway. Racing up the front steps, he saw a white piece of paper taped haphazardly to the front door. He took the final steps slowly and pulled off the note.

Dad
Gone 2 Frans
2 study
L

That was all she wrote. No 'Love, Lauren,' with a smiley face above the *u* the way she used to do it in grade school. No 'xxx ooo,' the way she signed her letters home from camp. Not even her full name.

Inside he sensed the static stillness of the house. He couldn't wait to get out of his dark suit, the uniform of death. He loosened his tie.

'Dad, you're home.'

Lauren came rumbling down the stairs, her long black hair flapping off in all directions. Like her mother's, DiPaulo couldn't help thinking for the hundredth time. After keeping it short for years, she'd grown it out this winter.

'It's before noon,' he said.

'Fran called. She wants to study together.'

'I thought you were gone.' He waved the note at her.

'Forgot my cell. Fran says the play within the play, you know, like with Bottom as the ass, doesn't make sense.'

'Want some lunch?'

'We're going to Pizza Pizza. Abdi and Leonard and Kamil are coming too.' She frowned. When she did that, the dimple in her left cheek popped out. 'This woman's supposed to have all this power over two men because of some dust in their eyes. Do you buy that?'

'It's a romantic comedy.'

She looked at her cell phone. 'Some lady named Chiara called for you. She sounded nice.'

Chiara had called on Tuesday morning and they were going for coffee on the weekend. His kids had sworn they wanted him to start dating. But as hard as they tried to be cool, there was still something there. It had been just the three of them for so long.

'She's a friend,' he said.

'You really helped me understand Puck last night. Thanks, Dad.'

Lauren kissed him on the cheek and was gone. The Houdini-like disappearing act of the young. It was so fast that for a moment he looked at the note still in his hand and wondered if she'd really been there.

Then he bolted, taking the stairs two at a time. He pushed open the bedroom door at the front of the house. Rushing up to the bay window, he reached for the blinds and parted them to get a view of the street below. He watched his daughter's back for four or five strides until she passed out of sight.

He heard it again. The smothering silence of his home. When he was alone, he'd taken to playing the stereo really loud. His son had introduced him to grunge music, and DiPaulo had fallen hard for Kurt Cobain.

There was another sound. A buzzing noise. Maybe a fly inside, was his first thought. He realized it was his cell phone vibrating in his pocket. He'd turned the ringer off during the funeral.

Get it together, he told himself. 'Ted DiPaulo.' He answered the phone the way he would if he was still at the office.

'Ted, it's Ari Greene.'

The detective sounded serious. DiPaulo had heard this same tone of voice many times from cops. It always meant bad news.

'Hi, Ari.' DiPaulo could hear that his own voice had gone flat.

'We're going to arrest your client.'

DiPaulo took a deep breath. 'I appreciate the call.'

'I gave you four days,' Greene said. 'She never came up with an alibi.'

'I told her this might happen.' DiPaulo avoided a direct response to Greene about the alibi. 'I'll bring her in tomorrow morning about six. She won't give you any problems.'

There was a pause on the other end of the line.

'Can't give you till tomorrow,' Greene said. 'I had to get my elbows out to stop them from arresting her at the gravesite. Get her here by two, or I'll have to send out a squad car.'

Do that and the press will be all over it, DiPaulo thought. 'She should be heading home now,' he said.

'She arrived two minutes ago.' Greene's meaning was clear: the police were following Samantha. They'd probably been tailing her from day one.

'She hasn't seen her son yet. He's at the nanny's apartment.' DiPaulo looked back to the sidewalk where his daughter had disappeared moments before. 'Her family lawyer was going to go to court tomorrow to try to get her access.'

Greene exhaled. Clearly he was torn. 'Here's the best I can do,' he said. 'Pick her up and bring her to the nanny's place. I'll follow in an unmarked car. We'll find a corner of the lobby and do the arrest. Upstairs she'll have fifteen minutes with her son. I won't be able to leave them alone.'

'Thanks,' DiPaulo said.

He hung up and tightened his tie. This was just what the doctor ordered: a big-time, center-stage, no-holds-barred, first-degree murder trial. To hell with sleep.

I deserve five minutes for myself, DiPaulo thought. He charged downstairs, blasted Cobain on the stereo, and danced around the vacant living room, playing air guitar like a young Tom Cruise. '"Here we are now,"' he shouted out at the top of his lungs, '"entertain us."'

CHAPTER 25

'**M**s Wyler, you know why we're here,' Ari Greene said, more as a statement than a question. He was standing in a side room of the lobby of Arceli Ocaya's apartment. Kennicott, who'd gone ahead and found this location, was at his side.

Samantha Wyler wore a pair of slacks and a blue work shirt. She had her left hand wrapped around her right wrist, manacling herself. Her shoulders were tight. Ted DiPaulo was beside her. Wearing a suit.

'Yes. Ted told me.' She flicked her head, moving her dark hair from her face.

A nervous tic, Greene thought. He motioned to Kennicott. 'Officer Daniel Kennicott is here to assist.'

Wyler was trembling.

Without hesitating, Greene clasped her shoulder. Gently. He always made physical contact with a suspect when making an arrest. There was something very human about it. Touch.

'Samantha Wyler, it is my duty to inform you

that you are under arrest for the charge of first-degree murder of Mr Terrance Wyler.'

She brought her fist to her mouth and bit down hard on the middle finger. Her breathing was rapid, but her dark eyes never left Greene as he informed her of her rights. When he finished, she pulled her hand away from her face.

'Are there handcuffs? This is all new to me.'

'Not necessary now.' You'll be shackled soon enough, he thought. 'We're going upstairs and you can see your son for fifteen minutes. I'll be there the whole time you're with him. No talking about what happened.'

'I know, I know.' Wyler nodded over and over. 'Ted explained everything to me. Thanks for this.'

They all went together, in silence, up the elevator. Ocaya's apartment was remarkably neat, even though an enormous number of things were stuffed into so little space. Spotless, just like Terrance Wyler's house had been when she took care of it, Greene thought. The front door opened into the kitchen, where there was a sink, a hot plate, a small fridge, and, on a tiny table under the only window, a round rice cooker. A tall, cylindrical blue plastic barrel dominated the far corner.

Greene had seen similar barrels in many homes over the years, and they always impressed him. Immigrant families, usually working two jobs at minimum wage, stuffed into tiny apartments in far-flung suburbs, somehow scrimped and saved to fill these large containers with all kinds of

166

goods – canned food, clothes, batteries, toys, tools, and other utensils – to send back home to their families.

Samantha and DiPaulo came in behind Greene. Kennicott stayed by the door. Billy barked, and Greene rubbed the dog behind his ears. Simon, who was playing in the adjoining living room, spotted his mother and rushed into her arms. 'Mommy, it's not your week.' He paid no attention to the other adults in the crowded kitchen.

Wyler clasped his little head to her body. 'Mommy won't be here next week. I have to go away for a while.'

'Oh,' Simon said. He wriggled free and led her into the living room. Greene sat at the edge of the kitchen, where he could see them. Simon picked up a building block. 'I sleep on this couch. It's comfy.'

Wyler kissed the top of his head. Her jaw was clamped tight.

Simon showed her a book, *Chugga-Chugga Choo-Choo*. 'It's a baby's book, but I can read some of the words,' he said.

'I'm proud of you.' She stroked his hair.

'Cely eats lots of rice. It gets stuck in my teeth.'

Greene glanced behind him. DiPaulo, Kennicott, and Ocaya were hanging back. He pointed to a sink and made a drinking motion, and Ocaya rushed over with a glass of water. 'Thanks,' he whispered.

The fifteen minutes seemed to go by in a few

seconds. Wyler must have felt the deadline approach, because as Greene was about to stand up, she held Simon. 'Time for Mommy to go,' she said. The boy's shirt had become crooked from her embrace, and she straightened it with both hands.

Greene looked back to Kennicott and DiPaulo and motioned for them to step outside.

'Bye-bye,' Simon said to his mother.

Her body seemed like a dead weight as she walked through the small kitchen to the front door. Ocaya slipped past her into the living room and went to hold the boy.

Greene followed Wyler to the door.

'Mommy, Mommy!' Simon yelled. He scooted past Greene and grabbed Wyler by the leg. 'Did you find my Thomas?'

'Your Thomas?' Wyler turned. Tears were in her eyes. 'No, I didn't.'

'It's missing. Uncle Jason told me he was going to go back to my daddy's house to look for it. Maybe he can find it.'

'I hope so.'

Greene stepped forward. 'The police will search for it too.'

Wyler looked over the child's head at Greene and mouthed the words 'thank you.'

'The police always find lost things,' Simon said. 'And bad guys too, don't they, Mommy?'

Wyler put her hand on her son's head. Her eyes were fixed on Greene. 'They always try their best to get the bad guys,' she said. 'But even the police sometimes make mistakes.'

'No, they don't. They're the police.' Simon looked up at Greene. 'Isn't that right?'

Greene knelt down so he was at eye level with the boy. 'Why don't you give your mommy the biggest hug ever.'

Simon squeezed his mother as hard as he could, the way a child does when he doesn't want to say goodbye.

PART II

SEPTEMBER

CHAPTER 26

When they appear in Superior Court for serious charges, such as murder, Canadian lawyers wear black robes, white shirts, and white tabs. The tradition of 'gowning' is a holdover from the British judicial system and Ted DiPaulo loved everything about it – his crisp shirt, gold cuff links, and the great swish of the gown that accentuated his big frame.

Like everything in law, there was a tradition to the legal robes. Years earlier DiPaulo had been appointed Queen's Counsel, an honorific for veteran lawyers. Being a QC no longer meant a great deal. The only vestige of status was a subtle difference in the robes they wore. Junior lawyers' gowns had a narrow sash across the left shoulder that had no apparent purpose. An astute observer would note a gap in the fabric near the top, designed so clients could discreetly deposit an envelope with payment enclosed. The robes of a QC were conspicuously flat across the back with no place to deposit funds. The reason: a senior barrister would never bother with anything so trifling as fees.

In the robing room during the tense minutes before court commenced at ten o'clock, the lawyers chatted away as they struggled with buttons and tabs. To an outsider the scene might appear to be quite genteel. But really it was no different from a boxers' dressing room before a fight. Mondays were always busy. Every lawyer with a case on the trial list was summoned to court at the beginning of the week.

DiPaulo was keyed up. It had been more than three weeks since Samantha Wyler was arrested, and he was about to step into the ring for round one: the bail hearing. He opened his vertical locker, took out his blue velvet bag with the initials TLD written in flowing white script on the side – Lando was his middle name – and laid out his clothes on the long table in the center of the crowded room.

A thin man with streaked blond hair spotted him. 'What've you got today?' His name was Clarke Whittle, a talented lawyer who always wore dramatic eyeglasses, of which he seemed to have an endless supply.

Like most defense counsel, Whittle loved to gossip. What've you got? was one of the two most common questions asked in the lawyers' robing room. It meant: What are you doing in court – a bail hearing, a pretrial with a judge, or a trial?

'Bail,' DiPaulo said, as if the case were nothing unusual. 'On a murder.'

Whittle pulled off his latest pair of glasses, a

combination of wood and metal, and polished them with a special cloth. 'Who you got?'

This was the second robing-room question. The 'who' referred to the judge on the case. Most of the talk every morning was about judges, their foibles, their strengths, what they liked to see from counsel, and any other goodies that could be thrown into the mix.

'Norville.' DiPaulo unbuttoned his blue work shirt. Another thing he liked about wearing robes was that he could dress in casual clothes coming to and from the courthouse. No need to put on a suit and tie first thing in the morning.

'Madam Justice No Decision,' Whittle said. 'Better you than me.'

DiPaulo unzipped his jeans and hung them in his locker and pulled on his striped black and gray court pants. 'Thanks,' he said.

Until her judicial appointment two years before, Irene Norville had been a family lawyer at a small, undistinguished firm with no trial experience in criminal matters. Her second husband, a partner in a downtown firm and a heavyweight in the Conservative Party, had lobbied hard to get her the job. The word on the street was that during trials, when a tough legal question came up, she'd phone him for advice – and would even get one of his juniors to do legal research for her – because she was too embarrassed to ask the more senior judges.

The upshot was that Norville was forever

finding reasons to take breaks during a trial. It drove lawyers – Crowns and defense – crazy. DiPaulo found the best way to deal with her insecurity was to overwhelm the judge with legal precedents that addressed even the most mundane issues.

In preparation for today, he had filed with the court a thick casebook with all the relevant passages highlighted in yellow marker. There were a surprising number of decisions in which people charged with murdering a spouse had been released on bail. Almost always they were women with no criminal record, like Samantha.

After a quick cup of coffee in the adjoining lounge, DiPaulo found a quiet corner and pulled out a clean pad of paper. He had two boxes of files back at his office, and his briefcase was packed with pretrial notes, but before going into court he liked to put everything aside and write all the key points on one page. If you couldn't do it in a page, he had taught young lawyers for years, then you didn't know your case.

At the top of a blank sheet he wrote, 'Samantha Wyler, née Samantha Frankland, Bail Hearing, September 14:'

PLUSES
- Mother, one child, Simon, age four
- Thirty-five years old, good work history
- No criminal record, no outstanding charges (note: can't say 'no police contacts'

because of e-mails and voice mails she recently sent Terrance)
- Plan for bail:
  - Live with mother in Cobalt – small town in northern Ontario
  - Report to local police station – daily if necessary
  - Leave town limits only with express permission of police and in the company of her mother or brother
  - Ask that she be able to use local libraries
  - Surrender passport
- Sam made no statements – only circumstantial evidence against her. No proof she had the knife. Question – do they have evidence she was in the house that night? Don't know – be careful. Reason why Sam <u>must not testify at bail hearing.</u>
- Justice Norville?

MINUSES
- Bad divorce
- No criminal record – but recent contacts with police – angry e-mails and voice mails to Terrance. Very bad.
- Motive
  - Family court trial slated for the next day
  - Jealousy – the new, famous girlfriend
  - Anger – e-mails and voice mails – see above

- Child custody?
- No alibi. She made no statement – i.e., she had motive AND opportunity
- Justice Norville?

DiPaulo sat with his notes. Let the time pass, his mind drift. Then he used his own little secret code to guess his possibility of success. He never wrote out a number, for fear that somehow his clients might see it. Instead, he used the election years of American presidents in the twentieth century. He played with his pen for a few seconds, and wrote 'FDR II.' Roosevelt was elected to his second term in 1936. That sounded about right – there was about a 36 percent chance, one in three, of getting Samantha out.

Then he had a thought. He pulled out the four-color glossy photos of Terrance Wyler's bloodied body on the kitchen floor. The multiple slashes in his white shirt were like lightning bolts across his chest. DiPaulo crossed out 'FDR II' and wrote in 'Herbert Hoover.'

Hoover won the election in 1928. That was closer. There is about a one in four chance, he thought, if I'm lucky. Just the kind of challenge he relished.

CHAPTER 27

'The first witness for the Crown will be Ms Arceli Ocaya,' Crown Attorney Jennifer Raglan said, standing tall at the long wooden counsel table she shared with Detective Ari Greene.

Judge Norville nodded from the chair up on her dais. She made a show of opening a red book and writing some notes on the first page. The large wood-paneled courtroom was packed. Most of the first two rows were taken up by the press, and behind them were a sea of spectators and a few lawyers in gowns who'd drifted in to watch.

The Wyler family sat in a specially reserved row of seats directly behind Raglan and as far away as possible from the defense table and Samantha. Raglan had met with them yesterday afternoon, and like most families of the deceased, they were upset and anxious. The oldest brother, Nathan, and the father were the most boisterous.

'You're telling me there's even a chance she could get bail?' Nathan demanded.

'Ridiculous.' The father's face was red with anger. 'Why's this taking so long?'

For people like the Wylers, who lived in a world of instant decision making and rapid results, the lumbering criminal justice system frustrated the hell out of them. Mr Wyler senior had seemed particularly agitated.

This morning, Mr and Mrs Wyler looked tense, Nathan was a case study in fury about to boil over and Jason, the disabled son, held his head high in defiance.

Raglan watched the nanny approach the witness stand. A small woman, about five feet tall, she moved haltingly. Last week Raglan had brought Ocaya here and walked her through the courtroom so she wouldn't feel too awkward today. Still, it was clear from her uncertain gait that she was intimidated by the august surroundings and the crush of onlookers.

Smiling down at her, Norville greeted Ocaya as if they were old friends newly reunited. 'Come right up and sit here beside me.' She patted the side of her desk next to her.

Ocaya sat in the tall witness-box and practically disappeared. Damn, Raglan thought. During their little tour yesterday she hadn't had Ocaya try sitting down. Mistake.

Norville frowned. 'You may stand if you like.'

'Is it permitted?' Ocaya asked.

'Certainly.' Norville glared at Raglan, her smile replaced by a scowl that said 'Jennifer, why the hell didn't you bring this poor woman into court before today so she could see what it was like?'

Great way to start, Raglan thought. The court registrar, who sat directly below the judge, was a wiry, balding man who always had a crossword or a sudoku puzzle tucked under his notebook. He swore the nanny in as a witness.

'Ms Ocaya, good morning,' Raglan said.

'Good morning.' Ocaya looked terrified.

'You remember last week, when I brought you here to show you around the courtroom?' Raglan shot the judge a sideways glance.

'Yes.' Ocaya's voice was weak. 'You were very kind.'

'Was that the first time you had ever been in a court of law?' Raglan made a point of not using contractions when questioning Ocaya.

'I have never been in any trouble in my life,' she said. 'I have done everything for immigration, and more community hours than requested to bring my family to Canada.'

Raglan smiled. No matter how many times you go over things beforehand, when an inexperienced witness hits the stand, all the insecurities are there to see, clear as day. In Ocaya's case, it all made her more believable. I wish I'd saved this for the trial, Raglan thought.

'You know all that is required is that you tell us the truth,' Raglan said. 'Can you do that?'

'Of course.'

For the next half hour she led Ocaya through her evidence: how she came to the country as part of the nanny program, how Mr and Mrs Wyler

181

hired her when Simon was born, how she'd become close with the boy, how she stayed with Mr Wyler when the couple split up.

'Tell us about Mrs Wyler,' Raglan asked.

'When she moved away from the house, I saw her at the pickups and drop-offs for Simon.'

Raglan waited for Ocaya to say more. In the witness interview they'd had last week, the nanny had gone into great detail about how Samantha Wyler was unpredictable, angry, and sometimes nearly out of control. But now she was freezing up. A woman like Ocaya wouldn't want to speak ill of someone in public, especially with Samantha Wyler sitting right across the courtroom from her.

The rules of evidence didn't allow Raglan to ask her own witness leading questions. She'd have to coax the story out. Moving from behind the counsel table, she strolled up to the witness-box. She crossed her arms comfortably. 'How about Simon. Is he a good boy?'

'Oh, yes.' Ocaya's shoulders relaxed as she talked about a safer topic.

'And was he close to his father?'

Ocaya looked down at her hands and gulped for air, her emotion real. All she could do was nod.

'Arceli,' Raglan said, putting her hand on the top of the witness stand. 'In court you cannot just nod. You need to answer with words. I know it is tough.'

182

'Yes. They were so close.' Her voice was a notch above a whisper. 'Mr Wyler was a good father.'

'What about Simon's mother?' she asked. 'Was she close with her son?'

Ocaya glanced at Samantha Wyler. 'No.' She looked away. The bitterness palpable. Believable.

'Why do you say that?'

'The mother was busy. With her job, then the business. Mr Wyler worked hard too, but he had time for Simon.' Ocaya's voice had found its steel.

'I see,' Raglan said.

'Mrs Wyler had a bad temper. She would yell at the child. Grab him by the arm.'

'Did you see that?'

'One time, yes I did.' Ocaya thrust her chin out.

There was the sound of a chair moving behind Raglan. 'Your Honor, I must object,' Ted DiPaulo said in his smoothest voice. Raglan turned to see that he was up on his feet, his tall frame dominating his half of the courtroom. He had on his most charming smile.

'This is a criminal court, not a family court,' DiPaulo said. 'My client is a thirty-five-year-old mother who's never been charged with a criminal offense. She doesn't drive, so I can't make a big deal about the fact that she has a perfect driving record. Mrs Wyler's not on trial for occasionally disciplining her own child. My friend knows this is totally irrelevant.'

In Canadian courts, no matter how vicious the arguments were between them, competing lawyers always referred to each other as 'friends.'

Raglan saw Norville nod at DiPaulo. With only a few words he'd emphasized his strongest argument – that his client was a mother with a clean record. Even made a casual joke about her not driving. His confident tone was meant to intimidate the judge into thinking he was absolutely right about the law, which he wasn't. Raglan was close to the line with her questions, but nowhere as far over as DiPaulo made it sound.

'Your Honor.' Raglan cranked up her voice. 'The accused is charged with first-degree murder, not shoplifting. At a bail hearing, character evidence such as this is both admissible and relevant. My friend neglects to mention that in the last weeks of the victim's life, his client, the accused, sent her husband a series of nasty e-mails and left him numerous angry voice mails.'

Raglan never referred to Samantha Wyler by name. Instead she called her 'the accused' and 'his client.' Terrance Wyler was 'the victim' and 'her husband.'

Up on her bench, Norville looked terrified. This was crucial evidence. She'd have to make a tough decision.

Raglan strode back to her counsel table and grabbed the bound blue book of materials she'd filed. 'If you'll please turn to tabs seven through nine, Your Honor will see the threatening e-mails the accused sent to her husband from July the thirtieth to August the twelfth of this year.'

She stood still. Confident. Not hurrying things. Raglan waited until Norville found the right page, then kept waiting. It would have been easy to read the text out loud, but she wanted to force the judge to read the e-mails herself.

When Norville finished, Raglan dropped the book on the table, where it landed hard. She had the judge's full attention.

'The anger of the accused is well documented. That's why this witness, the family's nanny for so many years, must be permitted to testify about any acts of ill temper she observed. Mr Terrance Wyler was stabbed seven times. Somebody was extremely angry at him, angry enough to enter his home and murder him.'

'Murder.' That was the word to emphasize.

Norville looked back and forth between the two lawyers with an expression that said, 'Why can't you two just get along?' She stared out over their heads at the packed courtroom, then turned to Ocaya. 'I can see the witness is shaken by her testimony,' she said. 'I suggest we take a twenty-minute break.' With that, Norville scooted off the bench, her flat-footed deputy tailing out behind her.

Off to call her husband, Raglan thought, looking

at the courtroom clock on the wall behind the jury box. It was only ten-thirty. She turned back to the front row. Nathan Wyler's face was red with anger. This was going to be a long day.

CHAPTER 28

Daniel Kennicott settled into the window seat of the train and pulled out the Samantha Wyler file. He was on his way up north to Cobalt, the place where she'd grown up. Detective Greene had waited to send him there until her family was down in Toronto for the bail hearing. It was a smart move. There weren't many secrets in a small town and people would be more likely to talk knowing that Samantha's mother and brother weren't there.

Greene's instructions were open-ended: 'Nose around, see what you can find out about her.' That was all the detective had said. Kennicott was learning that if the person you arrested remained silent, as Wyler had done, you had to figure out who they were by other means.

Who was Samantha? That was his mission. The Wylers had a one-dimensional take: she was self-centered, controlling, had alienated Terrance from the family. In a word, she was the 'bitch.' Friends? She didn't seem to have any in Toronto. At the bank where she'd been for three years, people said she'd worked hard. No one got to know her.

Kennicott tracked down some old professors who remembered only that she was smart and diligent about her studies. He even found her first-year roommate, Jocelyn Bathurst, a socialite from one of the city's wealthiest families. He had paid her a visit at her Rosedale mansion.

'Sam was invisible,' Bathurst told Kennicott after insisting on serving him a latte from her spanking new espresso machine. It would have taken up half the counter space in his little galley kitchen. 'Pretty, but she studied all the time. Came from some small town up north. Didn't even try to make friends.'

'How long did you know her?'

'First year. Everyone moved out of residence after that. Most of the girls got places together. She told me once that she had her own apartment. I'd see her sometimes in class. Final year, when everyone was interviewing for an internship program at one of the big banks, she didn't get an offer. Samantha had the marks. Better than me. I don't think she had what they were looking for. Only time I ever saw her angry. She ended up at some retail branch in the west end, and that's the last I heard of her until she married into the Wyler family. That was a shocker.'

The train pulled out of the station, heading east, hugging the shoreline before it swung north through the industrial edge of the city and the sprawling suburbs, and in minutes it was tunneling through the forested hills, gaining altitude bit by bit as it climbed onto the glacial remains that made up the great Canadian Shield. Ahead lay six hours of travel time, punctuated by the occasional stop in small towns, which grew farther and farther apart along the way.

Kennicott looked through the file for the folder that interested him the most. It was an interview another cop had done with Jo Summers.

Question: How did you meet Terrance?

Answer: Our families' boats were next to each other at the yacht club on the island. He was a few years older, but I was a good sailor even as a kid.

Question: How well did you know him?

Answer: Very well.

Question: What was the nature of your relationship?

Answer: Our relationship? We were close. As friends. Just friends. On Fridays we'd meet for lunch if I was free. That was it. Lunch and Christmas dinner once a year.

Question: I don't want to embarrass you, but were you involved romantically?

Answer: Romantically? Never.

The train whistle gave out two loud blasts. It was a sound that crept right into you. A moment later the whole car shuddered as an oncoming train whizzed past on the other track.

Kennicott had been studying statement analysis.

Looking closely at interviews to determine if people were telling the truth. Perhaps the most famous example was Susan Smith, the South Carolina woman who strapped her two young sons into her car and drowned them. 'My children wanted me. They needed me. And now I can't help them,' she tearfully told reporters when the boys were still missing. In contrast to Smith, who referred to her children in the past tense, the father said, 'They're okay. They're going to be home soon.' Police concluded, correctly, that the father believed his children were alive and the mother knew they were dead.

Another indicator of untruthfulness was stall tactics – words and phrases like 'to tell you the truth,' or 'honestly,' or repeating a question that had been asked instead of just giving a direct answer. It was obvious that Summers was stalling when asked about her relationship with Terrance. There was more there than she was telling the police.

Question: Did you know Samantha Wyler?
Answer: I only saw her once. They were shopping on Bloor Street. Terry – that's what everyone called him – was outside the Max Mara store with Simon in a stroller. Samantha was inside buying something for herself. She came out and he introduced me as an old sailing friend. Later, Terry said she kept asking about

me. He never told her about our Friday lunches because he said she'd be jealous. He wasn't allowed to see any of his old friends, especially female friends. That was hard for him, because Terry was such a friendly guy.

Question: What do you think Terry saw in her?

Answer: He liked good-looking women, and Samantha fit the bill. Terry always felt like the third wheel in the family. Nathan could do no wrong. Jason was sick and needed extra attention. Samantha convinced him he'd been hard done by.

Question: And Samantha? What do you think she saw in Terry?

Answer: He was her ticket. To money. To prestige. Don't forget, for years the Wyler Foods store was big in the city. And he was a wonderful man.

Kennicott was impressed with the way the interviewer switched from Terrance to Terry. Speaking Jo's language. Keeping his questions short, open-ended. Summers's answers here were direct.

Question: How'd Terry get along with his family?

Answer: His family? It was complex. Growing up, Terry had to get away. When he came back from the States, he wanted

191

to modernize things. Prepared food in the store. Get rid of those stupid bow ties. Change the ugly colors and that ridiculous logo. I think Mr Wyler and Nathan felt threatened, so nothing happened. Terry became frustrated and Samantha exploited that. But when she had him arrested for that stupid threatening charge, they were there for him. The Wylers are loyal. Like a clan.

What, Kennicott wondered, was so complex about Terrance's relationship with his family? Why had Jo gone back to being evasive?

Question: Why do you think they split up?
Answer: April Goodling wasn't the only reason. After Simon was born, Sam wasn't into being a parent. She was obsessed with the new store. Terry was desperate to have more kids and she flat-out refused. They fought a lot. When the business failed, everything went to pieces.
Question: Did you ever see Terry get violent?
Answer: Terry? Never.
Question: What about Samantha? Did he ever tell you about her being violent with him?
Answer: Sam was the one topic Terry refused to talk about. Even after they split. Frustrated the hell out his family that he wasn't more critical of her.

Question: I understand you had lunch with him on Friday, two days before the murder. And that Terry came over to your place on the island with Ms Goodling and Simon on Sunday afternoon. What did you talk about?

Answer: The upcoming divorce trial. He showed me the last-minute offer Samantha's lawyer had made. His lawyer and his family were pushing him to turn it down. Said he could win hands down at trial. He wasn't sure what to do.

Question: What did you say?

Answer: I thought he should take the deal. Think of his son. He said, 'Simon still needs his mother. Samantha's not the monster my family thinks she is.' That's the last thing he ever said to me.

Good advice, Jo, Kennicott thought. He put the Summers interview back and read through the rest of the file as the hours and the countryside passed by. The clouds grew dark and soon it was pouring great sheets of rain.

'Cobalt, former home of the world's largest silver mine,' the ticket taker said late in the afternoon. He was an energetic little man with a 1950s-style pompadour. 'Haileybury after that. Home of Leslie MacFarlane, the first author of the Hardy Boys books, using the pen name Franklin W. Dixon.'

A lovely old station came into view to the left as the train rounded the bend into town. The rain was still belting down, so Kennicott was relieved to see there'd be some shelter.

'That's my stop.' He pulled down his bag from the overhead rack and headed for the door. Although the train was about half full, he was the only one getting off. They glided to a stop. The ticket taker swung the door open and tossed out a metal step. The station was about a hundred yards farther down the track.

Kennicott pointed to the station, which featured an overhanging slate roof and a wide stone porch. 'Here?'

''Fraid so.' The man wore a blue-and-white-striped shirt with ONTARIO NORTHLAND across the breast pocket and the name HAMISH sewn in above it. 'Everyone says the same thing first time. Station's a beauty. Been closed for years.'

Kennicott looked out into the rain.

'Politicians keep talking about building a shelter,' Hamish said. 'Talk, talk, talk. Be grateful you're not here in the winter.'

'Thanks.' Kennicott stepped down. The rain was coming hard. Running over to the station, he stood beneath the eaves while the train pulled away, blowing its deep bass whistle. Warm and comforting, it echoed off the hills and across the wide river that bent out into the distance along with the tracks, following them into the horizon.

It was 4:20 in the afternoon and this far north the sun was still high. Hovering. Relaxed.

Growing up, Kennicott had spent his summers at his family cottage north of Toronto and was familiar with the late-summer sun, the rhythm of the long days. He wasn't intimidated by storms. The clouds were low, moving fast. The rain wouldn't last long. There was an expression they had in the north – you want a change in the weather, drive five miles or wait five minutes.

By the time he walked up to the Silver City Motel, which was up the hill and around the bend, the sky had cleared. His room on the second floor had just enough space for a bed, a bathroom, a TV mounted on the wall, and a view of the river. This was the only accommodation in town.

There was a tourist brochure on the night table. A hundred years ago Cobalt was famous. As the conductor said, it was the home of the world's largest silver mine. It had a population of thirty-five thousand, mostly miners, a large hospital, two theaters, an opera house, and a streetcar running up to Haileybury, where another thirty-five thousand people lived.

The rush lasted well into the 1920s. By the end of World War II, the mining had petered out, leaving behind hundreds of abandoned sites, decaying buildings, and a plethora of relics of what was. Unlike most old mining towns that died, somehow Cobalt hung on. Barely. The last grocery store closed about twenty years ago, two small restaurants were only open for breakfast and lunch, and there was a native Indian souvenir shop, a mining museum, a library, a school, a hockey rink, and one gas station, which Samantha Wyler's family owned.

Kennicott watched the shadow crawl up the far shore, leaving a dark blanket of silence in its wake. He could see why Samantha Wyler worked so hard to get out of this place and head south to make it in the bright lights of the big city.

CHAPTER 29

It was past noon, and Ari Greene had already made twelve pages of notes. The nanny, Arceli Ocaya, had testified for almost two hours. After her initial hesitation – and once Norville came back and made a ruling in favor of the Crown allowing Jennifer Raglan to ask more probing questions – the nanny had opened up and painted a damaging picture of Samantha Wyler as an inconsistent and unpredictable parent.

Jennifer Raglan had just called her next witness, the police officer who'd been on duty when Terrance Wyler made his complaints about Samantha's e-mails and voice mails.

Ted DiPaulo jumped to his feet. All smiles.

'I've prepared a transcript of all the calls,' he said, handing a set of bound documents to the court reporter and another set to the registrar. 'We can save a lot of time and simply enter them as evidence.'

The registrar handed the papers to the judge. 'Sounds like a good idea,' Norville said to Raglan.

'Your Honor, I submit that the court should listen to the actual voice mails,' Raglan said. 'The accused's tone of voice, which isn't conveyed by the written word, is evidence as well.'

Greene was impressed with Raglan in court. She always used the term 'I submit,' never 'I think.' The last thing in the world judges wanted was to be told what to do or, even worse, what a lawyer thought they should do. Instead, she used body language to get her message across. Back straight, confident, smart.

'The tapes are short,' Raglan said, as if the judge had already decided to let her go ahead.

'Play them,' Norville said, not even asking DiPaulo to respond.

Greene peeked over at Samantha Wyler. Dressed in simple clothes, she'd sat beside DiPaulo all morning, projecting an image of silent submission. She flinched when the static of the recording started and her voice carried out across the courtroom.

'*Terry, you scumbag. I can't believe what you are doing to me. And that lawyer of yours. She's a piece of work.*'

'*Terry, fuck you. I read your affidavit. Thanks a lot for making me out to be the bitch queen of the universe. You may not believe it, but I tried to be a good mother. Did it ever occur to you that Simon will see this garbage one day?*'

The only perceptible movement Wyler made was the way she tightened her jaw as her voice on tape shattered the controlled image she'd tried to portray. This was why Raglan had insisted on playing them.

198

Greene and Raglan had spent the last week preparing for this hearing. Since Wyler hadn't come forward with an alibi, they hadn't told DiPaulo about Simon's evidence that his mother had come into his room that night. They hoped Wyler would testify at the bail hearing and say she hadn't been in the house. If that happened, she'd be caught under oath in a barefaced lie, and the case would be as good as over. The fact that she'd never get bail would be a bonus.

That was the other reason Raglan insisted on playing the tapes in open court. They were hoping to scare her into the witness-box.

'You're a king-size asshole, you know that, Terry. You make me so angry sometimes I think I could . . . I could . . . fuck you, go running home to your mommy.'

Greene watched Wyler. It looked as if she was trying to swallow without any saliva. DiPaulo must have sensed this. He made a show of pouring her a glass of water from an ice-filled pitcher, hoping to create a minor distraction. Then he stood up.

Raglan hit the Pause button.

'Your Honor, really,' DiPaulo said. 'The Crown's had its fun humiliating my client. The tapes are all very colorful. Must we hear ten more? The defense concedes that Ms Wyler was angry. Not shocking, given that her husband was seeing another woman. Here's the key point that I fear will get lost in all this melodrama. Nowhere in these tapes, or in the e-mails, did my client make an actual threat. Commit a criminal act. It's perfectly legal to be mad at a philandering husband.'

DiPaulo had worked himself into an indignant anger. He'd taken the negative of the tapes and tried to turn it around on the Crown.

'Madam Crown. Do we really need to hear any more?' Norville went through the binder DiPaulo had given her. 'I've got the flavor of what was going on here.'

Greene watched Raglan rock on her heels.

'I'm not here today to judge guilt or innocence.' Norville was staring at Raglan. 'But I'm mindful of the fact that if Ms Wyler is not guilty, then she's in a nightmare scenario, looking at a prison sentence of twenty-five years and probably never seeing her son again.'

Norville turned to DiPaulo. 'I'm also aware that, to date, the defense has not produced any alibi evidence.'

Back to Raglan. 'I've heard enough.' Norville sat taller in her chair. 'Let's move on.'

'Thank you, Your Honor,' Raglan said. 'May I have a moment to confer with my officer in charge?'

'Take your time.'

Raglan's robes dangled down by her side. 'I'm glad Ted objected,' she whispered, her lips near Greene's ear. 'We have Samantha's skin crawling, but I was starting to feel like a real asshole playing those tapes.'

Greene could feel Raglan's breath. The heat of her body so close. 'Mission accomplished. Let's see if DiPaulo puts her on the stand.'

'I like working with you, Ari,' Raglan said before she straightened her back. She swished her robes back over her arm.

'Your Honor, that's the case for the Crown.'

Norville looked at the courtroom clock. 'We'll take a longer lunch than usual. Back at two-fifteen.' She rose from the bench and took her time striding out.

Greene kept his eyes on Samantha. As soon as the judge's door closed, she rolled both hands into fists and smacked the table in front of her. Damn hard.

CHAPTER 30

The moment court adjourned and Samantha was taken out by the guards, Ted DiPaulo rushed down two flights of stairs to the lawyers' lounge, grabbed a coffee, and hurried to the elevator that went to the cells. When the doors opened, the whole Wyler family was right in front of him.

This was always awkward for defense lawyers. Even in a large courthouse, inevitably you'd run into the family of the deceased. Innocent victims. People in mourning. And the lawyer who was standing up for the accused was often a lightning rod for their anger.

No one said a word. Mrs Wyler stood beside Jason, who was holding himself up on two canes, his strong arms and shoulders a stark contrast to his shriveled legs. Nathan Wyler and the father were in back. Tall, imposing men. Something moved, and DiPaulo realized it was one of Jason's canes. The rubber tip at the end came up and he efficiently pushed a button. In a moment the doors swung closed.

DiPaulo headed to the stairs and ran down to

the prison cells. A guard had already brought Sam into the interview cubicle. DiPaulo sat across from her and they both had to bend down to speak through the airholes near the bottom of the glass. She looked awful.

'You okay?' he asked.

'I'm never going to get bail.'

'We have a chance. And some good case law.'

'The judge hates me.'

'You can't tell.'

'I went to university with women like her. Believe me. I know.'

Wyler rubbed her hands together. They were rough. Scraped. She started picking at her nails.

'We have to stick to our plan,' DiPaulo said.

Wyler nodded with no enthusiasm. 'I know. You're going to put my mother on the stand. You don't want me to testify.' Her voice was drained of all emotion. 'But if I don't testify, how do I get out?'

In the middle of a bail hearing clients often panicked, prepared to try anything to get out of jail. They had no vision beyond the moment. Worse than teenagers, he thought. His job was to protect them, even from themselves.

'We've gone over this. Raglan will tear you apart,' he said. 'She'll play every one of those tapes.'

Wyler rocked back and forth, like a mother with a child. Except her arms were empty.

'Doesn't the judge want to hear from me?'

'Not necessary. This is about bail, not guilt or innocence. You'd be testifying under oath. One misstep, and they'll throw it at you in front of the jury, and the whole case is blown.'

'I need to go home,' she said.

'We both want the same thing.' It wasn't entirely true. In jail she was less likely to do something stupid, like leave more voice mails or talk to some guy in a bar who was an undercover cop. Sam would adjust to prison. Clients always did. She'd already read her way through most of the beat-up paperbacks on the nightly book cart and was talking about teaching some of the young mothers how to read.

Wyler stopped picking at her hands. 'The food in here's horrible,' she said. 'A stale bun with one slice of cheese for lunch.'

DiPaulo smiled. With all control of their lives taken from them, clients would focus on the most irrelevant things. Small bargaining chips to make them feel better. It meant he'd prevailed.

'I'll talk to the guards and see if I can get you some soup,' he said.

'I need to get back to Cobalt.'

'Cobalt?' He laughed. 'I thought you hated your hometown.'

'You're not hearing me.' She didn't crack a smile. More intense than ever. 'I'll agree to any condition they want. Just get me back up there.'

Clients always have a hidden agenda, DiPaulo thought when court resumed after lunch. He stood the moment Judge Norville took her seat.

'The defense calls Mrs Jacquelyn Frankland.' He motioned for her to come forward. DiPaulo wanted to move things along fast, change the tone after those devastating tapes this morning.

He watched Samantha's mother take the stand and be sworn in as a witness. There was something solid about Frankland. Dull dress. Sturdy shoes. Her maiden name, she'd told DiPaulo, was Cormier, and her English had a trace of a French-Canadian accent.

'Mrs Frankland, you're Sam's mom, right?' DiPaulo's choice of words was folksy as a small-town politician at a country fair.

'Yes, sir.' Her voice was nasal.

'And you live in Cobalt, Ontario. I believe that's north of North Bay.'

'North of North Bay, north of Temagami, south of Liskeard,' she said. 'Proper name is *New* Liskeard, but everyone calls it Liskeard. Know what I mean?'

'How long you lived there?' DiPaulo asked.

'Whole life.'

'You have two children.'

'Sam came first. Jimmy two years after. Jimmy's like me, knows how to fix things. Sam's like her dad, always in the books.'

'Your husband passed away many years ago.'

'Karl died Sam's first year in high school. She was crazy for her dad. He was at the gas station, changing the oil on his convertible, when the hoist broke. We had one of those old single-shaft ones.

Karl was always bugging me to get a double-shaft, but where was the money? Sam's the one who found him.'

Frankland spoke in the no-nonsense tone of a woman who knows herself. Great witness for the defense.

'I'm afraid I have to ask you a few personal questions, ma'am,' DiPaulo said.

Frankland turned to the judge. 'I got no secrets,' she said.

Judges hated it when witnesses spoke directly to them. And normally DiPaulo lectured them to always watch him – never, ever look at the judge or the jury. But Frankland was so unpretentious, he'd intentionally not mentioned this to her.

Norville smiled back at Frankland and nodded a few times before she caught herself. Clearly she was charmed by Samantha's mother.

'You're fifty-five years old, you have no criminal record, and you run the only gas station in town,' DiPaulo said without looking at a note. 'Silver Shores Motors.'

'Been doing it for thirty-five years. Jimmy works in Liskeard at the foundry. He's a grinder. Helps out on weekends. I do the tires. Lots of flat tires up our way. Ice in winter pops huge potholes every spring.'

DiPaulo put his hand on his client's shoulder. 'If Her Honor grants bail to your daughter, are you willing to have her home until this trial's over?'

'Where else she going to live?'

There was a murmur of laughter in the court.

'And could you keep her busy?'

'Sure. Sam's the smart one in the family. Straight-A student. Won that scholarship to the university here in Toronto. Did better than all those rich girls, but they're the ones got those jobs at the big banks.'

'You understand, Sam won't be allowed to leave town unless she's with you or her brother.' This was the third time he'd referred to his client by her first name. Make her sound like a small-town girl who wanted to go home and live with her family, not a woman accused of murder.

'That could be a problem,' she said.

Norville jerked her head up and looked at Frankland.

'What kind of problem?' DiPaulo asked.

'The libraries,' Frankland said. 'Sam lives in them. There's one in our town, but her favorite's the one in Liskeard.'

'I see,' DiPaulo said, as if this were news to him. Of course he'd spent hours going over this with Frankland before putting her on the stand. 'Well, if she went to one of the local libraries, how could you guarantee she stayed there?'

'Stay? She never leaves. Books and librarians are her best friends. Always researching something, the way her dad taught her. I could get Lillian to call me.'

'Lillian?'

'The librarian in Liskeard. She's here in the

207

court.' Frankland pointed back behind DiPaulo. A tall woman in the audience, sitting beside Samantha's brother, gave a little wave. Exactly as they'd planned it.

'She came down with you for the bail hearing?' DiPaulo moved out from behind the counsel table.

'On the train,' Frankland said.

DiPaulo approached the witness-box as if he had something difficult to confide in her.

'Do you have any travel plans?'

Frankland smiled. Her teeth were jagged. 'I got nowhere to go. I sent Jimmy down for the funeral. I haven't been south in ten years.'

'Is there room for Samantha at your house?'

She looked at DiPaulo as if he were a customer who'd asked a really stupid question. 'Her bedroom.'

This brought more laughter.

Frankland looked confused. 'Haven't touched it since Sam left after high school.' She turned to Norville. 'She won't let me move a thing in there. Know what I mean?'

The judge couldn't help but nod. DiPaulo saw she was scribbling away in her notebook. A good sign. Let's hope she's working out conditions for a release on bail. He waited until Norville finished writing. The evidence couldn't have gone in better.

He smiled his best smile. 'Those are my questions.' DiPaulo turned and headed back to his seat.

208

'Am I allowed to say one more thing?' Frankland said behind him on the witness stand.

Oh, no. She'd been perfect. What the hell did she want to add? Be calm, Ted, he told himself. No way you can shut up your own witness. Look happy. He pivoted to face the judge. Not quite Fred Astaire, but not bad. He plastered a smile on his face. 'What do you want to say?'

'There's something I didn't tell you, sir. Or anyone else. And I guess I have to.'

Keep smiling, DiPaulo screamed at himself. The key to this whole hearing was to get the judge to trust the person who was signing the bail. If there was even a whiff of suspicion that Frankland was hiding something, it was game over.

'You never told me about this?' In for a dime, in for a dollar, he thought. 'Even when we prepared for you to testify?'

'That's right. Sam might be mad at me, but I don't see anyone from Cobalt or Liskeard here except her friend Lillian and my son.'

'Please. What is it?' he asked. As obsequious as a hotel doorman.

'Sam teaches reading.'

That's it? The big secret? DiPaulo was ecstatic. But he had to keep calm. 'Oh, I see. And do the children like her?'

'That's the secret. It's not children. Adults. They're real embarrassed. Only me and Lil knows.' Frankland pointed back out into the audience. 'Whenever Sam's in town she meets with folks in

209

the library basement who can't read. Got to keep this quiet.'

Sure do, DiPaulo thought, suppressing the urge to whoop for joy. Run up and hug his witness. Norville was smiling, writing away.

'Thank you, ma'am. Those are my questions.' He sat down, the blood flowing again in his veins. He'd graduated to the Eisenhower line. Ike was first elected in 1952. About a fifty-fifty chance now. This was the greatest goddamn job in the world, when magic like this happened.

'Next witness for the defense?' Norville asked.

'No more witnesses needed.' He was determined to project confidence. 'I'd be happy to make submissions right now.'

The indecisive Norville looked taken aback. She turned to Raglan. 'Does the Crown wish to call any more evidence? A case like this, I'd like to hear everything.'

Norville was practically begging the Crown to give her more ammunition so she could take the easy way out and keep Wyler locked up.

Raglan made a show of looking at the wall clock. 'Your Honor,' she said, standing up, her voice polite. 'This has been a long day and the Crown would like some time to consider whether we'll call further evidence.'

Norville beamed at Raglan. 'Excellent suggestion. Further evidence and counsel submissions tomorrow morning. I'll make my ruling in the afternoon.'

Plenty of time over lunch to pick the brains of the top young lawyers in her husband's firm, DiPaulo thought. He scrambled to his feet, not wanting Raglan to get all the brownie points for good behavior. 'I agree wholeheartedly.'

Norville smiled at him.

Good, DiPaulo thought. Rule number one in court: keep the judge happy.

CHAPTER 31

A ri Greene always found the experience somewhat surreal. Here he was, sitting in a packed courtroom about to take notes on the next piece of evidence – the video of him in the child-friendly room at police headquarters, playing trains with Simon. Raglan had a big television screen on a movable stand and rolled it into position so the judge and everyone in the court could see.

After DiPaulo closed his case yesterday, Greene and Raglan had decided to play the videotape in court. Since Samantha wasn't going to testify, there was no reason to hold it back, and it was powerful evidence that might get Norville to deny bail. And even more important, it might convince Wyler that the case against her was overwhelming and set up a guilty plea.

The video was made on the afternoon of the murder, before Simon's family had told him the news. Up on the screen, the boy ran in through the door, holding a train he'd carried with him from home. The train's name was Percy, he'd told

Greene. He went right to the train basket. Greene saw himself come into view seconds later.

'Do they have Thomas? I lost mine.' Simon sat down on the carpet and grabbed an engine. 'This one's Henry.'

'I'm not sure,' Greene said. The squeak of little trains rolling back and forth on the wooden tracks and Simon making 'vroom-vroom, choo-choo' sounds vibrated out across the courtroom.

Simon fished out some bridges and track and started building. The boy was humming contentedly, his falsetto voice occasionally interspersed with 'clang-clang' and 'choo-choo' sounds. After a while Greene opened a square refrigerator on the far wall and brought out two juice packs.

'Apple or orange?'

'Apple, please,' Simon said. They sat on the floor and unwrapped the little plastic straws.

'Simon,' Greene said between sips. 'I need to talk to you about something.'

'I know,' he said.

'You do?'

Greene looked back at the glass, which was a one-way mirror. Daniel Kennicott was on the other side with the technician who was running the camera.

'That bridge.' Simon pointed to the one closest to him. 'One of the parts is broken.'

Greene put his head near the carpet to inspect it. One of the connector nodules was

213

missing. 'You're right. But it still works, if you're careful.'

'I didn't break it,' Simon said.

Greene watched himself smile up on the screen. 'Simon, I want to ask you about your mommy.'

'Oh.'

In court, Greene looked at Norville. She was glaring down at the defense table. Greene glanced over. Wyler was staring transfixed at her son.

'This morning, when I met you in your bedroom, we talked. Remember?' This had been the toughest part of the interview. If his questions were leading in the least bit, suggesting an answer to the child, the whole exercise could backfire.

Simon lay down and reached for a train. He rolled it back and forth on the carpet, not bothering with the wooden rails, intensely studying the movement of the wheels. One of his feet flopped across Greene's leg. This was painful to watch. The poor child. Somehow aware his world had changed, he had an innate instinct to protect his mother.

'Arceli doesn't have any trains at her apartment.' Simon's eyes were glued to the engine's little wheels, the sound of them going back and forth a constant backbeat.

'She doesn't?'

'There's no Thomas here either.'

'We'll have to get one.'

'My mom came into my room last night.'

Even though he'd seen the video at least ten

times, Greene's heart was beating. He remembered how he'd had to resist the urge to nod.

'What did your mommy do?' he asked, his voice almost cold.

'She kissed me and said she wouldn't see me for a long time.' Simon rubbed his foot along Greene's leg. 'Can I go home now and get my trains?'

Greene saw himself glance at the mirror. Looking toward Kennicott.

'I heard you're going to have a sleepover at your uncle's house for a few days.'

Simon looked at Greene. 'But there're no trains there.'

'We can bring yours from home,' Greene said.

Simon considered this. He shook his head. 'My mommy was crying. Why won't she see me for a long time?'

'Maybe she has to go visit some people,' Greene said.

There was a sniffling sound in the courtroom. Samantha Wyler was holding a tissue to her nose.

'My daddy always wakes me up before he goes away on trips.'

'Perhaps he was in a hurry.'

On the screen Simon sat up, lifted a train, and rolled it in his hand. 'This is Percy. I like him second best after Thomas. How long will Mommy be away?'

This was the question Greene had dreaded. 'I don't know,' he said.

'Can I go now?' Simon asked.

'Sure.' Greene pulled him up from the floor in one motion.

Simon stared at Greene, confused. 'First I have to put my toys away,' he said. 'My dad always makes me tidy up.'

A sigh of affection went up from the audience behind Greene.

Raglan stood. 'Your Honor, the tape goes on for a few more minutes.' She spoke over the bang-bang sound of Simon and Greene tossing trains into the bin. 'We've seen the relevant portion.' She turned the machine off and the courtroom felt unnaturally quiet.

Greene sneaked another look at the defense table. Wyler's face was buried in her hands. DiPaulo had a smile pasted on his face. Greene was sure the tape had taken him by surprise. DiPaulo would be glad he hadn't put his client on the stand and have her come up with some desperate, false alibi, claiming she hadn't been in the house the night of the murder.

DiPaulo must have sensed Greene's eyes on him. He looked over at the prosecution table. They locked eyes. DiPaulo nodded slowly.

Both men were experienced enough to understand what had just happened. With this evidence, there'd been a seismic change in the case. The question of Samantha Wyler's guilt or innocence was all but settled. The only real issues left were: Which charge would she plead guilty to and how many years would she spend in jail?

CHAPTER 32

Something as simple as a primary school report card could reveal an extraordinary amount about a person. Daniel Kennicott first learned this lesson in his rookie year as a cop. He was working on the case of a forty-nine-year-old pedophile named Herman Marchmount, who targeted girls between the ages of five and nine. A detective at the division suggested that Kennicott swear out a search warrant to get his report card. Sure enough, it described in vivid detail how at recess Marchmount dragged a girl from his grade-two class into the bushes and pulled her skirt up over her head.

And what am I going to learn about you, Samantha Wyler? Kennicott thought as he took his seat across from Corinne Tressider, head of guidance for Cobalt High School.

'We were all so shocked to hear about Sam – I mean Samantha.' Tressider sat comfortably behind a desk in her bright room. The school was on a hill above the town and the large windows on the east side looked out across the river beyond. 'Everyone called her Sam.'

'You remember her?'

'Never had a student like Sam, and I'm in my thirty-second year of teaching. Take a look at these.' Tressider opened a folder labeled SAMANTHA FRANKLAND – REPORT CARDS.

They were on identical pages, their horizontal boxes filled in with precise handwriting. Funny they still call them report cards, Kennicott thought, since they weren't on cards anymore, but on sheets of light blue paper. The letters in the boxes on the right-hand side jumped off the page: A–, A, and A+, for four straight years. Except for phys ed. In that she was a C student. According to the reports, she wasn't a team player.

There was a cup filled with sharpened pencils on the corner of Tressider's desk. She took one out and twirled it between her thumb and forefinger. 'I went to school with Karl, her dad.'

'I understand he died in an accident.'

Tressider tapped the pencil on the edge of her desk, which was spotless. The whole room had a Windex-like smell of cleanliness about it. She gave the pencil one last, hard tap and swirled her chair around.

'In our last year of high school we were on a team together.' She turned back to Kennicott with a photo in her hand of four students in a television studio, two boys and two girls. 'The show was called *Reach for the Top*. Everyone in the country watched it. Back then we had only two channels. It was what you'd call a trivia show today. Every topic you could imagine.'

She passed Kennicott a faded color picture in a black frame. It was obvious which of the boys was Samantha's father. He had the same long neck, big eyes, good looks. Tressider had blond hair in a Doris Day bob and wore a flowery dress. They sat beside each other. A banner overhead read REACH FOR THE TOP: NORTHERN ONTARIO CHAMPIONS.

'Karl and I are on the right,' Tressider said without looking at the photo. 'Harold, the other boy, went out to Alberta to work in the oil business. Hasn't been back for years. Gwen was the smartest of all. She went to med school in the States but then got ovarian cancer.'

Kennicott put the photo back on the desk.

'We were finalists in the provincial championship. It was the biggest thing in this town ever. We did car washes, raffles, bake sales to raise money. Took the midnight train down to Toronto and stayed in the Royal York Hotel, across from Union Station.' Tressider's eyes seemed to lose focus as she looked out the window.

'How'd you do?'

She snorted. Shook her head. 'We were wiped out. This team from a Toronto school – Neil McNeil. They were so fast hitting the Answer button. Knew everything. Karl took it the hardest. Swore he'd go back to Toronto and make it big. He got into that bank program down there, but it didn't work out.'

'What happened?'

219

'He'd never talk about it. The year he came back, I was away at teachers college. When I returned home, he was with Jacquelyn Cormier, and she was pregnant.'

Without warning, Tressider popped out of her chair and went over to the window that overlooked the town below and the train track running along the river. The sun was still low on the horizon and streaking in across the room. She brought the venetian blinds down almost halfway.

Kennicott looked around the office. Tressider had no other personal photos. No pictures of her and a man about her age. No snapshots of children. Often it was the things people didn't say, or didn't have, that told you the most about them.

'The first day Sam was in high school, Karl brought her in. She sat right in that chair you're sitting in. He was so proud of her. The year before, he'd taken her out of school for a week and they'd gone down to Toronto. Stayed at the Royal York. Took her to see all the bank towers, the stock exchange, the museum, the art gallery, some musicals, a Blue Jays game.'

Tressider was speaking without looking back. She scraped the pencil across the mullion in the middle of the window. 'Sam was a bright and fun kid. But when Karl died like that, she closed right up. Fourteen years old. A terrible time for a young girl to lose her father.'

Kennicott scanned the 'comments' sections of the report cards. All said she was a dedicated student. 'I've spoken to her college roommate. She said Samantha was a hard worker and a real loner.'

Tressider returned to her desk. She put the *Reach for the Top* photo back in its place before she sat down. 'Sam didn't make friends. She'd come here if she needed to talk.'

'What would you two talk about?'

'Schools. Scholarships. Her latest research project. She loved to borrow my *Newsweek* magazines. Sometimes she'd talk about her dad. How he didn't want her to get stuck in Cobalt.'

'Did she have any enemies? Ever get in a fight, get angry with anyone?'

'I knew you were going to ask me that.' Tressider flexed the pencil between her hands. It broke with a loud snap. 'Sorry.' She looked flustered. 'I'm not used to talking to police officers.'

'You're doing fine.'

Tressider opened her middle desk drawer, tossed the two broken pencil pieces inside, and slammed it shut, as if she were hiding incriminating evidence. 'Sam was smart, and impatient and I'll admit it, she had a temper. People thought she was a snob, but she didn't care.'

She reached for another pencil. 'I don't see how it's relevant, but once in grade twelve this boy named Brett Barton was taunting her. He tried to pull her into the boys' washroom.'

'What happened?'

'Sam was a strong girl. Cracked his nose in two

221

places. Punched him so hard she broke a rib too. Then she threw him against a locker and he lost consciousness. It was a minor concussion, but we had to call an ambulance and run him up to the hospital in Haileybury.'

Kennicott pulled out the grade-twelve report card. 'There's nothing in here about it. Was she suspended?'

'It was a week before the scholarship applications went in. We had a big meeting. Brett was known for pushing himself on girls and no one blamed Sam for standing up for herself.'

'So you left it out.'

'She deserved that scholarship. But . . .' Tressider tapped her pencil and didn't say anything.

'But you thought she overreacted.'

Tressider gripped the pencil tighter and kept tapping.

'Perhaps you weren't entirely shocked when you heard about this murder.'

Tressider's eyes looked tired. 'I don't know,' she said.

Kennicott left his seat and walked over to the wall opposite the window. There were two long rows of photos of students in caps and gowns under a sign that read TOP STUDENTS OF THE YEAR. The dated haircuts and the clothes made the series of photos look like a time capsule.

'Sam's up on the top row, third from the left,' Tressider said.

Unlike most of the graduates, who were grinning

at the camera, Samantha Frankland was serious. Kennicott turned back from the wall of pictures. 'Was she close to any other teachers?'

Tressider pulled out a piece of paper and started writing. 'No. Her only other friend was Lillian Funke, the town librarian up in New Liskeard. Lil brought in books for Sam from all over the province. This is her number. She's in Toronto for the bail hearing, but you can call her anytime.'

Kennicott took the piece of paper. 'Sam ever come back to visit?'

'Every time she's home. Which isn't very often. She's never had a lot in common with her mom, or her brother for that matter. It was her dad who had the brains.'

'Ever bring her husband and son?'

'One time, when the boy was a baby. After that she came alone.'

'Ever talk to you about her marriage?'

'No. Only about university, then her jobs. She was real upset when those rich girls from Toronto got the internships at the big banks. But typical Sam, made her more determined to make it. Prove she was better than they were.'

'When's the last time you saw her?'

'About a year ago. She'd split up with her husband. It was all over the papers that he was dating that American actress.'

'How'd she seem?'

Tressider tossed the pencil onto her desk.

'Upset. Like you'd expect in a situation like that.'

'Angry?'

Tressider picked up the pencil and put it back in the cup. 'Not angry like she was going to kill her husband or anything stupid like that. She was mad. At him. At herself. She said she should have been a better mother. You know, I think she felt like she'd never had a childhood, she was always working. I told her to enjoy having some time off for a change.'

'What did she say to that?'

'She smiled. Said it wasn't a bad idea.'

It was 11:05 in the morning when Kennicott emerged from the school into the bright sunlight. Sitting at the top of a long set of granite steps and looking over the town, he heard the whistle of the southbound train before the engine chugged into view.

He could imagine young Samantha Frankland sitting in this very spot, watching this train make its daily run.

The whistle blew again. Kennicott wondered if it would slow down. Let someone off. Pick somebody up. But instead the train rumbled through the town, whistle echoing off the distant hills even after it disappeared behind the trees.

CHAPTER 33

'Counsel, I'm prepared to give my ruling now,' Judge Norville said right after Ted DiPaulo and Jennifer Raglan had finished their submissions about whether or not Samantha Wyler should be granted bail.

DiPaulo glanced at Raglan. She was as surprised as he was. The time was twelve-thirty, and they'd both expected Norville to take an early lunch break and call her husband for advice.

The judge is tougher than people give her credit for, DiPaulo thought as he watched her reach for the book of cases he'd filed. He remembered something about Norville. She had one child, a girl who was developmentally delayed. When the baby was only two years old, her husband died, and she remarried nine months later. The woman was a survivor.

Raglan rose to her feet. 'If Your Honor wants to proceed before lunch, that's fine with me.'

DiPaulo stood. 'I agree.' What did Norville's sudden decisiveness mean?

'Will the defendant please rise.' Norville's voice was laced with a stern confidence.

Samantha Wyler stood up, unsteady on her feet.

Hearing judges read out their decision was the most painful part of being a defense lawyer. Even when victory seemed a foregone conclusion, until you heard the magic words 'not guilty,' or in this case 'released on bail,' you never knew.

When they gave their rulings, judges didn't worry about the poor defendants whose lives hung in the balance. Instead, to justify themselves every step of the way, they went into excruciating detail about their decision-making process. Judges lived in fear that the dreaded Court of Appeal would overturn their rulings. They never wanted to leave their posteriors exposed.

It was DiPaulo's practice, as the judge spoke, to draw a vertical line down each page in his court binder, about a quarter of the way from the outer edge. On the left-hand side he wrote the judge's words, while on the blank space to the right he noted the key points he'd need for an appeal, should he lose.

Standing beside him, Wyler raised her eyes to the judge. Usually when clients did this they looked rather pathetic, pleading. But not Samantha. She looked straight at Norville.

'This is one of the toughest decisions I've had to make since being appointed to the bench.' Norville furrowed her brow at Wyler. 'On the one hand, ma'am, if you are innocent, you're going through a hell that none of us in this courtroom could ever imagine. The father of your only child, dead. Your son, bereft. I'm cognizant of the fact that if I keep you in prison, you'll be cut off from him for months, maybe years, at a formative stage in his life.'

Okay, DiPaulo thought. Now tell us about on the other hand.

'On the other hand, if you are guilty,' Norville said, 'you are responsible for the death of a man with whom you shared this lovely son – his father – and all the grief that's left in your wake.'

Wyler put her hands behind her back. As if she were waiting for the handcuffs to go on.

'It is not up to me today to determine guilt or innocence. The only issue is if you're a good candidate for release on bail. There are three questions I must answer. First, will you come to court as required? As Mr DiPaulo said in his excellent submissions, you'll surrender your passport and live in Cobalt – a one-horse town with the only horse tied up, was how he put it. And, as he pointed out, you don't even have a driver's license.'

DiPaulo was writing furiously. Often it wasn't a good sign when the judge told your client what a great job their lawyer had done for them. Prelude to bad news despite a valiant effort.

'The second ground. Will you commit further offenses? Again Mr DiPaulo points out that you have no criminal record. And more important, I'm confident your mother will be an excellent surety. Once you go back to her house, I don't think you'll be a danger to anyone.'

Two out of three ain't bad, DiPaulo thought, but not enough.

'The last and most vexing question is whether or not releasing you would undermine public confidence in the administration of justice.' Saying that, she lifted DiPaulo's thick binder of cases and dropped it back on her desk with a thump. 'It's not unprecedented to grant bail to accused in murder trials, especially someone such as yourself, with no criminal antecedents.'

For some reason, judges loved double negatives. As if they were more nuanced. Why say 'it's not unprecedented' instead of spitting out 'there's precedent' for granting you bail?

DiPaulo's hand froze on his pen. He'd been gripping it so tight his fingers were in spasm. They were stuck. He let go of the pen and tried to move them.

He realized that Norville was silent. This was the moment of decision. He didn't dare look up. His fingers were numb. No one in the courtroom moved.

Please don't say 'but,' the dreaded word every criminal lawyer hated to hear, the fulcrum upon which a negative decision always turned. If the next word was 'but,' it was all over.

He looked up at the judge. Her eyes were on him.

'Mr DiPaulo,' she said. 'What arrangements are in place for your client to see her son if she's living up north and he's down here in Toronto?'

DiPaulo shot to his feet, his mind a jumble of emotions. There was no 'but.' Norville's going to let Wyler out. The videotape of the boy playing with Greene – DiPaulo thought it had sunk his case. Blood was coming back into his fingers.

Now he saw it. Norville didn't want to cut Simon off from his mother. When her first husband died, she must have seen what happened to a child who lost a parent. That was her focus. Why didn't I think of that? That tape of Simon playing with trains would be a killer at trial, but now it was going to get her bail.

Keep your cool, Ted, he told himself. Don't act like it's a done deal.

'Your Honor, that's an excellent question.' He was stalling for time to get his thoughts in order.

Raglan stood. 'Your Honor. I appreciate your concerns about the boy seeing his mother, but I want to remind the court that Simon will be a key witness for the prosecution. There's a real danger he might be unduly influenced by the accused. In a homicide case, this must be the court's paramount concern.'

Norville tapped her pen.

I'm losing her, DiPaulo thought.

'The Crown makes an excellent point.' Norville bit her lower lip. She shrugged her shoulders at him, as if to say, 'Sorry, Ted. Close, but no cigar.' 'Mr DiPaulo. I have grave concerns about separating mother and child, but . . .'

There it was. The 'but.'

The idea came to him in an instant. Damn the 'but.'

229

'I share Your Honor's concerns,' DiPaulo said, interrupting the judge, which was a real no-no in her court. Norville scowled. He kept talking. 'And I agree with my friend. We can't allow my client to be alone with her son—'

'Okay then.' Norville cut back in. 'Then I'm going to deny—'

'But, Your Honor, I have the solution. Hear me out,' DiPaulo said.

Norville had her mouth open. She was about to speak. Don't stop, he told himself.

'When Ms Wyler comes to Toronto to meet with me, I'll take her to see Simon in the play-room at police headquarters. The one in the video. Obviously the boy was comfortable there.'

'Hmm,' Norville said.

'It keeps Ms Wyler in touch with her son.' Come on, Judge, keep nodding, DiPaulo thought. 'It doesn't prejudice the trial. Just the opposite. It keeps my client totally visible to the police. Everything's recorded.'

Norville broke into a grin. Like a hiker who'd made it across a wild river, safe on the far shore. 'I was thinking of something along the same lines,' she said. 'Ms Wyler, I'm granting you bail, but believe me the terms of your release will be the strictest that I can fashion without keeping you behind bars. Step over the line once and you'll be in custody so fast your head will spin. Is that understood?'

'Yes,' Wyler said. It was stunning to hear her voice for the first time in court.

For the next twenty minutes Norville piled on every term and condition she could think of. House arrest, the only exception being allowed to go to the libraries in Cobalt and New Liskeard. No use of Internet or e-mail. No cell phone. No long-distance calls except to her lawyer.

DiPaulo dutifully made notes of every word on the left-hand side of the page. In the blank right-hand margin he drew an enormous happy face.

Round one to the defense. With Herbert Hoover odds, no less. Man oh man, he loved to win. And tonight he was going to get a very good night's sleep.

PART III

NOVEMBER

CHAPTER 34

Arceli Ocaya was worried about Simon. It had been three months since Mr Wyler was killed and the boy had stopped talking about his father. Any time she brought up the subject, the boy took out one of his toy guns and shouted, 'Bang bang! I'm police. Bad guys hands up!' Guns and police were the only things he talked about.

After the murder, Simon and Arceli had spent a few days at the home of Simon's uncle Nathan. The police sent over a social worker, and Simon started crying, saying he wanted to go back to day-care camp. They worked out a plan. For the fall Simon would live at Arceli's apartment during the week and spend the weekends at Nathan's house. Uncle Jason would drive them back and forth. In January they would move permanently to Nathan's place.

When the boy first went back to day care, many of the parents tried to help out, inviting Simon for playdates at their houses. Now they were complaining about all his talk of police and guns.

Every two weeks Detective Greene came by the

apartment and took Simon to police headquarters to see his mother. He loved the police radio. 'Copy that,' 'Ten-four,' 'Roger, we're on our way.' Simon used those phrases over and over again.

When the detective called the day before, Ocaya broke down and told him her concerns about all of Simon's gun talk. 'I am so sorry to bother you with this,' she said.

'You did the right thing,' he assured her. 'No more police cars, and I'll get rid of his guns tomorrow.'

The intercom from the downstairs lobby buzzed. Simon rushed over to push the Entry button.

'Police headquarters.' He stretched onto his toes to reach the speaker. 'Come in with your hands up.'

'Simon, stop that.' Ocaya pulled him from the wall.

'Why?' Simon squirmed away from her grip, rushed into the living room, where he slept on the couch, and grabbed the toy gun he kept under his pillow.

By the time he got back, Detective Greene was in the kitchen with a big white cloth bag in his hand. It had a large police logo on it. Billy barked and wagged his tail.

Greene bent his knees to get close to the boy's height. 'Good morning.'

'Did you find my Thomas?'

Simon had lost his train at the old house and asked about it every time he saw Greene.

'Afraid not. But I'm on a special police mission.' Greene pulled a long piece of paper from his coat pocket. 'Look at this.'

Simon put his hand on the detective's shoulder.

'This is called a search warrant,' he told Simon. 'See. Can you read that word?'

Simon looked at it closely. 'Simon. That's my name.'

'How about this one?'

'Arceli,' he said, proud of himself, and looked over at Ocaya.

She clapped her hands together. 'Good, Simon.' She always felt better when Detective Greene came over.

'How about this little word? It's only four letters,' Greene said.

'Guns. Did you bring me more guns?'

'Afraid not. This says I'm supposed to collect all the guns in the house and put them in this police bag. Time for another little boy or girl to play with them.'

Simon looked at the gun in his hand, then crossed his arms in front of his thin chest.

'No,' he said. 'I won't.'

'Simon, be a good boy,' Ocaya said.

'It's mine,' Simon screamed at Detective Greene. To Ocaya's amazement, he spun on his heels and ran out the apartment door. The dog ran right after him.

'Simon,' Ocaya yelled.

Greene didn't hesitate. He charged out into the

hall. Ocaya rushed to the kitchen drawer, grabbed the front door key, and ran outside. Simon was heading to the stairwell, the dog at his heels. The detective was running after them.

'Simon, please,' Ocaya shouted. She locked the door and by the time she turned back to the hallway they were gone. At the stairway she heard their footsteps heading down. She descended as fast as she could and on the fourth floor she saw them in a corner. Detective Greene was on his back with Simon on top of him, his arms wrapped around the boy. The dog was nuzzling them both. The floor was filthy. Poor Detective Greene was wearing such a nice suit.

Simon looked up. 'Daddy didn't have a gun,' he said. 'I need my gun.'

CHAPTER 35

Reason number nineteen to never work on a homicide, Daniel Kennicott thought, crossing off yet another name on the long list of witnesses Detective Greene had given him to go back and interview. Most of the work was boring. After the initial flurry of activity during those first few hectic days, the daily routine ground down to getting out and pounding the pavement, which was the backbone of any good investigation. Going over things again and again.

A lot of detectives would have hit Cruise Control in a case like this, given the piles of evidence that were stacked up against the accused. But not Greene – even though tomorrow was the judicial pretrial and the whole thing would probably end in a guilty plea. This morning he wanted Kennicott to return to Terrance Wyler's street and knock on doors yet again. Kennicott had been back twice and reinterviewed all the witnesses but one, a teenage boy named Brandon Legacy who lived next door. Both times he'd called ahead and left a message that he'd be stopping by, and both times Legacy's mother answered the door and said her son wasn't home.

'Don't call this time,' Greene said. 'Get there good and early.'

Kennicott drove past Legacy's house. Like Terrance Wyler's, it was built into the hill, with a steep stone stairway to the front door and a driveway snaking up the side and disappearing behind.

Kennicott thought back to the morning of August 17. The heat. The near empty street. Speeding over to the Ontario Food Terminal, telling Nathan Wyler his brother was dead, then rushing back to Terrance's house to help out. While he was gone, other officers had been doing door-to-doors, standard procedure in a homicide. The protocol was to touch base quickly with every possible witness, collect basic information, and do more detailed follow-ups later. Everything was recorded on preprinted interview sheets that Kennicott collated into one chronological log.

Another officer had been to Legacy's door first. The log entry read:

> August 17, 10:31 – 223 Hillside Drive. Knocked. Rang doorbell. Three attempts each. No one home.

Later in the day Greene had asked Kennicott to try the house again. This time Legacy answered the door. A tall teenager with a big mop of dirty-blond hair, he was just waking up. Classic, Kennicott thought. The interview was short.

August 17, 14:52 – 223 Hillside Drive.
Brandon Legacy, age 18, alone in the city,
parents at cottage. Working as lifeguard,
City of Toronto. Home last night. Playing
video games. Knew neighbor, Mr Wyler.
Babysat occasionally. Didn't notice any cars
or anything unusual on the street last night
or in the morning. Was asleep at 10:31 a.m.
and wouldn't have heard the doorbell when
first police officer came.

Kennicott got out of his patrol car. There was
a biting November chill in the air. He was determined to talk to this kid. The ringer on the front
door had a loud chime.

'Oh, hello, Officer Kennicott,' the boy's mother
said as she answered the door. They'd met on his
two previous visits. She wore a tight tracksuit.
Although probably in her mid-forties, she looked as
fit as a retired Olympic athlete. A workout bag was
slung over her shoulder and there was a water bottle
in her hand labeled QUAD EAST. 'You didn't call.'

'I need to speak to your son today,' Kennicott
said.

'He's still in bed. Teenagers. Gets up about two
minutes before he has to drive to school.'

Kennicott didn't move. Let his presence at the
door speak for him.

She glanced at her ultrathin wristwatch, the kind
that doubles as a heart monitor. 'I'm running late
for my eight o'clock spin class.'

'Ma'am, this is a first-degree murder investigation,' he said.

She unscrewed her water bottle and took a sip. 'I'll get him. There's a nine-thirty I can take.'

Twenty minutes later Kennicott was sitting at a wrought-iron table in the kitchen nook at the back of the house, sipping a cup of herbal tea the Legacys' nanny had prepared.

There were windows on all sides and the room was bathed in sunlight. The Legacys had a big backyard, and like the Wylers next door, their driveway curled around in back so it was level with the house. Three vehicles were parked there. Eighteen years old, and young Brandon had his own car, Kennicott thought. The neighboring lots were separated by a row of trees with a footpath running through it.

Brandon Legacy came in wearing loose-fitting jeans that flared out on the bottom, sneakers with a respectable number of holes and a tight black sweater. A white undershirt showed at the neckline.

'Here he is,' his mother said.

'I need to speak to Brandon alone,' Kennicott said.

'Oh.' She checked her watch before she turned to her son and touched his cheek. 'Honey, you okay if I go?'

He recoiled from her. 'Mom. Whatever. Don't miss your class for this.'

She grabbed her workout bag and practically

sprinted out of the room. Brandon watched her go through the slits of his eyes and sank into the chair across from Kennicott.

'Mom's a cardio queen, has to work out every day or else.' He spied Kennicott's teacup. 'That one of her fancy teas?'

'Handpicked from India, according to the package,' Kennicott said.

He shook his head. 'How can you drink that stuff so early in the morning? I need coffee. I hope you don't mind?'

'Go right ahead.'

The boy had a certain charm about him, despite his baked-on teenage persona. He settled back in his chair, a large mug of coffee in hand, and looked across the table. He wasn't defiant but Kennicott caught something. Maybe he was scared. Kennicott placed a micro-recorder in front of him.

'I tape all my interviews,' he said after he'd snapped on the recorder. 'Okay?'

Legacy gave a mechanical nod.

In fact, Kennicott didn't tape all his interviews. But it was a good way to get the young man's attention.

'This is Officer Daniel Kennicott. I'm sitting in the kitchen of the home of Brandon Legacy, age eighteen. It's November sixteen, and the time is . . .' He looked at his watch. 'Eight oh nine in the morning. Is that all correct, Brandon?'

'Yeah.' He hunched over toward the recorder.

'Brandon, when we talked back in the summer,

243

I asked you what you were doing on Sunday evening, August sixteenth, the night Terrance Wyler was murdered. You said you were home playing video games.'

'Yeah.' He sat back.

'Here's the question I didn't ask that first time. Were you alone?'

The young man took a noisy slurp of his coffee and looked out the window. Stalling, Kennicott thought. 'Not really,' Legacy said at last.

'What do you mean, not really?' Kennicott checked the little recorder between them to make sure the function light was on.

'Well, not like the whole night.' Legacy took another sip. Not slurping this time.

Kennicott looked straight at Legacy. 'Who was with you?'

'A friend.'

'Who was the friend?'

Legacy looked over his shoulder. The kitchen was empty. 'Do I have to tell you?'

'Your neighbor Terrance Wyler was killed right next door. You used to babysit his son, Simon.'

'He's a smart boy.'

'A boy who doesn't have a father. Forget what you see on *CSI*. We don't solve crimes in the laboratory, we solve them because citizens help out. I need to know who was with you.'

People always surprise you, Kennicott thought as a cascade of tears streamed down the boy's cheeks. There was a cloth napkin on the side of the table and Kennicott gave it to him.

'Thanks,' Legacy said.

'This is important.'

'I haven't been in Mr Wyler's house since they split up and Samantha left,' Legacy said.

'I was asking about who was with you in your house.'

'After my friend left, I was online. I went to summer school in Europe last year and met this girl from California. We chatted for at least an hour. There's this game called Flight Simulator. You can fly planes and copilot with people all over the world. After that I hooked up with this guy in Perth, Australia. I didn't get to sleep until about four. I saved everything. You can check the times. I never left this house that night. Ever.'

Giving extraneous information like this was a classic evasion tactic by a witness.

'Brandon, stop avoiding the question. Who was with you?'

'I really need to talk to my dad. Okay?'

'You're eighteen. Not a minor. I can question you without your parents present.' Kennicott looked out the back window and traced the path between the houses. He thought about Legacy's bell-bottom jeans and that swatch of blood down at the bottom of the back door of Terrance Wyler's house.

Legacy had followed Kennicott's glance next door. 'Samantha.' He sounded scared. 'She was here. But I swear, I swear, I never left my house that night.'

'How long was she here?'

He shrugged. 'A few hours.'

'Your parents were away, weren't they?'

He blushed. 'Yeah. They'll kill me if they find out.'

'What time did she leave?'

'I don't know exactly. Around one o'clock.'

'Where'd she go?'

Legacy pointed next door. 'Mr Wyler's house. He e-mailed her, said he'd accept her offer to settle their divorce stuff. Asked her to come over. I never went there. I swear. You can take my DNA, check my computer. Hook me up to one of those machines. I don't care. Anything. I haven't been in there for a year at least. I never went in there that night and I never saw Samantha again.'

CHAPTER 36

'How was the train ride?' Ted DiPaulo asked Samantha Wyler. She took her usual seat in his office, closest to the hallway. He shut the door and sat in the chair by the window. She wore black jeans, a flannel shirt, and a down vest. Made her look more like an older graduate student than the banker and businesswoman she'd once been.

'My mother fell asleep,' Wyler said. 'I sat there and read. Six hours.'

'How's it going at home?'

She gave her head an exaggerated shake. 'Lots of fun.'

When people got out of jail, they always swore they'd be eternally grateful to those who'd bailed them out. The gratitude usually lasted about a month or so. Then the day-to-day realities sank in. For Sam it meant that at age thirty-five she was living in her childhood bedroom, in a house with her mother and bachelor brother.

'What're you reading?' he asked.

She laughed. 'Divorce books. Parenting books.

Law books. Medical books. You know me, always researching.'

DiPaulo moved back behind his desk. A signal to her that he had something serious to talk about. 'The pretrial's set for tomorrow with Judge Norville. Even though she did the bail hearing, she wants to be involved with the case. I think she's taken a special interest in it.'

'Wants the publicity, like everyone else,' Wyler said.

'I doubt it,' DiPaulo said. 'Her first husband died when their daughter was very young, and I think she's worried about Simon. That's why she let you out on bail.'

'No matter what, I don't want my son to have to go to court.'

'Very unlikely. The prosecutor would look bad calling him as a witness. And the tape is all the evidence they need.'

'Need to convict me, right? That's what the judge is going to say at this pretrial, isn't she?'

'She's going to push like hell for a deal. She'll tell me how overwhelming the evidence is against you.'

Wyler hung her head.

DiPaulo picked up a silver letter opener his wife had given him for his law school graduation. It was engraved with his initials but the letters were fading. Silver, he'd learned, like gold was a soft metal.

'What would I get for manslaughter?' Wyler asked, still looking down.

He was glad she'd brought up the topic. 'The math is brutal. First-degree murder, which is a planned and deliberate killing, the sentence is twenty-five years. Mandatory. No parole. You're thirty-five. That means you'll be sixty when you get out. Sixty years old.'

She started to cry. 'It's unbelievable.'

'Second-degree is a minimum of ten years.'

She wiped the tears away and looked at him. 'I couldn't have another baby. Simon would never talk to me again.'

'Manslaughter's the last alternative. There's no minimum sentence, and you could get out on parole after one-third of your time. I'd ask for six to eight years on a plea to manslaughter.' He watched her closely. She was still staring at the floor. DiPaulo put down the letter opener, determined to wait her out.

'Six years?' she asked at last.

Clients only heard the lowest number. He'd deliberately given her the best possible news to get a foot in the door. Time now to drag her inside, kicking and screaming if necessary.

'I said I'd ask for six to eight. The Crown won't want you to plead to manslaughter. If the judge really twists their arm, they might take a plea. But for a much bigger number.'

'Bigger?'

'They'll want at least fifteen. Probably more.'

'Fifteen.' She writhed in her chair. 'Fifteen? Simon's only four years old.'

'Samantha, listen. I'll tell you again. Manslaughter, you can get parole in a third of the time. Second-degree murder—'

'I know, I know. Ten years minimum, twenty-five for first-degree. Still—'

'It'll be up to the judge. I'll tell her how well you've done on bail.'

'If I plead, I'll never get to see my son again,' she said.

'You don't know that for sure. Feindel's an excellent family lawyer. Maybe with time—'

'With time Simon will get older. You think when he's a teenager he's going to want to have anything to do with a mother who he thinks killed his dad?'

DiPaulo checked his office door to triple ensure it was closed, the way a nervous traveler checks and rechecks his passport in his breast pocket. This was a big step. She had almost confessed to him. Guilt, he knew, was a heavy burden to carry.

'I'm only a criminal lawyer.' He came around the desk and took his usual seat beside her. 'My job is to make the best I can of this situation. I'm terrified you'll be convicted of first-degree murder.'

She bit her lower lip and flicked her hair back. Teetering on the edge of her emotions.

'Twenty-five years,' he said.

Her breath was coming fast.

'I'm going into that pretrial tomorrow and I'll fight for you,' DiPaulo said. If he was going to ride this horse – make the best possible deal on a guilty plea – this was the moment. 'If the judge pushes them to offer me manslaughter, will you take it?'

'I . . . I—'

'I need an answer. Otherwise the Crown will go all the way.'

Wyler nodded a little.

'I'll keep saying it until I'm sure you understand. Twenty-five years. You will be sixty years—'

'Okay,' she said in a voice so thin, so tentative that if his eyes were closed, DiPaulo would have thought she was a child. It wasn't a lot, but it was enough.

CHAPTER 37

'I'll be there in five minutes,' Ari Greene said to his father, calling from his car when he was about a mile from his dad's house. At last they had time to repaint the railing of his front porch.

'I need some new brushes,' his father said. 'Can you pick up a few?'

'What's wrong with the old ones?'

'They're stiff.'

Greene chuckled to himself. His father hadn't bought a paintbrush in a decade. Every few years Greene brought new ones over, which always provoked a slew of comments about how the old ones were good enough. 'See you in about twenty minutes,' he said.

Instead of continuing north to the hardware store, Greene swung his Oldsmobile west, slipped through a few side streets, and parked a block away from the house he grew up in. He hopped out and walked to the old maple tree on the corner that he used to climb when he was a kid. 'Ari, you never stop being a cop,' an old girlfriend had once told him. I guess it's true, he thought as he hid behind the tree.

In a few minutes his dad's old Buick pulled up to the stop sign and turned in the other direction. Mrs Spiegel, one of the women who ran the synagogue sisterhood, was in the passenger seat. She'd been a widow for years.

Greene went back to his car and waited. It didn't take long for the Buick to reappear. He followed it down his father's little side street and parked behind it in the narrow driveway.

'I hear Mrs Spiegel's a good cook,' Greene said when they were both out of their cars.

'So, you didn't get the brushes,' his father said.

Greene kissed his dad on the forehead. 'Once a cop, always a cop, Dad.'

'Her husband died ten years ago.' His father shrugged. 'I knew her from the DP camp.' After he was liberated, Greene's father had spent two years in the displaced persons camp in Austria. The third day there he met Chana, Greene's mother. They were married four days later. 'It's not easy to find a man who still drives.'

Greene eyed his father. 'As long as he stays off the highway.'

His father grimaced.

Greene looked at the paved driveway. There were cracks in the black asphalt and this past summer more weeds than ever had poked through. 'You haven't resurfaced this since I was a kid.'

'Your mother bothered me about it for years.' They walked together up the concrete front steps. His father pulled out a big ring of keys. He had three locks on both the front and the back doors which he also braced with a metal bar.

'The Portuguese family that moved across the street said they'd give me a good price.' He walked inside. 'Leafs were terrible last night. Three goals against them in the first seven minutes. I told you that goalie from Finland would be a disaster.'

'He's Swedish.'

'He stinks. What's happening with your case?'

When Greene was on a murder, he'd talk to his dad about it. 'Judicial pretrial's tomorrow. Everyone else thinks it'll be a guilty plea.'

'Except you?'

'Except me. And Kennicott. We're both betting this will be a trial.' In the kitchen Greene pulled some dishes from his father's dishwasher and put them in the cupboards. Since his mother died last year, Greene's father used the dishwasher for storage. 'Why bother putting them away?' he said every time Ari asked him about it, mixing English and Yiddish. '*Zaytki arbet.*' Which meant extra work. As far as his father was concerned, he'd already worked hard enough in his life.

'This family. The Wylers. What do they say?' his father asked.

'They want it over. They have an aggressive family lawyer who's told them that if Samantha pleads guilty, even to manslaughter, she'll never see her son again.'

Greene opened two tins of tuna and mixed them with mayonnaise while his father set the linoleum table in the kitchen. There was a dining room on the other side of the wall, but Greene couldn't remember the last time they'd eaten there.

'The oldest brother, Nathan, was fooling around with his girlfriend the night this happened. I'm the only one who knows, and he wants to keep it that way. A guilty plea solves all his problems.'

'You haven't told anyone this?'

'It's not relevant,' Greene said. 'His alibi is solid. I checked it out myself.'

His father brought out a pitcher of milk and two glasses. 'But you think because of her son, this woman Samantha won't plead.'

Greene bit into his sandwich. Last week he'd bought his dad some rye bread and it was hard. Should have toasted it, he thought.

'What did the husband do when he lived in the States?' His dad did this all the time, asked a series of seemingly unrelated questions. It was impossible to discern where he was going with them, but often they'd lead to a whole new way of looking at things.

Thanks to the Nazis, Yitzhak Greene had no formal education. On the evening of September 22, 1942, their little Polish village was surrounded, and half the people – the two thousand Jews who'd lived peacefully with their two thousand Catholic neighbors for hundreds of years – were rounded up and shipped to Treblinka. He and two others were the only survivors. His first wife and their two daughters were killed. If given the opportunity to go to school, his father could have been anything. But he never complained that he'd had to spend his life fixing other people's shoes so he could raise a family.

'Went to college in Vermont.' Greene opened a jar of Strub's pickles he'd brought to the table. 'Stayed in the town when he graduated and ran his own health food store. Apparently he was good at it, made a lot of money.'

'He came back. Why?'

'They needed him. The middle brother couldn't work anymore because of his disease. And he met his wife, Samantha, back here,' Greene said. 'Dad, eat.'

His father was a slow eater. He'd weighed seventy-six pounds when the Americans liberated him. And always left a bit of food on his plate. 'He was away. How long?'

'Ten years.'

'Long time away from his family.'

At last Greene's father bit into his sandwich. 'Bread's stale,' he said. 'I should have toasted it.'

CHAPTER 38

When she was going to court for a judicial pretrial and not a trial, Jennifer Raglan didn't have to wear her robes. She knew Judge Norville well enough to know it was important to dress well, and besides, it felt good to put on a nice wool suit, great for a fall day, with a pin she'd inherited from her grandmother. On the weekend she'd had her hair cut and her roots touched up. There was this new lipstick she was trying, a softer red that worked well with her pale skin. And if the case settled, this could be one of the last times she'd see Ari Greene.

Even Gordon noticed when she came down for breakfast. 'Luncheon date today?' he had asked, lowering the sports section of his newspaper.

She shook her head. 'Pretrial with Judge Norville. She's very formal. Hates it when lawyers are casual about anything.' There was no need to tell him that Ari Greene would also be at the courthouse today. There'd never been a reason to tell him anything about Greene.

'Well, you look good.' Gordon put down his paper, got up, and leaned over to kiss her.

She turned her mouth so he had to kiss her cheek. 'Fresh lipstick,' she said by way of explanation.

'Good luck.' He sat down and disappeared behind his paper.

The best part of the outfit was her new pumps. She'd spent Sunday afternoon on Bloor Street with Dana, mother-and-daughter shoe shopping. It had been fun and she couldn't resist this Italian pair. They made her feel tall and confident as they clicked on the floor leading to the door where, up ahead, Ted DiPaulo was chatting with the court officer who would usher them back inside to see the judge.

'Morning, Counsel.' The older man was in full uniform, complete with a row of badges and metals. 'Her Honor's expecting you.' He pushed some numbers on a code pad before taking them down a quiet carpeted hallway.

Every few steps they passed a different judge's office. Big rooms, each with its own flooring and furniture. Judges hated to think of themselves as civil servants. As far as they were concerned, a judge was above the constraints and influences of government and they wanted their offices, which they referred to as chambers, to reflect their own individual styles.

'Good morning.' Norville looked up from her steel desk. The chambers of many of the older judges were rich in dark wood furniture and thick carpets. In contrast, every inch of Norville's office was ultramodern. The floor was covered in a thin,

258

light gray carpet accented by swaths of color, like a horizontal version of a huge modern painting. Her gray desk was brushed steel. The two chairs in front were metal too, angular and fashionably uncomfortable.

Norville, out of her gowns, wore a gleaming cotton shirt under a tailored jacket. She had on stylish aqua blue glasses – not the boring brown-framed pair she wore in court – that matched the desk and the chairs and the flooring. Her hair had the consistent styling and streaks that could only be achieved with weekly appointments.

Raglan perched herself on the edge of the chair closest to the window. DiPaulo sat beside her.

Norville sighed. 'I have all these forms to fill out if there's going to be a trial.' She touched the stack of papers on her otherwise empty desk. How do people keep their offices so clean? Raglan wondered.

'First, let's talk.' Norville took off her fancy glasses. They must have cost at least eight hundred dollars, Raglan thought, just for the frames. 'I'm determined to do everything I can to try to avoid a trial.'

Judges loved settling cases. Not only did it save precious court time – the one commodity in their pampered lives that was in short supply – but it gave them status with their colleagues. Finding that magic middle point made them feel proud.

DiPaulo glanced at Raglan but didn't say a word. They'd both taken the same negotiation skills

259

training courses. Rule number one was keep your mouth shut, let the other side talk first.

Norville sensed the deadlock. 'Okay,' she said, looking at DiPaulo. 'Ted, you have a huge problem with this case. The e-mails, the voice mails, the Hollywood girlfriend – and that video with the child is going to bury you in front of the jury. You'll be lucky if they don't convict her of a first. Twenty-five years for a young woman like that.'

'It's not the easiest case I've ever had, Your Honor.' DiPaulo put on his most charming smile. 'My client isn't entirely realistic.' He turned his face into a sad frown, as if to say 'What can I do?' The message was clear: make me an offer Samantha Wyler can't refuse.

Norville shook her head. 'She needs a reality check. I haven't heard a word about an alibi. Means she can't testify. This is her one and only chance.'

She swung over to Raglan. 'What are you looking for?' It was more of a statement than a question. 'This isn't a first. I don't even see a second here. Smells like manslaughter. The movie-star girlfriend. All those stab wounds. Scenario's obvious. Husband and wife on the eve of a divorce trial get together. Foolish. They talk. They fight. She loses it. Grabs a kitchen knife. Crime of Passion one oh one. Where's the premeditation?'

Raglan couldn't keep quiet any longer. For the last two days she'd huddled with Ralph Armitage and Ari Greene to hammer out a plan.

The Crown's initial bargaining position would be a plea to second-degree murder with an agreed sentence of twelve years, two above the minimum. Their fallback was a plea to manslaughter, but ask for eighteen.

DiPaulo was a master at the pretrial game. He had Norville totally under his spell. Raglan had to counterpunch. 'Best I can do is a plea to second, for a high minimum. Say fifteen years,' she said. 'The family's furious. Anything less than a first and they'll bite my head off.' Never mind that the Wylers didn't want a trial where their family business would be dragged out in public.

Norville cocked her head at Raglan and frowned. 'The family watches too much American TV. This isn't murder by a mile, first- or second-degree. Every judge in this building will have my head if I let this suck up valuable court time. I expect a plea to manslaughter.' She gave DiPaulo a big smile. 'Ted, how's your client?'

Norville had called him Ted again. As if they were best friends. She seemed more concerned about Samantha than her dead husband.

'Doing great on bail.' DiPaulo was piling it on and the judge was lapping it up.

'Wonderful.' Norville pushed aside the papers on her desk. 'It has to be a big number when she pleads. The public doesn't understand the difference between murder and manslaughter. But they know how to count.'

She said 'when,' Raglan thought.

'A woman like this will be a model prisoner.' Norville didn't give either of them an opening to interrupt. 'Be running the prison library in no time. Early parole will be a cinch, and she'll do most of her time in minimum security. I don't want any whining about this.'

DiPaulo looked chastened. Another part of his act for Her Honor. He was thrilled with a plea to manslaughter, although Raglan suspected that Samantha Wyler wouldn't be so pleased.

'We're only arguing about the name above the door – manslaughter or murder,' Norville said. She looked at her watch. 'The important word is "guilty."'

No one spoke.

Know when the tide is coming in and when it's going out, DiPaulo had taught Raglan. This was as good as it was going to get. And most important, in her heart she didn't believe it was murder. 'If it's a plea to manslaughter,' she said, 'I'm going to yell and scream for eighteen years.'

Norville slapped her desk with glee. 'Be my guest. Okay, this is what's going to happen.' She slipped her expensive glasses back on and clicked her teeth. 'The sentence has to be in double figures. The optics are lousy if it's anything less. Jennifer, you'll ask for eighteen. Ted, you'll ask for twelve. I'll give her fifteen.'

With a big smile on her face, she picked up the phone. 'Masoud, hello. Justice Norville here. How's my calendar this week? Sure, I'll wait.'

She looked up. 'The trial coordinator's a miracle worker. Ted, your client – is she here?'

'Outside the courtroom. My partner's trying to shield her from the press.'

'Goes with the territory,' Norville said. 'Excuse me.' Taking out a pencil, she opened her diary and made 'hmm' and 'uh-huh' noises for a few seconds. 'Tomorrow?' she said into the phone. 'Excellent. I'm doing that sentencing at ten. Perfect. Put the Samantha Wyler matter in for noon, mark it for plea and sentencing. Which court? Room 204. Wonderful. Thanks, as always.'

She smiled and hung up. 'Okay, Counsel. Tomorrow, noon, 204, we'll wrap this all up before lunch.' She made more notes to herself. 'Manslaughter. Fifteen years. That's the magic number.'

Raglan stood to shake the judge's hand. But really she was dying to slap Norville, see those expensive glasses fly across the room and wipe that shit-eating grin off her face.

CHAPTER 39

'Fifteen years for manslaughter,' Ted DiPaulo said to Nancy Parish, swinging into her office, not waiting for her to look up from her desk where she was sketching something on a white piece of paper. Parish had been an artist as a kid and was forever drawing cartoons.

'Deal of a lifetime.' Parish popped her head up. 'Grab it.'

'Norville barricaded us in her office and wrung a manslaughter plea out of the Crown.'

'Fifteen was about what I thought. Sam will be at one of those hobby-farm jails in no time.' Parish lifted up the drawing for him to see. A male defense lawyer was standing in court next to his female client, facing the judge. The client was leaning over to whisper in her lawyer's ear. 'Remind me again. Do I say "guilty" or "not guilty"?'

DiPaulo laughed. 'Like all good humor, there's an element of truth to it.' He rubbed a hand across his face. 'I hope Sam takes the deal.'

'She doesn't have an alibi.'

'I know. I need your help.'

'Sure. But don't keep me too late tonight. I have my first date in months.'

Parish's marriage had busted up a few years before. Since then she liked to say she'd been dating Mr On and Mr Off, mostly Mr Off.

'Sam'll be here in a few minutes. I need signed, written instructions that she'll accept the plea. And I need you as a witness.'

'Good idea,' Parish said.

Back in his office, DiPaulo cleaned off his desk, lowered the curtains, and started typing the instructions for the guilty plea. The bell rang in the front hall and he heard the sound of conversation. He'd told Parish to make Wyler wait a few minutes until he called for them. This was a change from his usual pattern of going to meet her himself. Keep her off balance. She had to understand he was no longer her defender, but her apologist.

When he was ready, DiPaulo looked down the hall. 'Come on in, both of you.'

Wyler entered first, followed closely by Parish.

'I've asked Nancy to join us.'

He motioned Sam to the seat by the window, away from the door, and for the first time she took it. She looked defeated. Parish sat in the other chair. He closed the door, effectively sealing Samantha in.

'I've prepared this for you to sign.' He went behind his desk and passed her a three-page document, neatly stapled in the top-left-hand corner.

'Read it carefully.' He gave a second copy to Parish and picked up the third for himself.

Wyler looked at DiPaulo, then at Parish. Not at the papers in her hands.

'The heading, as you can see, is "Instructions for My Lawyer Re: Guilty Plea – Manslaughter," DiPaulo said, moving right in. 'That's the good news. After much arm-twisting by Judge Norville, the Crown will agree to a plea of manslaughter. But the price is steep. Fifteen years. It could have been worse. They wanted eighteen.'

Wyler showed no emotion at this news. She looked at the papers.

DiPaulo read the document out loud. It stated that Wyler had been duly informed of all her legal options, that she was making the decision to plead guilty of her own free will. 'We'll put on a show trial. The Crown will pump up the moral outrage and ask for eighteen years. I'll be equally appalled and demand twelve. This way the judge gets to play Solomon and cut the baby in half.'

As soon as the last words were out DiPaulo realized he'd gotten carried away.

'Simon's not a baby anymore,' she said. 'I'll never see him again.'

He finished reading the document. A curdling knot was forming in his stomach. No one spoke. A part of him felt like ripping up the paper.

His first criminal law professor, a quirky Australian named Parker Graham, had warned the class, 'Get good at doing guilty pleas. That's how about ninety-five percent of your cases will end up.' It was true. But every time he did a plea, even in a hopeless case, there was that pit in his stomach. The feeling that maybe he could have won somehow. And the certainty that he'd be wide-awake at three in the morning, running different 'what-if' scenarios through his mind.

'Do I sign this now?' Wyler asked.

'Not yet.' The knot in his stomach should have loosened, but it tightened. DiPaulo distributed a one-page document to Wyler and Parish. Its heading was 'Agreed Statement of Facts.'

'These facts form the basis of your guilty plea,' he told her. 'I've negotiated hard with the Crown and watered them down as much as I could. This will be read out in court and the judge will only accept your plea if you acknowledge that the facts are true.'

Wyler was staring at this new sheet.

DiPaulo waited until she finished reading it. 'By signing this, you acknowledge that you're instructing me to enter a guilty plea on your behalf.'

Wyler nodded.

'I want to do this for real,' DiPaulo said. 'Let's all get up. Nancy, come behind the desk and play the judge. Sam, I'll stand beside you, like I will in court.'

When they were in position, Parish read:

'Agreed Statement of Facts
R. v. Samantha Wyler
Charge: Manslaughter

'In the early hours of Monday, August 17, the defendant, Samantha Wyler, age thirty-five, attended at the home of the victim, her husband, Mr Terrance Wyler, age forty.

'The home is located at 221 Hillside Drive, in the city of Toronto. The defendant and the victim were in the midst of divorce proceedings. Their family court trial was to commence later the same day.

'The defendant and the victim had been married five years. Their only child, Simon, was four years old. In the weeks before August 17 the defendant left the victim numerous voice messages and sent him many angry e-mails about the divorce and the victim's new girlfriend.

'The parties met in the victim's kitchen, and an argument ensued. The defendant became upset and, without planning or conscious forethought, grabbed a kitchen knife and stabbed the victim numerous times. One stab hit the carotid artery in his neck, and he died within minutes.

'Before she left the victim's house, the defendant went upstairs to Simon's bedroom. She told her son she wouldn't see him for a long time.'

Parish put the single sheet of paper on DiPaulo's desk. The room was silent. DiPaulo could feel Wyler by his side.

Standing beside your client in court was a simple, elegant gesture. Whether it was shoplifters or mass murderers, at the moment of truth every accused had their advocate by their side.

He didn't dare to look over. Wyler wasn't saying a word.

Parish folded her arms. 'I'll step out so you two can talk.' She looked awkward, like a teenager at a friend's house when the parents are having a fight.

'I'll sign,' Wyler said before she could leave. 'Let's do this fast.'

Two minutes later DiPaulo walked Wyler to the front door. She didn't say another word. He went back to his office, called Jennifer Raglan, and told her they had a deal. Professional courtesy. He offered to call Detective Greene, but she said she'd do it herself.

He headed to Parish's office, the signed instructions in hand, and slid into one of her client chairs. The cartoon was still on her desk.

'That was lots of fun,' she said.

'Guilt's a double-edged sword. It eats away at people. But hurts like hell when you pull it out.'

'Wasn't there a second bloodstain on the back

269

door?' Parish asked. 'Couldn't someone else have been there?'

'There's no way to date the blood.' He tried to stifle a yawn. 'Every case has a few missing parts. Nothing's ever perfect for the Crown or the defense.'

'You convinced?' Parish put the cartoon into a rectangular wooden box she kept on the credenza behind her desk.

'Not my job to be convinced.' DiPaulo tossed the paper onto her desk. 'Bottom line is, we have signed instructions.' He put his hands behind his head and closed his eyes. 'I always remember my client John Voelker. Charged with first-degree murder for shooting a guy in a park. Gang thing. After two years of battling, the Crown took a plea to manslaughter for eighteen years. To this day, I'm not sure if he did it or if he was covering for his best friend. Still keeps me up at night.'

'You never let a case go, do you?'

'Occupational hazard.'

'Who could Samantha be covering for?' Parish asked.

'I didn't say she was. The reality is we never really know.' He scooped up Wyler's signed instructions and rustled the document in his hand. 'That's why we have this.'

CHAPTER 40

Ari Greene's cell phone rang and he answered it on the first ring.

'We have a deal.' It was Jennifer Raglan.

'Manslaughter?'

'Right. Fifteen years. Tomorrow in 204 at noon.'

'Good work,' he said.

They were both silent. The implication of this news was clear. The two of them had worked closely together for months and, although it was unspoken, they'd gotten used to seeing each other every day. Even if nothing had happened between them. That would end tomorrow.

'Looks like I was wrong,' he said at last.

'About what, Ari?'

'I didn't think Samantha would plead.'

'You never know what's going to happen with people,' Raglan said. 'I guess it's all over.'

'Like you said in August, you're not doing murder trials anymore.'

Neither of them spoke for a very long moment.

'Ari . . .'

'I have to call the Wylers,' Greene said, almost at the same time. 'News like this travels fast.'

Last night he'd told the family that the case might settle at today's pretrial. Knowing how much families hated plea bargains, he warned them that the sentence might be much lower than what they'd hoped for.

'Ari,' Raglan said again. 'Make the call.'

The father, Mr Wyler, picked up the phone as soon as it rang.

'It's Detective Greene.'

'Yes.' Wyler's voice was cold. He'd been arrested twice himself, and like many people who'd been through the system, the man didn't like cops.

'I just spoke to the Crown Attorney. Samantha Wyler's going to plead guilty tomorrow. But not to first- or even second-degree murder. To manslaughter. She'll get fifteen years.'

'I see.'

'I know you'll all be disappointed, but fifteen years is much longer than a usual manslaughter sentence. I've seen them as low as nine or ten in a situation like this.'

Wyler didn't say anything.

'There was always the chance she'd be acquitted. It's a compromise. Ensures a conviction. Means your family doesn't have to go through a trial.'

'I'll tell them,' Wyler said after another long pause. He hung up without even saying goodbye.

Greene called Kennicott to tell him the news and thanked him for his hard work. Then he phoned Phil Cutter so the defense lawyer could inform his client, April Goodling.

'Thanks for the call,' Cutter said. 'Class thing to do.'

'You're welcome,' Greene said.

'Detective, things got heated there a few months ago.' Cutter paused, waiting for Greene to fill in the gap.

Greene held his tongue.

'Maybe one day we can go for a coffee,' Cutter said. 'There's more than meets the eye about this file, but trust me, none of it has anything to do with the murder.'

'Maybe,' Greene said.

'Oh, I forgot. You're the only cop in homicide who doesn't drink coffee.' Cutter's cackling laugh shrieked over the phone line. Greene's non-coffee-drinking ways were a running joke in the bureau, but he was in no mood to laugh it up with Phil Cutter.

'Ms Goodling has my number,' Greene said. 'Tell her I look forward to seeing her name on my call display.' He hung up.

The drive up to the Wylers' house was slow, the traffic bad even in the middle of the day. Keeping close to the victim's family was one of the things Greene liked most about the job. Finding a place among the living where he could make a difference. But explaining to them a compromised plea bargain like this was no one's idea of a good time.

This was the toughest moment for the families. Once the proceedings were finished there'd be no more phone calls, no more meetings, no more press to bother you, no more frustrations with how slowly the justice system worked, no more exhausting days sitting in court. Just the endless empty road ahead. And the promise of the detectives and Crown Attorneys that they would keep in touch – sincere, but never fully realized.

'Good afternoon, Detective,' Jason Wyler said when he greeted Greene at the door. He leaned hard on one of his canes. The second one was tucked under his arm to free up his hand. 'My parents are in the living room.'

Jason led him through the marble hall, moving with surprising agility. Mr and Mrs Wyler sat in the same place, closest to the door, where they'd been when Greene and Kennicott visited the day after the murder. No one was on the other two couches this time. Even though they were both tall, the couple looked small in the enormous room.

Jason stood at the edge of the sofa. With his strong upper body, standing looked to be a declaration of independence.

Mrs Wyler, who was seated closest to him, rose to greet Greene. 'Finally this nightmare will be over.' She didn't look as upset as he'd expected.

'Fifteen years is a long sentence for manslaughter,' Greene said. 'I have to warn you, she could be out on parole in five years.'

Mr Wyler rose slowly, his brow furrowed in anger. 'What a joke. Five years for murder.'

Victims' families always heard the lowest number, Greene thought.

Mrs Wyler shook her head. 'I called Terrance's lawyer, Anita Starr. She says that with this conviction, Samantha will never get near Simon. We can't bring my son back, but we can protect our grandson.'

Greene looked around the empty room. 'Where's Nathan?'

'At work, but he'll be in court tomorrow,' the father said. 'Was tied up with an employee issue. He said you'd understand.'

Greene remembered the red-haired cashier. Everyone has his own way of celebrating, he thought. Was that a knowing smirk on Mr Wyler's face?

'Jason has decided he won't come to court. The stress is too much for him.' Mrs Wyler reached out to touch her son.

Jason stiffened. 'It's not the stress, Mother,' he said. 'The place will be a zoo with all the press. I'm going to the cemetery. Say goodbye to my brother by myself.'

'That makes sense,' Greene said. 'A day like this is never easy. And it's good to go back to the grave of someone you loved without a crowd around.'

Jason looked upset. 'It's fifteen years, guaranteed?'

'The Crown will ask for eighteen. The defense

twelve. Judge Norville told both sides it'll be fifteen. The whole thing will take about an hour.'

'She's pleading guilty for sure?' Jason asked.

'According to her lawyer.' Greene turned to Mrs Wyler. 'How's your grandson doing?'

'Plays with his trains all the time. The social worker's been terrific. Recommended he stay at the nanny's place until Christmas. Keep him with all his friends. We're making the transition gradually. Jason picks him and the nanny up every Friday night and they're here all weekend. We love having him around.'

The zipper on Greene's old briefcase made a ticking sound as he opened it and pulled out some forms. 'If any of you would like to take the stand and talk about Terrance, you're more than welcome to do so. If you don't wish to speak, then you can write out what we call Victim Impact Statements. I brought a few that you can fill out.'

The three looked at one another. Often, testifying or writing out a statement could be cathartic for people, but everyone was different. You never knew who'd want to step forward.

'My brother can speak for me,' Jason said. His body was beginning to sag, but he looked determined to stay on his feet.

'I don't want to fill out any damn forms,' Mr Wyler said. 'Let Nathan talk for all of us.'

'I agree, dear.' Mrs Wyler put her hand to her

husband's cheek. It was, Greene realized, the first time he'd seen any physical contact between the two. She guided him down to the sofa and laid her head on his shoulder, the white stripe in her hair disappearing in the folds of his neck. 'I hope tomorrow is the last time in my life I ever have to see that woman.'

CHAPTER 41

The moment Margaret Kwon's plane landed on the runway she booted up her cell phone and scrolled through for the number she wanted.

'Ari Greene,' the detective said, answering her call.

'I need a dinner date tonight,' she said.

'Margaret?'

'Plane's pulling up to the terminal.'

'Why didn't you call before you took off? I would have picked you up.'

'Damn. I forgot how polite you Canadians are. I hear there's going to be a guilty plea tomorrow.'

Greene laughed. 'You have very good contacts. Tell the cab to take you to the House of Seoul, a Korean place on Bloor, west of Christie.'

'Don't tell me there's a Little Korea in Toronto too.'

'Eleven restaurants on one block,' he said.

When she arrived half an hour later, Greene was talking to the owner, a squat woman who was about four and a half feet tall. '*An nyeong ha seh yo*,' he said to Kwon when she walked in, giving her a kiss on the cheek.

'Hello to you, Detective,' Kwon said. 'That's the only thing I can say in Korean too.'

They sat on a bench seat. Paper-thin napkins were stuffed into a green cup on the table, along with cutlery – long-handled metal spoons and matching chopsticks, held in a plastic container. There were no tablecloths. Greene's was the only white face in the place.

Kwon kicked him under the table. 'You like it here because you're at least a foot taller than everyone else.'

As they ate Greene filled her in on the details of the expected guilty plea. He didn't seem very happy about it.

'Isn't a guilty plea what you wanted?'

'Let's see what happens.' He fixed her with his eyes. 'Any news about April Goodling?'

'Nothing. She's disappeared.'

'Want to go for a drive?' he asked.

'Sure. Where?'

'If it was my last time in New York, you'd probably take me to the Statue of Liberty. So I thought—'

'Niagara Falls? I've never been.'

The trip took about an hour. When they arrived at the deep gorge beside the Niagara River she heard a roar come up from over the edge. The windshield filled with specks of water and, after one last sweeping turn, the falls jumped into view.

The noise grew louder and Greene put on his wipers.

Greene drove to an empty parking lot near the edge, where there were RESTRICTED ACCESS signs all over the place. He parked at the curb closest to the water. Within seconds a security vehicle appeared out of the darkness.

An older man in ramrod shape jumped out. 'Evening, Detective Greene.'

'Gerald, this is Margaret Kwon, reporter from New York,' Greene said.

'Evening, ma'am,' Gerald said. 'Have a nice night.'

'Is there any place we could go where no one knows you?' she asked Greene.

'Probably not.'

They walked through the light mist. There was a wide stone walkway and a wrought-iron-and-stone fence along the edge. The dark water above the falls moved at a steady, powerful pace.

Greene led her to the spot where the sidewalk and railing turned. They were looking right across the top of the falls. The water was so calm a second before it hurtled down in a chaotic white froth, as if each drop had been taken by surprise, the floor under its placid world evaporating in a moment.

Most of all there was the sound. A primitive rumble from deep below. The spray on Kwon's face felt like a cleansing mist. She was transfixed by the black water. Flat and constant, hitting the edge, breaking up, turning to foam, disappearing from view. Over and over and over and over and over again. She lost track of time. Space. Drawn to something so unstoppable. The water. The movement. The darkness.

'Only the surface water from the Great Lakes comes over the falls. About three percent,' Greene said. It had been a long time since either of them had spoken. 'Some of the original glacial water is still there, down deep.'

Kwon hadn't expected to be so transfixed. She couldn't move. Couldn't talk.

'I went to Europe for the first time when I was thirty years old,' he said. 'Instead of flying, I took a freighter. We tooled up the St Lawrence River, and the land on both sides fell away, and the boat pushed out into the ocean. It was like I was being released.'

'The water never stops, does it?' she said.

'Never,' Greene said.

The spray was fogging up her glasses. 'I can see why you come here.'

'Sometimes I sit for hours,' he said.

She reached for his hand and he held it. They hadn't done this before. Part of her never wanted to let go. But they were both looking at the falls, at the point where the water always flowed over the edge.

CHAPTER 42

Good, good, Jennifer Raglan told herself, looking into the mirror in the female barristers' robing room. She clipped the white tabs onto the collar of her white shirt. Samantha Wyler was going to plead out today. Fifteen years for manslaughter. Great. Now Raglan could go back to small cases, work nine to five and be home for dinner, weekends her own.

Her daughter, Dana, was thrilled. At the beginning of September she'd joined an all-girls' hockey team. Either Jennifer or Gordon had to get home, toss Dana into the car, and battle through traffic to practices and games in far-flung suburbs. Because the trial hadn't ramped up yet, Raglan had been doing the bulk of the driving. Yesterday, when she was tied up preparing for the pretrial with Judge Norville, her husband had driven. Somehow Dana's neck guard had been left out of her hockey bag and she wasn't allowed on the ice.

This afternoon the team had a game after school, and since the Wyler case was going to be a guilty plea, Raglan was on driving duty.

Then there was Ari Greene. She'd been spending a lot of time with him during the last few months. He'd been steadfastly cool toward her – but never cold – sending her the message that the door between them was closed. The problem was, she was still rattling the handle. This morning she'd awakened at four o'clock, out of breath, the dream she'd had about his body so real she could almost touch it. This wasn't healthy.

Yep, all good, Raglan thought as she entered Norville's court. The big room was packed. The seats directly behind the Crown counsel table on the far right had been reserved for the Wyler family, with ropes across the rows, as if they were being saved for the groom's side at a wedding.

No special accommodation had been made for Samantha Wyler's family, Raglan noticed as she picked out the mother and brother, plus the librarian who'd been at the bail hearing. They all sat on the left-hand side.

It was always like this. Both sets of families staked out opposite sides of the courtroom and kept to themselves during long trials. Somehow they'd work out an unspoken choreography of avoidance, one group coming or going before the next, inhabiting different sides of the courtroom, finding their own nooks and crannies in the hallway during breaks, and sitting far from each other in the basement cafeteria.

Raglan took her place at the counsel table. Greene was already there, wearing a well-tailored suit. In the helter-skelter way people's lives criss-crossed in the courthouses of such a big city, she might not see him again for months. Maybe years. At the other counsel table, Ted DiPaulo sat beside Nancy Parish. A long red coat was draped over a third chair, which was empty. Raglan recognized it from a photo of Samantha Wyler in the morning paper, taken the day before when she was leaving court.

At Crown School they taught you to never make eye contact with the accused. Hey, I'm human, Raglan thought as she stole a quick glance back at the raised prisoner's box. Wyler wore a black dress and no jewelry. Her eyes were vacant, out of focus.

A staccato rap sounded on the oak door to the left of the judge's dais. It flung open, and a court officer in full uniform shouted, 'All rise.'

Raglan heard a rustle behind her as the specta-tors stood. Norville, her robes dancing, trotted up to her raised seat. Raglan got a glimpse of the judge's shoes. They were the same expensive Italian pumps Raglan had worn to the pretrial yesterday. Damn you, she thought.

'Oyez, oyez, oyez,' the court registrar said, rising from his spot directly below the judge. 'All persons having business before the Queen's Justice of the Superior Court of Justice, attend now and ye shall be heard. Long live the Queen. Please be seated.'

The courtroom settled. Norville instructed the registrar to read out the charge.

DiPaulo went to stand beside his client. It was obvious that he'd made every effort to have her look as ordinary as possible. Wyler stood, stooped over, as if invisible weights were bearing down on her shoulders.

Raglan looked away. She'd won. No need to humiliate the loser.

The registrar straightened his robe.

'Samantha Wyler, you stand charged that on or about the seventeenth day of August, in the city of Toronto, in the county of York, you did commit the offense of first-degree murder of Terrance Wyler. To the lesser and included offense of manslaughter, how do you plead, guilty or not guilty?'

The power of words always amazed Raglan. It all came down to one three-letter word to seal the fate of the accused. The difference between guilty and *not* guilty.

She waited to hear that magic word: 'guilty.' Instead, there was silence.

There's a natural rhythm of dialogue at a trial. Like a steady, underlying beat in a four-four piece of music. The mind grows conditioned to the sound. Expects the tune to continue. Silence felt wrong, like a radio station when the music goes blank and there's dead air.

Raglan looked back over her shoulder.

Wyler had her hands behind her back, her shoulders squeezed together, her lips tight. DiPaulo stood beside her. Tall and still.

'Ma'am,' the registrar said, his voice patient. 'Guilty or not guilty?'

A shiver raced through the courtroom. Raglan turned back and saw Norville pull off her brown court glasses.

'Guilty,' Wyler said in a voice so soft it sounded like a distant whisper carried on the wind.

Thank God, Raglan thought. I'll make it to Dana's hockey game.

CHAPTER 43

Ted DiPaulo's collar felt tight. He could sense Samantha Wyler next to him, wilting like an overextended flower.

Judge Norville fidgeted with her glasses. 'Mr DiPaulo, I assume that experienced counsel such as yourself has given your client the pre-plea warning.' Her voice was cutting.

'Your Honor, I have written instructions to proceed with this plea. I've told her that any final decision in this matter will be yours and yours alone.' He kept his voice resolute and calm. Judges always liked being reminded of their power.

'And did you understand those instructions, ma'am?' Norville was talking right to Wyler.

She gave a timid nod.

Norville shook her head at DiPaulo. 'Your client needs to say yes or no for the record. Gestures are not enough. Ma'am, you understand you are not obliged to plead guilty, that by doing so you give up your right to a trial and that I'm the one who will decide on your sentence?'

Wyler nodded and said yes in that same weak voice she'd used to say the word 'guilty.'

Norville exhaled loudly. 'Let the record show the defendant has both nodded her head and said yes.'

'Your Honor. Ms Wyler's never been in criminal court before.' Always try to find a positive in a negative, DiPaulo thought. Emphasize that Samantha was a first offender.

Norville turned to Raglan. 'Madam Crown, may I please hear the facts upon which this plea is based.'

Raglan read the agreed statement of facts. Even though DiPaulo and Wyler had rehearsed this in his office, hearing the words out loud in court sounded worse. More painful. More real.

'"Before she left the victim's house, the defendant went upstairs to Simon's bedroom,"' Raglan said, coming to the end. '"She told her son she wouldn't see him for a long time." That's the basis of the Crown's case, Your Honor.'

Raglan was good, DiPaulo thought, proud of his former student. Straightforward, serious. He'd heard she'd gotten back with her husband. She must be happy about this plea. Why would she want a big murder trial in her life right now?

DiPaulo and Wyler were the only people left standing in the large courtroom.

Norville took her time, perhaps chastened by DiPaulo's words about how tough this was for his inexperienced client. 'Ms Wyler.' She waited for Wyler to look at her. The courtroom was still. 'Are those facts correct?'

DiPaulo didn't dare look over. There are some doors you have to go through alone, a kind doctor had told him when his wife was near the end. You can walk right up to it with her, but you can't follow. That was how he felt now.

'Ms Wyler,' Norville said again. 'We only want the truth. Did you stab him?'

DiPaulo glanced at the judge. It was an excellent question. Simple and clear. Amazing, he thought, how all this could be reduced to four short words.

Beside him Wyler rocked back and forth.

'Ms Wyler,' Norville said, 'I know this is difficult, but I need an answer—'

'No,' Wyler said. 'I didn't stab him.' Her voice was surprisingly full. She threw her hands over her face and dropped back into the chair. DiPaulo heard a rising murmur from the courtroom.

'Silence,' Norville shouted. 'Registrar, strike the plea from the record. Members of the press, I'm issuing an immediate ban on publication of these proceedings. If one word of what happened here is reported you'll be in contempt. I'm going to call the trial coordinator immediately. I want this to start in January – February at the very latest.'

Norville flew off the dais, ran down the stairs, and yanked the door open before her deputy could get to it.

DiPaulo looked over at the Crown's table. Raglan's face was flushed red with fury.

At the defense table, Nancy Parish looked back at him, frowning.

Sitting by his side, Wyler sobbed uncontrollably. 'It's okay, Sam,' DiPaulo said, not believing a word of it. Inside his QC robes, for the first time in his career, he was shivering.

CHAPTER 44

There's a cold damp in Toronto in November, before the snow and blue skies of winter come. People's blood is not yet hardened to the lower temperatures and day by day the darkness creeps in. It was the month Daniel Kennicott hated the most, and on a gray day like this it was about the worst time to visit a graveyard.

At least he wasn't in uniform. He wore a long winter coat, corduroy pants, and a pair of Australian boots. He'd been waiting an hour on a park bench across from Terrance Wyler's grave and the chill had set in. It felt as if he'd be cold for months.

Coming here was his own idea, on his own time. He hadn't even mentioned it to Greene, who'd told him that Jason Wyler was going to visit his brother's grave this morning instead of going to court.

Kennicott had interviewed Jason at the Wyler house the day after the murder, and the man impressed him. His health was in steep decline, but Jason didn't complain about it. His mind was sharp. And he seemed determined to wring every-thing out of his final days. Now that the case was going to be resolved, meeting the man one last time felt like the decent thing to do.

Something drew Kennicott's attention to the road above the cemetery. A car had stopped and he heard a door open. Moments later Jason Wyler was standing against the metal railing right in the middle of the bridge, about where Kennicott had stood a few months ago to watch Terrance's funeral. Wyler seemed to be inspecting the concrete barrier and the two parallel metal rail-ings on top of it. Then he looked down at the road far below. It took a few minutes for him to raise his eyes to the grave. He noticed Kennicott, lifted one of his canes in greeting, and went back to his vehicle.

Kennicott rose from the cold bench to meet him when Wyler's car pulled up. The driver's door opened and he extracted himself with care.

'I heard you were going to be here this morning,' Kennicott said. 'I thought I'd pay my respects. Hope you don't mind.'

'It's good of you to come.'

Kennicott could see that Jason's decline had been dramatic since they'd met months before. 'Detective Greene taught me to put a bit of myself in every case. My brother was murdered too.'

'Have any survival tips?' Wyler asked.

292

'Wish I did,' Kennicott said. 'Sometimes I miss him more now than ever. Other times it seems hard to remember the silliest things. That's the most painful part.'

Wyler took a few slow steps to the bench and sat. His breath was labored. 'I've become much weaker.'

'I looked up SMA.' Kennicott sat beside him. 'Some people with it lead full lives.'

'Depends on your lucky number. I've got SMA three. If I had one or two, I'd be dead already. Folks with SMA four can go all the way. But the numbers aren't precise. It attacks the spinal column at its own damn pace.'

'I read that people with SMA tend to be very smart.'

'Brains not brawn. Technology helps. Computers, hand controls for the car. None of it's very romantic.' He pointed his cane over to his brother's grave. 'That was supposed to be my plot. Typical Terry, he got everything first.'

Kennicott got up. 'It sounds so trite. But if you ever want to talk . . .'

Wyler shook his head. 'It's not trite. It's good of you. Believe me, when I want to, I'll call you. Or Greene. He seems trustworthy.'

'That's Greene,' Kennicott said.

They shook hands. 'Did they ever catch the guy who murdered your brother?' Wyler asked.

Kennicott shook his head. 'No. That's why I'm a cop. At least you don't have to deal with never knowing who did it.'

'Yeah,' Wyler said. 'Lucky me.'

Kennicott gave him a final smile and walked away. He didn't look back. Jason deserved time alone with his brother.

CHAPTER 45

'What the fuck happened in there?' Nathan Wyler was pacing back and forth in Jennifer Raglan's small office. His parents were sitting on two cheap chairs. Raglan stood beside Ari Greene, a stricken look on her face.

During the ruckus in the courtroom after Samantha's aborted guilty plea, Greene had got Nathan out a side door fast. Greene knew that he would be upset, and he had to get him away from the press. Raglan came into the office soon after with the parents.

'Samantha didn't go through with the plea.' Raglan's voice lacked its usual confidence.

'Oh, really.' Wyler turned on her. 'You think I'm an idiot? Tell me something I don't know, like how the hell did this happen?'

Raglan's shoulders sagged. 'We can't make her plead guilty.'

'Sam gets to jerk my family around all over again. It's not bad enough that she killed my little brother. How much more do my parents have to take?'

'Nathan, keep your temper,' Wyler's mother said.

'Goddamn lucky Jason wasn't here.' Wyler's face was blood-red. 'Do you know what the stress is doing to his health? What do I tell him now?'

'I'm sorry,' Raglan said. Greene had never seen her look so shaken. 'We'll have to get ready for the trial.'

'Which won't be for months,' Wyler's father said. He was as mad as his son. 'Why can't we start next week?'

'Get this damn thing over with,' Nathan said.

Greene walked over to Nathan and put his hand on the big man's shoulder. 'In the world of criminal trials, a trial in late January is lightning speed,' he said. 'Let's go for a walk.'

On the broad steps outside the courthouse, the low November sky threatened rain. Wyler cupped his hands as he lit a cigarette. 'Sorry I blew my top in there with the Crown. This is eating everyone up.'

'I understand.'

'One brother dead, one brother dying.'

They walked through the big square in front of the new City Hall. The clock tower above Old City Hall across the street rang out. It was 12:45. This whole debacle had taken less than an hour. A swirl of falling leaves twisted and spun in a crosswind, dancing bits of red and yellow.

'There's something I should tell you if there's going to be a trial,' Wyler said.

296

Greene knew that people always held something back.

'Terry was only my half brother.'

'What?' Greene kept walking beside Wyler.

'My mother had an affair.' Wyler took a final puff and discarded his cigarette, not bothering to stomp it out. 'After Jason was born, she kept having miscarriages. Then Jason got sick, and the doctors couldn't guarantee that another child wouldn't get it. SMA's an inherited disease. Comes through the X chromosome. Means both my parents are carriers.'

Greene said nothing. It was best to listen.

'When Mom found herself pregnant, she told my father she'd had a special test and there'd be no problem. Which was bullshit, of course. But my father – all he knows about is fruit and vegetables.'

That explained why Mrs Wyler was so eager for a guilty plea, Greene thought. Bury her secret with her son.

Wyler dug out another cigarette. 'Think I have a temper? It's nothing compared to my old man. Mom lives in fear of him ever finding out.'

There's knowing with your head and knowing with your heart, Greene thought. He remembered his first meeting with the Wyler family. Mr Wyler saying, 'This was always my wife's greatest fear. To bury one of *her* sons.'

'How about your brother? Does he know?'

'Terry insisted that we both be told. We promised

my mother we'd never tell anyone if she was straight with us.'

'Do you know who the father is?'

Wyler looked at his unlit cigarette and stuffed it back in his pocket.

'Judge Summers had his boat moored next to us at the yacht club. One afternoon my mother asked him to take her out for a sail. When Terry was nineteen and his daughter Jo was fourteen, they had to tell them. Terry and Jo were furious. Didn't you ever wonder why Terry took off to the States for so long?'

My father did, Greene thought. They kept walking.

'This can't come out,' Wyler said.

Greene felt a fresh gust of wind and watched a bright red leaf buffeted here and there on its erratic descent to the ground. Chaos theory, he thought. He'd studied it in a physics class years ago. Trying to predict the unpredictable. That's what a trial was like. You could never tell where it would go or what damage it would cause.

CHAPTER 46

'Daniel?'

Daniel Kennicott had just walked into his flat and grabbed the ringing phone. It was the call he'd been praying he'd get today.

'Hi, Jo,' he said.

'I'm so relieved Samantha's pleading this morning, you can't imagine.'

'I think we all are.'

There was a silence. Made more awkward because they were on the phone. It had been three months since that Sunday night in August when they'd been together on the island. The heat. Floating together naked, touching. They hadn't made love, but in a way it was more intimate.

'How've you been?' he asked.

'To tell the truth, not great,' she said. 'You?'

'Greene's been working me night and day.'

'It's probably good for you.'

He laughed, but it felt forced. Was this just a social chat? A goodbye Charlie phone call? 'Probably,' he said.

'I came into the office, but they gave me the day off.' She sounded guarded.

299

'I'm off shift too.' There was no need to tell her that he'd met Jason Wyler at the cemetery.

'Can we go for coffee?'

'Sure,' he said. 'How about the Dip. It's just down the street from my place.'

The Dip was the Café Diplomatico, a neighborhood tradition in Little Italy for more than forty years. He hurried over and took a private table in the corner. Summers came in a few minutes later. She looked exhausted. As usual, her hair was up, but it was flat, as if even it were tired. They gave each other a tentative hug.

The waitress came and they both ordered coffees. Turned out they both took it black. When they were alone, Summers looked him straight in the eye and smirked.

'Looks like I'm the one who didn't call this time.'

'I figured it out. I was your alibi and you had to preserve that.'

She nodded. 'There's nothing I would do to jeopardize this case in any way. Ted DiPaulo's a brilliant lawyer. Give him an inch and . . .'

Kennicott's cell phone rang. He would have ignored it, except it was Greene's special ring. He put his hand up.

'Jo, sorry this is so rude. But it's Greene.'

'Great.' She lifted her coffee cup, inviting him to toast. He clinked her cup with his. 'It must be over.'

'Hello, Detective,' he said into the phone.

'She didn't plead,' Greene said.

'What?' Kennicott exclaimed, the word coming out louder than he intended. Across the table, Summers tensed.

'She wouldn't admit the facts. Said she didn't stab him. Norville's expediting the trial. We're on for January thirty-first. I have a few things to do. Meet me at the office in half an hour.'

This was classic Greene. No editorializing. Back to business.

Kennicott hung up and looked at Summers. She'd already guessed. 'Samantha didn't plead, right?'

'Said she didn't stab him.'

'My God, Daniel,' she said. 'What if she didn't do it?'

Good for you, Jo, Kennicott thought. All he'd been thinking was that it would be at least another three months until he could see her.

'Trial's set for the end of January. Greene wants me to get to the office.'

She looked ashen. 'Daniel. Before I disappear on you again, I have to tell you something. Take this as a measure of my trust in you.'

He reached across the table and took her hand. It was cold as a stone.

'You think I was seeing Terry, don't you?'

He shrugged. 'It's none of my business.'

She zeroed in on him. 'But that's what you think. Isn't it?'

Summers was a damn good cross-examiner. He thought of saying, 'That story you told the police about lunches and one dinner a year was unbelievable. The only reason for you even mentioning the dinner was because you knew I'd seen you two together that night before Christmas.' Instead, he shrugged. 'I read your statement to the police. Your answers about you and Terrance were evasive.'

'I know,' she said. 'I didn't want anyone to know. Terry was my brother.'

'Your what?'

'Half brother. His mother. My dad.'

Kennicott was so stunned he didn't know what to say.

'Raglan knows. It's not relevant to the case. If this gets out it will destroy a lot of lives. I'll do anything, even not see you, to make sure this case doesn't go off the rails.'

Kennicott's mind was running off in all directions. Jo's brother was murdered, like his. The trial was starting at the end of January. Samantha said she didn't stab Terrance. If it wasn't Samantha, who? 'Did Mr Wyler know about this?'

'I don't think so. He's a dangerous man. It would be terrible if he found out. But I don't trust her either.'

'Mrs Wyler?'

'Totally two-faced. Puts on a big show about caring so much for Jason. But it's all about her all the time. What's her alibi?'

Kennicott had worked so hard on the file he practically had it memorized. 'Typical Sunday-night

302

alibi. Home asleep. The family had dinner at Terrance's house. Left about eleven o'clock. You don't think she'd kill her own son, do you?'

'If she thought her secret was in jeopardy, I don't know what she'd do. The woman seduced my father to get what she wanted.'

Kennicott was still holding Summers's hand. Now it was warm.

'When does Greene need you in the office?' she asked.

'Half an hour,' he said.

'You and me,' she said. 'We have the world's shittiest timing.'

She squeezed his hand and they both laughed.

CHAPTER 47

'We have to get out of here,' Ted DiPaulo said to Samantha Wyler. She'd been curled up in her chair in the prisoner's box, hands over her face, for about half an hour. The court had cleared out, except for the officer by the door, who was getting impatient.

'Okay.' She looked up at him and took a deep breath. 'Let's go.'

'The second we walk out that door the press will be all over us.'

'But the judge said they couldn't publish anything.'

'This isn't about what was said in here,' Nancy Parish said. 'They want a picture of you walking outside the courthouse.'

Wyler shook her head. 'It's disgusting.'

'They call it the perp walk,' DiPaulo said.

'That's grotesque. What can we do?'

'They can't take your picture inside the court-house.' DiPaulo pointed to Wyler's red coat on the chair by the counsel table. He had insisted that she wear it yesterday when she waited for him during the judicial pretrial and again today. 'Put that on.'

Wyler stepped down from the prisoner's box, retrieved her coat, and slung it over her arm.

'No,' DiPaulo said. 'Wear it.'

She slipped it on. Her hands were shaking.

The moment the officer opened the courtroom door, they were set upon by a throng of reporters. 'Keep walking,' DiPaulo told Wyler as people pressed in on all sides, their questions coming fast and furious. 'How are you feeling, Samantha?' 'What made you change your mind?' 'What happened to the guilty plea?'

'My client and I have no comment at this time.' DiPaulo used his size to push his way through.

The crowd followed them, coming within inches of their faces. DiPaulo had been in many press scrums like this. Reporters had no regard for normal social distance. They shoved microphones and cameras right up against your nose.

'Ted, if you're not going to talk, which door you coming out?'

It was Zachery Stone, the aggressive little reporter for the *Toronto Sun* who looked like a cross between Danny DeVito and a Scottish terrier. He'd pounded the crime beat for the city's only tabloid for more than twenty years.

'Can't tell you.' DiPaulo kept moving. They were almost at the door to the barristers' lounge, their safe haven where no reporters were allowed.

'Come on,' Stone said. 'This much press, every door's covered. We're going to get the shot.

Nothing's worse than a perp walk when you're running away. Make her look guilty as hell.'

DiPaulo put his hand on the door. Stone had wormed his way right in under his shoulder. 'Okay, Zac,' he whispered. He checked his watch and raised his voice. 'Everyone, I need a cup of coffee.'

'Which door?' a chorus asked.

'The elevator that goes down from here. The barristers' exit,' DiPaulo said. 'I'll be there in twenty minutes.'

The reporters rushed away, moving as one, tapping on their BlackBerrys to colleagues covering the outside of the building.

DiPaulo led Samantha and Parish into the lounge.

'I guess you had no choice but to tell them,' Parish said after they sat down on a long couch.

DiPaulo smiled at her. He turned to Wyler. 'Sam, take your coat off and give it to Nancy, please.' He pulled a copy of *The Globe and Mail* from his briefcase and tossed it to Parish. 'You'll need this. And hand your briefcase over to Sam.'

As they spoke, a thin black woman in legal robes approached. DiPaulo stood to greet her. 'Ms Delacroix, meet Ms Wyler and my partner, Nancy Parish.'

Parish and Wyler looked up at him, confused. He chuckled. 'Sam, Ms Delacroix will bring both of you into the women's robing room, where you'll put on Nancy's robes.'

They sat in a tight circle as DiPaulo explained

his plan. Wyler and Delacroix, both dressed in robes and carrying briefcases, would take the lawyers' elevator up one floor to the law library, walk around to the main set of elevators, and go directly to the basement. A tunnel ran between the courthouse and Osgoode Hall, the historic building that housed the main law library and the Court of Appeal. Once there, Delacroix would call DiPaulo on her cell phone and tell him when the coast was clear. DiPaulo and Parish – who'd be wearing Wyler's long red coat – would take the elevator down to the barristers' exit. They'd step into the glassed-in rotunda, where all the reporters could see them.

Parish picked up the newspaper. 'Let me guess. I'll have my face buried in this.'

'Ms Delacroix, you'll take my client to a cab on University Avenue that's already waiting for you.' DiPaulo looked up at the three women and smiled. 'Not bad?'

Parish laughed. 'This has been a tough day. We deserve some fun.'

Delacroix and Wyler left, and DiPaulo got a cup of coffee.

'The press will be pissed that you lied to them,' Parish said when she returned from the robing room in street clothes and reached for Wyler's coat.

'Ah, ah, ah. I didn't lie. I told them that *I'd* be down in twenty minutes. I never said where Samantha would be.'

'Smooth. But how can you still represent her if she told you she was guilty?'

DiPaulo took a sip. The coffee was watery, and was too hot to boot. 'Samantha Wyler never told me she was guilty. Just the opposite. At our first meeting she told me she didn't do it. All I asked her, in your presence, was for instructions from her to enter a plea based on a set of facts. I never asked her if those facts were true.'

Parish laughed. 'How many lawyers can dance on the head of a pin?'

'As many as it takes to win.' He took another sip and looked at his watch again. It had been twelve minutes since Delacroix and Wyler left. His cell phone rang.

'There's only one reporter,' Delacroix said. 'She looks Asian.'

'Good. I'll call you when we're downstairs. That should draw her up this way. Don't move yet.' He turned to Parish. 'Shall we, *Ms Wyler*?'

They took the elevator down and walked into the glassed-in rotunda. Parish, in the red coat, newspaper opened and covering her face, was beside him. Lightbulbs started flashing.

'Now we stop,' DiPaulo said. 'The press will think you're getting nervous. Lean your head against me and I'll put my arm around you.'

DiPaulo looked over at University Avenue. After a few seconds he saw a dark-haired woman running up the road. He pushed a preset number on his phone. 'I see the reporter. Go fast and keep your phone on,' he told Delacroix.

He gave the crowd on the other side of the glass

a 'wait a second' gesture. Through the phone he heard the sound of steps on stones, feet running, air rustling past, then a door opening, metallic, and Delacroix's voice: 'Three ninety Bay, please. That's Bay and Queen, across from Old City Hall.'

He heard an East Indian-accented male voice say, 'Mr DiPaulo already gave me the address.' There was the sound of a car engine starting up and moving.

'Mr DiPaulo,' Delacroix said. 'We're clear.'

'Great work.' He closed his phone with a snap.

'Ready?' Parish asked from behind her newspaper.

'Time to meet the press.'

They walked through the barrier and opened the door. Reporters started yelling. More flashbulbs. DiPaulo took the newspaper out of Parish's hands.

The reporters gasped. 'Fuck.' 'Shit, cover the other exits.' 'I don't believe it,' he heard them say.

'Ted, you're making me look bad,' Zachery Stone said.

'Sorry, old friend. I said *I'd* be out in twenty minutes.' He held up his watch. 'I'm right on time.'

DiPaulo had a second cab waiting for them on University Avenue. When they'd shut the door, Parish turned to him. 'Counsel, ready for cross-examination?'

'Certainly.' DiPaulo tried to sound innocent.

'You planned this a few days ago, didn't you? Delacroix. The red coat. Two cabs on standby.'

Through the car window, DiPaulo watched the crowd of reporters recede. 'Perhaps.'

'You didn't think she'd go through with the plea, did you?'

He grinned. 'I pushed Samantha as far as I could. In this job you always have to ride more than one horse.'

The cab rumbled past city workers dismantling the flower displays that had adorned the broad avenue throughout the summer and fall. The street felt barren.

'I bet you're happy. You love trials.'

'I certainly do,' DiPaulo said as they bumped along on old shock absorbers. 'But only if I win.'

CHAPTER 48

'Come in, Detective, please come in,' the Honorable Justice Johnathan Summers, head judge of the Old City Hall Provincial Court, said. He jumped up from his red leather chair, slipped around his wide wooden desk, his black judicial robes swirling behind him, and pulled his office door all the way open for Ari Greene.

Greene had been in the big corner office many times and it always struck him that the judge's chambers were as over-the-top as his personality. A boisterous, bossy man, he ran his courtroom with a sternness that rivaled Captain Ahab. Summers loved to brag about his two great passions, on display in equal measure throughout the room: hockey and sailing.

Summers had been a minor hockey star when he went to Cornell, and his old number 9 sweater with a big *C* sewn in over the left breast was in a glass frame behind his desk. It was surrounded by signed photos of His Honor with well-known players for the Toronto Maple Leafs. A collection of signed hockey sticks dominated a corner of the office.

Before going to college, the judge had spent five years in the navy, and some people felt he'd never left the ship. His nautical obsession was reflected in the photos and drawings of boats and frigates that covered almost every inch of remaining wall space.

Most people assumed Summers was born wealthy, but Greene knew it wasn't true. The judge's father died overseas during the war, when his mother was pregnant with him, and Summers went into the navy ostensibly to pay his way through school. Greene suspected it was also to honor, and in some sense replace, the father he never knew.

'Sorry to disturb Your Honor on such short notice during lunch,' Greene said, returning the judge's powerful handshake.

'I hardly ever bother to eat during the day anymore,' Summers said. 'Get a yogurt or something, unless Jo happens to be free. There's a quiet little Thai restaurant up on Dundas where she likes to go.'

There were two high-backed chairs facing the judge's desk, and Summers motioned Greene to one while he shut the door.

'What can I do for you?' Summers took the other chair. Greene had wondered if he'd sit behind his desk. The fact that he didn't made Greene certain that the judge knew what this was about.

'As I think you are aware, I'm the officer in charge of the Terrance Wyler murder case,' Greene said.

Summers had a ruddy, full face that projected a confidence many people found intimidating. Despite the judge's bluster, Greene had seen the man bend over backward to ensure that trials held before him were conducted fairly, and he was surprisingly sympathetic when it came to sentencing. Especially first offenders. Some Crowns had even nicknamed some of his judgments 'A Summers Second Chance.'

He met Greene's eyes and leaned forward. 'I understood there would be a plea in that matter. Today, wasn't it?'

'I've just come from High Court.' The Superior Court at 361 University Avenue was across the street. Greene knew that the news wouldn't have reached Summers's ears yet. 'The defendant changed her mind and didn't go through with the plea. Judge Norville's not happy.'

Summers slumped back in the chair and put a hand over his eyes. 'I see.' His normally powerful voice was weak.

Greene looked away. Among Summers's sailing photos was a picture of the judge on the deck of a big boat, hoisting a two-handled trophy in the air amidst a crowd of smiling people. Hoisting the other handle was a young woman with a mane of blond hair and Summers's big-toothed smile. His daughter, Jo.

Outside the Old City Hall clock tower rang.

'You know, Detective,' Summers said when the ringing died down, 'in this job I see people at their worst. Every day. Oh sure, about twenty percent of them are hard-core bad apples, but most are quite normal. They go to work, shop, cook, raise their kids, shovel their sidewalks after a snowstorm. And they make mistakes.'

Greene sat still and waited for Summers to keep talking. But the man was silent.

'Nathan Wyler talked to me after what happened in court this morning,' Greene said.

'And that's why you're here, as you should be.' Summers lumbered up from his seat, strode slowly behind his desk, pulled out a bottom drawer, and handed a folder over to Greene. 'You're going to want to see this.'

Inside was a plane ticket for Justice Johnathan Summers and Mrs Dorothy Summers on Porter Airlines, the airport located on the Toronto Islands, dated August 15, Toronto to Ottawa, returning August 18. Next was a receipt from the Carlton Hotel in Ottawa for three nights, August 15, 16, and 17. Finally, there was a program titled 'National Provincial Court Judges Conference.' Greene opened it.

'I was the special guest speaker on the Sunday night,' Summers said. 'You need to know if I have an alibi. About sixty judges from across the country could vouch for me if it came to that.'

'I'll have to confirm all this, you realize,' Greene said.

'You're investigating a murder. I'm not asking for any special consideration.' Summers put his hands down on the desk and braced himself, teetering, unsure whether he should sit or not. 'As you can see from the documents, my wife was with me in Ottawa.'

'In every murder investigation I find out people's secrets,' Greene said. 'It's always a judgment call – what's relevant to an investigation and what isn't. But unless I absolutely have to, I won't damage people.'

Summers sat. 'After all these years on the bench, I've come to think we all have three lives. Our public life, our private life, and our secret life. We all have secrets. But when a crime like this happens all bets are off.'

Greene closed up the program and put it back into the folder. He knew Summers needed to talk.

'Funny thing is, I hear so much about people having affairs that go on for years,' the judge said. 'For me this was the one and only time. A sunny afternoon. A beautiful woman. I knew what she wanted. A child without that horrible disease.' He bit at a fingernail. 'I've probably sailed Lake Ontario a thousand times. That day the lake was calmer than I've ever seen it.'

Greene opened his briefcase with its noisy zipper and slipped the folder inside.

'The worst part was telling Jo and Terry. They were so young. She was only fourteen. I had to face that I'd disappointed my daughter. Burdened her with this secret. It would kill my wife if she found out. Jo was mad at me for a long time.

315

Moved to Central America for a few years. Finally came back and went to law school. When she became a Crown Attorney and was in court every day, I felt like I'd gotten her back. Then this happens.'

'Nathan just told me about this today. Last night, when I informed Mr and Mrs Wyler about the deal that had been worked out I expected they'd be upset,' Greene said. 'Most families want the maximum sentence. But they were happy to have this over with, especially Mrs Wyler. Now I understand why.'

'I'll tell you straight. That husband of hers isn't too bright or he would have figured this out. He's a violent man with a hell of a temper. She has good reason to be afraid.'

Greene stood up. 'I'll treat you as I would every potential suspect. That includes not causing any collateral damage that I don't have to.'

'In my dark days, I like to think that this made me a better judge.' Summers pulled his robes forward over his broad shoulders. 'I know I drive everyone hard in my court. Can't stand lawyers who don't do the best possible job. Every one of those accused people who come before me – you have to see who they really are, look past the mistakes they've made.'

Greene tucked his open briefcase under his arm and stood.

'I tried not to think of Terrance as my son. Felt it wasn't fair to anyone.' Summers looked over at the photo on the wall of himself and his daughter with the trophy.

Greene scanned the sea of faces in the background and this time he picked out Terrance Wyler, over to the side near Jo.

'But he was my son,' Summers said. 'And now he's gone.'

Greene let himself out of the door, closing it gently. Lunch break at a courthouse is always strangely quiet. The hallways empty out, like a school at recess. He sat down on a hard wooden bench and pulled the zipper on his briefcase. Tick, tick, tick, until it closed. Then he shut his eyes to take in the silence.

PART IV

JANUARY

CHAPTER 49

'You don't think I should let her testify, do you?' Ted DiPaulo asked Nancy Parish.

It was already noon on Sunday. The trial was starting in less than twenty-four hours and precious time seemed to be slipping away. They'd spent the weekend in the office board-room, which had been turned into their war room for the duration. Boxes and file folders were every-where.

'Is there ever a right answer?' Parish asked back.

To call your client to testify or not to call your client to testify – it was the Hamlet-like dilemma for criminal lawyers.

Every Canadian defense lawyer was haunted by the David Milgaard case. Back in 1969 Milgaard was convicted of the brutal rape and murder of a young nurse in Saskatoon, Saskatchewan. For twenty-three years while he was in jail, Milgaard maintained his innocence. He was vindicated when DNA evidence linked Larry Fisher, a known serial rapist who'd been in the city at the same time, to the crime. The ironic twist: Milgaard never testified at his own trial.

If Samantha Wyler never took the stand, she might suffer the same fate. And yet there were countless murder trials in which, as the saying goes, the defendants talked themselves into convictions.

'You can advise and cajole your clients, but ultimately, it has to be their decision,' DiPaulo said. He picked up a pad of paper. The title 'To Do List' was on the top of the page, which was filled with notes. 'She's determined to testify. I think the jury's going to hate her. A few days from now, I need you to do a mock cross-examination. See how she holds up.'

'Okay, but I want to cross-examine you first.'

'Go right ahead.'

'Mr DiPaulo, you have more then twenty-five years of experience as a criminal lawyer, both as a Crown Attorney and a defense counsel, correct?'

'Twenty-six years, in fact.'

'And rule number one for you is that a good defense lawyer should never believe everything his client tells him. Correct?'

'Correct.'

'And never, ever let yourself believe your client's innocent. Because it could blind your judgment. Correct?'

'Do I have to answer that?'

She pointed an accusing finger at him. 'In the case of Samantha Wyler, I suggest you've broken your own golden rule. You now believe she's not guilty.'

The outside doorbell rang. 'Saved by the bell.' DiPaulo grinned at his partner. 'Guess who's here?'

Samantha was in the reception room with a thick file in her hand. She looked excited. Clients were often strangely euphoric before their cases began, glad that their months of pretrial purgatory were ending.

She lifted the file. 'I think I've found something.'

'Come on into the boardroom,' he said, leading her back down the hall.

Wyler was the most involved client DiPaulo had ever had. Terrance had called her a control freak in his family law affidavits, and DiPaulo could see why. She insisted on seeing every piece of disclosure, reading each witness statement, and combing over all the forensic reports.

'I've been going through the autopsy.' She took a seat in the crowded boardroom.

'Dr Burns,' DiPaulo said, naming the pathologist.

'He says the fatal wound was the small cut to the neck,' Wyler said.

'Wound number two.' DiPaulo wanted Sam to know he was totally up on the file. 'Nicked the carotid artery. He would have bled out fast. Burns

323

estimates four minutes. I checked with two doctors I use as backup. Both thought that was about right.'

'Okay,' Wyler said, opening her file. 'Look at this.'

CHAPTER 50

Jennifer Raglan gazed at the seven evidence boxes stacked in the corner of her windowless office. The words R. V. WYLER were written on the side of each one in thick black letters. The consensus among her fellow prosecutors was that this was such an open-and-shut case that even a first-year Crown Attorney could win it hands down.

Crown Attorneys, of course, were not supposed to win or lose trials. They had a higher calling – to serve the general public interest, ensure that justice was done. This lofty goal was never easy to reconcile in an office filled with ultracompetitive type A personalities.

That's what made this case a nightmare. Win, and you'd get no credit. But God forbid if you weren't victorious – and with a jury, you never knew – she could imagine the whispers behind her back: 'Jennifer's rusty being out of court so long.' 'Think this thing with her husband distracted her?'

The reality was that for any murder trial, even a so-called easy case, you never had enough time to prepare. In November, Ralph Armitage told her to take two months for prep time – meaning she was supposed to be free of other duties. She scrawled a sign on a blank sheet of paper and taped it to the door of her office. It read DO NOT DISTURB – LAWYER TRYING TO THINK.

Within hours the sheet was filled with witty written comments by her colleagues about the dangers of advocates using their brains. By the second day, Crowns were drifting in without knocking to ask about a difficult judge, a complicated case, a pain-in-the-ass defense lawyer. Or, even worse, to register complaints about Armitage, accompanied by sighs of how wonderful it had been 'when you were in charge, Jennifer.' Finally, she insisted that they put a lock on her door.

It didn't help. The downtown office was in a perpetual state of siege. Most afternoons she was interrupted by all-hands-on-deck emergency calls that required the attention of every available Crown to run to this or that court. Midway through the third week, she moved home.

Overnight, endless hours stretched before her without interruption. She could accomplish twice as much in half the time. Best of all, this put an end to the daily e-mail battles with Gordon about who would get to the after-school program by six to pick up Dana or face the dollar-a-minute wrath of the underpaid staff who worked there.

She began getting Dana before six – at five, even four-thirty. Instead of stuffing her daughter into the car, they'd walk home hand in hand, tossing snowballs, stopping at her favorite café to share a butter tart and hot chocolate.

Today was Sunday, and with the trial set to begin the next morning, she'd been in the office all day. It meant she'd had to miss taking Dana to her hockey practice. But there was no way around it, especially because after months of negotiations, she was finally going to interview her most troublesome witness, Brandon Legacy, the eighteen-year-old who lived next door to Terrance Wyler.

It was obvious to Raglan and Greene that the reticent teenager had been having an affair with his former neighbor, thirty-five-year-old Samantha Wyler. His parents had done everything in their power to protect him. They hired a top lawyer, Canton Carmichael, who advised them that young Brandon had no legal obligation to speak with the police or the Crown. Which was true. When Legacy refused to talk, Raglan and Greene counterpunched. They began what was known in the trade as the witness dance.

Greene sent a police officer in full uniform to serve Legacy with a subpoena during lunchtime at his school. He was required by law to appear in Superior Court on the first trial date and remain there until he was called as a witness.

Predictably, Carmichael called Raglan to complain about the high-handed police tactics. 'You could have my client sitting in that courthouse for weeks,' the lawyer said.

'Weeks. Could be a few months,' Raglan said. 'You can never tell with a murder trial.'

'Young Brandon's in grade twelve. Doing the "victory lap," taking an extra year to get out of high school. His midterm exams are crucial. They start the second week of February.'

'If your client spoke to us, I could let him know well in advance when he'll be called. Schedule him in on a day when he doesn't have an exam. Glad to do it. But since we don't know what he's going to say, how can I predict when I'll need him?'

Carmichael laughed. The man was smart enough to know when he'd hit a brick wall. 'Jennifer, when did you become such a hard-ass?'

'Actually, I think you can credit Detective Greene with this idea. Why don't you have a word with young Brandon's folks.'

'I'll do that. Tell Greene I say touché.'

The parents eventually realized they were stuck with the Crown, just as Raglan was stuck with their son. As the days ticked down before the trial, negotiations with Carmichael intensified. Greene had Kennicott look at Legacy's computer to confirm the kid was playing video games all night. Legacy consented to a DNA swab, and forensics confirmed there wasn't a spec of his DNA in the Wyler house. He took a polygraph test and passed it without a hitch.

Raglan watched the gangly teenager amble into the boardroom. 'Hi, Brandon.' It was freezing cold outside, but all he wore was a thin black T-shirt, a ripped pair of flared jeans and running shoes with holes in them.

'Yeah, hi,' he said, his hair down over his face.

'Hello, Ms Raglan.' Canton Carmichael was an elegant black man, always beautifully dressed in hand-tailored suits, even on a Sunday afternoon, who often joked that he was the first to crack the white ceiling. It was true. Color had been no barrier to his representing rich and powerful defendants from every community in the city – wealthy whites included.

As part of the agreement they'd worked out, Carmichael would sit in on the interview. Detective Greene, who'd brought them into the office, would also be present. After everyone was seated, Raglan jumped right in.

'Brandon,' she said. 'Thanks to your cooperation with this investigation – showing us your computer, the DNA test, and the polygraph – at this time you're not a suspect. Given that, we've come to an agreement with your lawyer that the statement you make today is involuntary. That means anything you say cannot be used against you, should you ever be brought to trial. The exception is perjury. You lie to us, all bets are off. That clear?'

Legacy brushed his hair from his forehead, revealing a few red pimples. He turned to his lawyer and the two of them whispered together.

'Yeah,' the boy said, looking both contemptuous and bored at the same time.

Raglan's oldest son was two years younger than Legacy. In the last six months he'd grown half a foot, and recently there'd been bits of facial hair and a few pimples. There was a childishness about him. He'd still sometimes ask her to slip into his bed at night so he could snuggle up. But it was fading fast. Looking at the arrogant teenager across the table, Raglan thought, There's the future, in all its sweaty glory.

'Once you're on the stand and sworn in as a witness,' Raglan said, 'I'll ask you a few questions about yourself. Your age, where you go to school, what subjects you're studying, et cetera. To get you warmed up and give the jury some background.'

'Uh-huh,' Legacy said.

'There's no need to look at the judge or the jury. Look at me, or at the defense counsel when he's asking questions.'

'Uh-huh.'

'And in court, no uh-huhs. You need to answer yes or no. Okay?'

'Yeah.'

'Then I'm going to ask you how you met the Wylers.'

'They were neighbors. Moved in when I was a kid. I used to shovel their driveway sometimes. When I got older they asked me to babysit Simon.'

'How often did you do that?'

'Lots. Mrs Wyler was always at work. Mr Wyler liked to sail all the time.'

'How'd you get along with Simon?'

'He's a nice kid. Sometimes I played his dad's piano for him, so he called me Piano Man.'

'I understand the Wylers separated a year ago.'

'Yeah. Sam – I mean Mrs Wyler – moved out.'

Raglan took a look over at Greene. Carmichael moved forward in his chair.

'And did you continue to see Ms Wyler?'

'Uh-huh. We were like friends.'

'That's as far as my client is going on this line of questions,' Carmichael said.

'Maybe for now. But in court the defense is going to delve into this.'

'And you'll object, won't you?' Carmichael asked.

'On what grounds?' Raglan asked.

'How is it relevant?'

'If he was having an affair with Samantha Wyler and her husband is found dead next door, your client's in defense counsel's line of fire. Much better if I get this evidence out in chief and not leave him exposed on cross-examination. I'm not going to look like an idiot in front of the jury, objecting to things and being overruled.'

Legacy had his head down and was playing with his hair. 'It wasn't, like, really like that.'

'Brandon, don't answer these questions,' Carmichael said.

'Mostly we really were friends,' Legacy said.

For the first time since the interview began, the teenager looked at Raglan. She had a vision of him ten years from now – skin cleared of pimples, hair cut, neat clothes. He'd be a real winner, a lovely young man, except for this dark cloud forever in his past.

'Tell me about the night of the murder,' she said. Best to take what she could get right now. And perhaps Carmichael was right. If the defense really tried to point to this kid and claim he was the murderer, they'd look ridiculous. Brandon Legacy was an overgrown boy. She'd make sure the jury saw that.

'My parents were up north at the cottage. I had a job as a lifeguard at a city pool. Sam came over.'

'How did she get to your house?'

'I don't know. She doesn't drive. She likes to walk. Her apartment's about ten blocks away.'

Raglan caught Carmichael's eye. Sounded like Brandon was familiar with Samantha's place. 'When did she arrive?'

'Before ten, I know that. At ten we watched a repeat of *The Amazing Race*. It's her favorite show. This one was in Moscow.'

'That went until when?'

'Uh. Eleven. Show's an hour. We hung out for a while and she left.'

'Was that unusual?'

Legacy looked over at his lawyer. 'Well, kind of, yeah. Like sometimes she stayed, you know. Late.' The boy's voice was a whisper.

'Did you two have anything to drink?' Raglan asked.

He shook his head. Raglan didn't bother telling him he had to say yes or no.

'Any illegal drugs?'

He shook his head again.

'Did you do anything else?'

Legacy fidgeted and picked at his fingernails. 'We, you know. Played around.' He said it as if sleeping with a woman twice his age were nothing more than having a glass of milk. How long, Raglan thought, until her son was so casual about sex? 'Then she had to go.'

'Why?'

'She got an e-mail on her BlackBerry from Terry. I mean Mr Wyler.' Legacy's head slumped down. No longer a sloppy teenager, but a person who'd been at the edge of tragedy.

'Did you see the e-mail?'

'No.'

'Did she tell you about it?'

'Yeah.'

'What did she say?'

Legacy looked over at his lawyer. Carmichael nodded.

'She said, "That fuckhead. After all he's put me through, now he's going to accept my offer. He wants me to go over there to settle this, just the two of us." I said, "Why don't you?" She said, "I know how to settle this once and for all." Then she left.'

That's how I'll end my closing jury address, Raglan thought: ' "I know how to settle this once and for all." And that, ladies and gentlemen of the jury, is exactly what Samantha Wyler did.'

'What'd you do?'

'Went online and played Flight Simulator for a few hours. Checked my Facebook. I'd worked all day at the pool and it was hot. I was tired so I slept in late.'

It was almost four o'clock by the time they finished. After everyone shook hands, Carmichael checked his expensive watch and put his arm around Legacy.

'Time to get young Brandon home so he can study for his mathematics examination tomorrow.' Carmichael gave them an exaggerated wink over his client's shoulder before he slipped out the door.

Raglan was going to call Brandon Legacy to the witness stand. The jury wouldn't like him. But he'd make them despise Samantha Wyler.

CHAPTER 51

'Juror look upon the accused, accused look upon the juror,' the registrar called out into the packed courtroom. It was near the end of the first day of the trial and Ted DiPaulo was tired. Almost six o'clock, well past the usual end of the court day at four-thirty. They'd spent all morning and a long afternoon picking the jury and eleven had been chosen. With one more to go, Judge Norville was determined to finish selection before she adjourned the court.

DiPaulo watched the potential twelfth juror take her place on the witness stand.

'Juror look upon the accused, accused look upon the juror.' The same words were said to potential jurors at every trial, forcing them to make eye contact with the defendant, the man or woman they were sworn to pass judgment on.

Samantha Wyler stood at DiPaulo's side behind the counsel table. Judge Norville had agreed that she didn't have to remain in the prisoner's box during the trial. DiPaulo watched Samantha turn toward the witness, her deep brown eyes flat, emotionless.

The rules of jury selection in Canada allowed both the defense and the Crown to have twenty peremptory challenges, people they could refuse to allow on the jury without a word of explanation. With eleven jurors picked – seven women and four men – DiPaulo was in good shape. He'd only used up seventeen of his challenges. Jennifer Raglan, the Crown, had gone through nineteen.

Unlike in the United States, where jurors could be examined at length by counsel, no questions of substance were allowed. All that DiPaulo and Raglan had to go on were a potential juror's name, age, and occupation.

At the beginning of the proceedings DiPaulo asked Norville for permission to make some further inquiries when people gave generic job descriptions. The judge grudgingly agreed, and this led to a humorous moment before the lunch break when a middle-aged woman was called to the witness stand.

'If I may, Your Honor,' DiPaulo said. 'Ms Platt lists her occupation as operator. I'd like to inquire where she works.'

Norville shook her head. 'I don't see the point, but go ahead. Keep it short.'

'Ms Platt, where are you an operator?' DiPaulo asked.

Platt was a white woman with a stiff-set jaw. Her face flushed red. 'The marine unit of the Toronto Police Service,' she said. Everyone in the crowded courtroom laughed, breaking the tension that had built up during the long morning. Even Norville smiled.

Lawyers had all sorts of theories about how to pick jurors: Asians are law-and-order types, women tend to be less sympathetic to women, blacks are harder on fellow blacks, nurses are used to dealing with cops so tend to believe them, schoolteachers try to run things.

This morning Clarke Whittle, the lawyer with a thousand pairs of glasses – and, according to him, just as many girlfriends – told DiPaulo, 'I always pick at least one attractive woman, so no matter how ugly the evidence gets, I have one good thing to look at.'

DiPaulo preferred to focus on careers. Engineers, accountants, and computer geeks were his preference, people who could follow logic over emotion.

Most of all he used his own intuition. When jurors were called to the witness-box, he watched them closely. As the registrar intoned, 'Juror look upon the accused, accused look upon the juror,' DiPaulo zeroed in on their eyes. If they looked directly at his client, he often said 'Content' – the polite way of accepting a juror. But if they avoided eye contact, he always said 'Challenge.'

DiPaulo was happy with the eleven jurors so far. His two favorites were a thirty-nine-year-old Vietnamese male engineer – so much for the don't-pick-an-Asian theory – and a forty-six-year-old female computer programmer from some Slavic country. He had a hunch one of them would end up being the jury foreperson.

Potential juror number twelve lumbered up to the witness stand. Her name was Eunice Brown. A woman in her mid-twenties, she was extraordinarily overweight. Her mouth drooped in a permanent scowl. Another theory was that if your client was an attractive female, never pick an ugly woman. Pick as many men as you could. With only four males on the jury so far, he was planning to use one of his two remaining stand-asides on this woman. The next three jurors in line were all men.

Raglan swiveled toward DiPaulo so the jury couldn't see her face. She rolled her eyes. The math was obvious. If he cut the woman he'd have his choice of the next three men.

'Is the Crown content or does it challenge?' the registrar asked Raglan.

'Content,' she said without hesitation. Her strategy was to force DiPaulo to use up one of his three remaining stand-asides.

'Defense, content or not content?' the registrar asked.

DiPaulo had already put a black line through Brown's name. He was about to say 'not content' when he took another look at her. He was always decisive in front of the jury, but now he paused. She was still looking at Samantha. Most jurors gave the defendant only a quick glance and then looked away.

'Your Honor,' DiPaulo said, 'Ms Brown lists her occupation as student. May I ask what it is she studies?'

'If you must.' Norville was low in her chair.

'Ms Brown.' DiPaulo watched the woman's little eyes in her jowly face. She looked back at him. 'What are you studying?'

'Engineering,' Brown said. 'I want to be a dirt engineer. Build highways up north.'

'Content.' DiPaulo flashed the last juror his best smile. She didn't respond in any way.

Raglan raised an eyebrow at him. She turned her pencil around and erased something in her trial binder.

'Excellent.' Norville sat straight up. 'We have our jury on the first day. Good.'

Brown was sworn in, and Norville adjourned court. A few minutes later DiPaulo was back in the emptied-out lawyers' lounge, sipping another coffee and shaking his head.

Why did I pick her? he wondered, doodling with a pencil on a piece of paper. Pure instinct. In the end, that's what so much of trial work came down to. If I lose this case, he thought, I'll rue the day.

CHAPTER 52

Detective Ari Greene was usually the first person in court in the morning. He liked to have time to settle in. Get everything in order. Do a few crossword clues with the registrar, joke with the court reporter, chat with the older court officers. He sat at the Crown counsel table, took out a fresh pad of legal-size paper and a new pen. Nothing too fancy, but one with a spongy band around the bottom to make it easier to grip. He numbered the first page and wrote in capital letters R. V. SAMANTHA WYLER – DAY TWO, TUESDAY, FEBRUARY 1.

In Canada, every criminal case was titled 'R. v.' The *R* stood for Regina. The Queen. He'd explained this to Margaret Kwon when she started covering the trial.

'Here's what I don't get,' she'd said. 'You guys have Crowns and queens, where's Prince Charles?'

'Still at large,' he said.

Kwon was back in town and they were going to have dinner later in the week. There was still no news about April Goodling.

Right now his focus was the case. He'd been at

the courthouse since seven this morning, going through all the boxes of evidence, reviewing the witness list for the week, following up on some last-minute requests by Ted DiPaulo for bits of disclosure that were missing.

Jennifer Raglan slipped into the wood chair beside him. She looked good in her pressed white shirt under the black robes. Nothing like a woman in uniform, he thought. This morning was her opening address to the jury, a big moment. He'd made a point of staying out of her way.

'You look nice,' he said.

'Thanks.'

'You ready?'

'Little nervous,' she said. 'That's always good.'

'Morning, Counsel.' The judge came in and settled into her chair high up on her dais. She turned to the court officer. It was exactly ten o'clock. 'My jury, please,' Norville said.

Sounds like she's ordering her butler to get her car, Greene thought as he watched the jurors shuffle in, all wearing more casual clothes than yesterday when they were here for jury selection. Over the weeks of the trial, he knew their dress would grow even more relaxed.

The jurors settled into their chairs, the same ones they'd sit in every day. The Crowns always had the counsel table closest to the jury. Raglan took a few steps over to the wood podium, which was at the corner of the jury box farthest from the front of the court.

'Good morning, ladies and gentlemen of the jury.'

As she spoke, Greene took careful notes. He tried to listen to the Crown's opening and pretend he'd never heard the evidence before, like a juror. Listen for where it was solid, where it was weak.

Raglan started with the background. Terrance and Samantha Wyler. Married five years ago. She was a banker who had begun working at the family business, Wyler Foods, the year before they met. Their son, Simon, born a year later. Samantha and Terrance leaving Wyler Foods to start their own business, how that caused a rift between Terrance and his family. How that venture failed and the marriage unraveled. The eventual split-up and Terrance seeing the actress April Goodling. Greene and Raglan had decided it was best to meet this issue head-on, so it didn't look as if they were hiding anything.

Greene glanced at the jurors. A few of them were sneaking looks at Wyler, who, dressed conservatively, looked straight ahead.

Raglan was gaining momentum. She talked about how Terrance reconciled with his family after Samantha charged him with threatening her, and how he was found not guilty of the charges. Raglan moved on to Samantha's angry e-mails and voice mails and the contentious divorce proceedings. About the last few days before Terrance's murder. The family court trial set to start on Monday. Terrance's e-mail to Samantha on the Sunday night saying he'd accepted her offer and inviting her to come to his house.

'And you will hear, ladies and gentlemen of the jury' – Raglan cranked her voice up a notch – 'that Ms Samantha Wyler, the accused, was right next door, with her eighteen-year-old neighbor, a boy named Brandon Legacy, left home alone by his parents on the hot summer weekend. The last person to see Samantha before the murder.'

Raglan emphasized the word 'boy.' Some of the jurors were nodding, now not feeling so shy about looking at Wyler.

'And this boy, Brandon, will tell you that the accused was angry when she left, saying she was going to the victim's house to "settle this once and for all."'

Raglan stepped out from behind the podium and walked to the center of the jury box, no notes in hand. Taking her time.

'And you'll meet the Wylers' son, Simon. Only four years old. He won't be here in person, thank goodness. But on videotape, talking to that gentleman, Detective Ari Greene.' She gestured toward Greene. 'The officer in charge of this case, who's worked on it nonstop since early in the morning of August the seventeenth.'

Greene looked up from his note taking and nodded to the jury. Short and sweet. As they'd rehearsed it.

'On that tape you'll hear Simon talk about the night his father was murdered. Fortunately, he never saw what happened. But you'll see the pictures. And let me tell you, they're not easy to look at. Seven stab wounds. The victim, Mr Wyler, his body left lying on the kitchen floor while his son was upstairs in his bedroom.'

Raglan scanned back and forth across the jurors, like a slowly rotating spotlight.

'Simon tells Detective Greene that his mother came into his room that night. That she was crying. That she told her son she wouldn't see him for a long time.'

Raglan went back to Greene, who handed her a slim folder. Inside was a photo of Terrance Wyler on the kitchen floor, his body slashed. Back at the end of the jury box, she looked at the picture as if she'd never seen it before. The jurors were watching her.

'I'm only going to show you one photo,' she said, still holding it back from their view. 'And I'm going to read the e-mail the accused sent to the victim on August twelfth, five days before the murder.'

Greene glanced up at Norville. The judge was leaning forward.

Raglan turned the picture and held it low for the jurors on the bottom row, higher for those on the top. Jaws dropped, as if on cue.

At the far end of the jury box she put the picture down and reopened the file.

'Here's what she said in the e-mail.' Raglan spoke softly. Letting the power of the written words speak for themselves: '"August 12. One week from the trial and now your lawyer amends her pleadings and asks for full custody. Says it's not safe for Simon to stay overnight with me???!!! Who the fuck do you think you are? Just like you to stab me in the back. You want to go to war. Watch out. You're not the only one with a knife."'

She finished reading and whirled toward Samantha Wyler, raised her arm, and pointed directly at her. 'The Crown will prove that the accused used the victim's own kitchen knife.' Raglan's voice was loud. 'Stabbed him seven times. Committed first-degree murder.'

Pointing at someone in a public place is an extreme gesture. Combined with Raglan's contained fury, the effect was powerful.

Greene had an eye on Wyler, who had managed to look straight ahead the whole time Raglan was speaking. But now, with the finger directed at her, under the glare of all twelve jurors, she rotated her head in a slow, mechanical way, like an owl in no hurry to spy a noisy woodpecker, and she didn't even blink.

CHAPTER 53

'What's wrong, Ted?'

'Nothing.' Ted DiPaulo had tried to slip out of bed without waking Chiara. He'd checked the clock radio on his side table. It was three in the morning. 'I'm not sleeping much. Happens whenever I'm in a trial.'

'I can go home if you want.' She sat up, a pillow at her back.

In the new year, Chiara, DiPaulo's girlfriend – a word that sounded absurd given that he was turning fifty-one this year and she was fifty-three – had started spending the night at his house. Lauren had insisted that she was 'cool with it,' but DiPaulo still felt awkward having breakfast together, the three of them in their pajamas. But that had nothing to do with his inability to sleep right now.

'Please stay,' he said. 'The first week of a trial is always the worst for the defense. We've had three days of forensics, fingerprints, blood splatter, photos of the dead body, the bloody knife, the towel it was wrapped in. Then Samantha's angry e-mails and voice mails. It

346

keeps piling up. When they played the videotape of the boy talking to Detective Greene, saying that his mother had been in his room that night, the jury looked at me as if I were some beast defending a monster.'

DiPaulo was perspiring. Olive used to make fun of the flannel pajamas he always wore, and when Chiara finally spent the night, she'd laughed at them too. Poky, she called them, and Lauren agreed. It was nice to see his daughter and his 'girlfriend' form an alliance. He was glad to be the butt of their gentle chiding.

Maybe I should buy a lighter pair, he thought. The sweat layered on his shoulders and back. He walked to the window that faced his long backyard. His mind, as usual, was in overdrive. He always left the blinds open, since there was nothing back there but trees and the deep ravine at the end of the yard. It was what he loved most about the house, the sense of being alone. He could never imagine how people lived in those boxlike condominiums downtown.

The sky was black, as if an enormous blanket had been thrown across it. Early February, the deepest part of the winter.

'How's Samantha holding up?' Chiara was at his side. He hadn't heard her get out of bed. She slid her hand under his pajama top, letting in cool air.

'She almost lost it yesterday,' DiPaulo said.

'What happened?'

DiPaulo peered out into the darkness for a long time before he spoke. 'There's a little cafeteria in the basement of the courthouse. It's always over-crowded at lunchtime. This reporter, Zachery Stone, who works for the *Sun*, was in line and started pestering her.'

'You told me you never took your eyes off her in court.'

'I had to go to the library to look up some cases. I rushed down and Sam was at the cash register, her face all red. Stone was right beside her. He's a little guy, about half a foot shorter than she is.'

'Oh, no.' Chiara ran her fingers up and down his spine.

'She slammed her tray down and hissed at him, loud enough for everyone to hear, "Fuck off. Leave me alone."' DiPaulo shuddered. 'I got there just in time.'

'He can't put this in the paper, can he?'

'No. That's not what I'm worried about. Detective Greene was right behind them. He heard the whole thing.'

'What did he say?'

'Greene's a quiet guy but I know what he was thinking: Looks like your client has an anger management problem.' DiPaulo's eyes had adjusted to the darkness, and he spotted a weak strand of light in the sky.

Chiara was using her fingernails now. Almost tickling his skin. Not saying a word.

'And you're thinking, Ted – face it – he's right. Samantha's a very angry woman,' DiPaulo said.

Chiara intertwined their fingers.

'My first-year law school professor gave the best advice about being a trial lawyer: Forget the law. Make the judge or the jury like your client and they'll always find a way to acquit.'

'How do you do that with someone like her?' Chiara asked.

'Sam's her own worst enemy. A loner. Socially awkward. More comfortable teaching adults how to read than dealing with people who are her equal. She comes across as cold, uncaring. Her emotions are all bottled up, and they explode. Doing stupid things like sleeping with that teenage boy. Raglan's going to make the jury despise her.'

Chiara unclasped their hands and rubbed the inside of his forearm.

He heard a tiny click noise. 'I think Lauren's awake.' He kissed Chiara on the cheek and slipped silently into the hall.

A sliver of light was under his daughter's door. She must have heard him, because there was another small click and the gap under the door turned dark. DiPaulo and his daughter had been playing this little cat-and-mouse game since she was about four years old: Lauren reading all the time, DiPaulo trying to get her to sleep.

He paused for a moment. Not sure what to do.

'Lauren, you up?' He opened the door the tiniest crack. He heard her sniffle.

'Kind of,' she said.

'Can I come in?'

'Okay.'

The little light by her bed snapped back on. She'd been crying.

The worst part about being on a murder trial was the toll it took on your family. As if for weeks and weeks you were living on the other side of the moon. Even when he was home, DiPaulo's mind was elsewhere. Over the years the kids had learned to compensate. They'd say 'We can take care of breakfast, or dinner, or putting the recycling out for pickup on Wednesday.'

But with his son, Kyle, off at school, he'd had to leave Lauren alone so many nights. Despite her protestations that she was fine, that she had tons of homework and the revolving circuit of friends who passed through her Facebook page and their living room, he knew that for her as well, the big house felt lonely.

He sat on the edge of her bed. 'I know it's a drag. I've been so tied up with this case.'

She bit her lower lip.

'The trial will be over in a few—'

'Lenny and I split up.' She threw her hands over her eyes and wailed.

Lenny. DiPaulo searched in his mind for the name. He thought that part of her summer-school pack of friends included a Leonard. And he'd heard the name mentioned as part of the ever-long list of friends Lauren was 'hanging with' most weekend nights. But he could never keep them straight. At some point it had occurred to him that Leonard's name was popping up more than the others, but the thought had slipped away under the torrent of trial work.

Watching her cry, DiPaulo felt as if someone had sliced open his chest and torn a piece of his heart out with a scalpel. He put his arms around her.

'I didn't tell you we were going out,' she said between deep breaths.

'It's okay.'

'You were so busy with the trial, and . . .'

He couldn't remember holding his daughter this tight in the last few years.

'Everybody knows about it.' She sniffled. 'Lenny and Lauren. People liked making fun of our names.'

DiPaulo loosened his grip. 'When I'm on a trial, Friday's the only night in the whole week I can really relax. Let's go for sushi tonight. Just the two of us.'

'But, Chiara—'

'The one near Dovercourt that Mom loved. You can get your own spider roll.'

DiPaulo's wife had discovered the place a year before she'd gotten sick. Tokyo Sushi, tucked away in a grimy part of Bloor Street, was run by a young couple who worked seven days a week.

'Chiara won't mind?'

'She'll be happy about it.'

'Can I tell you a secret?' She reached under her

sheets and pulled out a beat-up stuffed animal. It was a koala bear Olive had brought back from their Australian trip. 'Sometimes I still sleep with this when I really miss her. I don't like to talk about Mom, because I know it makes you upset.'

DiPaulo stroked the bear's worn-down ear.

Lauren rubbed its legs. 'Chiara's great, Dad. But sometimes I miss Mom so, so much. It's not fair.'

He was holding her again. Rocking back and forth.

'I'm sorry. You're in this trial and everything. But Lenny was my first boyfriend.'

'I'm the one who should apologize,' he said.

Without a word, she slid over in her bed. He lay beside her, clicked off the lamp, and put his arm around her. The room was at the front of the house, and the light from the street filtered in through the corners of the curtains. DiPaulo found himself staring upward, knowing he wouldn't get back to sleep.

His mind drifted back to the book he'd most loved to read to his daughter when she was a child. Over and over again. *Madeline.* How it made Paris come alive in her mind. Two lines were his favorite:

And the crack on the ceiling had the habit
Of sometimes looking like a rabbit.

He felt Lauren's head settle on his shoulder. As she slipped into sleep, DiPaulo's mind wandered from the streets of Paris to Samantha Wyler in the courthouse cafeteria – her face contorted in anger – to Detective Greene's knowing grin. A loop that would keep playing until the sun came up.

CHAPTER 54

Forget TGIF, Jennifer Raglan thought, it was more like TGGIFF, as in Thank Goodness God It's Fucking Friday. She looked up at the courtroom clock ticking toward ten and felt like a kid in school waiting for the weekend. One more day of this. She was tired but satisfied.

They'd had three full days of evidence. The nanny, Arceli Ocaya, had been the first witness on Tuesday morning. Although nervous, she'd done well. The forensic officer, Zeilinski, came next. Despite her Polish accent, she was impressive. Raglan ended the day by passing around the bloody knife encased in a clear plastic box. Always good to send the jury home with something gruesome to think about.

The next day, she'd called Detective Greene. He put in the bulk of the evidence: background about Terrance and the divorce, Samantha Wyler's voice mails and e-mails to him, the late-night e-mail from Terrance to Samantha saying he'd accepted her offer, and her response that she was coming over. He ended with the videotape of himself and Simon building trains in the playroom at police headquarters. Good to send the jury home weepy.

Yesterday was the boring stuff. All the other officers who'd been at the scene: the photographer, the artist who'd produced the scale drawing that sat on an easel situated so the judge and jury and lawyers could all see it, various scientists from the CFS – the Centre of Forensic Sciences – who'd tested blood and hair and fibers. An easy day for Raglan, who'd mostly just asked, 'And what else did you find in your investigation?'

Sitting quietly at his defense table, Ted DiPaulo had been almost invisible all week. He asked each witness a few perfunctory questions – enough so the jury wouldn't forget he was there – flashed them his charming smile, but never objected, even when Raglan slipped into leading her witnesses. She sensed that he was holding his fire, waiting for the moment. Right now she had to get through this day and make it to the weekend.

'The first witness for the Crown will be Dr Arthur Burns,' Raglan said after the judge and jury were all settled.

Burns, the pathologist who'd done the autopsy, was an arrogant man. He firmly believed that he'd never met anyone who was as smart as he was, and he usually found a way to work that bit of information into the first five minutes of every conversation. He had a wandering right eye that never seemed to focus on anything, so when you talked to him, he appeared to be looking away. It was disconcerting. And he was extremely short. Perhaps that's why he loved to testify, because in the witness stand he was elevated two steps off the ground.

Raglan had received his postmortem report a few weeks earlier and passed a copy to DiPaulo. It was straightforward. Seven stab wounds to various parts of Terrance Wyler's body. Cause of death – blood loss.

Burns scurried from his seat in the front row, an elf-like creature with a battered brown briefcase under his left arm, and scooted up into the witness stand.

'Dr Burns,' Raglan said once he was duly sworn and faced her. He always stood, never sat. 'I understand you are a pathologist with the Centre of Forensic Sciences here in Toronto and have worked there for twenty-three years.'

'Yes.' Burns reached into his case and pulled out two thick folders. 'I've done more than two thousand autopsies, testified in court more than four hundred times, for both the defense and the Crown. I've also appeared in courts and coroners' inquests in every province in Canada, the Northwest Territories, twelve American states, and six other countries. I've prepared a copy of my curriculum vitae for Her Honor, as well as an extensive list of my publications. More than three hundred, translated into seven languages. I've provided copies of all these to the defense, naturally.'

Without being asked Burns passed his thick résumé over to the judge. She recoiled, as if the pages were infected.

'Doctor, if you don't mind, please give it to me,' Raglan said. This was typical of Burns. The smartest kid in the classroom, but you had to control him. 'I'll pass it to the registrar, who can mark your résumé as exhibits and give it to Her Honor.'

The little man looked at the jury and shook his head, letting them know he thought this was a waste of time.

'The Crown submits that based on his testimony and the materials filed, Dr Burns should be qualified as an expert in the field of forensic pathology for the purpose of testifying at this trial.' Raglan sat down.

She looked at DiPaulo and noticed a large stack of photocopied papers on his desk that weren't there moments before. Raglan had assumed that DiPaulo would agree that Burns was qualified. Clearly he had something else in mind.

'Defense counsel, any comments?' Norville didn't even bother to look up from reading Dr Burns's résumé, which the registrar had handed to her. She too thought this was a nonissue.

DiPaulo rose slowly to his feet. He waited until Norville looked up, an expression of surprise on her face.

'You object to the doctor being qualified as an expert witness?' The judge sounded shocked.

'I don't see this as a rubber stamp, Your Honor,' DiPaulo said. 'I have some questions for the good doctor.'

His voice was firm, filled with resolve. Oh, you're smart, Ted, Raglan thought. Play possum for a few days, and then when you finally start to growl, the jury is all ears.

'Go ahead.' Norville's curiosity was now piqued.

'Dr Burns, I'd ask you to turn to your list of publications,' DiPaulo said.

'Gladly.' Burns licked his lips. Relishing the prospect of talking about his favorite topic – himself.

'You testified that you have more than three hundred published works. By my count you've got three hundred and seven. Sound correct?'

'If you say so. I have my secretary update the list monthly, and honestly, I don't bother to count.'

'And you've written five books, correct?'

'Five I'm sure is the right number. All still in print, I'm happy to report.'

DiPaulo didn't even acknowledge Burns's attempt at bantering. He pressed on.

'I did some calculations. By my estimate you've written more than seven thousand pages. Assuming four hundred words per page, you've written more than two and a half million words. That sound about right?' Raglan knew that complex numbers were powerful things in court. They had the ring of factual truth about them.

Burns grinned. He was eating it up.

Pride before the fall, Raglan thought. She knew her old mentor was going somewhere with this, and it couldn't be good.

'Two and a half million words.' Burns smirked. 'Never thought of it in those terms. Has a nice ring to it, if I do say so myself.'

'You've written articles about gunshot wounds, poisoning, bludgeoning, accidental and intentional falls, asphyxiation, choking, blunt force trauma, drowning, burning. You've practically covered the whole gamut, haven't you?'

Burns's eyes squinted and his cheeks bulged, making his little face look grotesque. 'I like to think so.'

Shit, Raglan thought, seeing where DiPaulo was going with this.

'Everything but knife wounds, correct?' DiPaulo was speaking gently now, but his words were as hard as steel.

'Well, perhaps.' Flustered, Burns reached for his stack of papers and began thumbing through his lengthy list of publications. It was the worst possible thing a witness could do, Raglan thought. Far better to admit it.

'You can look for as long as you like, Dr Burns,' DiPaulo said. 'I can assure you, there are no articles about knives or stab wounds.'

'Well, I may not have written a specific article

about knife wounds, but I've done hundreds of autopsies of stabbing deaths. Testified in court about them many, many times. I consider myself an expert on them.'

'Perhaps we'll let the judge make that decision,' DiPaulo said.

'Well, yes. Certainly.'

'Two and a half a million words. None about knife wounds. Agreed?'

'I can't totally agree. I'm sure that I touched upon the topic, at least peripherally, in many of my publications.'

'I'm sure you did.' DiPaulo wasn't the kind gentleman lawyer anymore. 'But never in the title, right?'

'Well—'

'No further questions of this witness.' The way DiPaulo said the word 'witness,' it sounded as if the doctor were a total fraud.

Raglan stood up. To try to rehabilitate him, she ran Burns through his résumé and let him go on and on about how many times he'd done autopsies involving knife wounds. He's dying the death of a thousand cuts, she thought, the way DiPaulo had planned it.

When Raglan was done, Norville looked at both lawyers. 'What's the defense say about the qualifications of Dr Burns to testify at this trial as an expert witness?' she asked DiPaulo.

'I have no submissions at all,' he said.

Very shrewd, Ted, Raglan thought. Norville

would have no choice but to qualify Dr Burns as an expert, and Raglan was stuck with him.

She looked back at the clock. It was 11:30 Friday morning. The weekend couldn't come soon enough.

CHAPTER 55

'**D**r Burns.' Ted DiPaulo bounded to his feet the moment Jennifer Raglan sat down. It was three in the afternoon. She'd had Burns on the stand the rest of the morning and for an hour after lunch, going through his autopsy report and the seven knife wounds.

DiPaulo made a point of not looking at the jurors, but he could feel they were on the edge of their seats. They knew from his earlier attack on Burns's qualifications that he was up to something. His plan was to finish his cross-examination at the end of the day and send them home for the weekend with Dr Burns foremost in their thoughts.

'There were seven stab wounds, correct?' he asked.

'Yes, I just testified to that,' Burns said.

'You've numbered them on your autopsy report and on the blowup you've placed on the easel?'

'Standard procedure.'

'May I please see Exhibit Fifteen E?' DiPaulo asked the registrar. He grabbed Burns's autopsy report and moved swiftly to the witness stand.

'The wounds are numbered one to seven, but these numbers don't indicate any order in which they were inflicted. Do they?' He shoved the report right under Burns's nose.

'Correct,' Burns said, hesitant with this answer.

DiPaulo jumped right in. 'Let's be clear, Dr Burns.' It was important to keep the pace of this cross-examination fast. That way, when DiPaulo backed Burns into a corner and the doctor's answers slowed down, it would accentuate his uncertainty. 'There's no scientific or medical way to establish which of these knife wounds came first, second, or last. Right?'

'That's right.'

'And you can't even be sure if they were all done by the same knife, can you?'

This question took Burns by surprise. 'That's . . . true' – he stuttered – 'but . . . I would point out that wounds three, four, five, and seven are all puncture wounds with a single-sided knife, so there's some consistency there.'

'Even wound number one. It's superficial, but it was probably a one-sided blade. Correct?' DiPaulo wanted the jury to know that he understood the evidence as well, if not better, than the Crown's so-called expert.

'Yes.' Burns smiled. 'I thought to mention that, but I couldn't be entirely certain.'

DiPaulo gave him a broad smile. 'And since you're under oath in a first-degree murder trial, you want to be absolutely certain about any conclusions you draw for the ladies and gentlemen of the jury.'

'Right.' Burns's little face lit up.

'Now, time of death – that's one of those things we see on TV shows as something that can be easily ascertained. But that's a fiction, isn't it?' As he spoke, DiPaulo walked back to his counsel table and grabbed a stack of articles. 'In fact, Doctor, one of your more than three hundred papers was on this subject.'

DiPaulo handed a copy over to Raglan, then approached the bench and gave one to the registrar to hand up to the judge. At the witness-box he proffered a copy to Burns.

The little man held up his hands. 'Thank you, sir, but I don't need to see a copy. I remember what I wrote.'

'Well, let's see. Here on page four, Your Honor will see it's highlighted in yellow: "Estimating the time of death is the biggest mug's game going. In most cases of recent death, the best an honest pathologist can say is that the time of death was some time between the killing and the finding of the body."'

'Exactly,' Burns said.

'So,' DiPaulo said, 'in this case we have no estimate of the time of death.'

'None.' Burns flipped through his copy of the autopsy report. 'That's right.'

'We don't know when Terrance Wyler was killed, and we don't know in which order these seven knife wounds occurred. Agreed?'

'Well, yes. Agreed.'

'But you know which knife wound killed Terrance Wyler. It was number two on your chart, wasn't it?'

'Yes,' Burns said. 'That's an unusual feature of this case. It wasn't any of the big stabs that killed him, but this small wound to his neck. Hit the carotid artery. Just nicked it, actually.'

'And that could have been the last stab, or the first. No way to know. Right?'

'I can't see how it would matter.'

'Doctor, I have a suggestion. Why don't you let the judge and jury decide what matters in this case?' DiPaulo rarely let himself get angry in court but this was no act. The man was insufferable. He glanced over at Norville. She looked less impressed by the little doctor with the big ego. Guy should be renamed Dr Toolittle, DiPaulo thought, chuckling to himself.

'I . . . I didn't mean it like that,' Burns said.

DiPaulo walked away from Burns, went to the easel, and pointed to the neck area on the drawing. 'Let's try again. This stab wound number two, which I'll call the killing wound. It could have been the first stab. Right?'

'Well, when you put it that way, it is possible.'

DiPaulo raised his voice. 'Dr Burns, don't put words in my mouth. I'm asking for your evidence. It is possible that stab wound number two, the one and only killing wound, happened first. Yes or no.'

'Yes.' Burns looked unsure of himself.

'If this stab number two happened first, Mr Wyler would have died quite quickly. Right?'

'Yes. He would have bled out.'

'Four minutes, that's your estimate in your autopsy report?'

'Yes.'

'Enough time for the other six wounds to have been inflicted, after. Correct?'

'I suppose so.' Burns looked up at DiPaulo, afraid now. 'I mean, yes, that would be possible.'

He's on the run, DiPaulo thought. Time to move in for the kill. 'A stab wound to the neck like this doesn't require a lot of force, does it?'

'Not necessarily.'

'Please answer my question. A stab wound to the neck like this doesn't require a lot of force. True or false?'

'That is correct. I mean true.'

'It's an extremely vulnerable part of the body. For example, that's why we require that young hockey players wear neck guards. Isn't it?'

DiPaulo glanced over at Jennifer Raglan. Her older two boys had been hockey players, and she'd told him her daughter had started. She'd get it. So would the jury. Twelve Canadian jurors, there had to be a hockey parent among them.

Raglan kept her head down, making notes. But he was sure he saw her flinch.

'Yes, that's why they're called neck guards,' Burns said. He chuckled at his own little joke, but no one else in court laughed.

DiPaulo slid two fingers down the side of his own neck, under his ear. 'You can feel the pulse here, can't you?'

'Yes.' Burns mimicked his actions. DiPaulo knew that back in the jury room, the jurors would do the same thing.

'Skin's soft. Easily cut.'

'Yes. I suppose if an attacker knows where to put the knife.' Burns turned to the jury, smirking at the point he thought he'd made.

'Let's stop supposing. The neck is easily cut, even by accident.' DiPaulo said. 'Correct?' He didn't add yes or no. By now the jury would expect a straight answer. If Burns didn't give one they wouldn't be impressed.

'I don't think I'd call seven stab wounds an accident.'

'I'm talking about wound number two. The fatal wound – that could have happened first. Could it have happened by accident?'

'I don't see how.'

'Does that mean no? Are you testifying under oath at this first-degree murder trial that wound number two couldn't have been an accident? Is that your expert evidence?' DiPaulo was breaking a basic rule of cross-examination: never ask a witness more than one question at a time. Good, he thought. Rules are made to be broken.

Burns laughed. He turned to the judge, who glared back at him, stone-faced. Flustered, he looked out at the audience in the courtroom. 'I've never heard of this type of "accidental" stabbing. The answer is no, it could not have been an accident.' He'd retreated to sarcasm, trying to make the word 'accidental' sound like a childish notion. He looked proud of himself.

'You've never heard of an accident, such as two girls, sisters, cutting up some apples to make a pie with their mother. A knife flies out of the hand of the older one and kills her younger sibling?'

Burns looked at DiPaulo, trying to paint sympathy on this face. 'Sounds like a fantasy to me. I've never heard of anything like that.'

Bingo. I love this job, DiPaulo thought as he returned to his table and picked up a second stack of papers he'd placed face-down there. 'But you've heard of the *Journal of Forensic Medicine*, correct, Doctor?' He turned back to his witness, like a shark circling in on its wounded prey.

'I've published there many times.'

'Dr Andrew Flacks? Heard of him?' DiPaulo looked over at the jury. It was past four o'clock on a Friday afternoon after an exhausting week of evidence, and they all looked wide-awake.

Burns chuckled. 'Dr Flacks is one of the world's top forensic pathologists.'

'With expertise in knife wounds,' DiPaulo said. 'He's published fifty-seven articles on the subject. That sound about right?'

'Andrew's good with knives.'

'Take a look at this article he wrote last year.' DiPaulo distributed copies to Raglan and the registrar to give to the judge. He took a leisurely detour to give another set to the court reporter before he moved in on Burns. 'Please read the highlighted portion out loud for us, Doctor.' DiPaulo faced the jury head-on. He found himself looking at juror number twelve in the far corner. The dirt engineer in training. She was staring at him. 'Why don't you start with the title, Doctor.'

He could hear Burns fumble with the pages.

'The title is "Accidental Fatalities by Means of Knife Wounds." And it is by Andrew – I mean Dr Flacks. Published over a year ago.'

The jurors were looking back and forth over DiPaulo's shoulder at Burns and back to DiPaulo. Except for juror number twelve. She stared at him the whole time. He stayed steadfastly silent.

More rustling of papers behind him.

'I get hundreds of medical papers every year and certainly try my best to keep up with the literature,' Burns said. 'This does appear to be one of those rare cases you described.'

'Dr Burns, please. Read the passage.' DiPaulo was doing everything he could to keep his face neutral. Never, ever gloat in front of a jury.

The courtroom was a place of noise. The judge, the lawyers, the witnesses, someone was always talking. Even with the jurors, there were footsteps, the moving of chairs, the occasional cough.

It was stunning when a big courtroom like this, packed with people, became totally silent. And for DiPaulo, oh, so delicious.

369

In the audience DiPaulo heard a clattering, metallic sound. The jurors all looked. It was Jason Wyler. One of his two canes had tumbled to the floor. He pushed himself up as his mother reached down for the fallen cane, and he grabbed it from her before he hobbled out. His mother got up, gave a distressed look back, and accompanied him, step by step, to the exit.

No one said a word until the big oak door, which the officer on duty opened for them, had swung shut.

Never forget, with all the pomp and ceremony of the trial, that you are dealing with real people in real pain, DiPaulo reminded himself.

Dr Burns cleared his throat. 'It says, "Whilst the younger sister, Tabatha, was cutting into a russet apple, the knife flew from her hand. Contact was made on the left side of the neck of the older sister, Maria, penetrating the skin and the carotid artery. The patient expired within four minutes."'

DiPaulo allowed himself the slightest smile. The jurors were nodding at him.

It's an unnatural, one-way communication a lawyer has with members of the jury. One party is so talkative. The other is forced to be silent. Only through the eyes, and little head gestures, could they communicate.

DiPaulo looked from juror to juror. The message they were sending back to him couldn't be clearer if they'd shouted it out. The doctor's a conceited fool. Yes, it could have been an accident.

He turned from the jury box and walked up to Burns. The man's face was burning red. DiPaulo plucked the report out of the doctor's hands and ambled back to his table. Quit while you're ahead. That's what he'd been teaching lawyers for decades.

DiPaulo dropped the report. It landed with a satisfying thwack. He looked at the courtroom clock. It was 4:30. He'd opened up a fat crack in the Crown's case. The jury would have all weekend to think about it. So would Samantha. He'd thrown his client a lifeline and could only hope she'd grab it.

'Your Honor, I have no more questions for the Crown's *expert* witness.' His voice was dripping with sarcasm. And the jury knew what he meant: Dr Burns was an incompetent ass.

CHAPTER 56

There's a certain day-to-day rhythm lawyers fall into when they're doing a murder trial. Jennifer Raglan had been through this many times and it never changed. Before a case started she'd dread what it would do to her life. But after a week or two she'd begin to embrace it, knowing that when the case was over, for all the disruption it caused, she'd miss the amazing intensity. Stuck in the same courtroom day after long day, using every moment out of court to work, you developed a kind of Stockholm syndrome and learned to love your captors. In this case it wasn't armed terrorists, but the relentless pressure that kept her contained in the world of the trial.

As the days wore on, everything was defined by her life in court. Raglan even calculated time differently. Not in terms of hours or minutes, but by witnesses. How many had testified already? How many to go? And trial days. How many days had she been in court? How many lay ahead?

Maybe it was the routine of it that Raglan found comforting. Her days started at five-thirty in the morning. She'd go down to the kitchen table and spend an hour reviewing the notes she'd made the night before about the witnesses to be called that day. She'd make coffee for herself and Gordon and lunches for the kids – stuffing them with little 'I love you, Mommy' notes on different-colored craft paper – be in the shower by seven, and out of the house by seven-thirty. A half hour on the streetcar, where she'd read over more of her notes, and in the office by eight. The next two hours would go by in no time: getting every-thing ready for the long day to come, putting on her robes, strategizing with Greene. Court ended at four-thirty, and then there were witness inter-views, transcripts to review, legal research, cross-examinations to prepare, all the while eating a salad and pizza and calling the kids from the office to say goodnight. She tried not to get home later than ten, when she'd lay out the papers on the kitchen table. The next morning she'd start all over again.

The only break in the relentless pressure was this evening – Friday night. For a few hours at least she could forget about the case. I deserve it, she thought, putting her cheek up close to the bathroom mirror and taking a pad to what remained of her makeup. Most of it had worn off from the sweat and tension of another long day.

She brushed her teeth, turned the light out, and crawled into bed with Gordon, who she had to admit had been supportive through all this. Raglan was still keyed up, in need of release, distraction.

And horny as hell. Sex had become part of her nightly routine as well.

What was it? Maybe living full out like this, maybe dealing so closely with murder and death, but she found she had a near desperate need for sex. Every night. This had the additional benefit of keeping Gordon calm and happy, and on her side while he carried the extra workload.

He clicked off the night-light by his side of the bed and they were engulfed in wonderful darkness. Men are so easy, she thought as she reached down for him. It didn't take much to get Gordon ready. Good. She didn't want to wait.

She thought about the trial so far. The evidence had gone in well, except Dr Burns. DiPaulo had cut the arrogant little prick down to size, but what had he really proved? That Samantha Wyler had accidentally killed her husband? What, while they were making sushi together? And then carved him up six more times for the fun of it? Raglan couldn't see it.

Gordon was rolling on top of her. She pushed his shoulder back and, feeling playful, climbed on top and growled in his ear.

The case all depended on her next witness. Brandon Legacy, Samantha's eighteen-year-old 'friend.' What was the jury going to think of a woman in her thirties having sex with a teenager?

Gordon liked to say that he had strong fingers because he pushed a pencil all day. That it was the best thing about being an accountant. His hands were strong, she had to admit, and his fingers knew her body.

But Legacy was the wild card in her deck. Raglan and Greene had talked about not calling the kid to testify. If the defense put him up there as an alibi witness, then she'd have the advantage of cross-examining him. But if she didn't call Legacy, the defense might not call him either and the jury would never hear any of his evidence. It was too big a risk.

Raglan put her hands on Gordon's hips and rotated him around. She felt like lying down and the pillow felt good under her head. Last year, after they split up, Gordon started going to the gym. He felt firmer around the waist. She liked that.

Then there was Wyler's last comment to Legacy before she left his house: 'I know how to settle this once and for all.' That alone should secure a conviction for manslaughter. At least.

Defense lawyers were always being asked how they could defend someone if they knew they were guilty. But when he was her boss, Ted DiPaulo taught her to look at the other side of the equation. How could you prosecute someone you know is innocent? Or to be more subtle, not guilty of the crime they are charged with, but something less serious?

In the summer when Raglan moved back home, as a gesture of reconciliation, she'd gone shopping with Gordon for a new bed. It amazed her how many styles there were. They settled on one that had separate controls for both sides. Right from the start she hated the stupid thing, but her husband loved it. And at least it didn't squeak like the old one, she thought as she felt the weight of Gordon's body.

There was one other reason Legacy had to testify, even if he hurt the Crown's case. He provided direct evidence that Samantha was angry when she went over to Wyler's house. Add into the mix the evidence DiPaulo had extracted from Dr Burns – that the fatal stab wound could have been accidental – and it would be easy for the jury to conclude she stabbed Terrance in a fit of rage, not really meaning to kill him. A manslaughter verdict. This was going to end up as a manslaughter verdict, she'd bet on it. Especially if Wyler didn't testify.

Gordon rolled off beside her. His breathing soon leveled out and she felt him twitch, then go slack with sleep as he started to snore. Great, she thought. We've gone through all this, just to end up at the same place.

CHAPTER 57

The date was, literally, set in stone. It had been written on Ari Greene's personal calendar for months, a constant in his unpredictable world, hovering in the distance and ever closer day by day. It was the unveiling of his mother's grave, a Jewish tradition that saw the closest family members return to the cemetery when the headstone was in place, covered by a sheet. Because Saturday was the Sabbath, unveilings were performed on Sundays.

Greene stood beside his father at the grave. The headstone was large enough to cover two spaces, and the one beside his mother's was empty. Reserved for his dad. As he anticipated, a few men and women from the synagogue had come, as well as some people who had worked with his mother at the factory. He hadn't expected the chief of police, Hap Charlton, and Officer Daniel Kennicott to show up like this on a Sunday morning. Both stood respectfully off to the side.

The one person he didn't want here was Rabbi Climans. The man had been at the synagogue for more than a year and he annoyed the hell out of

Greene's father, who'd nicknamed him Rabbi Cliché. There was a fake sincerity about him, like a politician running for office. His sermons tended to be long on time, short on depth. Worst of all, Rabbi Cliché had a standard-form eulogy, especially for elderly Jewish women, that made Greene and his dad gag: 'For Mrs – fill in the blank with any woman's name – family always came first. Her beloved husband, her beautiful children, her treasured grandchildren were everything to her.'

The idea of Rabbi Climans speaking at his mother's grave was revolting to Greene. He had tried to get the older cantor, who sometimes stood in for Mr Zero Mostel, Jr – another of Greene's father's nicknames for Climans – to do the service. But last week his dad told Greene, 'Don't worry about it. I took care of the rabbi.'

'What did you do?' Greene asked.

'I told him if he gave the same "family always came first" speech, I'd jam the stone I was supposed to put on your mother's tombstone down his throat.'

'Dad.' Greene arched his eyebrows at his father.

'I said it in a nicer way.'

'That might work,' Greene said.

The grave was in a modest row of monuments, close to the neighboring backyards. A low fence circled the cemetery. Greene saw a mother, who looked to be Somali, with a round, beautiful face, holding a child and watching them with great dignity.

He thought about Kennicott and the funerals the young officer had been forced to attend. Both his parents, killed by a seemingly random drunk driver. Then his brother, Michael, murdered. Now there were questions about the driver, a guy named Arthur Frank Rake. He'd turned up in Gubbio, a hill town in Italy where Michael was headed the night he was killed. Daniel's trip there this summer hadn't been very successful. Rake had disappeared.

After Rabbi Climans chanted a few prayers, Greene and his father each put a hand on the thin veil covering the stone and broke the light strings that held it in place. The cloth was light, and it felt comforting. Greene had thought long and hard about the inscription for the headstone, and in the end chose the words CHANA GREENE – SHE LIVED.

For his whole life Greene had heard his parents referred to as survivors. He'd grown to loathe the term. Yes, they'd survived the camps, horrors Greene could never fully understand or know. Yes, his mother had lost her parents, both sets of grandparents, uncles, aunts, cousins, friends, and her little brother. But there was more to her than survival. She had lived a life. Not the life she deserved but, until the last few years, a good life, an important life.

Climans tucked the prayer book under his arm and stepped forward. 'It's an important ritual for the family members to come back to the grave of a loved one with a few close friends. This visit is quieter, more intimate than the funeral. Why do soldiers go back to battlefields? It's a fundamental human need we all have.'

Greene looked at the rabbi and thought, How many times have you said that before?

'When I first came to Toronto, I decided to go see some of the congregants who were most ill.' When Climans said the word 'Toronto,' he had a way of emphasizing the first syllable that was annoying.

'I never told anyone this until last week, when I spoke with her husband, Mr Greene,' the rabbi said. 'I visited with Chana Greene many times. It was difficult. A woman who had lived through so much, forced in her last years by Alzheimer's to relive the horrors of her youth. She had, of course, no idea who I was. One day she thought I was a Nazi guard and threw her bedpan at me. Another day she thought I was her brother, Chaim, and hugged me so hard I had to call a nurse to help me break free without hurting her. I remember her screaming, "Where is Chaim? Where is Chaim?"'

Seven years earlier, the disease had come upon Chana Greene with cruel speed. Within months she didn't know who her son was and soon didn't even recognize her husband. That Greene's mother was forced to spend the rest of her life in a helpless fight against these living nightmares made him dark with rage. The endless power of the past to destroy the future.

'One day I started singing an old Yiddish song my grandmother had taught me.' Climans was speaking louder, not that soft-focus tone he used most of the time. 'We held hands like children in kindergarten and sang the song over and over. Twenty, thirty times. I lost all track. It didn't matter. It was beautiful. I can't comprehend the life of Chana Greene. There was a courage in her that touched me, and I pray that will bring a measure of comfort to her family.'

In so many ways his mother had died years ago. But something in the rabbi's brief speech brought her back to life, for a moment at least.

Greene looked down and saw that he still had in his hand the piece of the cloth that had covered her grave. It was time, he knew, to let it go.

CHAPTER 58

Sunday nights were the worst time of the week for trial lawyers. Ted DiPaulo had spent the entire weekend barricaded in his office, getting ready for the upcoming five long days in court. Exhaustion loomed, and yet there were still too many items left to cross off his to-do list.

The boardroom turned war room looked more like a university dorm than an office. Pens, pencils, and highlight markers were scattered about. Two garbage cans overflowed with take-out pizza boxes, Coke cans, and coffee cups. The air was stale.

Samantha Wyler looked exhausted. Nancy Parish had just put her through a rigorous mock cross-examination. Although she'd done quite well as a witness, DiPaulo could see that being grilled like this had shaken Wyler's confidence. People who weren't used to being in court always found cross-examination intimidating.

This is what he'd hoped would happen. He was still riding two horses in this case. Thanks to Samantha's research, his cross-examination of Dr Burns meant that there was still time for her to drop her story about walking into the house and finding the dead body. It was time to make a final decision about her defense.

'Samantha, let's go talk in my office,' he said.

She flopped down in her usual chair nearest the door, which DiPaulo left open. He sat beside her.

'You see how tough cross-examination will be,' he said.

She bit her lip.

'There's one other alternative,' he said. 'Maybe you went to see Terrance and you two had a fight. Like you said in your family law affidavit, Terrance had another side no one else saw. He became angry. Perhaps he turned on you with the knife in his hand. You struggled. He was stabbed by accident.'

She didn't say a word.

'The jury hated Dr Burns. It's a story they could believe.'

She stared at him. 'Let's say "theoretically," I told you Terry was cutting up some fruit for Simon's breakfast when I came in.'

DiPaulo could feel the hairs stand up on the back of his neck. This was it. '"Theoretically," he attacked you first,' DiPaulo said. 'You acted in self-defense. After he was already fatally stabbed, in anger and rage, you kept cutting him.'

Wyler was silent.

DiPaulo didn't know where to look. He bent his head down and made a tent with his fingers.

'That makes me sound crazy,' she said at last.

'Not crazy. Just angry.' It will be a relief for her

383

to finally get this off her chest, he thought, looking at her. 'I know how tough this is.'

'No you don't.' She smiled. 'I was testing you. It's a nice theoretical discussion, but it's not what happened. As I told the judge, I'm not pleading guilty, because I didn't stab him. He was dead when I arrived.'

So much for the Dr Burns defense, DiPaulo thought. 'Well, who did?'

'I don't know.' She put her hands on her forehead. 'I keep thinking and thinking, and I don't have the answer.'

DiPaulo stood up. 'I'm sorry. I sound like a Crown. It's not our job to solve their case. They bear the burden of proof. Okay. I ask every client the same question when we get to this point: What haven't you told me? There's always something.'

He'd expected her to be angry. Instead, she looked back to the boardroom. 'Can we look at the list of witnesses for next week?'

They walked across the hall. DiPaulo felt oddly relieved. It was all or nothing now with Samantha's story. He had only one horse left to ride. He'd line up two other witnesses. A psychologist who would testify that Wyler's reaction to seeing Terrance dead on the floor – grabbing the knife, going to see Simon, walking for hours with no memory of what she'd done – was possible, especially in someone like Samantha, who'd experienced a similar trauma when she was a teenager.

And Lillian Funke, the librarian from New Liskeard. She'd put a more human face on Samantha, talk about her love of books, her teaching adults to read.

'Are they calling all these people, for sure?' Samantha asked, running her hand down the Crown's witness list.

'No. The list is a courtesy. They can change their mind at any time.'

She flipped over to the second page. 'What if we want them to call someone. Can we make them do that?'

DiPaulo chuckled. 'The opposite. If they think we want them to call someone, they won't. We have to put them on the stand, and they get to cross-examine.'

Her thumb stopped at a name. She smiled at DiPaulo, her eyes clear. 'You were right. There's something I didn't tell you. No matter what, make sure that Raglan puts this witness up there. And I'll tell you why.'

CHAPTER 59

Margaret Kwon watched young Brandon Legacy walk, his flared jeans making a swish-swish noise, from the back row of the courtroom to the witness-box. Now, this is juicy stuff for a Monday morning, she thought. And what amazing headline potential for the next issue of *Faces* magazine. She started writing some titles in her notepad: 'Sam's Boy Toy Testifies,' 'Brandon Baby Babbles.'

Kwon was still hot on the hunt for April Goodling. The actress had disappeared and no one had been able to find her for months. Kwon convinced her editor in New York that Goodling might turn up at the trial. She put her secret Toronto contacts on high alert, especially Goodling's regular limo driver. All last week the actress never showed, and Ari Greene was so busy with the trial they only had time for dinner one night. He took her to Little India on Gerrard Street and they ate at a wacky restaurant under a big tent – the Lahore Tika House. No tablecloths. Plastic cutlery, paper plates. Half the women wearing saris. And great food. Perfect for Greene.

'State your name, please,' the registrar said to the kid.

Legacy cocked his head and a shock of blond hair fell across his eyes. He didn't bother to brush it away. Boy, is he surly, Kwon thought. And yummy.

'Brandon Legacy.' His voice was deeper than she'd expected.

'Do you wish to swear on the Bible or affirm?'

The teen looked at the Bible in the registrar's hand as if it were some ancient artifact found in a museum.

'Uh, affirm,' he said.

Jennifer Raglan rose to her feet and fiddled with some papers on her desk. She didn't seem to have the same confidence about this witness that she did with the others.

'Brandon, have you ever testified in court before?' she asked.

'No.'

'Have you ever been in a courtroom before?'

'Yeah.'

'When?'

'School trip.'

Wow, Kwon thought. Brandon was really breaking out with a two-word sentence. She was enjoying watching Raglan get frustrated.

Raglan spent a few minutes asking Legacy about

his family – he was an only child; about his school – film studies was his best subject; about his favorite activities – skateboarding, computer games. He looked totally bored.

'I want to ask you some questions about your relationship with the accused, Ms Wyler,' Raglan said.

'We were friends,' Legacy answered before she had time to ask a real question.

'I see,' Raglan said. For the first time in the trial, she was staying put behind her desk. Kwon could see that Raglan was wary of Legacy, like a cowgirl who'd spotted a rattlesnake in her path. 'Brandon, I don't want to embarrass you—'

'There's nothing to be embarrassed about. I told you we were friends.'

A blast of energy rolled through the court. Kwon looked at the jury. They were riveted.

'And the nature of that "friendship"?'

'We played a lot of video games. She's real good at them. And sometimes we read books together. She reads a lot.'

Raglan nodded, like a teacher frustrated with an under-performing student.

'Was there an intimate nature to your relationship?'

'Objection. Clearly leading,' Ted DiPaulo shouted, flying out of his seat. It was the first time Kwon had seen him raise his voice like this in an objection. Everyone in the courtroom stared at him. 'Your Honor, Mr Legacy is the Crown's witness. She's asked him twice about the nature of this relationship and he's answered. The question is absolutely improper, and my friend knows it.'

'Your Honor.' Raglan's voice was high too, with a touch of anger. 'This is an inexperienced witness. We're talking about a complex thing, the relationship between two people, and I simply want to give this young man a chance to give all the relevant evidence to this jury.'

Both lawyers glared at Norville, who looked stricken. Kwon saw her glance at the clock above the jury. It was 10:15. No excuse to call a morning recess and phone her hubby's law firm, as Greene said she often did.

He'd also explained to Kwon that Canadian lawyers were not allowed to approach the bench and talk quietly to the judge. There were no side-bars, as there were in the States. Everything was said in open court or the jury had to leave, which took a lot of time and was a pain in the ass.

'Mr DiPaulo,' Norville said. 'I think the Crown makes a good point. We need to give this witness every chance to give us his evidence. But Madam Crown, Mr DiPaulo is right that the question itself is leading.'

Both lawyers nodded. Norville looked pleased with herself.

'Brandon, let me ask the question this way,' Raglan said. 'You were friends with the accused, you played video games with the accused, you read books with the accused – was there anything else you and the accused did together?'

Nice work, Kwon thought. Now everyone knew what she had in mind. Were you fucking the married woman who used to live next door? If the kid denied it, no one would believe him.

'We cooked sometimes,' Legacy said.

This is delicious, Kwon thought. 'Kid Cooks Up Cougar Omelette.'

'Cooked. I see.' Raglan was speaking slowly. 'Lunches, dinners, which meals?'

'No, I mean we cooked, you know. Got it on.'

Raglan stopped in her tracks. There was some muffled laughter in the court. Norville looked up, angry. Greene had explained to Kwon that Canadian judges didn't have gavels as they did in the States. But from what Kwon had seen, they didn't need them. Everyone in Canada was so damn polite. The lawyers, in their cute black gowns, bowing to the judge when they walked in and out of court, calling each other 'my friend,' even when they were pissed off with each other. You half expected the defendant to bring in a guitar one day so they could all sing folk songs together.

'In a court of law like this, Brandon,' Raglan said, 'sometimes we need people to spell things out clearly. When you say you got it on, you mean—'

'Sex. Once in a while. It wasn't a big deal or anything. Mostly we played video games.'

Wow, Kwon thought. 'B-Boy Preferred Xbox to Sex with Ex.'

'I see.' Raglan looked shaky. Kwon saw Greene look up at her, concerned. I knew it, Kwon said to herself. I thought there was something between him and Raglan.

'She didn't make me do it or anything, and it was only after they broke up,' Legacy said. 'Her husband was dating that slutty actress, so what's the big deal?'

Perfecto. Kwon smiled. 'Teen Lover: "April Is a Slut."'

Legacy ran a hand through his hair, throwing it back.

'Mr Legacy.' Raglan stopped addressing him by his first name. 'Please try to answer only the questions I ask.'

He cocked his head again and the hair moved back into position. For the next two hours Raglan extracted the story from Legacy of the night of the murder. How Wyler had watched TV with him, played a Flight Simulator game on his computer – 'Man, is she a good flyer,' Legacy said. 'Mom Plays Mile-High Games with Babysitter,' Kwon wrote – and how she'd received an e-mail from her husband saying he accepted her offer and she should come over.

'And did she leave your house after that?' Raglan asked.

'Yeah. As soon as she landed her plane in Morocco.'

'And what, if anything, did she say to you before she left?'

Legacy lowered his head. He was still and didn't say a word.

'Mr Legacy,' Raglan said. 'Previously you provided a statement. I have a transcript. Would you like to review it? Perhaps refresh your memory?' She moved up to the witness stand. It was effective.

He looked squarely at her. 'I don't need the transcript. I remember.' Legacy shot a glance over to the defense table at Samantha Wyler. 'She said, "That asshole. After all he's put me through, now he wants me to go over there and settle this, just the two of us." I said, "Why don't you?" She said, "I know how to settle this once and for all." Then she left.'

There was an intake of breath from one of the jurors.

'Teen Testifies Against Former Lover,' Kwon wrote. This wasn't a joke anymore. He was sinking her.

Raglan turned and walked back to her counsel desk. She looked pleased with herself. Kwon watched her wink at Greene as she put the transcript down. You flirt, Kwon thought.

'Sam said shit like that all the time,' Legacy said.

Kwon saw Raglan's brow furrow.

'She once told me she was a total chicken.' Legacy kept talking. 'The only way to get Mr

392

Wyler's attention was to yell and scream, but she wouldn't have the nerve to squish a bug.'

Raglan grabbed the transcript off the desk and whirled toward Legacy. 'You never said that in your statement, did you?' She was furious.

'Objection,' DiPaulo sprang to his feet. 'She's cross-examining her own witness.'

Canadian judges might not have gavels, but they knew how to yell when they had to.

'Counsel, Counsel,' Norville shouted. 'Both of you, please.'

The court went silent. Legacy looked over at the judge. 'No one ever asked me if she'd said things like that before. I mean, she got mad a lot. She told me she could never hurt anyone. In high school some guy tried to drag her into the washroom and she punched him so hard he blacked out. It terrified her, like when she found her dad dead. Said she was afraid of violence. Any kind.' He sounded confused. And honest.

Norville shook her head at the young man. 'Sir, you are not to speak directly to me.' She looked at the clock. It was 12:30. 'It's early, but we're going to break now and have a longer than usual lunch.' Judges always liked to get on the record how rare it was for them to take long breaks. 'I'll address this issue at two-thirty.'

'No need, Your Honor,' Raglan said. 'Mr DiPaulo's right. Mr Legacy's my witness and I

393

shouldn't be crossing him. I have no further questions.'

Clearly, Raglan wanted to get Legacy off the stand. But Kwon knew the damage had already been done. 'Boy Toy Brandon Gets Neighbor's Wife off Murder Rap.' What a headline.

CHAPTER 60

'That rotten little shit.' Jennifer Raglan threw her file onto her small desk and slammed the door behind her, missing Ari Greene's shoulder by inches as he followed her into the office. 'He set me up. Can you believe it? He set me up.'

Greene watched Raglan storm behind the desk and plunk herself down on her cheap civil-servant chair. He'd seen her angry before. But never like this.

'The two of them must have planned this all out.' She was yelling. 'Phone records. We have to get a search warrant. Samantha's stuck up in Cobalt, he must have been calling her.'

Greene calmly opened his trial binder and took some folded papers from the inside pocket. 'I had the same idea after you interviewed Legacy last week. So I swore out a warrant for both their phones.'

'You got the records? Great. What do they show?'

'Nothing.' Greene tossed the papers onto her desk. 'No calls to or from Legacy or to anyone in

395

Toronto except her lawyer's office. No e-mails or text messages either. Nada.'

Raglan put her palms to her forehead. 'Legacy was right. We didn't ask him if Samantha had ever said anything like that before, did we?'

'No. We didn't.'

'Or if she'd ever said anything about being violent.'

'No.'

'Or not violent, for that matter.'

Greene shook his head.

'Shit.' Raglan's face was flushed. 'I shouldn't have taken this case first thing back. I'm rusty.'

'We make mistakes on every file.' Greene took the search warrant papers off the desk.

'Ari, why are we even having this trial?' Raglan asked. 'Their marriage fell apart, he was with another woman, and like Norville said at the pretrial, she lost it. She should have pled to manslaughter.'

'You're worried the jury might convict her of first, aren't you?'

'Yes.' She ran her fingers through her hair. 'I'm not in the business of convicting people of crimes they didn't commit.'

'None of us are,' Greene said.

'I can identify with Samantha. Smart small-town girl comes here. I grew up in Welland, half a mile from the canal. A big day was driving out to the watch the freighters go through the locks. My parents loved waving at the Russian or the Nigerian sailors.'

'No one said this job is easy.'

'Why's everything so complicated? My mom colored her hair from a box she bought at Woolworth's.' Raglan rubbed her eyes. 'As soon as this is over, I have to take the kids out to see her. It's been months.'

'We're all tired.' Greene pulled out his trial binder. 'Which witness do you want to call next? All we have left are the brothers and Wyler's parents.'

Raglan sighed. 'Ted DiPaulo dropped in this morning to say hi and he gave me a real hard time. "Come on, Jen," he said. "You're not going to put one of the family members up there to cry for the jury, are you?" When he was a prosecutor, Ted hated doing it. Said it was cheap theater.'

'We don't have any choice,' Greene said. 'You can't end your case with Brandon Legacy.'

'You're right.'

'Besides, Jason, the middle brother, he has good evidence about the last time he talked to Samantha. How angry she was at Terrance.'

'I know. The jury has to hear the last words she said to him. I can imagine what Ted's going to say: "Putting a disabled guy up on the stand to finish your case. Jennifer – save me the melodrama."'

They stared at each other. She came out from behind the desk, and Greene stood up.

'I'm sorry, Ari,' Raglan said. 'I need you to hold me for a minute.'

He put his arms around her and pulled her across the room until his back was against the office door.

'This feels too nice.' She snuggled against him.

'Tell me about your kids,' he said.

'We started having Sunday-morning brunch.' She wrapped her fingers around his hand. 'Dana loves making waffles from scratch. I found this Swedish recipe. You make the batter the night before. The boys are into fresh-squeezed orange juice. We go through a whole bag in one morning.'

'Sounds delicious.' He opened his palm and their fingers intertwined.

'It is good.' With her thumb she rubbed the fleshy part on the top of his hand, between the thumb and forefinger.

'There's something I didn't tell you,' he said.

'What?' She pulled away.

'I didn't think it was relevant and I still don't. But you should know this before you put Jason Wyler on the stand.'

'Tell me, Ari.'

'Terrance wasn't Mr Wyler's son. The mother had an affair.'

'How'd you find that out?' She looked mad.

'Nathan, the oldest brother, told me in November, when the guilty plea fell apart. The two brothers are the only ones who know. Their father doesn't and that's a good thing. He's a hothead.'

'Shit,' she said. 'Shit, shit, shit. Why the hell didn't you tell me this before?'

'Think about what would happen if this gets out. Mr Wyler will have a fit. He's a scary guy. Mrs Wyler's been through enough. And Simon would hear this one day. It would damage the family even more.'

'So you hid it from me.'

'I protected you.' He was getting mad too. Neither of them raised their voice, for fear of being overheard. They spoke in harsh whispers. 'So long as you didn't know about it, you had no obligation to tell the defense. Most Crowns would be thankful.'

'What do you mean, "most Crowns"? You don't think I'm up to this case?'

'Don't say stupid things, Jennifer. You're doing a good job.'

'I don't need your protection.'

'I made a judgment call that this isn't relevant evidence. No need to disclose it. I still think that. We tell DiPaulo, he tells Samantha. What does that accomplish? What difference does it make who Terrance's father was?'

'You believe that?'

'I do.'

Raglan made a fist of one hand and punched it into the other one. 'You're mad at me for taking this case, aren't you?'

'Don't cross-examine me,' Greene said.

'You think I took it just to be near you?'

'You asked the question. Why don't you answer it?' He stared back at her. His heart was pumping. 'There are enough other murders around.'

' *"Of all the gin joints in all the towns in all the world, she walks into mine."* Isn't that what you think, Ari? Because every woman's supposed to fall in love with the handsome, mysterious detective. Right? So you can just walk away.'

Greene still had the binder in his free hand. He hurled it across the room and it crashed on the floor.

'I can get Kennicott to babysit the rest of this case.' He reached behind him and cracked open the door. 'I was never going to ask you. But you brought it up. Why are you on this case?'

Raglan looked away. 'Because of Jo Summers.'

'What?' Greene loosened his grip on the door.

'Jo. The Crown. Judge Summers's daughter.'

'I know who Jo Summers is.'

'Did you know Terrance was her half brother?'

Greene closed the door behind him with a bang. 'I knew who the father was. Nathan told me. But I wasn't going to tell anyone his identity, not even you. That's why when I told you Mr Wyler wasn't Terrance's dad, I didn't say who the father was.'

'Jo was terrified this would come out,' Raglan said. 'She begged me to take the case. That's the only reason I'm on it.'

'When did she tell you?'

'The day after the murder. I couldn't say no to her.'

'So we both knew it all along,' Greene said.

'You were protecting the Wylers. I was protecting Jo,' Raglan said. 'That day back in August, when

I saw you for the first time. When we were alone in that hot little room at Old City Hall. After that I was determined to get off this case. I was afraid to be this close to you. Then Jo called, and I was stuck.'

Their bodies were inches apart. Greene reached behind him and snapped the door lock shut. It made a cold click sound.

'Lucky we both know how to keep a secret,' Raglan said as she undid the top buttons on her shirt and slid his hand inside.

'Blame it on Judge Norville,' Greene said before he kissed her, 'and her unusually long lunch.'

CHAPTER 61

All through the lunch break Ted DiPaulo wondered what Raglan was going to do next. She hadn't come into court yet, and it was almost 2:15. This wasn't like her. Usually she was in court early. He had his fingers crossed that his little bluff this morning had worked. He was terrified that she was going to close her case, not call any more witnesses. This could be the turning point in the trial, depending on her decision.

The door swung open and Raglan marched right up to DiPaulo. She looked flushed. 'Ted, we have to talk,' she said.

'Okay.'

'Please tell Her Honor I need five minutes,' she said to the registrar. 'Something's come up and I have to speak to my friend.'

The registrar put aside his sudoku and reached for a phone. 'Okay.'

Raglan turned back to DiPaulo. 'Ted, I'm calling the middle brother, Jason.' There was no joy in her voice.

'The disabled one?' He frowned, acting disappointed.

'He has real evidence about his last conversation with Samantha. I'm not calling him because of his disability. You've read the disclosure.'

'If you insist, Jennifer.' He gave an exaggerated shrug of his shoulders.

Raglan frowned. 'I know you hate this kind of thing,' she said.

'It's your call.' He looked away from her. I deserve an Oscar for this performance, DiPaulo thought. He was thrilled. After what Samantha had told him on Saturday morning in his office, he desperately needed her to call Jason Wyler as a witness.

She sighed. 'Carotid artery. Neck guard. They're fanatical about them in Dana's hockey league. I'll admit, I can see it. Why the hell didn't she take the manslaughter plea?'

'I tried,' he said.

'Deal's still open. I'll sweeten it, ask for fifteen years, not eighteen.'

'That's against the office rules,' DiPaulo said, lightly mocking her. The Crown office rules were that once a trial had started, all plea offers were off the table.

'Fuck the office rules. We'll go in chambers. I'll even tell Norville to give her twelve. She'll be out in four frigging years. You taught me that the Crown Attorney never wins. Manslaughter's a just result. No way she'll get less. Once Jason Wyler testifies, it's all over for this family. The bitterness will ramp up forever.'

Raglan was right and they both knew it. What she didn't know was that with the new evidence DiPaulo had in his back pocket, it would be worse for the family than she could imagine.

'You're a good lawyer and a good person, Jennifer,' he said. 'I'm stuck. Client wants a trial.'

'Is she going to testify?' Raglan was angry now.

'I still don't know.' Little white lies were sometimes necessary in the heat of battle.

'Any other defense lawyer, and I'd say screw you.' Her eyes were blazing with fury.

'We don't choose our witnesses or our clients,' DiPaulo hissed back at her. He was pretending to get angry too. 'You know that.'

'Okay, if that's how you want to play it. But don't ever forget, I tried to settle this thing.' Raglan straightened up. 'We're ready for the judge now,' she said to the registrar with forced cheerfulness. 'There was a technical matter my friend and I had to work out.'

DiPaulo felt a flush of nervousness. This is going to be messy, he thought.

'The last witness for the Crown will be Mr Jason Wyler,' Raglan said once Norville and the jury were back in place.

Wyler had been seated in the back row. Like everyone else in the court, DiPaulo turned to look. Cheap move, Jennifer, he thought, putting the disabled man as far away as possible from the witness stand. And a not-too-subtle message:

404

make me fight this all the way and I'll pull out all the stops.

There wasn't a sound in the courtroom as step by painful step Wyler shambled up the aisle, his canes squeaking on the polished floor. DiPaulo caught Samantha's eye and looked down at his papers, silently instructing her to do the same. As Jason made slow progress to the witness-box, his breathing grew heavier. DiPaulo peeked at the jury. They were staring down, to the side, anywhere but at the man with the canes.

At last Wyler was on the stand. The registrar tilted his head toward him, asking the judge: Shall I help him? Norville gave a firm shake of her head.

'Ahh. Ahh,' Wyler said as he scaled the steps and steadied himself on the railing at the side of the witness-box.

Once he was settled, Norville turned to the registrar. 'Swear the witness,' she said, as if Wyler had run right up and stood beside her.

'Mr Wyler.' Raglan moved out from behind her counsel table once the Bible was put away. 'Terry was your brother.'

Nicely done, Jennifer, DiPaulo thought. Refer to the victim by his informal name. Sound real familiar.

'I'm the second of three boys. Terry was the baby.'

'Were you close?'

This was a totally irrelevant question. But

DiPaulo wouldn't object and Raglan knew it. The jury would be angry at him if he interrupted poor Jason.

'We're a close family. We were raised to stick together. All three of us work at . . .' He closed his eyes and shook his head. 'I guess I should say we *worked* together, before my brother was murdered.'

Raglan strolled to the witness-box. 'You know Samantha, the accused.' She was beside Wyler now, talking chummy, chummy. Raglan pointed to Samantha, just as she had in her opening.

'Six years. Ever since she left the bank and came to work for our family.' He was glaring at Samantha. DiPaulo had expected this and had instructed her to look down.

'I understand she met Terrance about a year after she joined Wyler Foods, when he came back to visit.'

'Terry was living in the States. We have an annual barbecue at the house for our employees every summer, and he was back for a visit. I couldn't work much anymore, so we needed him. He met Sam, and before we knew it they were together. My mother was planning a big wedding, and they eloped. Samantha's idea of course.'

'Why do you say of course?' Raglan asked.

'She took over his whole life. Simon was born a year later, and we hardly saw him. Mom would make Sunday dinner and Samantha always found

406

some excuse not to come. She made Terrance quit Wyler Foods and they started their own store. We all knew she wanted to alienate him from the family.'

With a witness like this, DiPaulo would only object once. He made his move. 'Excuse me.' He spoke slowly. 'I don't like to interrupt this witness. Perhaps Your Honor could instruct Mr Wyler that he's only permitted to tell this jury what he observed, and not to offer his or other people's opinion.'

Wyler shot DiPaulo an angry look. DiPaulo knew that juries learned the basic rules of evidence with remarkable speed, and they'd know his objection was reasonable. Whatever sympathy they had for Jason Wyler, they wouldn't like it that he was trying to embellish his evidence.

'Ms Raglan, Mr DiPaulo has a point,' Norville said, not even asking her to respond to the objection. Raglan wisely didn't put up a fuss.

Norville pulled herself over to the witness-box and spoke to Wyler as if she were confiding a secret. 'Mr Wyler, we all appreciate that this is difficult. But please, tell us only what you saw and heard, and nothing else. Okay?'

'Yes, Your Honor.' He didn't look contrite.

'Did you have a chance to observe them together very often, your brother and the accused?' Raglan asked.

Wyler lifted his right arm. His elbow was badly deformed. He pointed at Samantha before he replied. 'Almost every time I saw them together something happened.'

For the next half hour Raglan led Wyler through a litany of explosive episodes: Terrance and Samantha having a fight at his parents' house the first Christmas after they were married; Samantha walking out during their mother's birthday party and Terrance running after her; Terrance and Samantha having a screaming match at the yacht club.

'Did you ever see any physical violence between the husband and wife?' Raglan asked.

'I never *saw* anything, no.' Clearly Wyler was dying to talk about how he felt. DiPaulo's objection was the thumb in the dike, and barely holding.

'Did your brother ever talk to you about his relationship with Samantha?'

Wyler shook his head. His face was turning red. 'My brother was an open book. We used to share a room as kids. But Samantha. You couldn't talk to him about her.'

Raglan nodded. Understanding.

'How about the accused, Ms Wyler? She ever talk to you about your brother?'

DiPaulo felt as if the blood in his body had slowed down.

'Once,' he said.

DiPaulo glanced at the jury. They were eating up every word.

'What did she tell you?'

DiPaulo knew what was coming next. He'd read it in his disclosure and he couldn't prevent this evidence from going in. It was the price he had to pay for goading Raglan into calling Wyler as a witness.

'She said that sometimes she got so angry she was afraid she'd lose control.'

'And when did she tell you this?'

'The day before my brother was murdered.'

'Did she tell you what she was so angry about?'

'Everything. He'd left her for another woman. He never worked hard enough in her store. He was turning Simon against her. She hated my whole family.'

'Did she say anything else?' Raglan asked.

'She called. Asked me to talk to Terry. Try to get him to accept her last-minute offer.'

'What did you tell her?'

'I said I had tried, and would try again. But not to count on it. That he'd made up his mind.'

'How did she react to that?'

'She became angry.'

'Did she say anything?'

DiPaulo cringed. This testimony was going to hurt.

'She said, "Fuck you and fuck your whole family." Then she hung up.'

'Have you talked to her since?'

Jason glanced back at Samantha. She had her eyes fixed on him. 'They were the last words she ever said to me.'

'Thank you, Mr Wyler. Those are my questions.' Raglan walked back to her seat.

Wyler reached for his canes. He turned, about to leave the stand.

DiPaulo stood. 'Excuse me, Your Honor. I have some questions for this witness.' He could feel the jury despising him because he was keeping this grieving, disabled man on the stand.

Norville was swept up in the moment too. Content to have Wyler step down. She regarded DiPaulo with a cross look. Then she got it. 'Of course,' she said. 'Sir, I'm afraid you can't leave quite yet. The defense may have a few questions.'

How do you know it will only be a few? DiPaulo thought.

Wyler's body sagged. He looked spent. Without being asked, Norville poured some water and passed it over to him. Wyler took a long drink.

DiPaulo walked out from behind the counsel table. Standing back there would make him seem distant, aloof. But where to go? If he approached the witness-box, he'd come off as aggressive, threatening. The only alternative was to sandwich himself between the jury and the Crown's counsel table. It would be harder for the jurors to be mad at him if he was right in front of them.

He took his time moving across the court. He had no notes in his hand. The trickiest part of any cross-examination was getting that first question right. But no matter how much DiPaulo prepared, the question always came to him at the last second.

This jury would have no patience with him. He needed to make an immediate impact.

CHAPTER 62

Ari Greene watched Ted DiPaulo place himself right beside the jury and look straight at Jason Wyler in the witness-box. DiPaulo was an imposing presence. Now he was stepping right into the lion's den. The guy had guts.

Greene always tried to be neutral in court. Keep his head down, be constant with his note taking, and project for the jury an image of his own objectivity. But he couldn't resist watching. Witnesses never told Crowns everything. And DiPaulo wouldn't cross-examine a man with two canes unless he had something up his sleeve.

'Mr Wyler, since my client's arrest, she's made no attempt to contact you. Correct?' DiPaulo was calm, matter-of-fact.

'That's true,' Wyler said.

It was a good opening. Showed that Samantha had been respectful to the family since the murder.

'This is unusual, isn't it? For the last six years, the two of you have been in contact almost every day. That's true, isn't it?'

Anger flushed across Wyler's face. He cast a

vicious look at Samantha before he clamped his mouth shut. Greene saw the jurors ease forward in their chairs.

'You used e-mail and telephones. And once in a while you'd meet secretly on a secluded walking bridge over in Rosedale.' DiPaulo's tone was tougher. 'Right?'

Wyler glanced over at Raglan, then at the jury box. He looked trapped.

'It's true, isn't it, Mr Wyler?' DiPaulo asked.

'We were in touch sometimes,' he said.

Greene put his head down and wrote out his notes. A vague answer like this made a witness look as if he had something to hide.

'You set up an anonymous e-mail account for you and Samantha, didn't you?'

Without waiting, DiPaulo walked to his table, opened a file folder, and took out some papers. He dropped two of them in front of Jennifer Raglan, approached the registrar and gave him two copies for the judge, and gave copies to the court reporter before he made his way back to the witness-box. He stood square in front of Wyler and handed him one page.

'The company's called bigstring.com. This is their Web site. It says, "BigString Corporation has created a revolutionary new e-mail service that allows users to control their sent e-mail." And farther down, let me see, yes: "BigString gives you the advantage of private e-mail and secure e-mail."'

Wyler didn't even look at it.

'In other words, untraceable,' DiPaulo said.

Wyler remained mute.

'That's correct, isn't it?'

Wyler nodded.

'Your Honor, can the record please reflect that the witness acknowledged this by nodding his head?'

'Okay,' Norville said.

DiPaulo put the second sheet of paper in front of Wyler. 'And you used covercalling.com to hide your phone calls.' He read, ' "Covercalling.com makes changing your caller ID simple." This is how you disguised your calls to Samantha.' He wasn't even asking a question. He was stating a fact.

Wyler stared off into space, afraid to look out into the courtroom, where his family was seated.

Greene started taking notes again, but his mind was racing. After Samantha Wyler's arrest he had had Daniel Kennicott go through her BlackBerry and laptop and all her other phone records. Nothing was recorded as being to or from her brother-in-law.

Wyler finally spoke. 'We e-mailed each other. I like computers. That's what I do for our company. I can follow food prices all over the world. With BlackBerrys I'm in touch with my brothers – I mean, well, now, my brother – all the time.'

A rambling answer like this was typical of a witness trying to change the focus of attention. Greene glanced at Raglan. She was putting on a brave face, looking straight ahead. But he knew she was churning up inside. DiPaulo had fooled her by putting on a big act and pretending he didn't want her to call Jason Wyler as a witness. And she'd fallen for it.

'If I told you there were one thousand and forty-nine e-mails between yourself and my client over a seventy-two-month period, you wouldn't dispute that number, would you, sir?' DiPaulo spoke with no notes. It gave his words added authority.

'That's possible.' It was as good as saying yes.

'And you were never out of touch for more than ten days. Sound right?'

'I guess so. Samantha liked to talk too.'

'And she did research for you, didn't she?'

'Samantha took an interest in my disease. She's smart. Was always looking for new treatments, new medications.'

Sitting beside Greene, Raglan wrote a note on a piece of paper and slid it to him under her palm so the jury wouldn't notice. 'Fuck,' it said. 'Ted really conned me. When should I object?'

Greene glanced at the jury. Their eyes were glued to the witness-box. 'Don't,' he wrote back. 'Will look like you're protecting him. Makes it worse.' He slid the note under her elbow.

Raglan glanced down and gave a quick nod.

'I'm not suggesting there was anything improper about you having contact with your sister-in-law,' DiPaulo said. 'Just the opposite. You were supportive of each other. Kept in touch even after the separation.'

'We did.'

DiPaulo took a deep breath. 'You had nicknames for each other. She called you B.B., which stood for Big Brain, and you called her B.N., which stood for Big Nerd.'

Wyler's head bobbed. There was something about a courtroom, a kind of alchemy that sent people back into their minds, their pasts. You could see it happening now. As hard as Wyler was trying to stay in his angry present, he was slipping into memories.

'People misjudged Sam because she was nice-looking.' Wyler's voice was surprisingly loud. 'They didn't want her to be smart.'

Wyler's hand slipped off one of his canes and he began to waver. He grabbed the railing. A small shudder had gone through the court, the shifting of the tectonic plates of this trial, knocking him and in turn the whole prosecution off balance. He held up one of his canes defiantly. 'She didn't see these, like everyone else. She listened, I mean really listened. I thought she was a real friend.'

Judge Norville glared at DiPaulo, then at Raglan. Her look said, 'Where are you going with this, Mr DiPaulo, and when are you going to object, Ms Raglan?' The courtroom was dead silent.

'One moment, please. I think those are all my questions,' DiPaulo said.

Wyler was clearly embarrassed. Now that his secret was out, he'd be a tougher witness.

DiPaulo went behind his counsel table, bent down, and whispered into Samantha's ear, careful to put his body between his client and the jury. From his angle, Greene saw Samantha nod. She glanced up at the witness stand. Wyler didn't look back at her. It occurred to Greene that this was probably the last time in their lives these two people would ever see each other.

Samantha slipped a piece of paper to DiPaulo. He read it and patted her shoulder.

'Mr Wyler.' DiPaulo looked down at the note. 'I want to thank you for your courage and your honesty today.' His voice sounded stilted. Not his usual smooth and confident delivery. It was obvious he was reading the words of his silent client.

He bent over, about to sit down. Samantha, who rarely moved a muscle in court, shot out her hand and pointed to the note again. She was insisting that he read something else.

DiPaulo cleared his throat and tagged at his robes. 'Ah, one more thing.'

Samantha looked at the witness stand. This time Wyler looked back at her. Their eyes met for the first time.

'Thanks for your courage and honesty not only today, but always,' DiPaulo said.

Wyler held himself erect and nodded at Samantha.

DiPaulo fluttered his hands in the air. 'Sir, with

these robes, and all the formality in this courtroom, sometimes we forget that a trial is really
about people.' His voice was confident again. Back
in rhythm now. 'I'm sure everyone here under-
stands that this has been most difficult for you
and your family.'

Greene was certain that Wyler didn't hear a word
of DiPaulo's last off-the-cuff remarks. Instead, he
was staring transfixed at the woman who was
probably the best friend he'd ever had.

CHAPTER 63

'As its first witness, the defense calls Ms Samantha Wyler.' Ted DiPaulo fingered his thick notepad, which was filled with thirty-six pages of questions he planned to ask. His strategy was to get it all out in his examination in chief of Samantha – the good, the bad, and the ugly. Make it so the prosecution had nothing left to cross-examine her on.

While Wyler was being sworn as a witness, DiPaulo could feel the jury's hostility toward her. And their fascination. They'd been staring at Samantha since the first day of the trial and the only words she'd ever said were 'not guilty.'

The trick with every witness was to let them be their true selves. Warts and all. The jury would never like Samantha. At best, he could make them understand who she was, and in that context they might believe her.

He started by asking her about growing up in Cobalt, discovering her father dead at the service station, the scholarship to the University of Toronto. He moved on to her job at the bank,

Nathan's recruiting her to Wyler Foods, meeting Terrance, getting married, having a baby, opening their own store.

'Would you call your marriage a success or a failure?' DiPaulo asked.

She looked down, placing her hands together, the way they'd rehearsed it. 'The success was Simon. The failure was both of ours. Perhaps more mine. After our son was born I was working all the time at the new store. Not paying enough attention.'

DiPaulo waited until after the morning coffee break to start asking about Brandon Legacy. 'Ms Wyler, we've heard from the young man who lived next door.'

'Brandon.' As they'd practiced it, she crossed her arms in front of her. 'I was at his house that night, it's true. And he was right – the intimacy only happened occasionally. But that's no excuse.'

They'd spent a lot of time coming up with the right word to describe the sex. 'Intimacy' fit the bill.

She shook her head. 'I shouldn't have let it happen. But I blame myself, one hundred percent. I felt more like a mentor than a – a . . . I don't know what else to say about it.'

Wyler had hit the right balance between shame and bashfulness. They'd chosen the word 'happen'. A good passive verb that made it sound as if sex with a teenager were a natural event, like a sudden

420

thunderstorm, which mere mortals were hopeless to prevent.

'Let's talk about your anger. Those e-mails and voice mails.' DiPaulo painstakingly played each voice mail and read out every e-mail. It took so long it became boring.

When he was done, Wyler uncurled her arms and put her hands to her side, to signal how defenseless she was to control her own emotions. 'I admit it. There were days when the anger would overtake me. I'd write. I'd call. It was stupid. I don't have an excuse to offer. They're very embarrassing. I wanted some contact with my husband. Not to hurt him. But to be in touch.'

'Husband.' That was the word DiPaulo wanted. Let the jury see her as the woman left alone. Lonely but not murderous. They'd decided she'd keep her wedding ring on.

He filled in the rest of the morning with Wyler telling the jury about being with Brandon on the Sunday evening, playing video games, and then getting the e-mail from 'her husband' saying that he'd accept her offer.

Samantha was unflinching in her self-criticism and hour by hour the atmosphere in the courtroom changed.

'What did you see when you walked into the house?' DiPaulo asked as his first question after the lunch break. This was the one part he'd been careful not to over-rehearse. It was critical that her testimony be authentic. Spontaneous. Juries knew when a witness was reading from a script.

Her eyes fluttered over DiPaulo's head, seeming to look nowhere. 'It was like that day my father was killed in our service station. The hydraulic lift broke. I was the one who found him. It was the same thing when I saw Terry on our kitchen floor. The exact same.'

A tear rolled down her cheek.

'My whole body tightened up.' It was taking all of Samantha's effort to hold her head erect. More tears were falling but she ignored them.

Judge Norville proffered a box of tissues. 'Would you like one?'

Wyler shook her head. She wiped the tears off with the back of her hand, as if she were shooing off pesky mosquitoes.

'I rushed upstairs to see Simon. I was crying. I thought my life was over. I was in shock. I wrapped up the knife and took it with me. And then I walked. A few hours later I was at the door of my family lawyer's office and it was the morning. I don't even know how I got there. That's what I remember.'

DiPaulo hadn't scripted his questions for this part. There was great value in moments of high drama in court to let them have a life of their own. Be confident, he told himself. Use your instincts.

He looked at the clock. It was 3:30. If he

stopped now, Norville would break for twenty minutes and then Raglan would be squeezed. She could start her cross-examination at the end of the day or risk letting the jury go home with Wyler's good performance as the last thing on their minds.

On the stand, Samantha looked vulnerable. Determined. This is as good as it's going to get, his inner voice told him. 'Your Honor, those are my questions.' He turned to Raglan before he sat down. 'Your witness,' he said.

Norville looked at the clock. 'We'll take our afternoon recess.' She rose from her chair.

Jennifer Raglan shot to her feet. 'Excuse me, Your Honor.'

'Yes?' Norville looked cross.

'If it pleases the court, I'd ask for a small indulgence. As you have probably noticed, my officer in charge, Detective Greene, hasn't been with me since we came back into court after lunch.'

DiPaulo looked at the Crown's table. He'd been so concentrated on Samantha he hadn't even seen that Greene wasn't there. Where'd he gone?

'He'll be back in the morning,' Raglan said. 'I'd prefer to start my cross-examination at that time.'

Norville raised her hands in objection. 'Ms Raglan. You're experienced counsel. The jury is here and I don't want to waste valuable court time.'

'Your Honor, this trial has moved along quickly.' Raglan was standing her ground.

'Mr DiPaulo, what do you say to this?' Norville asked.

He didn't know what Raglan and Greene were planning, but if he forced the issue, she'd insist that the jury be removed, then say to the judge something like 'An issue came up when the defendant was testifying this morning, and Detective Greene is out investigating it. I can't and won't start until he reports back to me tonight.'

Norville would have to grant Raglan the adjournment. It would focus the jury on her upcoming cross-examination. Besides, jurors always liked leaving court early. Best to take the high road and score some brownie points at the same time.

'Your Honor, I really shouldn't editorialize,' DiPaulo said, 'but I suppose that since my client was such an impressive witness my friend might need some extra time to prepare her cross-examination.'

A few members of the jury chuckled.

'The jury will disregard Mr DiPaulo's editorial comment,' Norville said with a snicker. 'I appreciate seeing courtesy between counsel. Ms Raglan is correct, we have all been working hard. We will start tomorrow morning at ten.'

Tomorrow morning at ten, DiPaulo thought, looking at his client alone in the witness-box. It was like watching his children walk out into the world. He'd done everything he could for Samantha Wyler. Now she was on her own against the formidable skill of Jennifer Raglan. Add to that Ari Greene. Where had the detective gone? What had he found?

CHAPTER 64

It was the crunching of his boots on the snow that was so different, Ari Greene thought as he walked across the main street in New Liskeard. He'd spent most winters of his life in Toronto, where the temperature wasn't this cold, nor the air this dry. Tonight, in this small northern Ontario town, it was minus forty degrees, the point where Celsius and Fahrenheit meet. The air had a dry snap to it, making his footsteps sound hard and treble, but clean.

No one up here seemed bothered by the temperature. 'Ah, you get used to it,' the man at the gas station on Highway 11 had said at about seven o'clock when Greene pulled in to fill up his Oldsmobile. The guy didn't even wear gloves.

'I hate the cold in Toronto – too damp,' a woman at the central stoplight in town told him. She didn't even wear a hat.

The main street had an old-fashioned 1950s feel to it. It was all local merchants: a shoe shop, two women's clothing stores and one men's, a butcher, a barber, a jeweler's and an electronics store, a bike shop, a few restaurants. Not one chain store.

In the window display of the travel agency, a beach umbrella was stuck into a pile of white sand. A number of southern vacation books were circled around its base. *Cruise Vacations for Dummies* was prominently displayed.

New Liskeard was across the lake from Quebec, and in the store signs and the talk on the street, there was an easy bilingualism about the place. So Greene wasn't surprised when he spotted a bookstore named Le Chat Noir.

The store had a homey feel, with a touch of sophistication, including dark wood bookshelves, a well-preserved tin roof, and an Italian-looking café over to the side. At the checkout counter, a handmade poster announced that it was 'P.J. Party, Reading Night.' Greene watched a parade of children and parents wearing long winter coats take them off to reveal that they were dressed in pajamas. Slippers were pulled from carrying bags and everyone sat on a round carpet in front of the fake fireplace.

Greene found a seat in the café and ordered a herbal loose leaf tea, which came in a small French-press glass pot. It poured easily without spilling. An improvement on the thin metal teapots in most Toronto restaurants that seem guaranteed to leak all over the place. He settled in and looked at the Carnegie library to his left, across the street.

He'd read the historical plaque staked on the snow-covered front lawn before stopping in at the café. After the turn of the century, Andrew

Carnegie endowed libraries all over North America, and most shared the same classic architectural design – built with local stone, a wide front stairway leading up to a functional center hall.

With time to kill, he picked up a local newspaper, *The Voice . . . of the Shores*. MAN PLEADS GUILTY TO REMOVING ROAD SIGNS was the headline. Apparently an eighteen-year-old resident had been apprehended by the local constabulary, and a search of his bedroom had uncovered a collection of STOP, YIELD, and MOOSE CROSSING signs, plus a pile of hubcaps stashed in his closet. What a crime wave, Greene thought.

At about ten to eight a small stream of people walked out of the library, pulling their coats tight against the cold night air. All lights but one on the main floor were turned off.

Greene paid for his drink and bought a teapot for himself and, for his dad, a biography of Tim Horton, the late hockey player so well known for the ubiquitous coffee shops named after him. Horton, who was born in another Northern Ontario mining town, Timmins, was still a hockey hero up here.

Grabbing his coat, Greene slipped it on as he went outside. In the cold night air there wasn't any wind, only the crisp sound of snow underfoot. Greene crossed the street as Lillian Funke, the librarian, was locking up. He recognized her from the bail hearing, when Samantha's mother had pointed the woman out in court.

428

'We're closed,' she said, startled by the sudden appearance of a stranger out of the dark.

'My name's Detective Greene, from the Toronto Police Homicide Squad.' He pulled out his badge to show it to her. 'I need to speak to you.'

'It's been a long day.'

'This will only take a few minutes.'

She took a deep breath. 'Couldn't we talk tomorrow?'

'I'm afraid not. Can we go inside?'

Funke hesitated. 'Sam obeyed her bail when she was here. She taught reading in the basement and went home with her brother, or she'd take the tri-town bus. Sometimes she even walked. Sam loves to walk.'

Even though there was no wind, it was so cold that Greene was getting chilled. 'I have a search warrant.' He tapped his breast pocket. 'I'd rather not have to execute it on the New Liskeard Public Library.'

Funke looked torn between her friendship and her role as a public servant. 'Okay,' she said. 'I should be more hospitable. It's the northern way. Come on in and I'll make some tea. What do you need?'

The main foyer was packed with books and posters and warmth. This would have been my refuge too if I'd grown up here, he thought. 'I need Samantha Wyler's library card.'

The librarian stepped back. 'That's confidential information.'

Greene smiled. 'I couldn't agree more. Like Samantha, I practically grew up in my local library. At Bathurst and Lawrence down in Toronto. I still remember Mrs Calvert. She gave me *Animal Farm* when I was ten years old.'

'So you understand,' she said.

'I understand libraries and I understand privacy. That's why I didn't have the local police execute this warrant. I drove all the way up here so I could explain to you that this is different.' He held up the subpoena. 'Ms Wyler's charged with first-degree murder. This could be crucial evidence. It might help her more than hurt her. I don't know. All I can tell you is, you have to give it to me.'

CHAPTER 65

Most defense lawyers would have their client on the stand for an hour or two for the examination in chief and pray that they'd survive the cross-examination, Jennifer Raglan thought. But not Ted DiPaulo. He'd had Samantha Wyler testify for most of the day yesterday. It was a brilliant strategy.

Raglan had been determined to dislike Wyler from the moment she hit the stand. But as her testimony went on and on, Raglan felt herself warming to this hard woman, with all her compelling contradictions. There was something lonely and vulnerable about Samantha. Of course, this was why DiPaulo kept her up there for so long. Why he went over every last bump in the road of her life, so that by the time he sat down and said to Raglan, 'Those are my questions. Your witness,' it felt as if there was nothing left to ask.

This morning Greene was back and sitting at the counsel table. He'd done a twelve-hour round-trip and gotten back to Toronto at four in the morning. But you'd never know it. He looked as composed as ever.

Raglan knew the jury would be waiting for fireworks. Expect her to crack Wyler's far-fetched story wide open. But Raglan knew that Hollywood-style Perry Mason moments never happened in a real courtroom. Wyler wasn't going to break down and admit her guilt. Nor was anyone in the audience going to jump up and say, 'She's telling the truth. I did it.'

So where to start? Her goal wasn't to cut Wyler's story to shreds – but to poke a few big holes. Even one would do.

'Ms Wyler, you stabbed your husband seven times, didn't you?' She came out from behind the counsel table. Of course Wyler would deny it, but Raglan had to make it clear to everyone that the battle was joined right from the get-go.

'I didn't kill my husband. He was dead when I got there.'

'You're sure? No problem with your memory on that point?'

'I didn't stab him.'

'Answer my question. Do you have a problem with your memory on that point?'

'No.'

'But you were in his house that night?'

'After he was killed.'

'Ms Wyler, answer my question. Were you in the house that night, yes or no?'

'Yes.'

'You went there to settle things once and for all. Didn't you?'

'That's what I said to Brandon. I wanted to avoid the divorce trial.'

'Conveniently, you were right next door.'

'Convenience had nothing to do with it.'

'But you were next door, weren't you?'

'Yes.'

Raglan tried to make every question a leading question. Limit Wyler's responses to either yes or no.

'And the first thing you saw was—'

'Before I saw anything, I smelled something horrible.'

This was something new. 'You remember the smell?'

'Vividly.'

Raglan realized she'd made a mistake. Emphasized a piece of evidence that made Wyler's story believable: that she walked in and smelled a dead corpse. Raglan needed to counterpunch fast. 'You didn't mention that yesterday when you testified, did you?'

'I didn't think of it.'

'You didn't remember it?'

'I just . . . just didn't think of it until now.'

Raglan had to keep on the attack.

'But you do remember going up to see your son in his bedroom?'

'Yes.'

'And telling him you wouldn't see him for a long time?'

'Yes.'

'You remember picking up the knife?'

'I wrapped it up in a kitchen towel. It was red and white.'

'Is there anything you don't remember about that?'

'No.'

'It's all clear in your mind?'

'And my breathing. I remember the sound of it. After I turned off the music.'

'Music, what music?' As soon as she'd asked the question, Raglan regretted it.

'There was a CD playing. Billy Joel. He was Terry's favorite.'

'That's another thing you didn't mention yesterday, did you?'

'I didn't think of it.'

'You didn't remember it?'

'I remember the blood. I remember the smell and my breathing. I remember the music.'

There was always a risk of what lawyers called cross-examining a witness into credibility. Overdoing it. Raglan was in danger of looking as if she were nitpicking at someone who was doing her best to recall complex and shocking events. Time to switch gears. Go for Samantha's weak underbelly.

'You were rational enough to check on your son, weren't you?'

'Yes.'

'To wrap up the knife?'

'Yes.'

'As we've heard, you have no criminal record. Correct?'

'Yes. No. I mean, correct. I have no record.'

Wyler was starting to get flustered. Raglan kept up the pace of her questions. 'You've never been arrested before, correct?'

'That's right.'

'And when the police went to talk to you about those phone calls and e-mails you sent Terrance before this happened, they were polite, weren't they?'

'Very.'

'You've never complained to anyone about their behavior, have you?'

'No.'

'And you weren't afraid of the police, were you?'

'No.'

'But you say you walked into Terrance Wyler's home and found him stabbed to death in his kitchen and you didn't phone 911. Why not?'

Every once in a while it was good to break the rhythm of leading questions by asking one that was open-ended. And, after all, this is what the jury was thinking: Why didn't Samantha call the cops? Whatever answer Wyler gave, it was bound to look bad.

'It's my biggest regret.'

'You have no explanation, do you?'

'I was in shock.'

'That's it? All you can say about leaving your child, taking the knife, not calling the police, is "I was in shock"?'

Wyler ducked her head down. Her long neck turned red. I almost have her, Raglan thought.

'I didn't call the police,' Wyler said. 'I was, I was . . . I don't know.'

'You don't know? You didn't even lock the door, did you?'

'I don't remember locking the door, no.'

'You don't remember?'

'I was in shock. I wanted to get to my family lawyer. Let him take care of things. I was lost.'

'Oh. You remember how that felt.'

'Yes.'

'You want us to believe you have no memory of how you got downtown, what you did for the hours before your lawyer, Mr Feindel, showed up at his office. No memory at all?'

'I wish I did.'

'But you don't?'

'I must have walked.'

'You must have walked? You know there's no evidence of you on the subway cameras, no bus drivers remember seeing you, no cabs. Is there?'

'No.'

Time to hit her from another angle. Raglan grabbed the file from the table behind her. 'This folder contains your high school report cards. Straight As all the way through. You were even offered full scholarships at quite a few universities. Weren't you?'

'I was a good student.'

'Top student.'

Wyler didn't answer.

'Ms Wyler, let me get your story straight,' Raglan said. 'You claim you went into the house, saw your husband dead on the floor, picked up the bloody knife, wrapped it in a kitchen towel, and left?'

'It's not a claim. It's what happened. I was in shock. I took the knife away to protect Simon.'

Raglan shook her head. She wanted the jury to know she was having none of it. 'May I have Exhibit Four F, please?' She had prearranged with the registrar to have it ready. She grabbed the photograph and headed straight for the witness-box. 'Can you identify the item in this photo, ma'am?' Her voice was filled with contempt.

Wyler glanced at the picture for a second. 'It's the kitchen knife holder,' she whispered.

Raglan echoed her words. 'The knife holder.' She let her voice boom across the courtroom, a confident contrast to the witness. 'How many knives are in it?'

'Looks like six,' Wyler said.

'Well, count them.' She thrust the photo into Wyler's hands. 'You're a banker. Good at math.'

Wyler dropped the picture as if she wanted no part of it. She flicked the hair away from her face. 'There are six,' she said.

Raglan snatched the photo. She walked over to the jury box and took her time parading it before them. 'Didn't take any of these knives away, did you?'

'No.'

'You left six knives in the kitchen. And you walked out the door. Left it unlocked. And you did this to protect your four-year-old son, Simon? Is that your evidence?'

'That's what I did. Not what I should have done.' Wyler began to shake. For a moment Raglan almost felt sorry for her.

'You keep telling us that you were in shock.'

'I was.'

'You're not a doctor, are you, Ms Wyler?'

'No.'

'So how can you identify yourself as being in shock?'

'It's the only explanation I can find.'

Raglan turned to Greene. They'd carefully choreographed this. Greene had a cardboard box on the edge of the table, and one by one he pulled out copies of thick medical textbooks. Five of them. Their spines were turned so that Wyler, the judge, and the jury could see their titles.

Wyler stared at the table.

Raglan knew that there was nothing more effective in a court of law than physical evidence. Props like this were worth their weight in gold.

Up on her dais, Judge Norville was practically jumping out of her seat with curiosity.

'Ms Wyler,' Raglan said. 'You've been living with your mother and brother for the past months in your hometown of Cobalt, correct?'

Wyler nodded. Her eyes were fixed on the books.

'You need to answer yes or no, ma'am.'

'I've been living in Cobalt.'

'Detective Greene took a trip up there last night and stopped in at your local library. The one a few miles away in New Liskeard. You know the place well, don't you?'

'I teach reading there to adults.' Wyler's voice was monotone.

'You recognize these books?'

'I took them out when I was at home.'

Raglan went back to the table and pounded her hand on top of the pile before wheeling back to Wyler. 'Five medical texts. All books about shock. Right?'

'That's right.' Wyler's face was white. 'Lil, the librarian, had them shipped in for me.'

'Studying up, weren't you?'

'I was doing research. Trying to figure out what happened to me.'

'So you could make your story fit.'

'No. It was like when my dad died. I couldn't talk and I don't remember anything.'

'Oh, another time you couldn't remember.'

'I know it seems like—'

'It seems you wanted to study up.'

'No, I—'

'An "A" student. So you could come before this jury and fool them.'

'That's not—'

'Pull the wool over everyone's eyes.'

'Objection, Your Honor.' Ted DiPaulo was up

439

on his feet. 'Ms Raglan keeps cutting off my client. Ms Wyler is trying to explain herself.'

Raglan grabbed three books from the top of the pile, stormed up to the witness stand, and slammed the top one down. 'Okay, Ms Wyler, explain to this jury why you were reading a book called *Shock, How the Human Mind Works Under Duress.*'

'Objection,' DiPaulo said.

Raglan slammed the second book down. '*Shock, Trauma and Memory.*'

'Objection,' DiPaulo yelled this time.

'*An Alchemy of Mind.*' Raglan tossed the third one on the pile.

'Your Honor,' DiPaulo pleaded.

'Counsel, both of you,' Norville shouted, taken aback by the sudden flash of heat in her courtroom.

'I have no more questions for this witness.' As DiPaulo had done when he was finished with the pathologist, Dr Burns, Raglan made sure the jury heard her sarcasm when she said 'witness.' Made it clear that to her the word meant one thing: liar.

CHAPTER 66

Ted DiPaulo had spent the longest five days of his life waiting in the barristers' lounge for the jury to reach a verdict. It was Sunday afternoon, and the jury's lunch break had just ended. The courthouse was empty except for the odd cleaner who came through with a vacuum. DiPaulo was required to stay in the courthouse while the jury was deliberating, and since the call could come at any time, he stayed in his court clothes. During the day, when the jury stopped deliberating – over lunch or dinner – the registrar would call him, and for an hour or so he'd be free to leave, go for a walk, sit by himself in a restaurant, and try not to sulk. Try not to think of all the things he should – and shouldn't – have said and done. A dripping tap he couldn't stop.

Nancy Parish, Chiara, and Lauren were all supportive. They dropped in to see him, brought him homemade brownies and snacks. There was everything to talk about, but really nothing to say. DiPaulo knew he wasn't very good company. Mostly he wanted to be alone.

He'd just finished lunch and was trying to do a

crossword puzzle without much luck. His gown was off, his shirt collar and tabs undone. His cell phone rang. It was the registrar.

'Mr DiPaulo, we have a verdict.'

'Oh, okay.' His voice sounded loud, foolish.

'Her Honor wants you in court in twenty minutes. I've notified the press as well.'

DiPaulo called Nancy Parish, got her voice mail, and left a message. He ran into the washroom and threw cold water on his face, did up his shirt, put on his tabs, tossed on his robes. For a moment he stopped to look at himself in the mirror. What were his chances? A Herbert Hoover twenty-five percent? An Eisenhower fifty? A Gerald Ford seventy-five? He had no idea. But the next time I'm back here in this washroom, he thought, I'll know.

In court there was a rattle of the door handle and the jurors walked in single file. There are as many theories about how to read a jury when it comes back with a verdict as there are about how to pick the jury. Watch the jurors' eyes, some people said. If they're afraid to look at your client, you're in trouble.

DiPaulo preferred to look at their hands. Were their fingers relaxed or tense? Fists open or closed? As they filed in, he saw sets of hands that looked tight. Even worse, the last juror, number twelve, had hers in a closed, angry ball.

It was only seconds away now.

Where does your mind go at turning points in your life? DiPaulo asked himself. His memory went into rewind. His mother: '*Lando, Papa is in the hospital . . .*' A letter from Osgoode Hall Law School: '*Dear Mr DiPaulo, we are pleased to inform you . . .*' His wife, Olive: '*It turned pink, darling. I'm finally pregnant . . .*' The oncologist: '*I wish I didn't have such horrible news . . .*'

'Ladies and gentlemen of the jury, will the foreperson please rise,' the registrar said. His desk was clear of all signs of crossword puzzles, sudokus, brain twisters.

The Vietnamese engineer rose to his feet. Juror number three. One of DiPaulo's two guesses for who would get the job.

'Have you reached a verdict?' the registrar asked.

'We have.' The juror looked straight at the registrar.

Don't cross your fingers, DiPaulo told himself, his own reverse superstition.

'There are a number of possible verdicts that relate to the same incident,' the registrar said. 'I will go through them in descending order, commencing with the most serious charge. If you say "not guilty" to a charge, I will move on to the next one. If you say "guilty," then there will be no need to ask any further questions. Is that clear?'

His face was impossible to read. 'Yes.'

'To the charge of first-degree murder, what say you all?'

'Not guilty.'

A deep shudder went through DiPaulo's spine. He could hear Wyler exhale.

'To the charge of second-degree murder, how say you all?'

'Guilty.'

The word landed like a rock on concrete. Wyler sagged at his side. Every part of DiPaulo's body ached all at once.

'Thank you,' the registrar said. 'You may be seated.'

Juror number three sat down. It had all happened so fast, yet in a peculiar, clear, slow motion.

Wyler's breathing was sporadic.

'The defendant may be seated,' the registrar said.

DiPaulo turned to her. Tears pooled in Wyler's eyes.

'Here, sit down,' he whispered.

She shook her head. Not hearing him, he thought. He touched her arm. It felt like a dead weight. She turned to him. Those magnificent eyes. Dark. In such pain. 'But . . . but I didn't.'

'Sit, please sit.'

Wyler fell into her chair. DiPaulo saw two court officers approach, like a pair of sturdy castles on a chessboard, brought out from their corners for the endgame.

'Mr DiPaulo?' Norville said.

He stood up. 'Thank you, Your Honor. May I please poll the jury?'

'It's your right to do so.'

This was the grimmest of tasks. After your client is convicted, the defense had the right to ask each juror individually if they agreed with the decision.

Except when the foreperson stated the verdict, it was the only time the jurors were allowed to speak once the trial began.

The problem was, in ninety-nine point nine percent of the cases, the jurors all confirmed that yes, your client was indeed guilty. 'Feels like twelve people individually hammering a nail into the coffin,' was how his professor, Parker Graham, had put it.

Still. He had to hold out for that zero point one percent chance.

'Juror number one.' DiPaulo approached the jury box and looked her straight in the eye. 'How say you?'

'Guilty.' It was a thin woman.

'Juror number two?'

'Guilty.'

He kept asking each juror. The word 'guilty' repeated over and over, like an echo chamber in a bad movie. Your wife is dying, dying, dying. Your client is guilty, guilty, guilty. But if you'd insisted that she not testify, it might have been different. But you did. You did. You did. Guilty, guilty, guilty. In unceasing rhythm.

'Juror number twelve, how say you?' DiPaulo wanted more than anything to be out of this courtroom, out of his gowns, back home in bed, the covers over his head, the world locked out, Kurt Cobain banging away on his guitar. Singing: 'A denial. A denial. A denial . . .'

DiPaulo looked at the woman's narrow eyes. He

remembered her clenched fists when she walked in the door. Her hands were still tight. Why the hell did I pick her? he wondered.

Then DiPaulo heard it. The silence. She wasn't speaking.

My God, he thought.

Juror number three, the foreperson, looked at her. If he'd had a pair of scissors, DiPaulo felt he could have reached out and cut the tension between the two engineers. In all his years in court, he'd never seen this.

Juror number twelve took another deep breath. 'Guilty.' She tore the word from inside, as if it had ripped out a piece of her soul.

DiPaulo saw what had happened. The verdict had been eleven to one to convict Wyler of first-degree murder. The twelfth juror had held out for acquittal for five long days. Second-degree was the compromise deal.

He turned back to his counsel table. There was a clambering noise in the body of the court, and he had a vague notion that the reporters were scrambling to get outside. The two police officers had already turned Wyler around, fastening the handcuffs.

'I'll come down and talk to you,' he heard himself say. Samantha looked back at him for a moment before they led her out the side door.

'I'd like to thank both counsel,' Norville said as she packed up her books. At least she had the dignity not to flee the courtroom.

'Ted.' There was an arm around his shoulder. It was Parish. He didn't realize she was in court. 'I ran over when I heard your voice mail. I'm so sorry.'

'Did you see that last juror?' he said. 'She almost . . .'

He felt weak. Exhausted, the way he'd felt when the last visitor finally left the funeral home after Olive's visitation. He looked at the courtroom clock. It was 2:30 in the afternoon. That was the thing about trials. When they ended, there was a sudden blankness to the day. Empty time. He felt so tired.

'I miss working with you,' another woman's voice said. It was Jennifer Raglan, putting her hand out to him. 'It was a tough case. Don't eat yourself up about it. You did everything you could.'

Shock, anger, denial, bargaining. All the emotions were running wild through his system, like a roaring train. The words from a few minutes ago still reverberating. Not guilty. Then guilty. And then guilty, guilty, guilty, guilty, guilty, guilty, guilty, guilty, guilty, guilty, guilty . . . guilty.

'Thanks,' DiPaulo said to Raglan. 'You didn't miss a beat getting back in court.'

'I felt rusty,' she said.

'Didn't show.'

He sat down and Raglan sat beside him. 'I didn't want to prosecute that poor woman,' she said. 'I was terrified they'd come back with a first.'

'Tell me about it,' he said.

447

'Damn it.' She banged the counsel table with both fists, just as Samantha had done during the bail hearing in September. Five months ago. Felt like a year, maybe two. 'Why didn't she take that deal?'

DiPaulo closed his eyes and put his head back. He had no answer for her. Already he could feel a series of what-ifs lining up to invade his sleep, like an army of fighter ants. He had no idea how he was going to defend himself and, even worse, how he was going to live with Samantha Wyler's final words. 'But I didn't . . .'

PART V
APRIL

CHAPTER 67

'April Fools. I'm flying in,' Margaret Kwon said to Ari Greene the moment he picked up the phone. She didn't bother to say hello or introduce herself. 'Plane leaves in five minutes.'

'Margaret?' Greene asked.

Kwon chuckled. 'Yeah. I keep forgetting, I'm supposed to be polite, say hi, how are you, and stuff like that. I'll be in Toronto in an hour.'

'This time you'll get some real Canadian cold.'

She laughed again. 'But it's April.'

'The cruelest month,' Greene said. 'Last week people were out bicycling, but today the north wind's blowing. March went out like a lion. What's up?'

'April Goodling. It's her fortieth birthday today. Remember, "April Fools"? My source, a limo driver, tells me she arrived in Toronto early this morning.'

'Where is she?'

'Don't know. She told the guy to drop her off at a car-rental place downtown.'

'You have the name?'

'You think?' Kwon gave Greene the name, address, phone, fax, and e-mail of the rental company.

'Where're you landing?'

'Island Airport. I can take a cab.'

'Don't be silly,' Greene said. 'I'll be there.'

'Get this,' Kwon said before she hung up. 'When she rented the car, Goodling ordered a car seat.'

A little more than an hour later Greene watched Kwon get off the ferry that took passengers on the short trip to and from the airport.

'Boat's freezing,' she said. 'Why don't they build a goddamn bridge? This city's full of bridges.'

'It's a big political question here.'

'What, freezing your ass off?'

He put his arm around Kwon and walked her to his car, both of them hunching into the wind. She tumbled into the passenger seat.

'It's worse down by the lake,' Greene said when he started the engine. The car was warm from the drive down.

'You still tooling around in this old thing?'

'Safest vehicle on the road.' The heater was working at full blast.

'What do I know? Men in Manhattan don't own cars. I need coffee.'

'I know a place,' he said.

'What a surprise.' She gave him a poke in the ribs.

Greene drove east along the lake and cut up

Parliament Street, so named because it housed the province's first parliament buildings. Now it was a hodgepodge of upscale stores in old Victorian houses, cheap furniture shops, and ready-cash spots. He parked illegally and tossed his police guidebook on the dash.

The area, known as Cabbagetown, was populated by a mixture of the city's trendy elite, multihued immigrant families and the lingering poor white folks from the days when the neighborhood was an Irish slum. Jet Fuel Café comfortably straddled all the lines. With its stripped-down design, pounding music, and the ever-changing art on its high walls, the place was a dedicated hangout for bike couriers, local hipsters, and laptop-typing patrons. Despite the cold, numerous expensive-looking bicycles leaned against the storefront.

'You Canadians,' Kwon said. 'Riding bikes in this weather.'

'Hard-core types do it all year.'

'This café is so New York,' Kwon said when they made their way inside after passing through the gaggle of smokers circled outside the doorway. She ordered a latte in a tall, clear glass. Greene got a tea in a similar glass, with a slice of real ginger.

The latest art on the walls was a series of oversize photographs of a piano maker at work. Billy Joel was singing 'Piano Man.'

The front of the café was packed, so they moved

up a few stairs to the back room. It was more like an eccentric university study hall, with people at every table hunched over their laptops. A steady stream of patrons slipped in and out the back door on the south wall, letting in gusts of cold air and whiffs of marijuana smoke.

'Smells like the party's out back,' Kwon said.

'Been a long winter,' Greene said.

A customer with a bicycle hoisted on his shoulder slithered through the café and lowered it as he got to the back door. It was a tight turn and his rubberized kickstand caught on the bottom of the door frame, out of his line of vision.

Greene jumped out of his seat to free the bike.

'Thanks, man,' the patron said. 'Hope I didn't leave a mark.'

Greene looked at the bottom of the door. A small black smudge formed an upward swish on the white paint, a few inches from the ground. 'It'll wash off,' he said.

'You're so damn polite,' Kwon said when he got back to the table.

'True Canadian,' Greene said, more as a reflex than a thought. Because he wasn't really paying attention to what Kwon had said. Instead, he was staring at the mark on the bottom of the door frame. A few inches from the ground.

CHAPTER 68

Opening day for the Toronto Blue Jays was a big event for Jennifer Raglan's husband, and over the years, much to her surprise, she'd grown to enjoy the annual ritual. Even if it meant using up one of her precious vacation days.

Like everything with Gordon, there was a set routine. Go for a long breakfast at a French café on Queen Street East that had the best croissants in the city, take the streetcar across – because it felt like a real Toronto thing to do – and walk down to the ballpark. Now privately owned and known as the Rogers Centre, the stadium was formerly called the SkyDome. That was when the taxpayers had spent millions on the world's first retractable-roof facility, and as much as baseball purists complained that the facility was sterile, on a cold and windy day like this it was a treat to be inside.

When they started dating, Gordon had taught Raglan how to score a game. That was another part of their routine. He always brought two score-cards, two clipboards, and a bunch of freshly sharpened pencils.

She knew how much this meant to him. One afternoon after Dana was born, before her maternity leave was over, Raglan went on a cleaning binge in the house. On the top of a cupboard she stumbled on a hidden shoe box. What have you got in here, Gordon? she wondered as, feeling guilty, she opened it.

Inside were scorecards and game tickets reaching back to their first date. She sat and cried for almost an hour before returning the box to its secret spot.

'I'm buying the food today,' she announced after the third inning. It was a scoreless tie and the Jays' ace hadn't surrendered a hit yet. She knew Gordon wouldn't want to leave his seat.

'Thanks,' he said.

In an effort to bring some life to the concrete stadium, the new owners had tried to improve the concessions, with a modicum of success. Raglan ordered ridiculously overpriced noodles for Gordon and equally expensive sushi for herself. They always shared a bag of peanuts, so she got one of those too.

Halfway through the fifth inning the Jays were leading three to nothing, but the no-hitter had been blown. With two outs, the center fielder was at bat. Gordon put his pencil down and took her hand.

'You okay, Jen?' he asked.

'This is great,' she said.

'That's not what I mean.'

'Gordon, let's stop talking about our relationship. All this counseling and everything. It gets exhausting. Can't we just be together?'

He cracked a peanut and gave it to her. 'I wasn't talking about us. I'm talked out on the topic too.'

'What do you mean then?'

'I was asking about you and the Wyler trial.'

Raglan had never told anyone how she really felt about the case. How much it bothered her that she'd won because of her skill and not because it was the proper result. Well, she'd hinted to Greene. She could tell he felt uneasy about it too. But never to Gordon, that was for sure. It was best to play dumb.

'I know it's been bugging you since the verdict,' Gordon said.

'Why? We offered her a deal and she didn't take it. And I won.'

'That's my point.' Gordon put his pencil in his shirt pocket and dropped his scorecard on the concrete floor. 'You care about more than winning.'

Raglan felt a rush of tenderness toward him. Her eyes teared up. Somewhere she heard the crack of a bat. She reached out to throw her arms around her husband.

But like everyone else in the stands, he'd jumped to his feet. And all she got was air.

CHAPTER 69

'Ari, did you hear me?'

'Sorry, what?' Ari Greene said to Margaret Kwon. He was still staring at the bottom of the door frame.

'It's too loud in here.' She showed him her phone. 'My father called.'

'Let's go to the front,' Greene said. 'What's up?'

Kwon gave an exaggerated frown. 'Minor heart surgery. They have to correct a valve. The guy was tortured in a North Korean prison for years without a word of complaint, but get him near a doctor and he's such a baby. I'm totally unsympathetic, and it drives him crazy.'

'Sounds like my dad.' They walked through the café and he spotted two stools by the big front window.

'How is your father?' Kwon said.

'Crabbing about getting his driveway refinished.'

'He still drive?'

'Not on the highway,' Greene said.

'That's good.'

'Tell him that.'

Kwon's cell phone rang again. 'Daddy, wait a

458

second.' She hitched up her shoulder bag and slipped outside. Greene watched her through the window. She turned south to shelter herself from the wind.

He couldn't stop thinking about the kickstand on the bicycle hitting the door frame in the back of the café. It reminded him of the back door in Terrance Wyler's home. That extra bloodstain that had never been explained. It kept nagging at him, the notion that there'd been a second person in the house.

Greene heard the fizzy sound of the espresso machine behind the counter. An idea bubbled up in his brain. On the street, Kwon was doing a mock pout as she spoke into the phone. It was easy to read her lips. 'Poor baby,' she was saying, rolling her eyes.

'Baby.' He'd seen something like this before. It came to him so fast that without even thinking, he started waving frantically at Kwon.

CHAPTER 70

Daniel Kennicott was cruising north on Bayview Avenue, a wide, boring street in a rich, boring part of town. Why they called it Bayview was beyond him. There was no bay and no view of any bay to be seen. Just miles and miles of suburban homes.

Sometimes boring was good when you were a cop. It had been more than six weeks since the Wyler trial ended, and after the excitement of being on a homicide case for so many months, he was still adjusting to life back on the beat. Jo Summers had called him one night about a week after the trial. They talked for a long time, but that old reticence of hers was back.

Before they hung up, she said, 'Daniel, this has all been so horrible and exhausting. I don't want to be unfair to you, but I need my old life back. I can't handle anything else right now.'

'I understand,' he said. 'I've been through it.'

He wasn't sure if he was disappointed or relieved. Finally, he'd have some time to work on his brother's case.

Thanks to the cold wind, no one was around.

460

Kennicott drove past Hillside Drive, the street where Terrance Wyler had lived, and a thought occurred to him. He pulled a U-turn, and six blocks later he was in front of Wyler's former house. Detective Greene had taught him that it was a good idea to return to a crime scene a while after a case was closed. His theory was that you always missed something. Go look around again with fresh eyes.

Kennicott got out of his cruiser and took in the house in the bright April sun. A new family had moved in and the front was freshly landscaped. He tried to imagine that he'd never seen the place before as he walked up the driveway. He stared at the basketball net on a long stand, a big Raptors insignia on the backboard. His cell phone rang and he was shocked to see the name on the call display.

'Jo?'

'Daniel, it's an emergency,' Jo Summers said. 'Where are you?'

'I'm on shift. What's wrong?'

'You need to get to the cemetery. Right away.'

'Cemetery?'

'Mount Pleasant. Terry's grave. Where's Detective Greene?'

'I don't know. I'll call him.'

'How long will it take you to get here?'

He started walking back to his car. 'Ten minutes maybe. I'll throw on the siren.'

'Hurry. We're trapped here. He's on the bridge. And screaming that he'll only talk to Greene.'

461

'Who's on the bridge?'

She told him and Kennicott bolted down the driveway, hitting the auto-dial for Greene and praying he'd pick up.

CHAPTER 71

'Your camera. I need to see your camera,' Greene said the moment Kwon was back in the café.

'My camera? Why?'

'How long do you store your videos?' Greene asked.

'At least a year.' She reached into her bag.

'Show me the one of April Goodling at the Gladstone Hotel the morning she heard Wyler had been murdered.'

'You want the cover shot?'

'No. I want to see the video again.'

'Not so squeamish now, are you?' She rotated the camera around and within seconds played the short clip: Goodling in her room. Hands going to her stomach. Eyes bulging. Then her lips moving. Screaming.

'Play that again,' Greene said.

'The whole thing?'

'No. No. The part where she's yelling. You sure you don't remember what she said?'

'I was too busy falling on my face. Here, look.'

Greene watched. He concentrated on Goodling's

mouth, reading her lips. 'She's saying "baby,"' Greene said. '"My baby."'

'Baby?'

They watched the video together for a third time, heads touching as they focused on the little screen. He remembered meeting Goodling in Phil Cutter's office. How she'd held her copy of the affidavit in front of her body. Covering her stomach.

'She was pregnant,' Kwon said. 'My God, the car seat. Where do you think she's gone?'

Greene looked out the window at the cars and people going by. His cell phone rang and he looked at the name on the call display. 'You won't believe this.' He showed it to Kwon.

Her mouth dropped open.

'Happy birthday, Ms Goodling,' Greene said into the phone. 'I understand you're in Toronto. What can I do for you?'

CHAPTER 72

Kennicott put his car in gear. Greene hadn't picked up the first time he called. He'd left an urgent voice mail and was about to push redial when the phone rang. It was Greene.

'Detective?'

'Kennicott where are you?'

'Heading to Mount Pleasant Cemetery. Jo Summers just called and I was calling you.'

'April Goodling called me. She's there too. They're trapped. I'll be there in three or four minutes. What's your location?'

'Leaving Terrance Wyler's old house on Hillside Drive. I was taking a second look.'

'Boot it. I have to check something with records, so I'll put you on hold. Good move, going back to Wyler's place,' Greene said before he went off the line.

With his flashers blaring, Kennicott flew down Bayview and turned onto Eglinton Avenue, a wide commercial thoroughfare that should have been his fastest way. But the traffic was jammed by trailers from some film company on a shoot. He swung down the residential side streets and slowed. Be careful, he told himself, alert for kids running out of driveways. Rule number one: cause no more harm.

Greene came back on the line. 'Records confirms it. August seventeen, he got on the 407 at the Bayview entrance at 4:03 a.m. Exited at Highway 427 at four thirty-eight. I always thought someone else was in that house. How far are you?'

'About five, six minutes.' Kennicott spotted kids up ahead playing ball hockey on the street.

'You'll have to ditch your vehicle when you're two blocks away. Squad cars have already blocked off the street on both sides. He's demanding that I go there alone. Threatening to jump if anyone else comes near. Apparently he drove right up to the bridge, so his car might give you some cover from the north side. I'm coming from the south and I'll try to distract him.'

'Got it.' Kennicott hung up.

'Car,' one of the ballplayers yelled as he approached. The boy grabbed a flimsy goalie's net and pulled it toward the sidewalk, timing it so Kennicott didn't have to brake. 'Hey, it's a *police* car,' he said. A blue-and-white Toronto Maple Leafs toque was pulled tight on his head.

The kids parted. Boys, and a few girls, stood on both sides of the road, hockey sticks in the air like toy sentries. Up ahead the second net was yanked to the side, choreographed so he could glide right through again. At Mount Pleasant Avenue he came to a stop sign and checked his rearview mirror. The kids already had their nets in position and the game was back on.

CHAPTER 73

Margaret Kwon watched Ari Greene handle the cell phone, the police radio, and the siren as he sped through the crowded downtown streets. He was focused straight ahead. The guy was a cool cookie under pressure.

This story had taken a great turn, and she had a front-row seat. April Goodling having a baby with her murdered lover: 'April Fools – Carrying Dead Beau's Baby.'

Greene turned onto a ramp and the road opened up. They raced through a valley with beautiful old mansions on both sides. Going this fast, she had to admit his old car felt safe.

'We're on Mount Pleasant,' Greene said. 'The cemetery's a few blocks north of this hill.'

They hit a commercial strip with lots of cute-looking stores. One caught her eye. It was called George's Trains. An elderly man stood on the sidewalk in front wearing an old-fashioned railway conductor's uniform, complete with a puffy striped hat. He was passing out brochures.

I couldn't live here, she thought. These Canadians are too bloody sweet.

'Damn it!' Greene shouted. The traffic was totally backed up. A long row of cars, all with little FUNERAL signs stuffed in their hoods, was halted along with the rest of the traffic. 'Fuck!' Greene yelled as he threw the car up onto the sidewalk and yanked open his door.

'Detective, I'll call the language police.' Kwon grabbed her camera bag and jumped out.

'Shocking, I know.' Greene bolted across the road.

Kwon charged after him. The north wind was fierce and right in their faces. They ran to the top of the hill. Two police cars were across the street. Up ahead was the long bridge over the cemetery. Kwon spotted April Goodling down below, holding a baby in her arms. She was surrounded by the boy, Simon; the mother, Mrs Wyler; the nanny, Arceli Ocaya; and a blond woman Kwon didn't recognize. They'd formed a tight semicircle around Terrance's tombstone. Simon had flowers in one hand and a little railway engine in the other.

'Why are they here?' she asked Greene.

'Why do soldiers return to their battlefields?' he said. 'It's April's birthday. She wants to say goodbye to him without a crowd.'

A young female police officer with a dark complexion approached them. 'Detective Greene,' she said. 'He's demanding that you talk to him and no one else. His family down at the grave can't move. He told them he'd jump if they did.'

'Good work, Officer Mudhar,' Greene said.

The young officer smiled as they ran past her. Was there anyone in this city Greene didn't know? Kwon wondered. Up ahead there was the man on the bridge, his car parked up on the sidewalk behind him.

Greene stopped at the set of stairs leading down to the cemetery and grabbed his cell phone: 'Kennicott, I see him. I'm going to try to talk him down. The wind's coming toward me so sound will carry in this direction. Sneak up and grab him. Tackle him. Get him off that bridge.'

He clicked off his phone. 'Margaret, stay here. This is serious.'

She brushed her hand against him as he ran past. 'Ari, good luck.'

He looked back for a moment. 'Thanks.'

Once he was on the bridge, Kwon started down the stairs to the cemetery. At last she was going to catch up with April Goodling.

CHAPTER 74

'**D**etective Greene, welcome to my farewell party.' Jason Wyler was standing up on the concrete barrier on the side of the bridge. He'd jammed his two canes in between the parallel metal railings that ran atop it. The canes provided meager support for his stunted body. 'You heard I wanted to talk to you.'

'Jason,' Greene shouted, running at full speed. 'I know what happened.'

Wyler yanked one of his canes out and pointed it at Greene. 'Stop,' he screamed. 'Don't come any closer.'

Greene pulled up. The wind seared his face.

Wyler swung his cane down toward Terrance's grave, where the four women and Simon were staring up at him in horror. 'Such a lovely family reunion.'

'I know you went back to Terrance's house.' Greene glanced up the road. There was no sign of Kennicott.

'So nice to see all the Wyler women one last time. I told them they had to stay there and be quiet or I'd jump.'

'I just checked your license plate on the Highway 407 records.'

'Bad luck again. Had it right from birth. Four murders in one night and every other highway's blocked.' Wyler's voice was forced, each sentence clipped.

Greene cupped his hands so his words would carry. 'I kept trying to figure out why you left the court when Dr Burns was being cross-examined. Now I see Ted DiPaulo was right. This wasn't murder. You stabbed your brother by accident. Your family will understand.'

'My family. Ha. The Wyler clan. I'm the defective one, don't you see that?'

Greene took a step forward. 'An accident isn't murder.'

'I drove back to see Terry after I took the nanny home. He was cutting fruit for Simon's breakfast. My family had talked him into turning down Samantha's offer. I was going to lose everything. All I wanted was to keep Sam as a friend. Terry wouldn't listen. He kept cutting and cutting and cutting. Wyler Fresh. Wyler fucking Fresh. I grabbed the knife. He tried to pull it out of my hand. But I'm stronger than people think. And I slipped.'

Greene took another step.

'Don't.' Wyler swung his cane back at Greene.

'I've stopped.' Greene held up his hands as if Wyler had a gun. Out of the corner of his eye he looked again for Kennicott and still didn't see anything.

'If I loosen the second cane,' Wyler said. 'Bingo. It's more than fifty feet to the concrete. I measured it. You might survive this fall. Not me. Not a chance.'

'You slipped on the kitchen floor. It was an accident,' Greene said.

'No. I slipped on this.' Wyler slung the free cane under his arm and pulled a small model train out of his back pocket. 'Thomas the Tank Engine.'

'Simon's favorite,' Greene said. How many times had the boy asked what had happened to his Thomas?

'He must have left it on the floor,' Wyler said. 'I stepped on it with the knife in my hand and it came up right into my brother's neck. I didn't mean it.'

'Of course you didn't. Climb down. You can return the train to your nephew.' Greene caught his first glimpse of Kennicott. Two long blocks away at least. He was running full out.

'It's crushed on one side.'

'This is your family.' Greene pointed to the gravesite. Margaret Kwon had arrived. Oh, no, he thought. She's going to take pictures.

'My mother. Look, now she has another perfectly healthy grandchild. She'll be so glad to get rid of her defective son,' Wyler said. 'I knew April was pregnant. And I figured she'd come back here on her birthday. Say goodbye to Terry. I did the same thing the day Sam was supposed to plead guilty. That's when I came up with this plan. And now

473

my dear mother can see all this happen. Live and in color.'

Greene watched Kwon put her arms around the women and Simon. She was turning them away. He stole a look up the street. Kennicott was coming fast, but still had more than a block to go.

'What will this accomplish?' Greene asked.

'Everything.' Wyler looked back at Greene. 'Terry was bleeding so hard. There was no way to save him. "Damn it," I yelled at him, "don't fucking die." Made me so mad. He always had everything. And now he was ruining it all.'

'Jason, listen to me—'

'I cut and I cut and I cut him.'

'Jason—'

'When it was all over I used his BlackBerry. I sent e-mails to Sam pretending I was Terry so she would come to the house. It was the perfect crime.'

Greene looked at the rubber stopper on the bottom of Wyler's cane and thought about the mark and the wisp of blood low down on the door frame. 'You parked behind the house and left by the back door.'

'I could never use those steep front steps. After, I drove my car around the block and hid behind a tree in a place where I could watch the street. A while later Samantha walked by. Then nothing happened. I wasn't sure what to do. I think I fell asleep. Suddenly it was late. Then all those highways were blocked. I had to take the 407 to get home before the stupid gardeners arrived.'

Greene remembered the silly plastic sign on the Wylers' manicured lawn. 'Early-Bird Lawn – Weekly Maintenance – Monday, August 17, 5:00 a.m.' He'd wondered why someone as smart as Jason had taken the toll road.

'Your family will support you.' Greene sneaked another look. Kennicott was a block away.

'A crime against the Wyler family is unforgivable,' Wyler said. 'Unless you're Terry. He can take off, come back years later, start his own store to compete against us. No matter what, he was always welcomed back. Our very own prodigal son. You know why? Because he was clean, not deformed like me.'

Kennicott was about half a block away now.

'Samantha was your friend. Why did you do this to her?'

'Best friend? I was supposed to be her best friend. All those nights we'd talk together. The two of us all alone. Not one goddamn kiss. But she could run off and screw that teenager. How fair was that? I was going to do this the day after she pleaded guilty. But when she changed her mind, I thought, let her suffer a little more.'

'She wouldn't want you to do this.'

'I was a coward. Letting her stand trial like that.' He yanked the second cane halfway out. His body wobbled over the edge before it flopped back, like a puppet let loose, then pulled up by its strings.

Kennicott was maybe thirty feet away, running crouched over like a cat. Greene had to keep Jason looking at him.

'Nathan loves you,' Greene said. 'You're the only brother he has left. He won't want—'

'If Sam had won the trial, everything would have been perfect. This is my Plan B. I just had to wait for April and her baby to show up. I'm almost dead anyhow. Samantha's suffered enough. She should be free.' Wyler's voice was angry now.

'Jason, we can talk.'

Kennicott was at the back of Jason's car.

'She's innocent.'

'Okay, Jason. We'll release her.'

Kennicott was about twenty feet away.

'You promise?'

'Yes. Now stop—'

Kennicott was almost there.

'This is what everyone wanted, isn't it? The guilty plea.' Wyler jerked his second cane all the way out.

'No!' Greene yelled.

With all his support gone, Wyler's small body jackknifed forward like a deflated life-size doll, bending fast at the waist. He disappeared over the railing, his jagged feet flipping up in the air like a swimmer doing a deep-sea dive.

Kennicott lunged for him. Threw his arms over the railing. Greene ran up. Kennicott's hands came back. Empty.

The crashing, tumbling sound exploded from the concrete below, carried by the cold wind.

'I was so close,' Kennicott said, gasping for breath. His hands clenched in frustration. 'So, so close.'

CHAPTER 75

There are the blues. There is the night. There's darkness. And then there's losing a case.

Ted DiPaulo had many sleepless nights during Samantha Wyler's trial, but they were nothing compared to the night sweats he'd been going through for the past six weeks since the guilty verdict. Night after night, like clockwork. Two-thirty every morning he'd snap awake, his T-shirt soaked, his hair wet, his head pounding. It was like a great infection raging through his body and he was powerless to combat it.

What if he'd pushed Samantha harder to take that deal? What if he hadn't let her testify? And, my God, what if he hadn't picked juror number twelve? His stomach ached when he thought how close his client had come to going to jail for twenty-five years. What if, what if, what if?

After the verdict, everyone in DiPaulo's life had been supportive, just as they had when Olive died. Said the usual platitudes – you did a great job, it was a tough case, don't blame yourself, there was nothing more you could do with a client like that.

For a few days he hid in bed, blasting Nirvana CDs at full volume. He broke things off with Chiara, telling her that he wasn't there yet. Not ready to really commit. When he dragged himself back to the office, among all the usual boring mail there was a thin rectangular package. Inside was a beautiful silk tie and a note from Chiara: 'You are a good man, a great father, and an excellent lawyer.'

On his first day back in court, DiPaulo ran into Clarke Whittle in the lawyers' robing room. Whittle had on yet another pair of stylish glasses, made of thick gray steel.

'Excellent effort, Ted.' He clapped DiPaulo on the back. 'Remember what Casey Stengel said when he managed the 1962 New York Mets, one of the worst teams in baseball history.'

'What was that?' DiPaulo cringed as he waited for the punch line.

'"I managed good. They just played bad."'

Everyone in the room laughed. It said it all.

'*Courage, mon ami.*' Whittle had a credible French accent. He was cleaning his glasses with a light orange cloth. 'You'll bounce back.'

Everyone said things like that. At least tonight he wasn't alone in his bedroom. DiPaulo pulled himself up from his window seat in the airplane and made his way to the small washroom at the back of the cabin.

He looked at his unshaven face in the tiny bathroom mirror. He was wearing a button-down blue shirt and Chiara's tie. Pushing down hard on the little taps, he tried to get out some hot water but it wouldn't really heat up. He lowered his head, and as he splashed his face, the plane jerked, spilling water all over him. 'Damn it,' he growled through clenched teeth. This anger. He couldn't get it out of his system.

Thank goodness for my children, DiPaulo thought, wiping his face with the rough paper towel. He tried without success to dry off his shirt and tie. His son and daughter had conspired with Nancy Parish to plan this trip. He was being shipped out, like a FedEx package. Urgent delivery. One big, broken-down lawyer. Destination: April in Paris.

Back out in the cabin all the other passengers were asleep. He checked his watch. It was 1:45 Toronto time. The plane was only about a third full, so he had his own three-seat row. Sitting down, he looked out the window into the deep darkness.

Sleep. Ted, when will you sleep?

'Sir, I am very sorry to be bothering of you.' The air hostess came from out of the darkness. She was bent over the empty seats beside him.

Air hostess. The term felt awkward. But stewardess was out of the question. Some words felt wrong. Like widower. It sounded like an add-on to the real word: widow.

'I see you are not sleeping.' She had a lovely French accent to go with her Air France uniform.

'I don't sleep much, I'm afraid,' he said. She was attractive, not beautiful, but there was a gentleness to her.

Sleep. Everyone he knew in the world was asleep right now. The kids were asleep. His partner, his colleagues, the Crowns, the judges, his clients, even Samantha Wyler at the penitentiary for women. For a few hours she'd be asleep.

He was the only one awake. And now this pleasant woman. Don't be silly, he told himself. She's more than pleasant. In the plane's half-light she looked pretty.

'You are Mr DiPaulo, that is correct?'

'That's right.' He wondered how she knew his name. The passenger manifest, he supposed.

'I have a message for you—'

'Something wrong?' My kids, DiPaulo thought, his spine seizing up.

'Oh, *non. Pardon.* Excuse me, please. Nothing is wrong.'

Was she blushing? Hard to tell. He noticed for the first time that she had a piece of paper in her hand.

'We have a message to be given for you. The copilot wrote it in his English. A detective in

Toronto, Monsieur Greene, said to give it to you as soon as you are awaken.'

'Monsieur Greene?' I sound foolish, he thought. And charmed by her French accent.

'Yes. He said telephone to him when you are arriving in Paris.'

DiPaulo could feel his pulse jump as she handed him the paper.

'You will be staying in Paris, no?'

'Yes.' He straightened up.

'Here,' she said. He heard a click overhead. A cone of light came on, illuminating for a moment her shoulders and her breasts in the crisp uniform.

Ted

Wanted you to hear this right away. It appears Samantha didn't kill Terrance Wyler.

Wyler's brother Jason confessed. Looks like you were right. He killed Terrance by accident with a knife. Then stabbed him six times after in anger. Set Samantha up by using Terrance's BlackBerry.

Sadly, he committed suicide.

I've called your partner Nancy Parish. We will get your client into court tomorrow so she can be released.

Call me when you land. I'll explain all.

Paris me manque.

Ari

P.S. April Goodling was pregnant with Terrance's baby. A boy she named after him.

DiPaulo stared at the piece of paper in the airplane's dim light. Samantha not guilty. Jason the killer, by accident. He'd committed suicide. April Goodling had Terrance's child.

His hands were shaking. '*We will get your client into court tomorrow so she can be released . . . Paris me manque.*' I miss Paris.

'You are okay, Mr DiPaulo?'

Who was speaking? Oh, it was the stewardess. The air hostess. The woman with the beautiful accent.

'Thanks, yes. Fine. Nice of you to give this to me.'

He wanted to touch her arm for a second. Convince himself this wasn't a dream.

'Excuse me,' he said. 'I have to go to the bathroom.' Half standing, the way you do on planes, he brushed his hand against her forearm. The material was coarse. Real.

Back in the airplane bathroom, he smelled the forced air. He took off Chiara's tie, rolled it up, and put it in his back pocket before turning on the water. It was that same lukewarm temperature. He wet his face and used the greasy little bar of soap. He felt its harsh smell, almost acidic.

'*Looks like you were right. He killed Terrance by accident with a knife.*' This wasn't a dream. It fit. DiPaulo remembered Jason Wyler leaving the court while he was cross-examining that arrogant pathologist, Dr Burns. The clatter of his canes. The swatch of blood at the bottom of the back door. The other person in the house.

The air hostess was waiting for him in the aisle when he got back to his seat. She was holding a blanket and a pillow. No one else in the plane moved. They were all asleep.

I was wrong, he thought. Everyone else in my life is awake, not asleep. Samantha Wyler walking her cell for the last night. Nancy Parish, up with excitement. Jennifer Raglan, padding the floor, confused that she'd used all her skill to convict an innocent woman. And Ari Greene. Thank you, Ari.

'A pillow? A blanket?' the woman asked.

'That would be lovely.' He slipped past her to his seat. Perhaps he could ask her to sit beside him for a moment. He was shaking.

'You are certain you are okay?' she asked.

'Shocking news,' he said. 'Good news. But it's a shock.'

'Here is the pillow,' she said.

Shock. He thought about Sam. Finding her father dead in the service bay of the garage when she was a teenager.

'Would you like to read something, perhaps?' the air hostess asked.

Read. Like Samantha reading all those medical books. Trying to figure out for herself what had happened. How Raglan had used them to destroy her in cross-examination. He remembered that engineer as the foreperson.

He thought about Jason Wyler. Poor man. Exposed during the trial as Samantha's secret correspondent. A traitor to the family compact. His confession made sense. A lonely, dying man. He was in love with Samantha. How could he live with letting her suffer for his mistake?

Out the window he searched the sky for a sliver of light, but it was only black. DiPaulo thought of the last thing Samantha had instructed him to say to Jason when he was on the witness stand. She'd insisted on the words being said exactly as she'd written them: 'Thanks for your courage and honesty not only today, but always.'

'But always,' DiPaulo whispered.

'Monsieur?' the woman asked.

'Oh, excuse me,' he said. 'It's nothing.'

What if Samantha had a hunch about Jason? And this was her signal, a call to his conscience. The real reason she was so desperate for him to be called as a witness at the trial.

'The pillow. You can use it, perhaps?' the air hostess asked.

DiPaulo hadn't realized he'd been holding it in his lap. He put it behind him.

'Lie down,' she said. 'I will put the blanket over the top of you. It is more comfortable like this. No?'

He felt the softness of the pillow on the back of his head. A wave of warmth rolled across his skin as the blanket draped over him.

485

DiPaulo heard a cranking sound.

'This will be feeling nice,' the woman said. Cool air came from above. He smelled a hint of something. Was it perfume?

At last his eyes drifted shut. Now, even he could sleep.